Kate Harrison was born in Wigan, and attended more than a dozen different schools – the perfect preparation for writing a book about a class reunion. She trained as a journalist, and now works in London as a TV director ... that is, when she can be dragged away from surfing the net for the latest updates on Friends Reunited ...

Old School Ties is her first novel.

Old School Ties

Kate Harrison

PIATKUS

Copyright © Kate Harrison 2003

First published in Great Britain in 2003 by
Judy Piatkus (Publishers) Ltd of
5 Windmill Street, London W1T 2JA
email:info@piatkus.co.uk

The moral right of the author has been asserted

A catalogue record for this book is available from the British Library

ISBN 0 7499 3387 9

Set in Times by
Action Publishing Technology Ltd, Gloucester

Printed and bound in Great Britain by
Mackays of Chatham Ltd

The idea of one day writing acknowledgements seemed as unlikely as being published. But now the fantasy has become reality – and writing this has proved almost as hard as finishing the novel. At the risk of sounding like Gwyneth Paltrow on Oscar night, I'd like to toast all these lovely people ...

For providing endless encouragement, great critiques and the odd medicinal glass of Merlot ... Bristol Women Writers, Noeleen, Dominique, the Annual Writers' Conference, and the GOT crew, especially Sooz and Russ ...

For supplying generous advice, the inside track on what it's like to be published, and the occasional revitalising white wine spritzer ... Allison, Chris, Clare, Crysse, Leslie, Michael and Pete.

For believing in me and the book – and for providing the best buzz ever experienced over a cup of coffee – everyone at Piatkus, especially Gillian. And for making me feel like I'd drunk a bottle of champagne at 11 o'clock on a Wednesday morning, Barbara ...

For being fantastic mates, for listening to me obsessing about plot and for sharing creativity-enhancing Cosmopolitans ... Carrie, Lisa, Lynne, Sarah, and all the WDI crowd; Lynn and Emma for being the UK's Best; Jane, Andrea and Shelley for being slim-line versions of Boris; and Adele, Alison, Betsan, Kath, Liz, Mary, Rachel, Trudi and, of course, Geri and Jenny ...

For being there – no alcohol required – Pat, Pete, Grandie, Toni, Mum and Dad ...

And for reading this book and indulging my beverage-themed acknowledgements,

Thank YOU.
Kate Harrison

Chapter One

Last night, when the third gin and tonic finally knocked the sharp edges off the day, I dared to look in the mirror. And there, just below the problem family of white hairs breeding in my fringe, were the eyes of Tracey Mortimer. The most popular girl in the school.

I thought she'd gone for good.

When I was Tracey Mortimer, the whole year group belonged to me. Kids gossiping on the bus would say, 'Guess what happened in Tracey's year ...' Once a teacher told my Mum, 'we're all hoping that Tracey's year is a bit of a hiccup. Half the staff-room would retire tomorrow if we thought this was the way children were going to be from now on.'

If we'd had a yearbook, like they do in America, I reckon I'd have been on every page, and would definitely have been voted the girl most likely to succeed. I'm not boasting. You look at me now – plain old Mrs Dave Brown – and maybe you can't believe it, but I really was top dog. Not swotty – I would never have made it to head girl, but then again we didn't have a head girl, it wasn't that kind of school.

What I had was the knack of getting right in at the centre of things, without pissing people off. Saying the stuff everyone else was thinking, but making it funnier. Knowing what we should be wearing, way before it hit the pages of *Jackie* or *Just 17*. And, of course, giving the teachers just enough of a hard time to wind them up, but not enough to get detention more than once a month ...

I poured myself another drink, and took it to bed with me (unlike Dave, a G and T doesn't answer back). I propped his pillows on top of mine, nestling down in the hope that some tipsy memories might send me off into sweet dreams. His smell drifted up from the pillowcase, and I imagined him lying alone in his lodgings, a sad smile on his face, thinking of me ...

But I wasn't drunk enough. Before I could stop it, my imagination revealed the freckly back of some Irish tart lying asleep next to him.

And as the taste of the tonic turned chemical on my tongue, I realised. *Everything* since school has been shit. How I failed to notice for so long is a bloody mystery, but maybe life's like wrinkles. It creeps up on you.

Sitting up in bed, as I tried to compare the good bits in my first sixteen years to the good bits in the last sixteen, it was so obvious. The sodding Youth Training Scheme, the endless nights on a fruitless quest for Mr Right, and the getting excited about getting engaged and getting married and then getting wise to the reality that all it means is more ironing, and having someone different to shout at.

As for the fulfilment of motherhood, what a con. Sure, my two are the most beautiful children alive. But the other mothers? OK, I've had a few laughs in the antenatal group, that's almost like the old days, only they're a bit of a dopey bunch compared to Class 1G, too easily led for my liking. I used to enjoy a challenge. The only challenge that gets the new mums going is the race to finish knitting another pair of pink bootees. And now Kelly's started school, it's like salt in the wounds. She's not like I was, too shy, and I want to take her place. She hangs on to me like a strip of Velcro in the mornings. I try to shoo her off, but she hates every minute of it.

You know those films, *Big* and *Freaky Friday*? That's my dream, to swap places like Tom Hanks or Jodie Foster. Kelly'd love to sit at home doing the dusting, watching daytime telly, eating biscuits and playing with Callum, and I'd give anything to be at school, surrounding myself with a little gang, kissing the boys and making them cry. I want to go back in time. And I bloody can't, and I bloody hate it.

At least, I didn't think I could. And now, you know, I reckon there might just be a way ...

Alec hit pause on the remote control, then threw it across the table. A still frame of a bespectacled man with ginger hair hovered on the widescreen TV at the end of the production company meeting room.

'What an idiot. Do you think he's actually got any old school friends who'd want to meet him ever again?' Alec sighed deeply. 'I don't see why this is proving so hard. Reunions are the new sex, aren't they? Everyone's at it, shuffling around to Spandau Ballet. It's not rocket science to find me one single decent case we can follow.'

'Alec, we've got half a dozen reunions in the file—'

'Yes, but I'm not looking for dysfunctional retards. I want feelgood people. This isn't *Panorama*, but judging from this lot, you want to make some sort of gritty documentary.'

Jenny bit her lip. Better to let him finish when he was having one of his hissy fits – she'd learned that much in the last year at Smart Alec Productions.

'The clue –' he was now banging the file up and down on the desk to emphasise certain words '– is in the

3

commissioning document. It's *entertainment*. Go on, hazard a guess. What do you think that means we want the programme to be?'

He waited, but Jenny really couldn't tell if it was a rhetorical question or not. Annabel, the researcher, had her mouth open to answer, and Jenny kicked her under the table.

'It means ...' Alec had dropped the file on to the floor, and was speaking as if to an ill-disciplined child '... that it should be *entertaining!*'

Annabel gulped. She seemed to be blinking back tears.

Jenny took a deep breath. 'Alec, I know you're frustrated, but you're being a bit hard. Annabel and I are meeting another possible tonight, and a couple more over the weekend. But getting the right people takes time.'

Alec stared at her. 'Time, Jenny, is precisely what we don't have. If the BBC get their reunion show on air before us, it'll be my head on the block.' He paused before giving her a vindictive look. 'And yours, of course.'

There are times when I don't think I'll ever get out of the house. You'd think kids would get less dependent as they get older, but it's just not like that. Kelly acts as if I'm about to go on a year-long Space Shuttle mission instead of down to All Bar One.

'Don't go now, Mummy. I want to read to you.' Like I want to listen. I know it's what you're meant to do, and I do my duty once a day, make encouraging noises, but frankly it's no great thrill listening to the same old rubbish about bunnies and fairies. She's a much better reader than I was when I was six, but it's not exactly *EastEnders*.

Meanwhile, Callum's hanging off my leg to stop me leaving. His fingers are covered in banana yoghurt, so my one pair of decent glossy black tights now look like part of a wasp fancy dress costume.

My mum's babysitting but she's no help.

'Poor little Callum,' she coos, and he reacts like any toddler getting unexpected sympathy. He milks it without shame.

'Maaaaaaaaaaaaaaaauuuuuuuuuuuummmmmmmmmmmmmy.' He starts quietly but raises his voice to a high-pitched ending which interferes with my ears, and makes me nearly lose my balance.

But I manage to stagger out of the house, and when I look back, I can see Mum standing in the front window, giving me a dirty look. After thirty-three years of practice, it's easy enough to ignore her.

At least all the domestic grief has stopped me thinking too much about the interview. But while I wait for the bus – I daren't drive because I'm going to need a drink or two – I finally have time to get wound up.

I can only remember feeling nervous twice in my life. First time was on my wedding day, because Dave did the traditional thing, had his stag do the night before, instead of months in advance like any sensible person, and I was terrified he'd oversleep or be tied up naked in a mail sack on a sleeper train to Aberystwyth, when we were meant to be taking our vows. Mind you, I think the humiliation of being stood up at the altar would have been preferable to what's happened since, but you can't predict the future, more's the bloody pity.

Second time was before I had Kelly, and that was partly fear of pain, but mainly the fear that at the end of all that agony, she'd be ugly. I'd waddled off the week before to see a girl from antenatal, and her baby boy looked like Mr Potatohead; not that she seemed to realise. Kelly's hardly the life and soul of the party, but she's been a looker ever since she emerged, a bit squashed, from my tattered nether regions.

So I guess this adrenalin-induced nausea puts my

meeting right up there with two of the most significant events of my life. Which I admit is faintly ridiculous. Or rather, the boring Tracey Brown grown-up bit of me admits it's ridiculous.

But the girl that used to be Tracey Mortimer reckons this could be even bigger than the marriage and birth thing, in the excitement stakes.

I pay the bus driver, and the newspaper cutting flies out of my purse. My denim skirt feels too tight as I kneel down to pick it up. I know the advert off by heart now, anyway, but I have a feeling that this meeting might make everything different, and it's nice to keep souvenirs of the stuff that changes the course of your life.

Dear reader, it says, *are you itching to head back in time to those days when the worst thing you had to worry about was double Maths? We could make it happen.*

This sounds a bit bonkers, and I nearly didn't read on, but it made a change from the usual stuff that fills the letters page in my local paper, all about dog shit and corrupt local councillors.

So then it says: *We're making a programme for Channel 5 about school reunions, and if you think it would be fun to organise one, we'd like to hear from you. You supply the friends and the memories – we pay for the party!*

Now you're talking.

The last bit goes on about nostalgia and remembering the 80s and all that, before it finishes: *if your reunion's underway then it's thanks, but no thanks – we want to be in at the beginning. So, if that trip down memory lane is still just a glint in your eye, get in touch with Jenny or Annabel at the address above!*

I haven't thought about anything else for two weeks. And tonight I'm going to charm Jenny and Annabel, like I haven't charmed anyone since I set out to snare Gary Coombs in the first year.

Just hope I haven't lost my touch.

The barman had poured too much red wine into the glass, and it splashed over the rim as he placed it next to the mineral water.

'Four-fifty, please.'

'Can I have a receipt?' Jenny said, handing over a £20 note.

'You're not going to claim for *my* wine on expenses?'

'Oh, Annabel, my love, you've got a lot to learn.' Jenny picked up the drinks, and led the way through the empty bar, towards the plate-glass windows. The table she chose had the number 13 stencilled in black paint on the top. 'This one's got a good view of anyone walking in. And don't worry, I'm sure the number's not an omen. We've had enough bad luck on this programme to last a lifetime.'

Annabel took a huge glug of red wine before speaking. 'It's fucking pants, isn't it? I really thought that Sandra woman was going to be the one.'

'Yeah, well, she could have been, if it wasn't for Alec's irrational hatred of people from Coventry. So all we need now is a Page 3 stunner who isn't ginger, who isn't too boring or too interesting, who lives South of the Watford Gap, unless Alec's now decided that northern warmth is what'll make the film. Oh, and if she'll shag him, then even better ...'

Annabel took another gulp of wine.

'Oh, Annabel, you haven't?' Jenny shook her head, but she wasn't that surprised. Alec hadn't really embraced the idea that these days the casting couch was too politically incorrect even for Hollywood, never mind for a low-rent production company in East London. Fortunately for him, most would-be researchers hadn't realised either.

'I haven't had *sex* with him.' But she was looking away.

7

'What, like Bill Clinton never had sex with Monica? Come on, Annabel, wise up, don't you think twenty-two's a bit old to pretend to be a bimbo?'

Annabel sniffed, raised the glass to her lips and drained it.

'OK, there was a blow job involved. But it's just how things are, isn't it? Don't tell me *you* haven't occasionally done things that the careers officer wouldn't have recommended?'

'Um, excuse me. I've never used sex to get a job.' Then Jenny grinned. 'Maybe if I had, I wouldn't still be an associate producer at the ripe old age of twenty-nine.'

Annabel smiled, but it was clear she expected to be an executive by twenty-five, and given her enthusiastic approach to job-hunting, it could well happen. She looked down into her empty glass, and the smile disappeared. 'I suppose we ought to wait until this Tracey gets here before we can get another drink.'

Jenny looked up towards the windows, where a woman with wavy blond hair was pretending to study the menu, but kept sneaking looks inside the bar.

'I think this is our girl.' said Jenny. 'Well, she's not ginger, so that's one point in her favour. Let's just hope she's as committed as you are to keeping the producer happy!'

Chapter Two

I'm a bit late, but at least that means they should already be here, so I won't have to stand around like a tart. Though these new places aren't nearly as bad as proper old blokes' pubs, where you can't take two steps without being stared at, or pestered for your phone number. There's a girl I used to work with in the shop, who says All Bar One has about as much atmosphere as MacDonald's, but I get so few nights out that it looks pretty bloody exciting to me.

There's hardly anyone in here, so I reckon the researchers must be those two women over by the wall – they look too trendy to be from Bracewell, and one is irritatingly pretty.

The other one's seen me and she's getting up.

'Hi, you must be Tracey, I'm Jenny.' She's grinning away like my dental hygienist does before she goes at the scale and polish.

'Let's get you a drink, then I'll introduce you to Annabel. She's already started on the red wine, but then these youngsters can't go five minutes without a drink, can they?'

Considering Jenny looks about twenty, this is hard to stomach, but then I know from our phone conversations that she's about to hit thirty, and feeling paranoid about it. Either that, or her whingeing about age is part of an 'all sisters together' campaign to get me on side. It's quite flattering that she's making so much effort. Reminds me of a first date.

I go for a G and T, and Jenny suggests I have Bombay Sapphire Gin, which looks great in theory, but is a huge disappointment, because when the girl pours it out, it's got no more colour than bog standard Gordon's.

'Story of my life,' I tell her, 'This drink is a real fur coat, no knickers job,' and she laughs so enthusiastically that I nearly drop the glass.

We go to sit down, and Annabel starts jabbering on. She's got a cut-glass accent but every second word is 'fuck'. And there's the same need to be liked.

It's getting on my tits. I mean, bloody hell, it makes a nice change to be courted, but this air of desperation, before they even know me, is putting me off. All the most exciting relationships of my life have at least started with both of us playing hard to get, so this is too easy. I want to misbehave. But I've got to fight that instinct, or I'll do what Mum's accused me of doing since I was old enough to talk. And cut off my nose to spite my face.

'Have you brought the pictures we wanted to see?' Jenny asks. I pull the photos out of my bag and lay them on the table.

When I got out the album to choose the best ones, I was amazed at just how awful we all looked when we were eleven. I hope Kelly and Callum never get that bad.

'Fucking hell,' Annabel splutters as she picks up the group photo of class 1G in all its glory. 'I didn't realise you went to a special school!' Then she frowns, worried she's gone too far. But it just makes me smile.

I remember when it was taken, the week before Valentine's Day 1980. I was wondering if I might get a card from Gary – I already had my eye on him; he was the only decent-looking lad in my year, and so it stood to reason that he'd want to be with me, the best-looking girl in 1G.

Of course, it was only when he didn't show the slightest interest that I got seriously determined.

Aged eleven, I tower over him by a good four inches. You forget how short the lads were. And we look such ugly ducklings. I don't know whether it's the body's way of saving energy for puberty, but it's all extremely grim, from the outsize noses, to the orang-utan arms hanging too far down our stunted little bodies.

Someone must have done scientific research on the school uniform colours, fabrics and designs most likely to curb the ardour of the hormonally challenged. The Crawley Park Comprehensive version involved a mint-green acrylic v-neck jumper, white polyester shirt, navy skirt and – the pièce de résistance – a canary yellow tie. I would challenge anyone to come up with a less seductive outfit.

In the picture, we're all wearing our ties the same way, the thick end rolled round and round and round so the knot's roughly the same size as a fist, with a tiny tail of fabric poking from the bottom.

'Not hard to spot you, Tracey,' says Jenny, and she's right. I'm in the middle – as usual – and though I look rougher than I ever realised at the time, at least I'm smiling, and my hair's not that different from how it is now. It's always been one of my best features, and it stands out a mile among the other Brillo-pad hairdos. In the photo I'm half-child, half-woman, and the hair's definitely the latter, cascading like Rapunzel's on to my shoulders.

'So, talk us through your classmates, then?' Jenny's still bright as a sodding button, brimming with enthusiasm at the prospect of hearing all about a bunch of bizarre-looking children she's never met, who probably grew into equally bizarre-looking adults.

'Louise Shrimpton.' I point at the girl standing next to me in the photo, her jumper hanging off her, with fingers like single blades of straw poking from the scarecrow cuffs of her blouse. Her mousy hair sticks out at right angles as though she's been doing a science experiment with static electricity. 'Shrimp. My best mate.'

Annabel's already drawn a diagram on her notebook, with circles representing every child on my photo. She's marked my position with an X, and now she's writing Shrimp's name alongside the appropriate blob.

'She came from this huge family, she was the second youngest, and they were permanently broke. I mean, it's not like my mum was loaded, but compared to Shrimp, I felt like a millionaire.'

'So, are you still in touch?'

I look at the picture, and realise Shrimp's the only child in the class with black circles under her eyes. They didn't sleep much in her house; there was always someone screaming or laughing or wanting to play. Couldn't have been more different to ours, me and Mum always sending each other to Coventry.

'No. Shrimp died. She was run over.'

'Oh, God. When?' Jenny sounds sympathetic. It's the first time I've seen her show anything like a genuine emotion.

'Second year, just after Hallowe'en.' Her parents bought her a second-hand bike for her birthday. Once they'd scraped enough money together to pay for it, it saved on the bus pass. But she got knocked off on her way home, in the dark. Kids wear cycle helmets these days, don't they, but then it wasn't cool and I don't suppose the Shrimptons would have been able to afford one as well as

12

the bike. Her older brother, Ricky, told me that when he saw her lying in hospital before they switched off the life-support machine, the crown of her head had been flattened, like a pumpkin lantern with the top left off.

But when I saw her in the coffin before the funeral, she just looked like Shrimp, minus the black circles. Though there was this sickly smell of vanilla, and when I copied what the adult mourners had done, and went to kiss her hair, I realised her face was thick with make-up. I think they'd even drawn her freckles back on, because there were more than I'd remembered.

So one day Shrimp was mucking about with me, and the next there was just an empty chair, and I thought I'd never get over it. We knew what the other one was going to say before they said it, and I was more in love with Shrimp than I have been with any bloke. Not in a lezzy way but, you know, she was my mate.

I reckon she must have known that too, even after the last argument. That's what it's like when you're close to someone. We would have made it up. I know we would, the way we always did, if only ...

Jenny and Annabel are shifting in their chairs, so I look in the picture for my next best friend.

'Melody Tickell.' Until Shrimp died, me and Melody co-existed, but it wasn't that comfortable. Our class wasn't really big enough for two rival girl gangs, so it was natural that she filled the gap left by Louise – or she tried to.

'She was my bridesmaid as well,' I say, and this seems to perk Jenny up.

'And that was in ...' she looks at her notes ' ... 1992, is that right?'

'Yes.' It's odd to think that the TV company have got a computer file on me somewhere, and that she's probably adding to it mentally as we talk.

'Did anyone video it?' she asks, trying to sound casual, though it's obvious from all the conversations we've had on the phone that anything extra – photos, cards, and most importantly, film – could tip the balance in favour of my reunion being featured, rather than someone else's.

'Yes, it's brilliant stuff.' I see Annabel add a couple of ticks to her diagram.

Melody and I always looked good together, total opposites, almost like two porn actors specially selected for contrast in the girl-on-girl action. There's me with my blue eyes, blonde hair and curves in the right places, and her with the French-style pointy cheekbones and pointy bobbed hair and pointy eyes, in matching shades of charcoal.

In the photo she looks intense and studious, eyeballing the camera like it's a dare. But she was never into learning. To tell you the truth, she wasn't that intelligent, and the defiant act was a good cover. Loads of the teachers thought she was capable of more than she achieved, but they assumed she just couldn't be arsed. In fact, if you'd spent as much time as I did with her, you'd know that she operated on a kind of base animal instinct, which was usually right, but involved no logic or even any extended thought. She was the first of our class to start smoking, and that also gave her an aura of being a tortured soul, whereas in fact the only thing that tortured Melody was figuring out what the lyrics meant in Madness songs.

'She'll be easy to get in touch with, anyway,' says Jenny, and she will, I know she still lives somewhere in Bracewell. I don't mention that I haven't seen her since my wedding. But that's my business.

'Who's the fatty?' Annabel asks me.

Poor Boris. She always meant well. 'Helen. Her nickname was Boris.'

They look at me blankly. 'I know, it's a long story. Her

surname's Morris, and someone watched a film with Boris Karloff, and it rhymed so that was it. But she never seemed to mind.'

'And what about the lads?' Annabel asks me.

'OK. Well, that's Briggsy,' I point to the chubby bloke in the front row. Next to Boris, he looks positively anorexic. He was also my first snog, God help me, but we were both under the influence of Old Spice from an aerosol, sniffed through our jumpers. Don't try that one at home. It wasn't the perfume we were after, of course, and I can't even remember how we worked out it would give you a high. But I do wonder what the chemists thought was going on as their stock of canned body spray was rapidly depleted by teenaged shoplifters.

'And then Gary was my first love . . .'

'This one?' Annabel is laughing. 'He looks so young . . .'

'Well, it was sixteen . . . no, seventeen years ago.' I keep forgetting it was my birthday last month. Not surprising when even my husband couldn't be bothered to buy me a card.

'Um . . . well, I hate to mention it, Tracey, but if this is you guys in the first year, then this was actually twenty-two years ago.' Jenny says, and I take a big swig of gin when I realise she's right. Maths was always my worst subject. 'So are you still in touch with him?'

'No.' There's an awkward pause as I struggle to say something that'll throw them off the scent. 'He wanted to be a policeman.' Though I think he buggered his chances – with a bit of help from me.

'And this was your teacher, Mrs Chang?'

Height-wise, Mrs Chang was on the same level as the rest of us, pretty sad considering we all had growth spurts to come. She was our form tutor, and taught biology. She also happened to be pregnant.

When we got to the birds and the bees session later that first summer, she was really showing, and it was hard to avoid the unpleasant conclusion that Mrs Chang, our *teacher*, who must have been at least *thirty*, had actually had sex within the previous six months.

'Yes, though she left at the end of the year.' I guess they'll love this story. 'We had our first sex education class with her, and she was trying to be open with us, so I asked her the question we all wanted answering. "Miss, what's it like to have sex?"'

Jenny and Annabel have adopted vacant smiles, waiting for the punch line.

'So she went a little pink, and she coughed to clear her throat, and she said, "Well, for da woman, it hurts a leetle at first, but then you get used to it. And after a while, you might even enjoy it."'

I stay deadpan, and then the women choke with laughter, and I join in, and I think maybe they're not that annoying after all.

Of course, if I really wanted to clinch it, I could tell them about Mr Carmichael, and his more proactive approach to sex education. But some things are better left in the past.

'I like her. Do you think Alec'll like her?' Annabel waited until Tracey had disappeared into the loos.

'Well, she's the best we've seen so far. Good-looking, good anecdotes. And it's not too far from London for the filming. I dunno, though. There's something I can't quite get my head round . . .'

'Oh God, Jenny, whatever it is, don't tell Alec, I don't want to have to do this all over again.'

'I'm sure it's nothing, but you know Alec's banging on about how all the people we've found who want reunions are pretty odd individuals, all a bit screwy because they want to relive the past?'

'Yeah, but Tracey's funny and pretty and married and normal and sympathetic and – well, she was the most popular girl in the school!'

'But if she's really that normal – and was really *that* popular –' the door to the Ladies opened, and as a flash of blonde emerged, Jenny lowered her voice, 'then how come she's not in touch with a single person from the Good Old Days?'

Chapter Three

I'm having a *Casualty* day.

When you watch *Casualty*, part of the fun is wondering what's going to happen next. Maybe there's a young career woman skipping off to window-shop in her lunch-hour. Are her stiletto heels about to get trapped in the escalator, dragging her 10-deniered legs into the mechanism? Is that cheese and pickle sandwich going to trigger a life-or-death anaphylactic shock because the woman in the bakery allowed some peanut dust to sneak into the bread mix? Or – as she looks the right kind of age – maybe she's ignoring the stomachache that is in fact a symptom of a potentially fatal ectopic pregnancy?

Well, today I'm having one of those days when it feels as though Kelly, Callum and I are all TV characters, and everything we do could have grisly consequences. So Callum's adorable chipolata fingers are groping around the kitchen, and I'm convinced they're about to close in around the blade of a sharp knife I've forgotten to put away, slicing them off, so that they land on the laminate floor, still twitching and pointing out my appalling maternal neglect.

Kelly's wandering round with her shoelaces undone around her ankles. I haven't had time to tie them yet, and even though I know she's got rubber limbs, I've started to wonder if the random aches and pains she's been moaning about this week are actually early symptoms of a rare bone-crumbling disease. So when she trips over, instead of grazing her knee, she'll fall to the floor with multiple fractures, and will have to spend a year of her life in a plaster-cast like a junior mummy.

Meanwhile, *my* hands feel independent of my body, as if they're about to do something I've got no control over. I move very slowly and purposefully, in case my hands decide to pour too much boiling water into the coffee cup, and it runs down the sides like Niagara Falls, and scalds me, and Callum too, because of course, he'll choose this moment to stand under the worktop and start licking the underside where all the manky bits of food collect.

The bread's got stuck in the toaster and sets off the smoke alarm, which drags me back to reality. When I return to the kitchen after resetting it, there's this stinking haze of carbon that makes me choke, and my hands grasp the butter knife and they're about to plunge it into the orange-glowing elements inside the variable thickness slots to remove the offending dough, when my mind goes into fast forward.

I see myself leaping into the air in an electric shock, my body surrounded by a Ready-Brek style forcefield, before I plunge to the floor and the kids poke me mournfully, but can't rouse me, and then Kelly remembers from school that she should call 999, and an emergency crew arrives, and as they take me away on a stretcher, the kindly ambulance man, who looks like a cross between Josh and Charlie Fairhead, gives Kelly a lolly to congratulate her for being such a brave girl. And when I open my eyes, I can see her choking on the lolly, but no one else can, and I'm too weak from the shock to move or shout out and then ...

Anyway, in the split second it takes me to imagine all this, I make my mind override my hands, and force them to unplug the toaster at the mains before I go delving.

I used to worry that I was going mad, but then I talked to some of the girls at the tumble-tots where I take Callum, and they said they felt pretty much the same.

We're a generation of Paranoid Parents. I certainly don't remember my mum's cupboards being full of a million different cleaning sprays and foams and creams and impregnated cloths. I read in a magazine that scientists think the reason that so many of Kelly's age group have asthma is because we keep them in this hermetically sealed environment. As soon as they come into contact with anything even remotely grubby, their systems collapse from the strain.

But there's no way out, because if you don't put everything they touch through a sixty-degree wash every other day, someone'll probably report you to social services and you'll be left alone in your festering home, while the kids are handed over to more deserving parents.

Now there's a thought.

In a way, though, I find it kind of reassuring that I worry at all. I can see Mum looking at me sometimes as if I'm a monster when I shout at them, or even if I raise my eyebrows at Kelly when she blushes about the boys at school.

Mum doesn't think I'm much of a mother, and maybe she's right. Surely I shouldn't feel so frustrated? I know I love them more than Dave does; there's the pull in the pit of my stomach if Callum falls over on the patio, or if I see the glaze of tears in Kelly's eyes as she's watching something sad about animals on TV. But I'm not sure I like them all the time. Especially not Kelly. Is it right to want to shake her now and then, to want to tell her to pull herself together? That's not something I can ask anyone . . .

But maybe my nightmares prove I do love them, even if I'd never win Mother of the Year. And at least I haven't failed Mum's ultimate test, and become a *single parent,* responsible for dragging up society's dregs, kids destined to become junkies or jailbirds.

I think she should be quite proud of me, when you think *that*'s the way I could have turned out.

I check the kitchen clock, and realise I'm running out of time to get Kelly to school, and then get back before the film crew arrive.

I kind of knew they'd choose me, but it's still pretty exciting. Today is stage one, they're going to record an interview, then film me playing with Callum, looking at those photos again and trying to work out how to get the reunion up and running. The party's scheduled for July so they can show the programme as part of some Back to School season on Channel 5, so that only gives us three months to get in touch with everyone and organise it all. But then again, my new chums Jenny and Annabel will be sorting most of it, so all I have to do is be the centre of attention . . .

'Kelly, Mrs Fellowes will be very cross if we're late again.' Sometimes fear is the only way to get her out of the house, but when I've done their shoes and checked I've got the keys, locked up and then belted her in the back, put Callum in his baby seat, then double-checked all the locks – because it's a *Casualty* day – I catch a glimpse of her holding hands with her brother and biting her little cherub lips, and I wonder what she's done to deserve a mother like me. Not to mention a father like Dave.

PC Gary Coombs nuzzled his girlfriend's neck, but she snaked away under his arms and towards the bathroom before he could start fondling her breasts.

'Gabby . . . don't be mean. You know I can't resist it

when you're not wearing a bra. Gazza wants a cuddle.'

'Gazza'll be lucky to escape without a knee in the balls at this rate.'

'Oooh, you know how it turns me on when you get angry . . .'

He opened up his dressing gown to reveal a bulge in his counterfeit Calvin's. Gabby looked at his groin, shrugged and finished her tea in one swig. 'Much as I'd love to help you out,' she said, in a voice which suggested it was about as tempting as clearing the slimy hairball from the drainage tray of the shower, 'I have an urgent family case conference to attend to.'

'Awwww, Gabby. This is pretty urgent, too.'

'Well, once I've done my teeth, it'll be all clear in the bathroom, so don't let me stop you. Just clean up after yourself, would you?'

He pouted at her back as she squeezed out a pea-sized blob of toothpaste, and then headed back into the kitchen, buzzing around as she finished loading the washer, adding powder and then setting it going. It was the biggest difference he could see between men and women. He'd never met a man who did anything else while they were brushing their teeth, while women couldn't bear to do just one thing at once.

'Ga—zzy,' she mumbled through the vibrating brush, 'You're such a – buzzzz-baby. And I don't understand how you can be randy-zzzzzzzzz after a night shift anyway. Aren't you meant to be knackered?'

'All those women in uniform.'

'Yeah?' She spat the foam into the basin. 'Well, why can't you get THEM to give you a hand job before you get home, save you harassing me?'

'I did, love, but you know me. Insatiable.'

She pulled on her coat, the smart case-conference one, rather than the deep down and dirty council estate one she wore for home visits, then moved right up close to the chair where he was sitting, pulled his dressing gown open, grabbed his hand and stuffed it up her sensible skirt, so he could tell she was wearing her lacy g-string. She gave him a brief, too brief, tongue down the throat kiss, before turning round and running to the door.

'See you later, lover boy. And if you can drag yourself off the bloody Internet for a few minutes, that ironing is not going to do itself.'

He considered a last-minute leap to the door to stand in her way, but his legs had gone all wobbly, so instead he just grinned as she blew him a final kiss.

Domestic bliss, he thought, as he pointed the remote at the telly and settled down to ogle the showbiz reporter on *Lorraine Live*.

I like my lounge, especially since I painted over the nasty peach sponging. Paint effects had seemed such a good idea when I was just married; it took me hours to get it right. Now I've covered it with a more forgiving mauve satin emulsion, Violet Sprig or something. With the light brown laminate flooring, the room looks kind of low-maintenance Scandinavian, and there's only the cream sofa to give me grief. But even that's not doing too badly, considering it was the first piece of furniture we bought as a couple, when we hadn't the slightest idea that white and kids didn't go. I've washed the covers more times than I can remember and it's only really the Ribena stain that still shows.

But the crew hate the whole room on sight.

'Oh, bugger,' says Jamie, the cameraman, who has nice brown eyes and a cute bum, but a mouth that curls down at the edges. He's my age, so I'm pretty surprised I fancy him – I tend to go for the older model.

'We're gonna need a couple more blondes and a

23

redhead,' he shouts into the hall to Cliff, who is apparently the soundman. Cliff, who has a kinder face than Jamie, whistles through his teeth when he comes in, shakes his head like a mechanic doing a 12,000-mile service, then screams through the window to Frankie, the sparks, 'Two blondes and a redhead.' Frankie nods. He has the look of someone dropped on his head on to concrete at an early age. Nice muscly arms, though.

Jenny looks apologetic. 'They're talking about their lights. I've never heard them ask for a brunette,' she says sadly, stroking her own straight brown hair. She heads back out to the van, and I can see them pointing and shrugging; they seem to be giving her a hard time, and I wonder if she's apologising for my bad taste.

Annabel's in the kitchen playing with Callum, but I can tell he's pretty suspicious. She's keeping her distance to avoid getting her designer jeans dirty. It winds me up, mainly because I can remember the days when I didn't know how to play with babies either, and frankly I'd rather be in her shoes than mine. Especially as hers are ultra-cool leather slip-on trainer-mules, and mine are reindeer slippers that my mum bought me last Christmas.

It turns out that it's not the decor they hate, but the enormous picture windows at either end of the living-cum-dining room. Light, it seems, is the bugbear of camera crews, or at least uncontrolled light. In an ideal world, Jenny tells me later, they'd do all their interviews in a bunker with a storeroom full of different lamps next door, because then they can play God.

We're on our third cup of coffee, but they're still not ready so we're keeping out of the way. Callum's getting pretty fractious over the procession of men. I didn't feel nervous before, but the noise of the front door opening and shutting is starting to wind me up.

Then there's a knock at the kitchen door.

'Hellooo?' says a male voice. A head appears. This, I presume, must be Alec, the producer. The girls have warned me that he's a bit of a shark, but *hello* – I don't think I'm going to mind one bit.

Tall, sandy hair, forty-ish but trying to look younger, with twinkly violet eyes that I'm sure aren't coloured contact lenses, and laughter lines that bunch up around them when he turns on full beam, which he's doing to me now.

'Tracey! Lovely to meet you at last – I've seen your photo, of course, but it doesn't do you justice.' He shakes my hand and seems reluctant to let go. 'I feel like I know you so well already,' and he winks at me.

It's such a seamless routine that I know he's probably used it on a million women, but that doesn't make it any easier to resist. I catch the two girls exchanging glances. It's all very well for them to judge, their lives must be full of premieres and night-club openings, but this is pretty much the most glamorous thing that's ever happened to me, so I don't see why I shouldn't enjoy it.

'If you'll excuse me just a second,' he says, as though he can't bear to tear himself away from the company of a dowdy thirty-something and her chocolate-coated toddler. 'Are they through here?' he asks Jenny, before disappearing through the connecting door. I deliberately don't look at what they've done to my living room, but I catch a peculiar blue glow from the corner of my eye.

'Boys!' I hear him shout. 'I'm so glad we've got you on board for this one. It'll be just like *Dream Weddings* all over again.'

'Except we're not in sodding Bermuda, we're in Bracewell new town.'

'Yeah, but who needs the sun when you've got your mates around you?' he gushes. But the lack of response from 'the boys' makes me wonder if Alec's any more popular with his crew than he is with his researchers. Still, being the boss makes it hard to be friends with everyone.

He pokes his cheeky chappy head back round the door. 'Are you ready for us now, Tracey? Because we're ready for you.' And there's something wonderfully naughty in the way he says it.

'God, he makes me want to vomit,' said Annabel.

'You've changed your tune.' Jenny rinsed out the cups, and refilled the kettle.

'Not really. I never said I fancied him. I just wanted a job. But it's working on our Trace, bless her suburban cotton socks, so with any luck that'll let me off the hook.'

'He hasn't tried it on again?'

'No, but I can see him looking at me, and I know what he's thinking, oh, she's done it before, she'll do it again, if there's something in it for her, something to make it worth her while ...'

'I don't know he does think like that, you know. I think he thinks he's just so attractive that women can't help themselves, so it wouldn't be fair to deny any one woman of the gift he has been endowed with by God.'

'Endowed?' Annabel raised her eyebrows. 'I don't think he was near the front of the queue when it came to endowments. Unless you're talking mortgages.'

'That's not even funny. But I must admit I've heard the same about his ... um ... assets from some of the other girls in the office.'

Annabel wrinkled her nose up.

'Annabel, you're hardly the first, and you won't be the last, so stop looking like that. Or I'll be thinking you're jealous.'

'It's only the thought of how many others have been there.'

'Mummy?' Callum looked around him. It had registered

on his radar that Tracey was out of range. 'Mummy?' This time he sounded panicky.

Jenny squatted down to pick him up. 'Well, Callum, with any luck, your mummy might be the next lucky lady to take Alec for a ride.'

'And take the pressure off me,' mumbled Annabel as she led the way into the living room.

Chapter Four

This filming business is more boring than I could ever have imagined. They've turned the living room upside down, blacked out the sunlight and the garden with this thick black cloth, and the stupid one, Frankie, is holding up what looks like a circular space blanket so it reflects light on my face and makes me squint. And there's no one to do my make-up. Alec flashes me this grin and says 'you look fantastic as you are,' but I've got my suspicions that they want me to look dog-rough now, to achieve some kind of *Pretty Woman* transformation. Except in my case, it'll be middle-aged mum to Prom Queen.

Not that anyone gets middle-aged any more. When we did an essay in English once about what we thought we'd be doing in 2000, I couldn't believe I'd ever get this old, but actually, it's no big deal. I've got the sprogs, I've got the semi, I've got the boring part-time job in the shop, and I've got the face creams weighing down my bedside table, but in my bones, I'm the same as I always was. People don't change, do they? When it comes to the reunion, I'll bet you a tenner a time that Melody will still be a dopey cow with come-to-bed eyes, Gary'll still be a pushover, Helen Morris'll still be a fat pig ... who else? Bodger Lewis will still be bad at maths and still have heavy metal hair, Suzanne Sharp will still be an insufferable swot with nasty red curls, and I will still be the one and only Tracey Mortimer and they'd better bloody believe it ...

'Speed,' says Jamie for no apparent reason, and then Alec gives me another killer smile and says, 'So, to start with, Tracey, tell me what you're hoping to get from your school reunion?'

'Ummm,' I start, and realise my throat's gone dry and I feel self-conscious, because everything's facing me – Jamie, Cliff, Frankie, Alec, Annabel, Jenny, Callum, plus the camera, a long microphone coated with fake fur, and more lights than you get at Blackpool illuminations.

'Take your time, Tracey,' says Alec, but there's already irritation in his voice. I'm starting to go off him.

I had stage fright once, in the school play, and it was the strangest experience. I'd never thought being on stage was a very cool idea, and had gone round telling everyone else in 1G the same, until Shrimp told me she'd found out Pete from the fourth year was playing Joseph, so then I changed my mind, and decided that actually unless you were in the school play, you weren't cool, triggering a last-minute auditioning frenzy.

I had the power to set trends, and I loved watching the effect I could have as the word spread through school like ripples in a pond.

'Shrimp,' I said at lunch, as I finished off all the sultanas I'd saved from the chicken curry, 'I've decided to audition for a part in *Joseph* tonight.'

She grinned at me, and nodded towards the entrance of the dinner hall, where Pete, who was also a prefect, was marshalling hungry kids with the natural authority that I'd recognised and admired from afar since our first week. Just along the table was Melody, plus her mate Fran, and they overheard, and obviously decided they'd have to do

29

the same – remember, we weren't best mates then, it was Before the Accident.

By the time we went in for afternoon registration, the word was out, and I kept hearing my name being spoken alongside random words like 'Joseph' or 'audition' or 'Mr Aaronovitch', who was the drama teacher. The news was fizzing around the room like Chinese whispers, as Mrs Chang tried to get everyone's attention.

'What is matter wid you lot?' she snarled, then said, under her breath but we could all hear her, 'What additives they put in your orange squash today?'

Everyone did *Joseph* in those days, didn't they? Even *Grange Hill* had it as their school production in the same year; I seem to remember the fat kid and Tucker Jenkins getting involved. Actually, it's a rubbish play to put on in a mixed school because all the parts are for boys, and quite effeminate boys at that, what with all that coloured cloak bollocks. But Mr Aaronovitch was smart enough to cast Pete as Joseph, because he played rugby and was hairy, and even though his voice had broken, which meant he couldn't reach a lot of the notes in the solos without making funny gurgling noises, no one was going to accuse him of being a pansy. And Mr A gave the part of the Pharaoh to an enormous black fifth-form girl called Karin, who had this bluesy voice that made everyone shiver, and he made sure three of Joseph's brothers were played by girls, and also announced that there'd be a special part of a wife for Joseph at the end. Hardly the cutting edge of feminism, but it was better than nothing, and of course when we heard this, it was Melody against me for the privilege of being Pete's missus.

'Right,' said Mr A, after rubbing his eyes as if he couldn't believe the turnout to the first and second year auditions, 'this is going to be in three parts. Singing, dancing, acting.'

Shrimp nudged me; she'd heard me sing once in juniors, and she pulled a face. So I decided to hide for that bit, figuring that if I disappeared for a little while, they'd assume I had actually done the singing already, and it wasn't memorable or awful. Because they'd certainly remember if I *did* sing, and not for the right reasons.

So Shrimp waited until the singing had finished, then nipped back into the girls' toilets to fetch me. She always looked after me. I wish I'd done the same for her, when it mattered.

'Melody was quite good, I'm afraid,' she told me, as we headed back into the hall.

Mr A was obviously getting bored by this time, it was taking so long to get all the little would-be's through, so he decided to combine the acting and the dancing. He counted the boys and the girls, and divided us up two girls to every boy.

'Right, you've all learned about Egypt, even the first years, so I want the boys to be pharaohs, and the girls to be court dancers ...' He was thinking on his feet. 'And ... er ... I want you to work on an improvisation where ... let's see ... the girls have to dance for their lives in front of the boys, who then have to send one of you to death, and take the other for his wife.'

I'm pretty disturbed when I think about this now. I wonder if Mr A is now lurking on some kind of sex offenders' register, but at the time it seemed fair enough. And I suppose it's nothing compared to what happened with Mr Carmichael later on.

In Mr A's defence, he put us in groups according to our ages, and there was no way any boy of our age would want to touch any girl with a bargepole.

It ended up being me against Melody, in front of a bemused second year called Larry. I didn't know what sexy was, not properly, but I'd watched Pan's People, and so when the music teacher started playing some sort of slithery music on the piano, I just moved my hips about and tossed my hair – which was much better for that sort of thing than Melody's, which hung like a blackout curtain – and ended up throwing myself to the floor in front of the poor lad, who four years later became the first ever fifth former in our school to come out as gay. Wouldn't surprise me, looking back on it, if my little performance had something to do with it ... anyway, Mr A obviously preferred blondes, and so I got the choice part of Pete's lovely Egyptian wife, while Melody was a sheaf of corn. Ha ha.

On the opening night, we had a right laugh with the make-up, I had these brilliant blue and black eyes like Tutankhamun, and vivid lipstick, all on top of a white Pan-stick base. That oily, earthy, baby powder scent still takes me right back; you get thick foundation sticks that smell the same, and once, when I was feeling very old, I bought one from Boots and it made me remember being eleven, and I just sat sniffing one and crying into my wine, as I tried to get Callum to settle down for the night.

Anyway, I was convinced this seductive make-up – along with the fantastic midnight blue cape Mrs Whitstable from home economics had made as my costume – would win over my Pete. Poor bugger. Although he was a prefect/rugby player/fifteen-year-old pin-up, he seemed pretty shy with girls, and very embarrassed at having this irritating first year limping around after him.

I had loads of time to get nervous, because I didn't appear until right at the end when Joseph comes back to Egypt wearing his lovely Big Mac, which is what some wit had decided to call the coat. I started feeling a bit sick while he was croaking his way through 'Close every door to me' and by the time he was having his weird dreams, I wanted to go home.

But it wasn't until he nipped out the back to prepare for

the grand finale, and I saw him SNOGGING one of his brothers – a stunning girl from his class who'd apparently been wearing a bra since junior school – that I finally realised that the last thing in the world I wanted to do was get on stage in front of all those people and say my lines ...

I raced around looking for Shrimp, who was hovering around in the background as an Egyptian extra/choir member, and tried to persuade her to take over from me. But then Pete, displaying a masterful streak that would later feature in some of my early hormone-fuelled fantasies, dragged me on to stage with the words, 'We're on now, you wally.'

Instead of the elegant procession at the side of my heroic Joseph, I tripped my way on to stage, and blinked into the hot yellow lights that I'd found scary enough at the dress rehearsal, but were now even worse because behind them were people, barely visible except for the greasy wet whites of their eyes, that all seemed to be fixed on ME.

The choir sang the bit about Jacob turning up in Egypt, as Daniel Grogan shuffled from the wings, wrinkles painted across his forehead and a grey woolly wig propped on the top of his No 2 cut.

A couple of slaves dragged Joseph's golden chariot onto the stage, heralding one of the many moments where Mr A, dissatisfied with the lyrics of a musical that made millions all over the world for Rice and Lloyd-Webber, had added some extra lines of his own.

'And Joseph brought his wife to meet the celebrating crowd,' his version went, and then it was my line,

'I'd like to say my husband will make all of Egypt proud ...' which Mr A originally expected me to sing, but once he'd heard my voice, gave me special dispensation to speak.

I opened my mouth. And nothing came out. There's a first time for everything, as my mum always says when she tells this story ...

Everyone was looking at me. The audience, the cast, Pete, Mr A, the orchestra and the conductor. The conductor decided to give it another go, re-cued the orchestra and the choir, who repeated the line about the celebrating crowd. This time I was determined.

'I'd like to ...' I started to say but no one could hear me, and even Pete was whispering the words in my ear, trying to be helpful. I knew exactly what I should have been saying, but the words stuck in my throat.

The conductor saw me trying and decided to give me one last go ...

'And Joseph brought his wife to meet the celebrating crowd,' they sang, willing me to get that last line, before the rousing finale.

This time, it was going to be all right.

I opened my voice and from nowhere, as clear and confident, came the memorable line ... 'I'd like to say my pub band will make all of Egypt loud.'

There was a pause which seemed to last for ever, then all I could hear was giggling from Pete, who tried desperately to regain his composure to sing the final moving reprise of 'Any dream will do'.

He failed, and all I can remember is my face getting hotter and hotter, and the music getting more and more jerky, as the conductor lost control of the orchestra in the most impressive display of collective hysteria ever seen at a Crawley Park school production.

Mr A begged me not to audition next year, and funnily enough, I didn't take much persuading.

Alec is still sitting there looking at me, with as much sincerity as he can muster, which isn't much. And it's all flooding back – the panic, the humiliation, and then, oddly enough, the hero-worship from everyone else in the cast. To have suffered stage fright, to have come through it and to have sparked this unforgettable moment in stage history, was suddenly the most brilliant thing I could have done. I think it was around about this time, December 1979, that the first year suddenly became 'Tracey's year.'

'Shall we just stop the camera again for a second?' Jenny suggests.

I nod, and they switch the lamps off, to stop the living room getting even hotter, and suddenly I feel totally different, back to normal.

'That's what it is,' I say, 'it's the lights in my face like this.'

'Oh, great,' says Jamie 'if we lose them, we won't be able to see your face.'

'No, it's not the fact there are lights there, it's because they're facing me directly, shining in my eyes.'

He sighs so deeply that Cliff, who has headphones clamped to his ears to monitor the sound levels, jumps up in shock, but then Jamie fiddles about with the lights in a grumpy way, and they decide to have another try.

'So,' says Alec, in the same voice I used when I was potty-training Kelly, 'Tracey, in your own time, what are you hoping to get out of your school reunion ...'

And this time, we don't stop until I've been talking for about an hour and filled two tapes, with Alec barely getting a word in edgeways.

I need chocolate now, so I go back into the kitchen to unwrap the Kit-Kats I'd bought for the crew.

Jenny comes in. 'I think it'll look best in here, more natural.'

'It'd also save any more lighting trauma, there's barely room to swing a cat, never mind put up any lights,'

Annabel says. I think she's a bit of a bitch, behind all the fake niceness.

Jamie and Alec join us, and look suspiciously at the biscuits. I shrug. 'I would have baked you a cake, but I don't do baking. That would be way too domesticated.'

Alec shoots me a lightning-bright smile. 'Hey, but you're cooking on gas this morning. That interview was brilliant stuff.'

'Once you got round to it,' Jamie mumbles.

'Yeah, this'd be good,' Alec says. 'We could set the laptop up here by the breakfast bar, and then maybe have little Connor–'

'Callum.'

'Yes, little Callum sitting alongside, eating his lunch or something. Nice cutaways.'

I give him a doubtful look. Another grown-up without a clue about children. 'I'm not sure I'd recommend filming him eating. Can be a bit messy.'

'Hey, what's a few rusks on the keyboard between friends?'

'It'll still need a couple of lamps,' Jamie moans, but heads off to get the stuff ready. 'Can you make yourselves scarce while I sort it?'

'Sure – why don't we have a bit of a dry run on the old computer? You have brought it, Annabel?' Alec nudges me. 'Can't get the staff these days, you know.'

Jenny finds a socket, plugs the machine in and connects the modem. 'Have you used computers much before, Tracey?'

I sit down in front of it. 'No, not really. My mum's got an old one she does her accounts on, and Kelly's quite good, but I've never surfed the Web.'

'Well, why don't we have a trial run?' Jenny sits next to me, and reaches across to a knob in the middle of the keyboard. 'This controls everything that goes on, just through your fingers moving across here. So – if I want to go on the Web, I put the cursor – the arrow here – over the E, which stands for Internet Explorer, which is a browser, and double click, and then–'

She's lost me already. 'Um – sorry, Jenny, but this is making less sense than double Physics . . .'

Jenny frowns. 'OK. Um, well, why don't I set it all up for you then you can have a play . . . Right, now we're connected, and we'll go straight to the site that's started the whole reunion craze. Friends Reunited – there you go, it's loading . . . and we've already done a bit of preparation on this laptop, so if I click here – bingo. Crawley Park comp, year of leaving 1984 . . . recognise any names?'

Chapter Five

Bloody hell. Bloody, bloody hell. Names I'd forgotten I'd forgotten.

'Is the whole year group on here?'

Jenny says, 'It's only the people that have actually signed up to say they're interested in meeting old pals. So it depends on the size of the school. Look, we've set you up already, so you can have a look round and maybe e-mail some people for the filming this morning.'

'E-mail?' I feel very dense. I know people do it all the time, I even saw a film about it with Meg Ryan, cheesy rubbish as usual. But when would I have had time anyway, with the kids? 'I don't know where to start.'

I've never seen the point before, but looking at the screen, now I really want to learn. There was a mammoth number of kids in our year, the tail end of the baby boom. So this long list – there must be twenty-five or more on the screen – is only about a tenth of the total, and some names I really don't recognise. But there are a few – like Boris.

Jenny says, 'If you see any that have got this little symbol next to them, that means there's more information about them.'

'I knew this one – Helen Morris. Remember – the fat

one I showed you on the photos?'

She clicks on it, and up pops this little screen. I read it out loud 'Hiya, Helen "Boris" Morris here, well I was Morris and now I'm Norris, ha ha, only one letter out, hardly had to change my signature. Married to Brian, I work in IT, quite senior actually, you'd never believe it, and we're expecting a new arrival in the summer, which means I'm about to give up work, and I'll be bored at home so would love to hear from any of the old gang, love Boris!!'

'She works in computers?' I just can't imagine roly-poly Boris as a high-powered executive.

Jenny nods. 'Yeah, I've found most of the first people who put their names on here have something to do with IT. Maybe it just makes them more likely to be online. Or they're a bunch of lonely gits with no friends.'

I think about Boris, and reckon it might be the latter, but then again she is married and up the spout, and at school, no bloke would look at her.

Jenny says, 'Due in the summer, eh? She might be fun to invite to the reunion.'

'Hmmm.' I look down the list, and I half expect to see Shrimp's name there, then I tell myself off for being soft.

GARY COOMBS

It leaps off the page and burns a hole in my eyes. 'Gary Coombs—'

Jenny grins. 'Yes, we saw that, when we checked it after our first chat.'

I'm dying to see what he's up to. 'Get his info up!'

'Oh, he's a bit more reticent. No biog or anything. A lot of people don't put any details up on the site, they'll only accept e-mails, and then decide whether to reply. Do you fancy a go at e-mailing him?'

This is so strange. Is he single? Has he got kids? Did he ever get over me? What's he doing for a living? Where is he living?

WOULD HE STILL FANCY ME?

Alec wanders in. 'I think we're ready now.'

They move everything through, and I pull Callum into the high chair, bung the bib round his neck and heat up a jar of chunky lamb and veg korma, which he really likes, but I hate because I know I'll pay the price at changing time. At least it'll keep him quiet. When the camera starts rolling, I load the food on to his plastic spoon, and pass it to him so he can get on with spreading warm orange gloop across every bit of exposed skin from the top of his downy head to the creases in his wrists. I turn back to the screen.

'Just talk to me while we film,' Alec says. 'So what are you up to?'

'OK, well, I've just logged up to-'

'On to,' Jenny whispers.

'I've just logged ON to this site thing, Friends Reunited, and I've never seen it before, and I'm going to have a look through, it shows all sorts of names I haven't even thought about since we left in 1984. Which is a scary amount of time.'

'Maaaaumm.' Callum's looking irritated, and is obviously still hungry, not surprising as he keeps missing his mouth with the spoon – he hasn't quite got the hang of feeding himself yet. I shovel a bit of the sludgy food into him, and he gives me the wonky-toothed grin that always makes me melt, and Alec has to whisper, 'Keep talking.'

'And, um. Well, I thought I'd try an e-mail. I've never sent one, but I've been shown what to do, so here goes. It's to my first ever boyfriend. Gary Coombs.'

Gary stared up at the TV, unable to believe that there was a woman with her tits out on *Richard and Judy*. OK, she was doing something to do with breast cancer screening, but they were nice, pert specimens. The cameraman kept zooming into her nipples, which were quite stiff, but that made sense, because she was demonstrating how to examine the breasts, which meant having a good old feel.

He felt annoyed that he'd probably missed her getting undressed, while he'd been looking at some of his favourite web-sites. He opened the history page on the browser and then started deleting the addresses from the morning's surfing, one by one, without looking away from the TV. It was one thing Gabby knowing he looked at porn sites – how many blokes didn't, after all? – but he didn't particularly want her to know which ones. There was nothing that dodgy on the sites he liked – he wasn't a pervert after all – but it was strictly between him and his hard drive.

It wasn't something he was proud of, but what else was he meant to do when everyone he knew was at work? That, and chat rooms kept him sane.

Wilbur the cat – Gabby's cat, really – wandered along the coffee table sniffing at the row of seven dirty mugs, before settling at the glass, which had a couple of inches of water at the bottom. He stuck his head into the glass, ears folded back, so that his chin nearly reached the liquid, and then poked out his pink tongue as far as it would go, just breaking the surface of the water.

Actually, the girl with the tits wasn't that cute. In one of the close-ups he could swear he could see a hair as thick as a pube growing out of one nipple, and one breast was definitely bigger than the other.

'It's quite normal,' said the expert 'for the shape and size to be slightly different on either side. It's the same with our hands, or our feet.'

The computer beeped, and he looked down, he'd deleted all today's pages. Quick e-mail check, then a sarnie, then maybe bed, he was on shift again in another five hours.

Your dick as big as a cricket bat, one promised. Delete.

41

No need of any help in that direction.

College girls in the showers, they don't know you're watching!!!!!!!!!!!! – Could be worth a look later.

Friends Reunited. You've got mail.

Hey, this was a laugh. He'd had a couple through so far, no one he remembered that well, but when Gabby signed up, he'd done the same, no harm in it. He clicked it open.

Gary
Remember me? I remember you ...
Get in touch – if you dare.
Tracey Mortimer xxx

The cat had given up on the remaining water, and started competing with the laptop for Gary's attention.

'Fucking hell, Wilbur,' Gary said to the cat. 'What does that bitch want?' The cat purred at the attention.

Gary reread the message then shrugged.

'If she thinks I'm running back to her, after all these years, she can fuck right off,' he told the cat, deleted the message, and went to find a clean mug for another cup of tea.

Chapter Six

The secret of a lasting marriage is spending as little time as possible together, which is why Dave and I are still, on paper, a couple.

Sadly, every now and then, there's some kind of Irish bank holiday, and Dave's dad sends him and all the other builders back to England. There's no excuse, now it costs less to fly back than it would to take the train from here into London.

'Daddeeeeeee, Daddy,' Kelly's shouting at the top of her voice, while poor Callum doesn't seem to recognise the balding fat bloke in his bright pink fleece. Wish I could have a memory lapse too, then I might be able to get away with shutting the door in his face.

'Hello, sexy,' he says to me. There's a faint Irish lilt softening his annoying nasal tones. Sadly, it's not the only souvenir he's ever brought back from the Emerald Isle.

Must have been like this in the war, when the heads of the household came home on leave expecting this amazing welcome, and the women resented the way all their plans and routines, as well organised as any military drill, had to be swept away so the man could muscle back in.

If only Dave was off to the Front Line, then he might

not come back alive. Instead of which he'll be home for an entire, almost unbearable, three days and then bugger off back to the front line of Dublin's property boom, where the biggest danger he faces is a pickled liver. Even then, he's always moaning about how expensive the booze is over there, and because my dopey father-in-law negotiated the contract in Irish punts, believing all that stuff about the Tiger economy, they hardly make any money out there. Whoever heard of a Tiger in Ireland? I suppose the Spud Economy doesn't have the same ring to it. . .

So Dave makes up for it when he gets home, straight down the pub with his mates, which would suit me fine if he didn't then come rolling back expecting a shag.

We used to have the same battle over it every time, like characters in a bloody soap opera, but since he brought back a dose of genuine Celtic crabs, I've had the moral high ground. When he gets too drunk to respond to logic, I sneak into Kelly's bedroom and sleep on the bottom bunk. She's always annoyed when she wakes up because she says the bed belongs to Jolene, her imaginary friend. I don't know how to take that, I really don't. I never needed imaginary friends when I was her age, I had quite enough real ones.

The only good thing about Dave's return home this time round is that the local paper want a photo of my lovely family for this article they're doing about the reunion and the programme. They can put it across two editions, the one that covers the scummy old Crawley Park estate, and the one for round here (which is the much posher bit of town).

'It might help drum up a few more ex-pupils,' Jenny said when she rang me to tell me the newspaper wanted to do a feature. I think they're a bit worried about the response from the e-mails I've sent so far.

'Yes,' I agreed. 'I think the problem is that most of the

kids I got on best with in the year are too interesting to go off and work in computers, so they're not even on that web-site.'

What's terrifying is that now I've got the loan of this laptop, I'm turning into a computer nerd myself. Though I'm disappointed at the response, too. I'm surprised whenever I log on, which is roughly once an hour, that I haven't got a full inbox. I've sent about twenty messages now through Friends Reunited, and I've had precisely two back. One was to this kid I vaguely remembered because Melody snogged him at a house party in the fourth year, and he e-mailed back to say sorry he didn't remember me, though he remembered Melody: 'wasn't she the school bike?' which was spot on, but not very charitable. He'd be quite interested in coming to a reunion, though, and if I wanted to pass on his name to the production company, he'd give them a quote to build a web-site just for the programme, because that's what he does for a living.

The only other person to reply is Helen Boris-Morris-Norris, who was sickly sweet in her e-mail; she'd been one of the first people to put her name down on the site and she was really chuffed that more ex-Crawley Parkers were joining up. She'd had about a dozen people contact her via the Web now, and it would be lovely to catch up on the good old days.

'I don't get it, Callum,' I said, when I'd read the e-mail a couple of times. How come Boris has got all these e-mails, and I haven't? I reckon she's exaggerating, but anyway, she said she'd put the word round. She's feeling pretty isolated, because she's moved with her husband to a village ten miles away, and he's away a lot, and she's had to give up work early, because her blood pressure's been on the high side since she's been pregnant. Just you wait, love. You ain't seen nothing yet. Welcome to the glorious world of mummy martyrdom.

The non-reply I'm most pissed off about is Gary's. Though I suppose I can't blame him.

'Some of the e-mail addresses on here might be out of date,' Jenny said, and she could be right, I guess. And the lack of info about him on the message boards means all I can do is fantasise.

Which I'm ashamed to admit I do rather a lot. Sometimes we're back at school, and he's much the same as he is on the photo I've got of us all on the day trip to Brighton in the fourth year, except his skin is clear. In reality, just as Gary's handsome jaw started emerging from the pretty-boy puppy fat, he was struck by acne. He was still the best-looking lad in the year, everyone knew that, but all those hormones had to find a way out, and so they erupted in volcanoes of red and yellow on his chin and cheeks. No one dared to call him pizza face, not with me as his girlfriend, but I did have nightmares sometimes that when we were kissing, a pustule might explode, and bind us together a bit like those rubber suckers you get to stick hooks to the wall.

It's a mystery to me when I think about his acne, not to mention the whole mint-green uniform thing, how any of us ever got past the hand-holding stage. But in my fantasies, we are on the same trip to Brighton, and we go down to the end of the pier and he gets down on one knee and proposes, and I agree, provided we can travel the world together. And then it all kind of goes fuzzy, like in a film, and we're sipping cocktails on Bondi beach, or another time we're on top of the Empire State Building, or he's buying me an engagement ring at Tiffany's.

There's no sex in these fantasies, not really, only the kind of soft-focus canoodling they used to put in the black and white photo-stories that made us crease up.

It's funny because it's so different from my daydreams then. Me and Melody and the others, we were constantly wanting to get to the next stage of being grown-up, and because it was what the teachers warned us about, we figured that next stage was fags and booze, and sex. Mainly sex. So we mocked the kids like Suzanne, who thought carefully about their options and even paid attention in Careers lessons. We couldn't believe it when she said once that she wanted to go to university but before that she was going to save up and go travelling, to Australia and India.

It was like she'd stepped off another planet, and we never let her forget it. She kept quiet about her plans after that. We couldn't see why you'd bother to sit on a plane for days when we all knew the only down under worth exploring was located midway between the waist and the knees.

I guess now I've done enough shagging to realise that it doesn't make the earth move, all it does is take you on a one-way ticket to stirrups and the speculum, whether the end result is a baby or a nasty rash ... suddenly that other Down Under seems unbearably appealing.

'I can't believe they're putting you on this programme,' Dave says, as the photographer tries to coax Callum into joining us in a charming family scene around the dining table.

'Why not?'

'Well, for a start, you'll bore everyone to death like you do me, with all your stupid stories about school.'

I can't stop myself snarling back. 'I think you'll find it's my amusing anecdotes that made them choose me, actually. It's a bit more interesting than tales from the building site, you loser.'

I look at my miserable husband, and wonder yet again what Gary's doing now? He can't have joined the police, not after what he did. They won't take anyone with a record, will they? Maybe he's gone into car dealing or something. He always did have the gift of the gab.

I could have been living in a lovely detached house, nothing vulgar, maybe something Victorian, with a gorgeous BMW or a Merc in the drive. Except do Victorian houses have drives?

'... and when we meet the troll, he'll give us Cadbury's buttons.' Kelly is sitting quite still, talking to Jolene, who in her imagination is obviously sitting just to the left of my head.

If I'd had Gary's kids, I bet I'd have had a boy first, and the photographer would probably be taking photos outside while Gary and – what would suit the surname Coombs? God knows I used to play around writing our future children's names on my pencil case all the time in lessons. Jason, that sounds nice. So while Gary and Jason kick a football around on our large decked garden, I'd be standing proudly next to them with a cafetière full of fresh-brewed coffee. And at my side, there'd be an angelic little girl with gold ringlets, and a 'butter-wouldn't melt' smile the same as mine, offering the reporter and photographer cups of tea from an antique dolls' tea set.

I turn to the reporter. 'She's not normally any trouble. Kelly, stop chuntering.'

'I'm only talking to Jolene.'

'That's her little friend, you know, a made-up one. My mum's got all the old Dolly Parton LPs, so that's who we've got to thank.'

The reporter nods. I don't think he's listening. 'Can I just run through a few things with you for the article, then Derek'll take a few pictures, and we'll leave you in peace?'

'Sure. What do you want to know?'

'Jenny from the TV company says you're planning the reunion for July, is that right? Seventeen years after you all left?'

'Uh-huh. That's right. We were the class of 84.'

'And how many people are you hoping will make it?'

'Well. There were getting on for 250 in our year group, but it's obviously been a long time, so I'd be pleased if we got anywhere between 150 to 200.'

'Right. And are there any people you're hoping you might see that you've lost touch with completely?'

Who do I want to see, except Gary? The person I miss most is the real Tracey Mortimer. But she doesn't exist any more. Years of nappies, arguments and cashing-up in the stationery shop have made sure of that.

And after that, I miss Shrimp. But even the Internet can't do reincarnation.

'God, it's so hard. I'd like to see any of them, anyone from the days when 5G ruled the world! You tell them to get in touch with me – have they given you the e-mail address?'

'Yep, I've got it here. And what about you –' the reporter checks his notes '– uh, Dave? You're not worried Tracey might hit it off again with an old flame, childhood sweetheart?' He looks at us mischievously, his pen poised to jot down any good quotes in his notebook.

Dave turns to me, then back to face the journalist.

'I don't think anyone's going to meet Tracey now, and wish they'd not let her slip through their fingers, do you?'

And as the reporter and photographer exchange nervous looks, unsure whether this is a joke, Dave helpfully tries to clear things up. 'But if they do, they're welcome. And please print *that* in your paper. Could be my lucky day.'

Chapter Seven

'Don't wanna get up,' Kelly says yet again, and it's one of those times when I almost sympathise with people who leave their children on church doorsteps. Only 'almost', of course, because otherwise I'd be a horrible parent and deserve the most terrible punishments, but I really wish it was acceptable to use a dummy to shut a six-year-old up.

'Kelly, there are a lot of things in life we don't want to do, but unfortunately we still have to do them.'

Holy shit, where did my mother appear from? Except I never moaned about going to school, it was always homework or tidying my room or going to see her dad in the hospital at Christmas, because he used to want to play peek-a-boo and that scared me because he was sixty-three.

Kelly's got worse since Dave went back to Ireland, so that's another thing I can blame on him. Except, for all his faults – and there are plenty of them – he doesn't seem to carry the shyness gene any more than I do. It must be some kind of throwback to a previous generation, and I wish they could breed it out, because it's very hard to know what to do. To be fair to Kelly, it doesn't look like a hell of a lot of fun for her either.

Every morning she wakes up with a personality change. I put her to bed and she does as she's told, and she makes the right kind of noises when I read a story, and kisses me nicely, and doesn't wet the bed.

But then overnight, she's transformed into a six-year-old teenager. She's moody and surly, and everything's a battle. Getting her out of bed is the first skirmish – she insists she's ill or feels hot, and yet she's always a nice temperature, biscuity skin, not clammy or chilly. Her attempts to look poorly – half-closed eyes and fake-limp arms – are always betrayed by the colour in her cheeks

Then it's prising Bear from her, this disgusting toy that was once the colour of honey, and is now the colour of mud. I occasionally manage to wash it, but only if she can sit and watch it going round and round the machine. She waves and sings Dolly Parton songs at Bear, as it bounces about in the foamy water, and if she doesn't see its face for more than about ten seconds, she panics, and we both sit on the floor holding our breath until the revolution of the drum propels its cracked plastic nose back towards the window.

It probably took scores of Third-World child slaves less time to make her uniform than it does to cajole her into it, and that's not even counting her shoes. She moves downstairs a step at a time, as though each one is a huge ordeal, and it's the same with every single spoon of her cereal. She went through about a week of deliberately spilling food on to her pinafore dress; I think she thought perhaps it would get so late by the time I'd managed to clean her up that I wouldn't have the energy to ferry her to school, but I shouted at her then, not that I'm very proud of it, but it was so frustrating to have to clean her up as well as Callum. I stopped it by making her wear a baby's bib. She might be soft, but at least she has *some* pride.

'Not hungry.' That's the latest variation, and it's slightly more effective in raising my stress levels, because they say anorexia can affect the under-tens these days, and it's just a hunch, but I'd say Kelly's got the right kind of stubborn nervous temperament to get herself into that kind of mess.

We had an anorexic at school, Rachel Clark, and she was quite handy to have as a mate because she never spent her dinner money, and when word got back that she didn't buy any lunch, her mum would send her in with all sorts of goodies – Wagon Wheels, Dairylea triangles, those tiny packets of SunMaid raisins – and she was desperate to offload them.

There's another guest for my list. I'm keeping one on the fridge of people I suddenly remember, so Jenny and Annabel can have a go at tracing them. They've got this amazing computer program that means they can type in someone's name and it'll come up with their address or phone number, or all the people of that name in Britain, anyway. Works better with blokes, obviously, because they don't change their names.

I haven't asked them if they've looked up Gary yet. Half of me wants him to turn up at the reunion, sweep me off my feet. And half of me's too worried that I couldn't deal with the disappointment if he didn't live up to my expectations . . .

Alec hadn't said a word, and he was already sitting down when Jenny came into the meeting room, so it wasn't even the way he walked. But he oozed malevolence from every pore.

Annabel hovered with the tray of coffees, fearful that even the noise of them clinking together would set him off.

'Put the fucking thing down.'

'Come on,' Jenny started, 'It's not that bad, we're starting to build up a good guest list and the agents for a couple of the bands have–'

'Not that bad?' Alec snorted so fiercely that she wouldn't have been surprised if flames had poured through his nostrils. Though Jenny thought that level of nasal aggression was high-risk behaviour for a guy with such a heavy coke habit. 'Not that bad?'

They waited.

'Not that bad, that we're now two months from this bloody reunion and (a) we don't have a band to play, (b) we don't have any human interest stories and (c) the woman you assured me was the most popular girl in the school has so far failed to make contact with any of her enormous group of so-called best mates. Yeah, I suppose you're right really. At least we don't have to fix the hole in the ozone layer as well, or we really would be in trouble.'

Jenny sighed. 'I know it looks a lot to sort out on paper, but look at it another way. A month ago we didn't even have a reunion or a school to work on. The head teacher's said yes to us holding the party in the hall, we've got the registers from all the tutor groups in Tracey's year, she's great on camera and we've got loads of interest from the press. We can make a virtue out of necessity, like the local rag did, kind of "help Tracey in her trip down Memory Lane".'

'It's not in the proposal.' Alec hated deviating from the carefully crafted commissioning document that had sold the idea to the channel in the first place.

'Sometimes things don't work like the proposal,' Jenny said, gently, as though she was explaining the truth about the tooth fairy to a four-year-old. 'But that just makes things more fun. And Annabel has been checking out some other ideas.' She nudged Annabel, who looked nervous.

'Yes, yeah. Um, for example. Well, why don't we take Tracey back into school? That'd make a nice sequence as she meets the new staff, and the kids from 1G these days? There are a couple of teachers who remember her.'

Alec doodled on the side of the manila file, grinding his pen in zigzag patterns. But at least he hadn't interrupted them.

Jenny checked her notes. 'And I know you're worried we haven't heard back from Melody, but this other girl, Helen, she was in the same class and she's very sweet and willing to do filming, plus she's pregnant, so that might be nice. And it means she's got time to do all the "looking for an outfit" stuff we'd got planned.'

Alec snorted, but less ferociously than before. 'We still need the band. We still need an old boyfriend.'

'Well, Annabel has had some encouraging noises from Madness, and you know that they're the ones we had in the original pitch to Channel 5. We might even get Suggs to be the compère. And we think we've tracked down Gary. There's quite a few on the electoral register, but the most likely suspect is living in London, and we're going to write to him. So that's cool. And we had another idea.'

Alec buried his head in his hands, but then peered out between his fingers. 'Oh God, am I ready for this?'

'Annabel and I thought that, you know how in *Big Brother* they had those psychologists, that kind of made it look a bit more upmarket? So we thought, why don't we take Tracey to meet one, interview them herself and then she might have some amazing insight and even if she doesn't, we've got another sequence to pad out the film.'

Annabel was nodding enthusiastically. 'And you can bet BBC2 haven't thought of it!'

He looked at the two women and then up at the ceiling. 'OK. Whatever. But it's still down to you both to get it working. As the most experienced member of staff on this programme, I'm not taking the rap for cocking up just about the most straightforward commission Smart Alec Productions has ever had.'

*

54

Roger was bloody hard work compared to Gary's usual sidekick, but since Colin had been nutted by a football thug, and was being used as a test case for mental injury by the over-ambitious Police Fed. rep, Roger was as good as it was going to get.

'Oh, great,' Roger said as two Japanese women with dyed pink hair headed purposefully towards them, wielding a camera. 'I can't believe any tourists would stay on the Central line as far as Acton. I knew I should have combed my hair before I came out.'

'Come on, Rog, there are worse things than posing with a couple of students.' One woman's nose was pierced with a safety pin, probably at one of the hi-tech joints in Soho that true body art enthusiasts would reject for being far too hygienic. The other, who had matching black nails and lips, proffered her camera.

Gary stepped into position between the girls while Roger tried to work out which button to press. Pierced nose turned to Gary in irritation.

'No, no, with cuffs, with cuffs.'

Roger raised one eyebrow. 'Who's the fat bird that's taken over from Jeremy Beadle? You sure this isn't a set-up?'

Gary looked nervously at the tourists, then unbuttoned his jacket far enough to be able to flash the handcuffs. Pierced Nose lunged for them but he moved aside. 'No, you're not having them. It's this or nothing.' She moved back, and stood sulkily while Black Lips grinned for the camera.

As they walked off, waving, Gary shrugged. 'It's nice to keep the public happy, though, isn't it, Rog? Mind you, those Japanese kids all look like clones to me.'

'Don't let anyone hear you say that, you'll get chucked out of the Met.'

Not with a mixed race social worker as my girlfriend I

won't, thought Gary, but he decided it might be best not to share it with Roger. Colin was cool about it, but he suspected Rog would see it as a double whammy of political correctness, and be even less conversational in future. If that was possible.

It was bound to rain soon. This bobby on the beat stuff – sorry, high visibility community policing – was fine for about a month a year, in between the spring showers and the August heatwave. But May was unpredictable.

He racked his brains to think of something to talk about. Colin and him used to natter for hours about nothing in particular; they were as bad as old women, and even had pensioners' names for each other, Gladys and Colleen, but Colin wasn't going to be back for at least a month, longer if the Fed bloke had his way.

Hobbies. Well, when did Gary have time for hobbies? Roger probably fished or train-spotted, but Gary struggled to think of his own prime non-work occupation. Drinking? That only counted as a pastime if you went for the fine wines option (hardly possible on a constable's wage, even with overtime) or the real ale option (not much better than angling). Porn. That was the closest Gary got to a hobby, and he didn't want to risk telling Roger. Either he'd freak, or he'd divulge his own particular preferences. Horrible thought.

Indirectly, due to it being such a prime source of porn, the Web was also his hobby, but something told him Roger was a Luddite. There was precious little he could relate to when he watched *The Bill*, but they'd got Reg Hollis right. And Roger would have been his twin separated at birth.

Then he thought of something anyone could relate to.

'Rog? Are you still in touch with anyone you went to school with?'

Roger thought it over, as they trudged along the side of the little row of shops with their baskets of over-sized fruit and veg, sitting exposed to the pinching fingers of passing shoppers and the poisonous fumes of passing lorries.

Roger always looked like a masticating cow, even when he had nothing to chew.

'No one.' Then he stopped, peered in through the window of a mini-mart, making everyone inside freeze as if they were playing grandmother's footsteps, until he looked away again. 'Unless you count my missus.'

'Your wife? You were at school with your wife?'

'Only in the juniors. Went to a boys' school after that.'

'So was it love at first sight?'

'Wouldn't say it's love any time. She's a good sport, though. Doesn't moan like most women.'

Gary watched Roger as he carried on chewing the air. Mrs Roger was clearly a saint.

'Morning, Mr Mirchandani,' Gary said, nodding at the guy standing in the doorway of his newsagents' shop, who stood there most of the day, chain-smoking Marlborough Lights, and probably most of his profit margin.

They walked a bit further, and it was clear Roger wasn't going to return the question.

'You see, I've been thinking about some of the people I was at school with, lately.'

No response at all. But Gary thought it still helped to say things out loud, especially stuff you weren't sure about, even if the other person wasn't listening.

'Well, one particular person, actually. My first girl-friend.'

Roger allowed himself a wry smile. Or what Gary thought was probably meant to be a wry smile but looked more as though the imaginary grass he'd been chewing over had got stuck in one of his teeth and he was trying to suck it out.

'So. Yeah, you see, this girl. Tracey.' He found it hard not to say the word without spitting. 'Suddenly, out of the blue, this e-mail. You know, on the computer. Like it hadn't been seventeen years since she'd last been in touch, just "hi, how are you?" Or something like that.'

Remember me? I remember you ...
Get in touch – if you dare.

He'd tried to forget the message, but it kept popping up again in his head. Especially those last three words. *If you dare.* They taunted him when he was doing the washing-up, teased him when he was bored after the night shift, mocked him when Gabby told him to watch the speed limit. Poor Gabby would probably never get in a car with him ever again if she knew the truth.

God knows it had taken him long enough to get Tracey out of his system when they were sixteen, and it felt now as though she'd never gone at all, had just been lodging somewhere in his body, like the cold sore virus, waiting to reappear when he was at a low ebb.

'I mean, what made her do that? This is what I can't work out. I never could work her out. Women. But then it's not all women really, to be fair, because my girlfriend, she's totally predictable. In a nice way.'

Roger stopped again. 'Lad,' he said, and Gary braced himself for what Rog obviously thought was going to be the wise counsel of a man of the world. 'Lad, if you haven't heard from her in seventeen years, and she's got under your skin like that again after all that time, I've only got one suggestion.'

'Yeah?'

'Move house before she comes looking for you.'

Suzanne Marshall-Sharp clicked back on to the one-week view on her PC organiser screen, then shook her immaculately conditioned red hair.

'Charlotte, we're going to have to cancel the Women's Institute. I don't like to let them down, but they're a bit of a captive audience already, whereas the CBI...Well, we're not going to get a platform like that again in a hurry, never mind right before Tony's keynote speech.'

Just outside the window, a pigeon stopped on the ledge and peered in through the enormous warehouse windows.

'It's weird how you never see *baby* pigeons, isn't it?' Suzanne chewed her Cross fountain pen, then pulled off a Post-it note, and wrote 'Baby Pigeon'. 'I might use that. "Like baby pigeons, we want our young to be neither seen nor heard until they can fend for themselves." It's quite a nice analogy.'

Charlotte scratched behind her left ear, as she always did when she was stressed. 'I suppose I'm going to have to ring them and break the news?'

'Well, er, that is your job, Charlotte.'

'I know, but I hate turning people down, especially when there's hardly any notice for them to find anyone else.'

'OK, look I'll call Floella, she loves those things, she might do it for the cause. Don't suppose *she's* got an invite from the CBI.'

The three office phones rang suddenly, and the pigeon flapped away. Suzanne stared at the flashing light, then looked meaningfully at her PA, the unspoken 'it is your job, Charlotte', hanging in the air between them.

'Millennium Child Campaign, good morning!' Charlotte said brightly.

Suzanne smiled in satisfaction at the greeting; it had just the right combination of popular appeal and sincerity. Bit like Princess Diana. Now she would have been the perfect patron.

Charlotte waved at her. 'Hello, Mrs Sharp. I think she's available, let me see if I can put you through.'

Suzanne felt her neck tighten as the extension on her desk started to purr. She took a deep breath.

'Hi, Mum. Bit busy right now. Sorting out some more speeches.'

Mrs Sharp's London overspill vowels spilled out of the receiver. Suzanne had adopted a modified version of the accent, a hint that her background had more to offer than Roedean and Trinity College, without the ugly certainty of new town vowels.

'Yeah, too busy to talk to me, I know. That's all right. But I thought you'd be interested in this.'

Suzanne doubted anything her mother could tell her would be interesting, but there was an inevitability about the conversation. It would happen now, or tomorrow, or, worse still, at home, and despite being her own boss, she still preferred to deal with personal calls in 'work time' because she liked the fact that no one could tell her off.

'It's Crawley Park. Your school.'

Well, yes, obviously, even my memory's not that short, thought Suzanne. Probably about to get a government hit squad, or be closed, assuming the little buggers hadn't burned it down already.

'Not just your school, but your year, the ones who started in 1979.'

1979. The first year of Thatcher's reign of terror. The year that, if you traced it back, probably started Suzanne on her journey, via college and psychologist training, to Chief Executive of the Millennium Child Campaign (supported by Cherie Booth QC).

'Hmm, what about them?'

'Well, they're having a reunion in July. And it's going to be on telly.'

Oh God, any minute now she'll suggest I should go, Suzanne realised, and started inventing midsummer weddings and pagan rituals and dinner parties in Downing

Street to cover all thirty-one days of the month.

'And I wouldn't even have called you but then I saw who was organising it.' Mrs Sharp paused, as if she knew the effect the two words would have. 'Tracey Mortimer.'

Charlotte watched in astonishment as the colour drained from her boss's face.

Chapter Eight

You know those surveys of the most hated professions . . . it always amazes me that teachers don't feature, along with dentists and insurance salesmen and tabloid reporters and politicians. People slag off dentists for being sadists, and the rest for being a nuisance, but I think there's a certain mentality that makes you want to dominate and terrify small children, and it's not altogether healthy.

There are exceptions – the odd teacher who treats you as an equal, like Bob Carmichael. But generally, I think the profession stinks.

I'm just hoping it doesn't show. Mrs Fellowes, who has perfected a martyred smile worthy of Mother Theresa, has summoned me to school, and I know the one thing guaranteed to bring out the worst in teachers is 'lack of respect'. What makes them think they deserve it automatically I have no idea, though maybe it's something they teach them at training college – an unshakeable belief in their own superiority.

Mind you, I can't deny that my heart leaped when Kelly gave me the note. I suppose your average mother would hate the idea that their little darling was causing enough trouble to merit a letter home, but for me, it's the first sign that she might be a chip off the old block, after all.

I was always in trouble. I remember that feeling, a mixture of dread and excitement, that took over when I knew Mum was on her way home from yet another appointment with the head teacher. It never bothered me, but it can't have been easy for her. I can imagine the nudges from the two witches in the school office, the comments, 'You again, *Mrs* Mortimer?' and the whispers that she was meant to hear, as she waited outside the head's office. *'On her own, she is. And you know what they say about the lack of paternal influences...'*

Most of the time she'd arrive back and just give me this look. It wasn't even anger, but a lack of recognition, as though she was completely confused by the idea that she could have played a part in creating a child that could do whatever it was I'd just been accused of. Maybe she told herself it was all from my father's side. None of it was a big deal – fights in the sand pit, kiss-chase, playing tricks on people – but I denied it all. Much easier that way, and anyway half the things that Mum would repeat back to me in this weary voice, I didn't even remember doing, so it felt as though I hadn't done anything anyway. They only found out about roughly a fifth of what we got up to, so it was easy to pretend that the things they had uncovered were terrible miscarriages of justice.

The only time I remember in any detail, I wouldn't have been much older than Kelly, maybe I'd have been seven by then because it was June, and I'd have had my birthday already in April.

I was being quite good, considering, trying hard not to let anyone know I was upset while everyone around me made their Father's Day cards, pretending to myself as much as the others that if I concentrated hard enough, I could make a card so special that Dad would actually appear. My fantasy dad, tall as a giant, with big hairy arms and a deep gruff voice that would only go gentle for me, as he pulled a box from beside his back and un-ravelled the bow holding the lid on, letting me open it up to let out the kitten inside.

My card had a cut-out of a man, a film star, and a box I'd painted in bright orange, and a kitten from the Victorian pictures the teacher had brought in for the occasion. And as a finishing touch, I was going to add blue glitter, sprinkled all over it like magic dust, to make it real.

Shirley Bishop, who thought she was a cut above because her mum was the secretary, nudged me, and nearly knocked over my glue pot.

'Dunno why you're making a card at all,' she said, loud enough for the whole table to hear. 'My mum says you don't even have a dad.'

'So do.' I snarled back, after a few seconds passed, and the shock wore off.

She'd seen it in my face, though. 'You so DON'T.'

I could feel my eyes stinging, and a tear dropped on to the box, smudging the orange lines. 'DO!' I shouted this time. It should have been a warning.

'Do-on't have a daddy,' she laughed back at me, sing-song provocation.

I picked up the vial of blue glitter, poured a little bit on to the glue trail I'd made for it around the edges of the card, sprinkled off the excess, and then threw the rest of the tube's contents as hard as I could into Shirley Bishop's eyes. Her scream was the most satisfying thing I'd ever heard.

Mum was angry with me when the teacher told her, and she got angrier when I tried to explain. After she sent me to bed early, I could hear her crying downstairs, and then Granddad arrived, and brought me up toast. He under-stood. That must have been just before he started going senile and they had to put him in the home.

It was the Christmas after that when Mum told me Dad would never be back because he had died in a crash, after he'd gone to live with the other lady. I wasn't upset after that, because at least I never expected him to be there. And if anyone asked why I didn't have a dad, I could just say he was dead, not that he'd left us.

I always make Father's Day cards with the kids, even though Dave doesn't deserve one. I don't think they make them in school any more, not when half the kids come from one-parent families now.

Some things don't change, though. Kelly's school smells of cabbage and disinfectant, as every school should, and the buildings are every bit as traditional. The brick walls are painted in shiny cream and khaki, and the floors are grey and slippery from millions of plimsolled foot-steps. I admit I like the uniform, the mole-coloured pinafore dress and the pale blue blouse with the round collar; she looks adorable in it, but I know I would have hated it at Kelly's age. Not that she makes a fuss ...

They've made an effort to brighten things up, with the obligatory drawings and projects, endless variations on the same themes: the Romans, mini-beasts (known in my day as insects) and Harry Potter. But the primary colours can't really disguise the fact that it's not fun, it's education, and they're two very different things.

I can see Mrs Fellowes through the glass panel in the door, and when I knock, it rattles in the frame. She smiles as she looks up, which surprises me, because I was expect-ing a hard warning stare.

'Hello, Mrs Brown, thank you for coming in,' she says and smiles again. She has tiny teeth; perhaps she was such a careful little girl that she never even lost her milk teeth.

'Do sit down.' She gestures towards the only other adult-sized chair in the room. From this distance I realise she must be much younger than she looks – there are no wrinkles that I can see, and she's not wearing any make-up. All I can smell is a sickly perfume, Lily of the Valley or Hyacinth, the sort of scent that you usually only smell combined with an acid top note of urine, in old people's homes . . .

'Now, what I want to talk to you about might be a little bit of a shock to start with, so I want you to know that it's quite natural for you to feel upset, or even a little angry. But what we need to do is concentrate on what's in Kelly's best interests.'

Her face is all bunched up like a hamster's and I don't have a clue what she's talking about.

'Um, OK, yeah, well, that's what I want, obviously,' I say, then I wait.

'Kelly's a lovely little girl, really lovely,' and she pauses, as if I'm likely to disagree. I notice that I feel very cold, even though it's a mild day and the monster-sized radiator along the classroom window is blazing.

'Very bright. And very hard-working,' and she smiles as though she is bestowing a huge compliment. But there's something about the way she's emphasising my daughter's goodness that is making me uncomfortable.

'I wonder? Has Kelly said anything to you at home about how she feels about school?'

It's never even occurred to me that she might. Can you really talk to a six-year-old? We have so little in common that what we talk about is favourite colours and why she can't have a guinea pig.

'No. She's not really a chatty child, but . . .' I rack my brains to find a comment that might show I do take some notice of my first-born child. 'I know she enjoys her reading, doesn't she?'

'Yes, she does. She's doing very well in the literacy hour.' Mrs Fellowes doesn't look very happy now. 'So you have no real concerns, then?' Her eyes narrow as she

66

looks at me and it's clear she thinks I should be concerned. And something tells me it's got nothing to do with misbehaviour.

I shake my head and Mrs Fellowes takes a weary breath. 'Well, Mrs Brown, you see, I – not just me, actually, I've spoken to the playground supervisors and the head. So, WE are rather concerned that ... well, there's no easy way of saying this –'

SO JUST BLOODY SAY IT, I'm thinking.

'We think Kelly may have fallen victim to bullying.'

Suzanne read the menu of her favourite restaurant for the fifth time, and realised there was nothing there she wanted to eat. She threw it back on to the marble-topped table.

Christian reached out to touch her hand, tickling the underside of her palm before she snatched it back.

'Christian, it's no use you trying to understand, because you won't.'

'Suz,' he said, gently. 'I don't think that's very fair. You haven't even tried to tell me. All I know is that there's a school reunion and you're pissed off about it. So try explaining.'

She still couldn't quite believe that she was married to this perfect specimen of New Manhood, but this was the first time she'd ever felt a problem would be beyond him. The one disadvantage of Younger Men.

'It's not that I want to keep anything from you. But ... OK, what's the worst memory you've got from school?' Suzanne sat back and waited, while he screwed up his adorable hazel eyes, concentrating on the past. Of course, in Christian's case, it was much more recent.

'Well, um ... I was pretty miserable when I first started boarding.'

There was always that, the suffering of the small boy sent away from his parents to beatings and buggery. But it was a particular variety of upper-middle-class suffering so universal in Christian's contemporaries that it became more of a badge of honour than something to be ashamed of.

Suzanne shrugged, then gave in to his open face, and stretched both hands back across the table towards her husband. 'I'm not denigrating that, I think it's cruel and unnecessary and unforgivable–'

'Well, you would say that, wouldn't you? Otherwise you head-shrinkers would go out of business.' He was teasing her.

'Yeah, yeah. It has messed with your head, otherwise you wouldn't have turned into a toyboy, would you? But it's not the same.'

The waiter approached them. 'Order for me, Christian,' she said, and he selected comfort food, bruschetta and risotto.

She traced the patterns of the marble with her finger. 'It's so hard. It's so bloody ridiculous as well, I've always talked for a living, haven't I? About exactly this kind of thing. It's probably why I even ended up doing the whole psychology degree and the public speaking and...oh, God.'

Christian was concentrating with every cell of his twenty-five-year-old body, willing her to explain, and himself to understand.

'I suppose what I'm saying is that actually, what I am now, it's mainly down to that fucking bitch.' Suzanne banged the table in frustration, then looked around her in embarrassment, suddenly aware of how loud her voice had become.

Christian smiled at her. 'Well, darling, in that case, I for one would love to meet Tracey Mortimer, and thank her very much indeed.'

*

'Bullying?' It makes no sense. Kelly, being bullied. She's six, for God's sake.

'Yes, I know it must come as a bit of a shock.'

It would be a shock if I actually believed her. But it's stupid to talk about kids of six being bullied, especially my Kelly.

'You've got it wrong. Kelly's fine. I'm the first to admit she's not the most out-going kid, and it's bizarre, because you can't shut me up, or her dad. But bullying?'

'Mrs Brown, I'm not talking about anything physical, so please don't worry about that. We're just concerned that Kelly is ...' Mrs Fellowes is waving her hands around now, and it's almost making me laugh because she's flustering over something that's clearly complete rubbish.

'Is what?'

'Kelly's ... different. Yes, she's quiet and there's nothing wrong with that – in itself. I – I mean, we are worried that maybe she doesn't really have the, how shall I put it, the social skills to make the most of school?'

Now this is getting surreal. First of all she's saying that this school is some kind of war zone where infants go round threatening each other, and now she reckons Kelly's a retard.

'What the hell is this about? Is this because I'm not in the bloody PTA or something?'

'Mrs Brown ...' Every time she says my name I want to punch her, and I'm really not a violent person. But the way she drawls, it's as though even speaking my name is tiring her out '... I don't think this is going to help. Now, we're sure that Kelly's at no risk at the moment, and we're introducing Circle Time into classes right across the school anyway, which gives all the children a chance to explore how they're feeling, so it could all blow over. But I thought it was right to let you know, and see if you might want to have a chat with Kelly. And depending on what she says, we might think about doing some...work with her.'

'Work?' This woman talks double Dutch, and she'd win the World Patronising Championships without any problem.

'The school has a close relationship with the Educational Psychology Service, and we do find that early intervention can prevent an awful lot of problems that might –'

'A psychiatrist? You think my daughter ought to go and see a shrink? You're off your head yourself.'

She gives me this long, long stare, then sighs and stands up. 'I don't think we're getting anywhere here, Mrs Brown, but it does seem this has come out of the blue.'

She rummages around in this enormous handbag she's got on her desk, and pulls out a leaflet. I look down at it, and there's a cartoon picture of various children, different colours, all very jolly, grinning like maniacs, and a big heading saying 'Does your child need special help?'

'Mrs Brown, maybe you could take this away with you, think about it and then if you're interested in what you read, well, come back to me. And we'll keep you in touch about how things seem at school.'

I really want to snatch the booklet and tear it up in front of her and stamp up and down on it, but something tells me she'd absolutely *love* it if I did that, so instead I tuck it away in my coat pocket.

She sighs again. 'We're only trying to help Kelly enjoy her time with us ... and we do really need your co-oper-ation to make that happen, Mrs Brown.'

I can't bring myself to reply to her, and it's a good job, actually, because I think if I was capable of speech at this exact moment, what I'd say would not be very mature. It's all I can manage to get out of the door and not slam it so hard that the glass smashes out on to the floor.

'Good choice,' said Suzanne, as the rich risotto started to work soothing carbohydrate magic on her stressed nerves. 'Sorry to be so moody. I can't believe that just hearing her name has such an effect after all this time.'

'Kind of proves your case about the consequences of a crap time at school, though.'

'I did think I'd left it all behind. I suppose I never will. God, she was such a cow, but I don't think she had the ... humanity to know what she was doing. Every single bloody day, I used to hope she wouldn't be there, that she'd be ill or move or ... Well, I think I wanted her to die, actually. Or if she didn't, maybe I would.'

Christian leaned across the table to kiss her cheek. 'Poor Suz.'

'And you know, I've met enough kids since who've had it so much worse, really, unimaginable stuff, and I think if it did that to me, and still does it to me now, what can I do for them, what hope have we got of helping them to get what they need out of their lives?'

'That's so typical of you, Suz, thinking about other people at a time like this.' They shared the smile of a couple utterly convinced that no one else was as lucky as they had been, in finding one another.

'Years of conditioning.'

'But maybe, Suz, maybe it's just that you needed something like this, maybe it's fate that it's happened now, so that you can finally put it behind you. Perhaps now that we're thinking about bringing our own little Suzes and Christians into the world. . .?'

She played with the remaining clumps of risotto on her plate. 'I'm sorry, Christian. But all this makes it even less likely that now's the right time.' It was their one source of disharmony, and there was little sign of progress.

Christian pouted sadly. 'But, you said it yourself, at the inaugural charity dinner, in fact, we have to move on from our pasts, into our futures ...'

Just occasionally, his naiveté failed to be utterly charming.

'I know. But that was before ... and now that Tracey Mortimer seems to have come back into my life, I dunno, perhaps you're right and it is fate ... but this time round, she's not going to get the upper hand ...'

Chapter Nine

Boris is coming to tea, though you'd think it was the whole Royal Family, the way Jenny and Annabel are behaving. Of course, they're recording the entire thing.

'She's really keen,' Jenny told me on the phone when she rang to fix a date, 'and we think it'll make a nice sequence for early on in the film.'

That's all they talk about, 'sequences' and structure, and I feel more and more like a performing seal. I mean, I always knew there was bound to be more to TV than you see on screen, but it's unbelievable the amount of acting they want me to do . . . I think I should be eligible for an Oscar at the end of all this.

'Could you try to look a bit more enthusiastic?' Annabel says, while I butter some rolls, and I wonder what makes her think that making sandwiches should produce a state of ecstasy. She seems pretty unimpressed by the idea that anyone should be 'just' a housewife, yet also seems to expect me to exhibit the satisfaction of a 1950s fantasy domestic goddess. But Nigella Lawson, I ain't.

Alec's busy in London doing whatever producers do – which according to the girls mainly involves illegal substances – so Jenny's in charge of the filming today. I definitely get the impression they're disappointed in me.

She's going around with the look of a parent who's invested a fortune in public schooling, only to find out that actually their little cherub is going to live on a commune. I haven't lived up to expectations.

'I'm sure it's going to be fine,' she says, in a voice which suggests the opposite. 'But we thought it would be nice to get you and Helen together now, and also of course, Helen does seem to be in touch with a few more people, so we thought she might spread the word.'

Which seems like a nice way of saying, where are all your mates? I must admit I thought it would be easier than this, but I suppose the thing about people like Helen is that they're classic Christmas card senders. At school, she was kindly and bovine, and even in those days, sent cards to everyone, birthdays, Easter, any excuse, cheap Woolworths specials, full of cheery insincere messages signed off with 'lots of love and kisses'. She even gave them to Suzanne, and most people wouldn't even speak to her, never mind give her cards.

I might even have had a few in the early years after we left, and she's so bland that you tend to return them out of politeness. So she's bound to have an address book full of old school friends and a hundred other acquaintances from holidays or long train journeys. But she would make a seriously boring TV programme – which is, of course, why they've picked me.

They've given me one of those microphones you can walk around with, with a mini radio attached to the back of my jeans, so I can talk and move at the same time, without having to watch out for a cable tethering me to the camera.

'Tracey, can you tell me what you remember about Helen?'

I know the routine by now, they like me to look at the camera, and natter on 'as though you're chatting to your best mate'. Except, I suddenly realised when Jenny said that, I haven't had one since 1992. Me, Tracey Mortimer, the most popular girl in the whole of Crawley Park. How the hell did I let that happen?

'Helen?' I pause to butter another roll, there's a pile of them now that would feed a village of Kosovan refugees, but they've told me to keep spreading, for continuity's sake. 'Well, Helen was in 1G right from the start, like me ... and, well, I hope she won't mind me saying this, but she stood out because she was quite ... big.'

In other words, porky. But I don't want to sound like a bitch.

'We used to watch her, and I don't think she ate more than us at lunchtimes, but there was no way she was just big-boned ...' I peer down at the sandwiches, and add an extra layer of butter.

'She was kind of fat, but happy ... You know the kind. Everyone's agony aunt, someone to talk to, and I think maybe because she was big, she was never competition when it came to the lads, so she managed to stay out of all the nastier arguments.'

I wonder how she ever found a bloke willing to take her clothes off and delve around enough to impregnate her.

'So did she have a nickname?' Jenny knows she did, of course, it's in the huge file she brings with her every time she comes, but for some reason she thinks if she pretends she doesn't, it'll make for a better answer.

'Yeah, Boris, which is–'

'Er, Tracey?' Jenny interrupts me and looks as though I've made some kind of really obvious mistake. But I'm buggered if I can work out what it is, so I just wait for her to put me right.

'Full sentences?' They told me at the beginning to try to speak in complete sentences, because they often edit the questions out. It reminds me of French lessons with

Madame Higginbottom. 'Zut alors ... toujours complete sentences, 'ow many times must you all be told?'

But hang on ... 'Well, yeah, sure, Jenny, but if you ask me questions like "did she have a nickname?" then it's kind of difficult to answer anything BUT yes or no.'

She glares at me. 'OK, let's try it again. So, Tracey, tell me if Helen had a nickname?'

'Yes ... oh shit. Hang on ...' I pause, and formulate a whole sentence. 'Helen had a nickname, it was Boris. Because her surname was Morris, you see, and she looked a bit like Boris Karloff, the guy who played Frankenstein, so being eleven and a bunch of smart arses, we made the connection. It really made me laugh on the web-site that she's only gone and married a guy called Norris, so it still fits.'

She always seemed to take it quite well, Boris did, but I wonder if she hated it really. I only remember seeing her upset once, and that was in the weekly team-picking exercise in PE; it was winter so it must have been hockey. You know how it goes, the two sportiest girls get made team captains and they choose whoever they want on their side, and it's a game of brinkmanship, because naturally they go for all the ones who play in the school teams first, and then for people like me and Melody, who couldn't give a shit, but have got enough co-ordination to hit the ball if there's really no way of avoiding it. And then it gets to the last half dozen, the swots and the lard-arses. And you can see the captains working out tactics, normally a struggle for them because tactics require intelligence, and most of the really sporty ones were probably already off doing a cross-country run when God got round to handing out brains. They did all their thinking with their feet.

Anyway, the implications were quite far-reaching – was a really hopeless four-eyed brainbox preferable to a team member who couldn't run without hyperventilating? If your attack was stronger than the other side's, could you afford to put Boris in goal in the hope that they'd never get up your end of the field, and if they did, then at least her bulk gave her a very slightly higher chance of blocking the ball?

Well, this time round, they'd chosen the swots first – maybe Suzanne bloody Sharp had managed some fluke contact with the ball the previous week – and Boris was the last to go.

Gillian Palmer looked defeated. 'So I guess I'm left with Boris. Go and get your pads on, Boris, I'll have you in goal.'

But instead of trudging off to get kitted out, Boris stood firm for a second, and then I noticed that tears had started running down her face. They must have been icy on her cheeks in the freezing weather, but she didn't even seem to have the will to wipe them away.

Gillian hadn't noticed, though. 'Oh, for goodness' sake, Boris, you're slow enough during the game, shift your fat bum into position, will you?'

One of Gillian's team-mates nudged her, but before she could do anything, Boris turned on her.

'Fuck off,' she sobbed, and Boris NEVER swore. 'Fucking fuck off, Gillian. It's all bloody very well for you, isn't it ... with your place in the county side and your skinny legs, but you never, never think what it's like.' Snot was running from her nose now, and the whites of her little piggy eyes had gone a violent pink colour. But she didn't seem so much upset as mad with rage. 'Well, I've bloody had enough of you all laughing and of being a joke. I don't care if I get detention every night for ever, I'm never playing again and you can try and force me and I won't, I won't.'

It was incredible, and Miss Knowles, the PE teacher, who'd been messing about with equipment at the other end of the hockey pitch, had noticed something was up, and was jogging over to us. But before she could put her oar in, Boris had turned around and was walking slowly towards the changing rooms. None of us went after her, but Boris never came out for team games again. I don't know if she got a note from her mum, but even the sadistic Miss Knowles didn't seem to want to take her on, despite the fact she normally wouldn't accept anything less than the amputation of both legs as an adequate excuse for bunking off games. Not long afterwards, the PE department grudgingly introduced 'soft options' like trampoline and keep fit and badminton, which me and Melody used to mess about with, and which kept the sport princesses happy because they could play with themselves without having to bother with us.

Jenny's waiting for me to say something.

'Sorry, can you repeat the question?'

'Just, are you looking forward to meeting up again?'

'Yes – no, sorry, hang on, talk in complete sentences, I know ... Boris and I were never that close, but, yes, I think I am looking forward to catching up, for old times' sake. Can't wait to see how she's changed ...'

'Good afternoon, ladies and gentleman. Cast your mind back to being a child. What are your most powerful memories?'

Suzanne cast a long, meaningful look around the hall, making eye contact with as many members of the audience as possible. A hundred or so men and women, worthy types with such a commitment to society that not only had they volunteered to become school governors, they'd also co-opted themselves on to membership of a national organisation guarding the morals and mental health of young people. How boring must their personal lives be?

'Now I ask that question a lot, and I tend to find the

answers fall into two main categories. Put simply, the memories are generally extraordinarily happy, or overwhelmingly miserable. Ring any bells?' A mild chuckle passed around the room.

'I don't propose to turn this afternoon into a Jerry Springer style confessional, but I am going to do something I've never done in public before. Tell you about *my* childhood.'

It was a pretty safe bet. Governors and Pastoral Education (GAPE) was such an insignificant little group that there wouldn't be any press in the audience, but it was a good chance to try out the speech that had been fermenting in Suzanne's mind since the shock of finding out about the reunion. And if it went down well, there might be a repeat performance at a higher-profile gathering. Maybe even the CBI?

'Of course, in an ideal world, all psychologists, and, in fact, all children, would have a blissful time at school, a riot of fun and learning, so enjoyable that they can hardly bear to leave, and yet also the ideal preparation for a life brimming with satisfaction and achievement.

'Well, it wasn't like that for me. And if I had to blame anyone – not that blame is in my professional repertoire – it would be a classmate I'll call Stacey . . .'

Jenny is insisting on this really complicated way of answering the door when Boris arrives. She wants to capture both our reactions on video, but she can't do that because she's only got one proper camera, which Jamie's using, so he's going to lurk outside to film Boris walking up the path. But I'm not allowed to answer the door the first time. Instead, Annabel will open it from inside the house, and catch Boris's face on her little portable camera, and then Jamie will come in here, and they'll ring the bell again, and he'll follow me to the front door and then try to film both of us or something mad like that. Kind of takes the spontaneity out of it ...

The doorbell rings and Annabel skips past me to do the first bit. Callum's in his playpen, because it's the only way I can stop him diving face first into all the food on the dining table. It's a frenzy of Mr Kipling's exceedingly good cakes, along with those impossible mountains of rolls filled with ham, cheese and egg mayo out of a tub. Then they've insisted on orange squash, which is taking this whole nostalgia theme too far in my book. Gin and tonics would make for a more interesting afternoon, but then again Boris is pregnant, so I guess it would only be me drinking them. Not that I'd object.

Kelly's standing on my plastic stool, doing the washing-up. They wanted her to stay in her school uniform, because it's cute. She's cleaning the same bread board over and over again, pulling it out of the bowl every so often to check whether all the grease stains have gone. I'm not sure this perfectionist tendency is very healthy in a six-year-old.

'Mummy, the water's going cold.'

Ever since that meeting at school, I can't help myself looking for the signs that she's not normal, and I'm really pissed off at Mrs Fellowes for making me paranoid. A couple of days ago I even hid at the edge of the play-ground behind some of the other women, and tried to watch her coming out, to see if there were any signs of bullying. And there was the usual stream of little girls running out first, marching around with their mates before responding irritably to the calls from their mums. And then the boys; there seemed to be more loners among them, but the ones on their own had intense looks of concentration on their shiny faces, as they focussed on kicking stray Coke cans, or completing some world-saving mission on the Gameboys they snatched out of their pockets as soon as the bell went . . .

And there behind the straggling boys was my Kelly. She walked out as though she was in a bubble, avoiding any contact with the other kids, and her head was down towards the tarmac until she was safely past the clusters of friends gathered at the classroom door. When her path was clear, she looked up, searching the mass of mothers for me and Callum. Her eyes were wide with fear.

I don't want to admit to this, but alongside the urge to rescue her, to grab her and take her somewhere where no one could ever hurt her again, there was something else, another emotion . . . I don't know how to describe it – no, that's wrong, I don't *want* to describe it. But I know the last time I felt it. Or the last person I felt it about. Suzanne Sharp.

It only lasted a fraction of a second, and then I found myself rushing forward through the ranks of pushchairs to hold my little girl before we both burst into tears. But mine were more about guilt.

I've tried to work out what it is about Kelly, but I can't tell. With Suzanne it was obvious . . . ginger hair, glasses, inability to catch or hit a ball, and being an appalling swot. She couldn't have been more of a target if someone had painted her Day-Glo orange and stuck a dartboard to her back. When I saw her, I tasted fear, and it made me *itch* with irritation. I never hit her – that would have been bullying – but it was impossible not to pick on her – just like it's impossible not to squeeze a spot, or run your tongue over a loose tooth repeatedly until the thread of gum that keeps it dangling gets thinner and thinner and eventually gives way . . .

But Kelly's pretty, she doesn't wear specs, and she's not been at school long enough to be branded a swot. I think the teachers might be making it up. I've checked her clothes every day, and there's no sign of any rips. And when she was having her bath the other night, I looked closely and I couldn't see a single bruise. But it's making me jumpy, I even made her hold out her hands straight after school yesterday, pretending I was checking for dirt, but I was looking for red marks on her wrists from Chinese burns. I used to give them often enough in primary school.

'You all right in here?' Jamie pokes his head round the door, his camera braced on his fantastic shoulders. He's wearing a short-sleeved navy T-shirt, and his arms are tanned and taut. He's incredibly cocky, but gorgeous with it, and you don't begrudge him the attention he gets. Even Kelly can't stop herself grinning at him, and Callum responds to him man to man, when Jamie punches him gently on his lovely chubby arm.

I nod, and he says, 'They're going to ring the bell again in a minute, so why don't I film you arranging the cakes on the plate, and then when you answer the door, I'll let you go in front of me, and then squeeze past you to get the two-shot. Yeah?' I feel pretty excited about the prospect of him squeezing past me, and I wonder if he feels the same, or if I'm just another daft, deluded woman he has to flirt with for professional reasons.

I take up my position moving a fondant fancy a couple of inches to the left, and the doorbell rings . . .

'Stacey was the queen bee of our class. But she made every day of my life a misery. She never hit me – now and again one of her friends who had a bit less class would take it too far, and push me around a bit, but there was no real physical abuse. No, this was the Chinese water torture version of bullying, the commonest and the most insidious.' As usual, Suzanne had her key points printed neatly on to a handful of index cards. But this speech came from the heart.

'I'm not even sure if Trace ... um, Stacey realised quite how bad it was, the way that every morning I felt sick before I left for school, and the way that every evening when I shut the bedroom door behind me, I just wanted to stay there.'

It was strange how easy it was to talk about now, but then it had been the most humiliating experience; the way her digestive system churned so violently before she stepped into the form room, she was sure everyone could hear her stomach giving away how scared she was. The way she would tell herself over and over again before she fell asleep that tomorrow would be the day she'd stand up to Tracey, the day when life would become normal and someone else would be in the firing line. She didn't really care who it was – not a very honourable instinct, but one shared by victims the world over.

'But I was lucky. Yes, it was a miserable five years, and you know, you don't even get that for armed robbery these days. But I moved on – found friendships and confidence and formed loving relationships, and a happy marriage. We know from our research at Millennium Child that many thousands of young people feel so profoundly damaged by their experiences that they find it impossible to contemplate trusting anyone.

'I was also lucky because despite the effect on my education – and there's no doubt that it was affected by ending up too scared to raise my hand in class, or worrying my marks were too high – I made it to college and into a career I love. Our research also shows that tens of thousands of adults have been left unemployed, and potentially unemployable, because they either refused to go to school due to bullying, or were so badly traumatised by their experiences that they learned virtually nothing.'

She had them. Some of the audience were nodding in recognition, all were paying her complete attention.

'And I was lucky, more than anything else, because I survived – unlike more than a dozen schoolchildren in the last year alone, who took their own lives.'

Suzanne paused as it sank in. They knew the figures, but it was still shocking.

Had she ever considered suicide? Sure, she'd wanted it to stop, but going through the careful calculations working out how many pills, or how many storeys, or how much rope . . . she'd never gone that far. The thought made her shudder.

'Thankfully, most victims of bullying grow up. In a strange way, I think Stacey's responsible for me being here now. If it hadn't been for her endless taunts, I would never have started thinking about what makes people tick and would probably have never thought of psychology. I certainly wouldn't have become involved in the fight to make childhood a safer place for all our kids. And I wouldn't have the opportunity, no, it's more than that, it's a privilege, to work with people like you to achieve that.

'So – I'd like to thank Stacey, and to suggest that it's not just the bullied but the *bullies* we need to help. I'll never know what drove her to behave as she did, but knowing what I know now about human behaviour, I don't suppose she was much happier than I was.'

Suzanne had wondered, while she was writing the speech, what had turned Tracey into such a bitch. There was normally a reason. She remembered that Tracey's dad wasn't around, but that was too convenient an excuse. And hadn't she started behaving worse after that skinny poor girl got run over, and she joined forces with dopey Melody? Suzanne had counselled bullies, too, and sometimes their stories affected her as badly as the experiences of their victims. But with Tracey, she couldn't summon up any sympathy.

She paused again, building up to the grand finale.

'Then, bullying was seen as a fact of school life. All of us have a responsibility to change that. And I hope if I ever come across Stacey, whatever she's doing now, we could shake hands, and work together to make sure bullying is consigned to the history books, where it belongs.'

She looked down at the lectern and as the applause started, smiled back shyly at the warmth of their response.

The last bit wasn't strictly true. The only way she'd ever want to shake hands with Tracey bloody Mortimer would be if she knew in advance that the bitch was living in a B and B, had a job sexing chickens and had put on at least four stone. Sometimes forgiveness couldn't possibly match the appeal of sweet, straightforward revenge.

And there she is. Helen Morris. Slimmer in the face, fatter round the midriff, but undoubtedly Boris.

'TRACEY!' she squeals, and my cynical core melts away as she seizes me with the enthusiasm I remember her showing for everything, from centre-spreads in *Smash Hits*, to the weekly serving of chocolate sponge pudding in the canteen.

She's gripping me so hard that I can hardly breathe, but where her distended stomach meets mine, I'm sure I can feel her baby's heels making contact with my belly button. And all of a sudden, I want to cry.

'Boris,' I manage, when she finally lets me go and we hold each other at arm's length, scanning each other's face to see who has the most wrinkles, 'Boris, it's good to see you.'

And to my astonishment, I mean it.

Chapter Ten

This programme is like a full-time job, and it's not even as if I'm getting paid for it. As soon as one day's filming is out of the way, Jenny or Annabel are back on the phone with another bright idea and it's impossible to refuse.

Which is why I'm waiting for a cab to take me back to Crawley Park Comp for the first time since 1984. On the plus side, my sidekick for this latest trip down Memory Lane is the irresistible Jamie, and his trusty camera.

I think we're reaching an understanding. He's certainly less bad-tempered than he was early on in the filming, and I love the way he raises one beautifully bushy eyebrow at me whenever Annabel says something stupid – which is pretty often. But I know it's a hopeless, harmless flirtation; Jenny told me he's a serial shagger and he seems to have imposed an upper age limit of twenty-five. Though the way she said it made me wonder if he'd made an exception for her, at the grand old age of twenty-nine.

Only Boris seemed unmoved, but then she was so excited about seeing me and catching up, that I think Brad Pitt and Ralph Fiennes would have been ignored as well.

'You're still so gorgeous,' she told me, as soon as she'd released me from her manic embrace. 'How have you done it, Trace? With two kids and everything and oh, this is lovely,' she was skipping through the hall into the kitchen, with me, the crew and the girls sucked along in her wake like the debris from a hurricane. 'I would LOVE to have a kitchen like this and –' she stopped short as though someone had hit her across the face 'And this has to be Kelly! She's ADORABLE!'

Kelly was still in the middle of her washing-up and the sudden arrival of this banshee – albeit a well-intentioned one – produced a look of sheer terror. Before she could even open her mouth to protest, Boris had thrown her dinner-lady arms around Kelly's waist, and was throwing air kisses around her in every direction.

'Look at her nose, and those baby-blue eyes. God, Trace, she's the spit of you, except I might even dare to say she's prettier. Aren't you, my pet?'

Kelly had gone so red in the face I couldn't tell whether she was having an asthma attack, or was simply about to die from embarrassment. Poor Kelly, making her the centre of attention is just about the worst thing you can do to her. So I decided the only tactic was distraction, and hauled Callum from his playpen up to Boris's eye level. It's exactly the same technique I use in the supermarket when I'm trying to move the kids away from the break-ables that they gravitate towards like magpies. Only in Tesco it's sweets that I use as bait.

'Oh my word, the little man.' One second she was a human cocoon around my daughter, and a split second later she was virtually licking Callum's face like a puppy.

'Oh, he's like a cherub and a miniature bouncer rolled into one. Can I take him home?'

Fortunately Callum's a tart like his dad, so he was enjoying the attention she'd switched from Kelly.

'If my little one –' and she patted her belly in a way I'd normally find sickening but with Boris I just found myself grinning '– is anything like as gorgeous as these two then

I will be so thrilled I won't be able to speak for months
. . .'

'I find that hard to believe,' I said, then instantly regretted sounding so bitchy in the presence of such unadulterated joy.

She stopped, like Bambi caught in the headlights, but then her face rearranged itself into an even bigger beam. 'Oh, God, Trace, you're so right and it's such a relief that you haven't changed a bit. I'd have hated it if you'd gone all . . . soppy in your old age. Nasty is so much more fun!'

Then she stopped again, and seemed to realise what she'd said, but instead of stuttering an apology, she clamped her hand to her mouth for a second, then when it came away, she began to giggle. And it was so infectious that we all succumbed – first Callum, then Kelly and finally me – erupting into these uncontrollable spasms of laughter, only interrupted by gulping attempts to breathe.

It's only last week, but I really can't remember most of what we talked about, it was so daft and gossipy. I just know that judging from the state of my stomach muscles afterwards, we didn't stop laughing until she left.

'Tracey? The taxi's here.' Jamie's got all his gear ready for the off in the hall.

I check my lipstick in the mirror. 'I'm coming.'

Alec was running out of patience with the local radio reporter.

'Obviously we'll do what we can to accommodate you,' he said, his tone suggesting the exact opposite, 'and I do understand your deadlines, I spent a little time in the regions myself.' Alec spat the word 'regions' as though it was the worst possible insult. Which, to him, it was.

The reporter, a short man approaching a bald middle-age, shifted his weight from one foot to the other, and it seemed to be the only way he was controlling his irritation. 'But it was your press office that told us to turn up at 11.30.' He peered sadly at his radio car, the mast proudly extended, but with nothing to broadcast. A small group of children, all wearing vivid mint-green jumpers, had gathered round to watch.

Alec snarled. 'Not OUR press office, Channel 5's. There is a difference. But then I suppose you wouldn't know that, would you? The point is, you can see Tracey isn't even here yet. And when she gets here, we'll have filming to do which will take some time, and it's not cheap having a whole crew out here in the sticks. So we can't hold things up, can we? I'm sure you understand.'

Or, thought Jenny, what he really means is I couldn't give a shit if you understand or not. He'd been in a foul mood for two days, ever since he saw the unedited rushes from the filming at Tracey's house. At first she'd thought it was because he hated the way she'd directed it. But then he turned on her and Annabel, and said: 'Why didn't you find me bloody Boris before? The programme should be about her, not about that hard bitch Tracey?'

They'd spent the last week arguing about whether to start the whole filming all over again, with Boris at the centre of the show, until Jenny pointed out that Boris was likely to give birth just before the reunion AND it would cost too much AND, most importantly, being such a nice person, Boris would never go along with the idea of stealing Tracey's thunder.

So here they were, waiting for Tracey without any great enthusiasm. Alec was worried that his programme lacked warmth, Annabel found her annoyingly suburban and spiky. And Jenny? On the surface they got on well, and though she hated to think about it, there was only just over three years between them in age, so why did she have a sinking feeling every time Tracey appeared?

Only the local radio reporter was actually looking

forward to her arriving, and the way things were going, he wouldn't even get the chance to talk to her.

'Bloody hell,' mumbled Alec, checking his Rolex. 'You'd think with all we're doing for her, she could at least bother to turn up on time!'

Jamie's told me to look wistful while he's filming the journey, so that's what I'm doing, but it's hard not to look gormless at the same time.

I'm trying to work out how many times I've been past the school in the last few years: it's only three miles away, but it's not on the route to anywhere I need to go. Unlike my primary school. Not that the Pines Junior and Infants is there any more, it's now a supermarket, so if they wanted to do a reunion there, we'd have to call the register in the in-store bakery, and sing hymns in the freezer section. Mind you, if I mention that, they'll probably want me and Boris to go there so they can do exactly that.

I can't have driven by Crawley Park more than three or four times. But from what I can see out of the open taxi window, it hasn't changed. The property boom in the south-east has bypassed this part of town, because even the most desperate first-time buyer knows that this place is never going to be desirable.

Yeah, there's the litter and the smashed-up cars and the graffiti on the bus shelters, but it's more than that. It's this kind of apathy that hangs over the place: everything's the same colour, this mid-grey, even the little turfed embankments are grey; the grass has been worn away by kids pacing up and down like those polar bears you see on TV who've spent too long in a cage.

The driver takes a short cut through the estate where Shrimp used to live, and there are a couple of kids by the slightly larger than average strip of grass that she called the park. Bunking off. I did that a couple of times every term, but not for whole days, just when I couldn't face French or Chemistry or whatever the most hated lesson was that year. The rest of the time, I wouldn't miss the chance to play up, do my thing. Every hour mattered. I wonder if I kind of knew even then these really were the best years of my life.

The kids can see me staring at them as the taxi slows to negotiate the chicanes the council must have put in to try to stop the joy-riders.

'What chew fucking looking at?' the tall girl shouts at me; she's maybe twelve, and the other one gives me the finger. They look like the children in the video for 'I don't like Monday's', the one where they're all out of it, mouthing the words as Bob Geldof towers over them wearing these weird sunglasses.

'Little bastards,' the driver says, catching my eye in his mirror. 'It's like Beirut round here.'

I never saw it like that when I was growing up, but he's right. In my memories, it's only school that has any colour in it – the uniform and the wall displays and the discos – everywhere outside the gates is black and white. It's no wonder that we all had such a horrible shock out in the real world, and for all the crap he's put me through since then, at least Dave took me away from the grey to the side of town where the grass really is ... well, not greener, just green.

Because he was glamorous, Dave was. Or so I thought. A little of his dad's money went a long way when it came to convincing me that here at last was my route out. But there's a fine line between glamour and sleaze, and I was so blinded by his charm, I couldn't see the difference. Mum did, but I never listened to her, and by the time I realised she was right – somewhere between taking my vows and throwing my bouquet – it was too late. The funny thing is, I think she only saw Dave for what he was because she'd fallen for the same lines with Dad. Maybe we've got more in common than I want to admit . . .

And there it is, in the distance, with all the architectural sophistication of a nuclear power station. Crawley Park Comp.

He's racing past, our driver, like he's worried we're about to get ambushed, so I can only just make out the landmarks – the chip shop where we ate our lunches when we could afford it, and the newsagent next door where they sold us Slush Puppies so long as we only went in two at a time. The house with the proper front garden, where the couple had built little raised borders, and chosen a variety of jolly gnomes to nestle among the bedding plants. Even the worst lads in the year, the ones who were on probation by the third year, left the garden alone, though there was a time when someone kidnapped a fishing gnome and another one with a wheelbarrow for a whole afternoon, before peer pressure forced them to put them back.

Here we are . . . at the gates we ran through the day after our last official assembly with this feeling that we were the grown-ups: we could do what we liked, we could earn a wage and buy what we liked and mess about.

And of course, the same gates we crept through again the following day, for the first of our CSEs. Actually, the teachers entered me for a couple of 'O' Levels as well, but I kept that as quiet as I could. Being in the top set for anything was seriously uncool, and I managed to avoid it in almost every class. Except History. And that was more about the teacher than the subject.

And then they were the same gates we hung around in the weeks when we hadn't found jobs and didn't know whether we would ever find them, because we were Thatcher's generation after all, and we didn't know what the hell to do with ourselves except hang around the school we'd been so desperate to leave, and taunt the kids who were still there, who weren't free to do what they wanted, like we were free ...

But the sign's changed.

Crawley Park College for the Performing Arts.

And underneath, in smaller letters, it says 'a specialist school'.

What the hell's that about?

'Tracey, when the car pulls up, wait till I come round your side with the camera before you open the door, so I can film you getting out,' Jamie says, and then tells the driver we'll probably have to reverse back on to the road and do it all again.

'Whatever, so long as you keep paying me.'

By the main entrance, I can see a little reception committee of Alec, the girls and Cliff, who's travelled ahead with all the camera equipment. But I'm enough of a pro now not to wave or do anything to spoil the shot. They're all obsessive about maintaining this illusion that somehow it's just me on my one-woman mission into the past ...

And there's another guy standing next to a white estate car that's utterly ordinary except for one important detail – the staggering erection sprouting from its roof. It's some kind of mast, but it looks bizarre, like a Greek postcard featuring one of those brass statuettes with enormous great willies, so out of proportion it makes you wince.

We do the shot of me getting out, then Alec pulls Jamie aside to talk about how they're going to film me approaching the front entrance. The guy with the radio mast sidles up to me.

'Tracey?' he asks, which is a bit dopey because presumably if he's here to meet me, the fact I was the one being filmed must have been a giveaway.

'Yeah. And is that a mast on your car, or are you just

pleased to see me?' OK, pretty feeble but I couldn't resist it. I wonder if it's hanging around Jamie and all his pheromones that's making me sex-obsessed . . .

The guy looks embarrassed. 'Hi, I'm Tone, I'm from the BBC, local radio?' He's speaking so quietly and so uncertainly that I wonder if he's telling me or asking me. 'I know you're busy doing your filming, but I wonder if you could spare me a couple of minutes to do a live interview.'

I feel quite flattered really, this guy's here just for me, when Alec sees him talking to me, and strides over.

'I've already told you, mate, unless you want to hang around until we've finished then forget it.' I don't know how I could have fancied Alec, even for five minutes. He's so cocky, so patronising to this bloke who is only trying to do his job, that I instantly decide to do the interview.

'Wow, I listen to you all the time, what's that DJ in the mornings?' I say. It's not terribly convincing, and Tone looks even more embarrassed.

'Um, well, we don't really play music, we're more of a speech station.'

'Yes, of course, yes, I didn't mean . . . anyway, well, I'm sure we've got a couple of minutes, haven't we, Alec?'

He returns my glowing smile with a snarl, but he knows when he's beaten. Jenny's been listening in, and she steps forward.

'It might help with finding some more of Tracey's class,' she says, but Alec has already started walking towards his car, a red sporty thing with wheels so wide they look as though they belong on a tractor. We watch him go, and I wonder if he's going to drive off in a huff, but instead of the engine firing, the sound of The Verve starts blasting through his sunroof.

I turn to Tone. 'Let's get this show on the road then,'

I say, and I don't think he could have looked more excited if I'd just suggested an orgy.

Linda Jacobs was a thoroughly modern head teacher, and she'd had her doubts about the reunion programme, because somehow looking back felt wrong when her vision for Crawley Park was all about looking forward.

But then again, the two women from the production company seemed sane enough, and, as they'd pointed out, a TV documentary would be the perfect way for a new College of the Performing Arts to raise its profile. And when they started talking about a significant donation, in return for hosting the party itself, she decided the pros outweighed the cons.

She watched the crew through the slats of her aluminium blinds, which she'd picked up from IKEA to complete the make-over of her office. Local radio was hardly a novelty, her marketing strategy took care of that, but it was good to keep the profile up, and soon there'd be national press there too.

'Right, you two, I think you should get in position.' Mrs Jacobs had taken her time in choosing the pupils who'd show this woman around. Rav and Kathryn were both attractive and confident – he had the best singing voice in the school, and also reflected the multicultural dimension of school life, while Kathryn was third-generation Crawley Park; her father had been in the fifth year while Tracey was in the first.

'Treat Mrs Brown as you would any guest and don't forget you're ambassadors for Bracewell, for Crawley Park AND for yourselves.'

The politics might have changed, but it was a statement that any of Linda Jacobs's four predecessors would have been happy to endorse.

*

I'm pretty good at this media stuff, you know. I sent Tone away after the interview looking happy, and he said he knew they'd want to come back on the night of the reunion itself.

And now this is it, time for the tour. I'm standing on the steps that lead to reception, and despite the flash sign, it doesn't seem that different. I think councils must have bought designs for schools off-the-peg over the years and around the time this one was built, they probably had the choice of the red-brick mausoleum look, or the Lego-style wooden box effect. They went for the latter at Crawley Park, and it hasn't worn that well. I can only ever remember the paint around the timber window frames chipping away, and it's still peeling, though caretakers must have applied several new coats over the years, or the whole building would have crumbled away.

Of course, we were never allowed to use the main entrance, that was strictly for staff and visitors, so it feels really odd to go back through those doors. I feel I should be nipping into the side entrance of the Humanities block, as we did day after day after day to go to registration.

I step into the hall and come face to face with a six-foot-high water feature, and a five-foot-high power-suited woman who is just as gushing. This must be Mrs Jacobs.

'Mrs Brown,' she thrusts a manicured hand towards me, and shakes mine with a fierceness that seems over the top. 'Welcome back.'

Standing next to her are two kids, a girl of about eleven and a tall Asian boy ... well, he's not really a boy, he's far too tall and good-looking to be wearing that ridiculous mint green jumper. Still, it's nice to see they've kept some of the traditions, however horrific. Though the canary tie is knotted as tightly as a city banker's – I'm sure he'd be traumatised by our floppy, rebellious version.

She nudges them and they introduce themselves, as I

peer round the rest of the room, with its glass bricks and the marble reception desk that looks more like a bar counter. The water-feature, I notice, is labelled the 'fount of wisdom', which seems pretty naff, especially when Mrs Jacobs seems so tastefully understated.

Our tour begins, led by the frighteningly self-assured Rav and Kathryn. It's quite a convoy with me, Jamie, Cliff, Alec and Jenny following them. Annabel's been relegated to guarding the sports car. It's probably the only sensible judgement Alec's made all day.

I suppose I've been expecting some kind of flashback, like stepping into a time machine, but it's not happening. Sure, the sights and sounds and smells are what I expected, but they're not transporting me to 1979, it's as though there's this invisible barrier between then and now, and however much I want to, I can't cross over.

Maybe it's about experience. And I've got too much of it.

Rav is telling me that he decided to come to Crawley Park even though it involves a change of buses to get across town. He says it's worth it because of the facilities: the recording studio and the video editing suite and the full stage lighting rig, and it strikes me that some things have changed, after all.

But then I need the loo, and nip into the ones that used to be closest to our form room, and I realise as my bum freezes when it makes contact with the cracked plastic seat that some things have stayed the same.

Finally we reach the first-floor corridor leading to our form room – not Mrs Chang's lab, which we left when she went on maternity leave, but Mr Carmichael's History class, our home from the second year till we left.

This is the room where I grew up.

As I approach the door, past a row of pegs that were never used, because no one would be stupid enough to leave their valuables unsecured at Crawley Park, I'm almost expecting to see Bob Carmichael darting around at the front, firing questions off in his deep brown voice, and nodding so hard when some kid finally understands what he's getting at, that his head should by rights fall off, and go bouncing along the floor, still talking and still nodding.

Except, of course, I know it can't be him. If anyone should know that, it's me.

But this is still the closest I come to that 'back to the future' experience ... because when I peer through the window, it's not Bob but there's Dick Phipps, who was already deputy head of Humanities when we were there, standing at the front lecturing a class full of mint-jumpered kids. And instead of the timelines, and the portraits of Kings and Queens on the walls, there are maps and pictures of rocks. I wonder if he's done anything else in the seventeen years since we left him there, and when he turns in response to the knock on the door, I decide he probably hasn't – his face looks exactly the same, except it's a couple of shades greyer.

He comes towards us, and makes an attempt at a smile, but there's no hiding the fact that as far as he's concerned, any reunion with me in this lifetime would be far too soon.

'Well, well, Miss Mortimer ...'

He's been expecting me.

'I never thought I'd see you again ... I don't imagine you've been anywhere near a school in recent years. Unless it's to deal with your no doubt numerous offspring.' He's always had this affected upper-class way of speaking, even though everybody at school knew he'd grown up by the canal on the Clematis Estate, the roughest part of the roughest side of town.

'Hello, Mr Phipps,' I say, but then I run out of ideas, so decide to maintain what I hope will look like a dignified silence.

'Guess what, children. Young Miss Mortimer used to be a pupil here, and now she's brought a TV crew along with her ... and why is that, Miss Mortimer? Because, perhaps, you run an international company, and they want to see how you came to be a successful entrepreneur from humble origins?'

'No,' I say, quietly, feeling it's pointless to interrupt his flow.

'OK. So perhaps it's because you're a leading light in the arts world, and your experiences here at Crawley Park set you on your creative path. Let me guess ... a modern artist in the mould of, I don't know, Tracey Emin?'

I know he knows I don't know who he means. I sigh. 'No.'

He is loving this so much, and I can't believe I've been stupid enough to walk in on this situation. I want to tell him to fuck off, but even if it wasn't being filmed, I wouldn't dare, and he knows it.

Surely Jenny and Annabel don't know?

'Well, you really do have me foxed on this one. Please, put me out of my misery. What incredible achievement merits your presence and that of your charming colleagues?' He's standing there, arms folded, with one hand resting curiously on his chin, like a bust of Shakespeare.

'It's a reunion. I'm having a reunion, and they're filming it.'

He nods. 'Ah ... ah, and why you, Miss Mortimer?'

'I don't know. I suppose ...' and he is going to love this even more '... it's because I'm pretty average.' And I realise as I say it, that that's exactly why they've picked me, Mrs bloody Average, two average kids, an average semi, and your average adulterous husband. I've never felt average is anything to be ashamed of, but now it's like I am standing in front of a High Court judge looking down his nose at me, preparing to pass sentence.

'Average, Miss Mortimer?' He turns to his captive audience. 'Well, well. I must say, you HAVE exceeded my expectations.'

And he smiles that sarcastic smile, as I fight the urge to punch him, because we both know there's more to his dislike of me than a few excuses over late homework.

Chapter Eleven

I'm thinking of pulling out.

I know they'll be fed up, but that's not my problem, and they seem to prefer Boris to me anyway, so I reckon they could go ahead with the programme, using her instead. The whole thing is getting too stressful.

It's not just Phipps, though that didn't help. Afterwards, Alec and Jenny were like, 'oh, what rattled his cage, I guess you guys never got on,' but I'm pretty sure they don't suspect there's anything more to it than that. And they said they're unlikely to use any of what he said, way too sarcastic for a feel-good show.

And at least I know he's not going to let on, after all those years. Phipps and Bob have got way more to lose than me.

I dunno. I don't have the energy for this any more.

Dave's just left after one of his lost weekends in the pub, and we were talking about the programme – well, we never have what you could truly describe as 'conversations' but he cottoned on to the fact that I was feeling a bit grumpy about the whole thing, and he said something sensible. Always a shocker when that happens, but fortunately it's not very often.

'Sometimes,' he slurred at me, because it was after the

pubs had shut, and I think he was trying to get in my good books for the usual bloody obvious reasons, 'it's best to leave the past, in the past.'

'Oh, thanks for that stunning advice,' I snapped back, out of habit and to stop him coming sniffing round me, but it's so bloody simple, it's stuck in my head, and now I think he might just be right.

Then there's Kelly. So much for all the flannel about let's see what happens, these things usually blow over, because last week I got this letter saying the school's made her an appointment with the educational psychologist.

Meet my daughter, the nutcase.

I don't know what to think about it, so I try not to think about it at all. But it feels all wrong to be messing about with this reunion rubbish when school is such a bloody nightmare for her. I feel I've failed her somehow.

It's all very awkward.

And I hate to admit it, but what's scaring me the most is – what if after all this fuss, none of my *real* school friends even bother to turn up?

'Thank you,' the middle-aged man said, pocketing his change. His manners were as out of place as he was in the seedy hotel bar. His bear-like frame sank an inch or so into the soggy patterned carpet as he walked across towards one of the booths. This was a man who couldn't be unobtrusive if he tried.

'Sorry, Dick, it's not exactly going to win pub of the year, is it?' Bob Carmichael put the two pints down on the table.

'Well, we're not really here for the atmosphere. And it's certainly private,' Dick Phipps said.

Bob peered around the room. 'You wouldn't bother coming to a place like this unless you were up to no good, would you? Though chance'd be a fine thing these days.'

Dick grinned. 'So how is life at the top?' Neither of them wanted to start talking about the real reason they were there.

'Bloody over-rated, mate. Though the money's good. And the dinners. But you probably spotted that.' He looked down at his belly, which protruded a little way through his linen shirt, but still appeared to be more muscle than blubber.

The men laughed briefly, then Bob took a swig of his beer. 'So. Christmas cards for a decade and then it takes bloody Tracey to bring us face to face again. There's no escape from that one, is there?'

'You didn't even sound surprised when I rang you.'

Bob shook his head. 'No. I'm relieved, if anything. I always knew it'd come out somehow or other, and at least this way ...'

'It's not come out at all. And it needn't ever come out. You just had to know she was sniffing around, that's all. Silly bitch.'

'You don't actually believe that, Dick, that we can keep it hidden? You don't know what it's like, they're crawling all over everybody for sleaze.'

'But you're not even an MP.'

'The way the papers see it, I'm even bigger prey than MPs, and I can see their point.'

Dick grinned. 'Who'd have thought it, though, eh? You an adviser to Number 10. Hobnobbing with the rich and powerful. So have you been to one of these parties, the ones you see the celebs at in the magazines?'

'One or two. They're not a lot more interesting than the PTA barn dances, to be honest, though the food's better.'

'Hey, it's quality stuff at Crawley Park too these days – garlic bread, hummus, the works. Now we're a specialist school.'

'I bet Tracey loved that,' said Bob.

'Funnily enough, I didn't ask her. You amaze me, Bob. She nearly fucked your whole life up, and you still act as though it's a joke.'

Bob shrugged. 'I never could get angry at Tracey, could I? You were angry enough for both of us.'

'I wanted to hit her when she came into my classroom last week. YOUR old classroom, it was –'

'Yes, and if it wasn't for Tracey, I might still be there.'

'Like me, you mean?'

'Dick, don't be daft, I didn't mean it like that. Sometimes I wish I was still there – mainly when I'm sitting in the Joined-Up Thinking forum. Someone like Tracey would have sorted them out in two minutes, but I have to sit there listening to them droning on and on ... that's when I envy you.'

Dick had picked up a beer mat, and started peeling it apart. 'Well, we could reminisce like this for hours. It's not why we're both here, though, is it? I think you need to put a stop to this.'

'I suppose I've worried about the press getting hold of it for so long that if it's finally coming, then I almost feel relieved.'

'But it doesn't have to come out. I think what you – we – need to do is scare her off. It's not just you that stands to lose. Does she really want to look like a scrubber on national television? She was bloody quiet in the classroom when she saw it was me; she knew exactly what was going on, and she definitely didn't like the idea of me sharing a few anecdotes with the TV crew.'

Bob sighed. 'I never got anywhere telling her what to do seventeen years ago, and I don't suppose it'd be any different now.' He wiped condensation off his beer glass. 'Does she look any different now?'

'I can't believe you even want to know that. She still looks like a scrubber. Just an older one.'

'Dick, I know you think she was in the wrong, but I was the teacher, *she* was the pupil remember? I was older and wiser.'

'Only chronologically speaking. She knew what was what.'

'Maybe she did. But so did I, and I knew what the consequences would be. Maybe it's time to give in gracefully.'

Dick cleared his throat. 'All right then, if you don't care, what about the rest of us? How do you think it's going to look when the press are crawling all over the school? I don't think it's going to reflect well on any of us.'

Bob stared at his old boss. 'Oh, Dick, how disappointing. There I was thinking you had my welfare in mind, and the only thing that's worrying you is how it's going to affect *your* career.'

'That's not fair. It was me that made sure you could resign – you don't suppose you would have got where you are now with a sacking on your CV, do you?'

'I might not have lost *her*, though.'

Dick shook his head. 'I don't believe you. You're still letting your John Thomas rule your head. Did you forget to grow up?'

'Maybe.' Bob frowned. 'I don't suppose you'll be wanting another drink, then?'

Dick downed the last of his beer. 'No thanks – *mate*.' He stood up. 'Fine. Go ahead, then. Destroy yourself. But do me a favour, and don't take the rest of us with you.'

Trouble is, if I give up on the programme, I might lose the computer. It's my new best mate ... in fact, I feel lonelier when Dave is around for the weekend and I can't log on because he takes the piss, than I do during the week when the kids are in bed and I can surf to my heart's content.

I wouldn't have believed that a keyboard and a screen could become so important, and I hate the fact it has, but I can't break the habit. Every time I go into the kitchen for a coffee or, after seven, for a gin and tonic – and why shouldn't I drink anyway, round Crawley Park there were women who kept their kids despite serious smack habits – it's winking at me on the breakfast bar, flirting with me to come over again and have another delve into the Net.

Most of the time I give in. It doesn't seem nerdy to me any more, even though a month ago I would have dismissed the Web as the haunt of tragic no-hopers with no mates and nothing better to do.

Maybe I've just joined them.

Time disappears when I'm on the Web. Seeing (1) in my inbox gives me a thrill every time. To start with it was always from Jenny or Annabel, with a schedule for the latest bit of filming. Now, mostly it's Boris, but she's told me about these other sites where you sign up for e-mails, and I've got loads of them coming in now – with the latest on Brad and Jennifer, or details of fantastic holidays I could take tomorrow if only I had the money and didn't have Kelly and Callum to look after.

I was talking to Jenny about it, and she said 'I bloody hate all that rubbish they send you, it's worse than the stuff you get through the letterbox promising lottery prizes, because at least you can chuck them straight in the bin.'

But I don't see it like that – every bit of gossip or suggestion about how to change your hairstyle or your sofa or your life is a bonus. I can't quite believe it's all free. I've got horoscopes coming in, two different ones, so I can pick and choose whether today is going to be a good one for staying at home or going out to do the shopping.

I haven't dared log into any chat rooms yet, but I spend ages lurking around, reading what people have written.

Women with too many lovers, women who want one but can't find one, women who want to rewire their bathrooms. It's so brilliant eavesdropping on all these lives, and one day I'll put mine up for inspection.

Though God knows why I'm being so shy about that, when I've agreed to spread most of my life all over the TV this autumn. Another reason to dump the whole idea.

I had a look at porn. Late at night, after three drinks, I went to one of the search engine things and typed in sex, and had a surf around. It was like visiting the zoo, one where all the exhibits were bright pink. There's nothing attractive about people with their bits out.

Tonight my eyes are sore; I think I've been surfing so much lately. Maybe I should e-mail Jenny and tell her I've been thinking about whether to stay on the programme. Or maybe I should e-mail Boris first. She might look a bit daft, but there's more to her than fat . . . I log on to my e-mail.

GARYANDGABBY

Who's that? I click on the e-mail.

Tracey
What a bolt from the blue. Sorry didn't come back to you straightway, been busy at work. I'm a copper now, would you have believed it. How about you?
So what's made you get in touch now?
G

Gary Coombs.
Gary bloody Coombs.
What took him so long, cheeky bugger?
How the hell did he get into the police, with his history?
Who is Gabby?
And does she know he's e-mailed me?
Maybe I do want to stay on the programme after all.

107

Chapter Twelve

What do you wear for your six-year-old daughter's first appointment with her shrink?

I've dragged the dinky suits from the back of the wardrobe, the ones I wore to work before Kelly caused those snail trails on my belly. Despite the stretch marks, the little skirts and boxy jackets still fit, but they look so wrong: pastel colours and shoulder pads went out with the Tories. And they belong to someone flirty and fun, the kind of secretary I always pretended to be, the one who'd shag the boss in the gents and still nip out at lunchtime to buy his wife a birthday present. I managed the mascara and the push-up bras, but let's face it, marrying at twenty-four didn't exactly enhance my promotion prospects. I had quite a moral attitude to monogamy in those days, even though Dave was knocking off other people's secretaries in the site offices of his Dad's firm within a year of our wedding.

So the suits are out.

My usual collecting-Kelly-from-school gear – the tidy jeans and the pressed casual shirt that scream Racing Green – doesn't seem to reflect the seriousness of the occasion. But I don't have much in between that and my hen night outfit, which last had an airing over a year ago when Marsha from the shop took us all out clubbing at Kisses in Slough. And though bias-cut red dresses have a lot to recommend them, I don't suppose they'd go down too well with the local psychiatrist.

Actually, she's not a psychiatrist, she's a psychologist, so it's not quite as bad as it seems – they don't tend to admit infants to mental hospitals for being a bit grumpy in the playground. But even so, the red dress would not be a good look.

A toned-down version of my Christmas ensemble seems the best bet – black skirt, my sexy black boots, plus a check shirt. Maybe it's a bit hot for late spring, but it's also not slutty irresponsible trailer trash, or the look of some power-crazed career woman who regards her kids as accessories.

It's unthreatening – I think that's what people in authority prefer. Teachers, doctors, social workers, policemen . . .

Gary. It's not what I'd wear for a date with Gary.

Then it would definitely be the red dress. With the black bra – the lacy one from Marks and Spencer's that snuck into my basket on Friday below the new pyjamas for Callum and the strawberry-patterned pants for Kelly. And I'd wear matching knickers. Or – even more daring – no knickers at all.

I've had sex on the brain ever since I got that e-mail. It's a sad indictment of my life that a few stray words (thirty-five, to be exact, I counted them when Boris, being a computer whiz, told me that the art of e-mail flirtation is always to reply with fewer words than they did, to show how casual you are about it) from a guy I haven't seen for more than half my life, have sent me into a hormonal frenzy.

But he's been misbehaving too. I bet this Gabby doesn't know he's e-mailed me. And I know that he's off duty this morning. So while I'm taking Kelly to have her head examined, I could be at home exchanging ever shorter messages with a member of Her Majesty's constabulary, and fantasising about the moment when we are reunited.

If we ever are. We're both avoiding everything contentious – his relationship, my kids, whether he's going to turn up in July, not to mention the events of June 1984. I'm learning that e-mail is perfect for staying away from things you don't want to think about.

Like getting old.

'I don't know why any of you bother,' Dick Phipps snarled as half the staff room gathered around the school copy of the *Times Educational Supplement*. 'None of you are going anywhere, with this place on your CV. The only way out of Crawley Park is death.'

Carol Price, head of English, peered up from the paper. 'Shut up, you horrible old git. What makes you think we're looking at the jobs pages anyway?'

'Two things, Carol. One – who the hell reads that rag for the curriculum updates? And two, I can read upside down and the page you're all looking at is headed VACANCIES.'

Carol shrugged, as the bell rang, and the paper was left abandoned on the leatherette chairs, along with Dick, blessed with a free lesson for departmental admin. Suddenly, the dry old *Times Ed* and its Humanities section seemed strangely desirable.

He walked over to the kettle, and made himself another cup of coffee from the dregs of the catering-size drum of 'Golden Aroma' or whatever unspeakable granules they'd got from the cash and carry.

It was all primary stuff on the front page, as the nation's eleven-year-olds grappled with assessment tests, and their teachers moaned about exams stifling children's creativity.

Get used to it, Dick thought. Outside, a few remaining kids were heading for class, dawdling and play-fighting. Kids only need imagination for the important bits of school life ... to invent excuses for late registration, late homework, late periods ...

Page 3, and the Inspector of Schools wants improved standards of literacy and numeracy in trainee teachers.

Don't we all? But someone's going to have to be cannon fodder for the comprehensives, and if you have half a brain, you're going to think twice. Dick grinned at himself. Getting old was crap, but at least you could stop pretending to be cheerful, and embrace cynicism without embarrassment. And bloody hell, sometimes, it felt *so* good.

Page 5: 'Broader sports curriculum "would reduce obesity" '. Yeah, maybe, but then who would the sadistic PE teachers laugh at on the cross-country finishing line?

Page 7 – who can be arsed with the even-numbered pages – 'end bullying, pleads charity chief'. Like how, he thought, and went to turn the page, but something about the picture, a surprisingly young woman grasping her podium with a faraway expression, made him look again ...

'The chairwoman of one of Britain's newest charities to promote juvenile mental health, the Millennium Child Campaign, made an impassioned plea to school governors to act to rid the education system of bullying.

'And Suzanne Marshall-Sharp confessed to her own personal agenda – having been bullied throughout secondary school, the former comprehensive pupil wanted to thank her own bully for giving her the motivation to succeed.'

Suzanne Marshall-Sharp. He spoke the words out loud, trying to trigger a memory he knew was there.

'Ms Marshall-Sharp, now a key member of the government's pastoral care working group, confided in delegates to the GAPE conference that her experiences of being bullied had given her a unique insight into the experiences of the thousands of children her organisation represents.'

Sharp. Sharp . . . he stared at the snappily dressed woman, gazing coyly from the photograph.

Suzanne Sharp. Fuck me. Thanking Tracey Mortimer, presumably.

How bizarre, that you could go years without thinking about any of your old pupils, especially not that bloody troublesome bunch from 1984, and then suddenly, there they all were.

Suzanne Sharp, a government adviser. Weird that Crawley Park should have produced two people who thought they had anything to tell the rest of the world about education. Suzanne, the original prig until the rest of the kids bullied it out of her, and Bob, immortalised in school gossip for being just that bit too dedicated to teacher-pupil interaction . . . Not that Suzanne was any less irritating than Tracey; he'd never had much time for goody-two-shoes . . .

He went to turn over again. And then, with his hand holding page seven in the air, he had an idea.

'Hello, Kelly, Mrs Brown! I'm Sandy Hunter.'

The woman in front of me can't be much older than twenty-one, and has this terrifyingly bright smile, like an updated version of a Girl Guide leader. Any minute now, she'll say that this is going to be fun.

'Now I know you might be a bit nervous –' she's talking to Kelly, but what about me? I'm nervous. 'But I promise I don't bite, and with a bit of luck, when we get to know each other, we might even have some fun!'

I feel my eyes both heading for my nose in a kind of cross-eyed, I don't believe this, piss-take expression, but of course, there's no one to share my contempt, because Kelly looks like all her Christmases have come at once. Someone to play with, even if she is fifteen years older and is getting paid for it.

And suddenly, I hate myself so much. How can I think like that about my own daughter? She ought to have *me* to play with, except I'd rather spend my life sending e-mails to old flames and giving TV interviews to people who really couldn't give a shit.

Great mother I am.

'Now, Kelly,' says the glowing Sandy Hunter, 'why do you think we're here?'

'Um,' Kelly stares at the carpet. 'Um, is it because I haven't got many friends?'

Oh God.

Kelly's gone pink, and refuses to look at me. Sandy shoots me a glare, and I realise that the touchy-feely-smiley personality is a put-up-job to fool the kids. I suspect us parents get an altogether rougher ride.

'And what do you think, Mrs Brown?'

It's such a shit question, and she knows it. 'I . . . I think . . . we're going to help Kelly feel happier about school, aren't we?' And I nudge Kelly gently with my elbow, and watch as she recoils slightly. And I see that bloody Sandy's seen it too.

'Yes. *We* are,' she says.

Suzanne stared at the paper. 'God, Charlotte, trust the bloody *TES* to be in the audience. It's really buggered my plan to recycle that speech.'

Charlotte shrugged. 'No publicity's bad publicity.'

'I know, but the *TES* . . . The broadsheets won't want to report it when I trot it out again at the CBI, if they know it's been printed already. What a waste of all that suffering, eh?'

The phone rang.

'I'm not talking to anyone but Number 10.'

'Millennium Child Campaign? Yes, I'll just see if she's in, hold on.'

Suzanne whispered 'Didn't you hear me? I hope it's Cherie at the very least.'

'No ... but it's an original excuse. Guy called Richard Phipps?'

'Name rings a bell. Some tedious union person, I suppose. OK, bung him on, I can probably manage one more moron today.'

Charlotte punched in Suzanne's extension to transfer the call. 'Well, he says he used to teach you Geography ...'

I thought I'd get my own back on St Sandy by asking her what exactly *she* thought we were aiming to do with Kelly, but she deflected it nicely, saying 'That's up to Kelly, but we know it's going to be enjoyable.'

So Kelly's playing a game, well, we all are, involving various rather creepy dolls that Sandy unpacked from her rucksack. They're the same size as Barbies but with bigger heads and no bosoms, child-like I suppose. I have a horrible feeling that they might be anatomically correct under their brightly coloured skirts and trousers, and I start thinking about what else the dolls are used for, and the kind of things Sandy must deal with day to day. It also makes me angry. How come the school is targeting me and my daughter, when there must be hundreds of horrific sexual or physical abuse cases to sort out?

She's just shy.

Isn't she?

Kelly is concentrating really hard on showing Sandy what happens at lunchtimes, and the doll that she's chosen to be her is skipping happily.

'What about your friends?' asks Sandy, and I hold my breath.

Kelly concentrates even harder on the doll. Eventually she whispers 'Jolene stays with me.'

Sandy looks at me hopefully. 'Jolene?'

I feel incredibly disloyal when I answer 'It's her imaginary friend.'

'Oh ... right. Right. OK then, Kelly, I think that's it for today. But I have got some homework for you.' Sandy reaches into her bag, and pulls out a small notebook with coloured pages. 'Mrs Fellowes tells me you have lovely neat handwriting –'

Kelly beams at this.

'So I'd like you to write me a list before we meet again. A list of things that make you happy, and things that make you sad. Can be as long or as short as you want. OK?'

Kelly takes the notebook, excited at the prospect of showing off, and failing to realise that she's being manipulated.

'OK, Sandy.'

'Right, and I'll see you in two weeks. Now get off back to your class, and I'll just have a word with your mummy. Bye, Kelly.'

We both wave as my little girl leaves the office, and when Sandy turns back to face me, the smile has faded. So has mine.

'Very clever,' I say. 'I suppose you're trying to uncover some kind of trauma at home so you can blame me for her being a bit shy.'

'This isn't about blame, Mrs Brown,' she sighs. 'But your daughter is obviously an unhappy child, and I'd have thought you'd be as interested as I am in finding out why.'

She's got a point, but it just irritates me all the more. 'Of course I do. But don't you think that she's too young for therapy? She'll make friends if she's left alone – it's natural.'

'I wish I could agree with you, Mrs Brown. I've seen

115

too many children who are much older than Kelly who've never learned how to make friends, and they'd tell you there's nothing natural about it. But Kelly's young enough for us to work with and move on with … though I have to warn you, I will need your full co-operation.'

What can I do? I can hardly refuse, but there's something about this woman's smug manner that makes me want to pull a face, throw her the v-sign, then run out of the door.

She delves around in her bag again. 'I have got a questionnaire here for you too, if you don't mind, though it's more of a tool for you. And, yes, it does look at your home situation, your own attitudes and so on. Relationships between the most important adults in a child's life are bound to influence their behaviour, don't you think?'

Relationships? I'd hardly describe what goes on between Dave and me as a relationship. Maybe I'd be better off shagging someone else, at least it might cheer me up. And surely a miserable mother would also 'influence a child's behaviour …'

I thank her for the leaflet.

'No, no, thank you for coming, Mrs Brown. It's so important to have your support – after all, this is a partnership and we've all got Kelly's best interests at heart.'

Annabel put the phone down and wandered across the office to the viewing room, where Jenny was logging the videotapes from Crawley Park.

She looked up from the TV. 'Hi, Annabel.' She took a bite of her sandwich. 'I really don't get this thing with Tracey and that teacher. Weird shit, the way he's laying into her after all that time … unusable, though. So, how's it going?'

'Bit of a result actually!' Annabel squeezed herself on to the table, which was already piled high with cassettes.

'Yeah?'

'Well, you know we've not been having much luck with the psychologist idea? I've just had a call from the boss of one of the country's big kids' psychology charities ...'

Jenny shrugged. 'Hmmm, it's not really *child* psychology we want, is it? It's grown-ups and why they want to go back in time? Unless she's really brilliant, I can't see us being interested-'

'No, it's better than that. She does sound pretty good, actually, but this one has the best CV for our programme. Not only is she a psychology hotshot – she also went to school with Tracey!'

Jenny looked up from her notes. 'Ah ... now that's different.'

'And she really, really wants to do the programme. Couldn't shut her up. I think it's what you'd call killing two birds with one stone!'

Chapter Thirteen

Have you ever had that feeling of dread when someone says they've organised a something they 'just know' you're going to love?

Annabel called me last week, soon after I'd arrived back from my meeting with the appalling Sandy, and said – book yourself a babysitter, we've got a treat for you a week on Saturday.

For a start, anything involving filming is unlikely to be a spontaneous fun-filled night out. It was even more ominous when I asked her what I should wear, and she said 'Oh, nothing special. We'll provide any extras you need.'

So now I'm thinking maybe we're going ice-skating, or to one of those dry ski-slopes or a go-karting track, except I can't see what that's got to do with the programme.

Oh, I forgot, Boris is coming too.

So, now I think about it, that rules out anything too physical. She's still got two months to go, but she's clumsy enough at the best of times, and I can't see anyone insuring her for dangerous pursuits.

At the back of my mind, I've been wondering if they might have tracked down another one of our classmates, and are doing something connected to it – perhaps a mini-reunion to prepare us for the real thing. Jenny's been saying they're worried about filling two half-hour programmes – the first one's meant to be the preparations, and the second one the party itself, but she reckons that despite all the time they've spent hanging round, and asking the same question over and over, they might be struggling to make episode one interesting enough.

And then the little demon that's now taken up residence in the penthouse in the back of my mind, keeps saying . . . if they *are* taking us to meet someone, what if it's Gary?

I don't see how it could be, realistically, because I haven't told them about him getting in touch. I know I should have done, but this is one blast from the past I want on my own terms. Once I've decided what those terms should be.

It's become even more of a fixation since that conversation with Kelly's shrink. I haven't filled in the questionnaire yet, but I know what it's going to ask – are you and your hubby presenting a good, stable example to your kids? Is there anything you do that might upset them/give them the wrong idea about relationships/turn them into lifelong victims and emotional retards?

And of course, we do the lot. No physical affection, constant sniping – on the rare occasions he's around – followed by loud arguments in the middle of the night, fuelled by his booze and my boredom.

It's so bloody unfair. I've done it all by the book. Calmed down when I realised I wanted to get married, chose the right kind of bloke – easy-going, well-off, but not out of my league – and played the courtship game. Didn't live with him before marriage, traditional wedding, promised to obey as well as the other stuff, ignored the signs that might as well have been painted a hundred feet high, and kept working at being the loving partner, waited until it seemed like the right kind of time to try for babies, kept myself pretty up to the births, between the babies and then afterwards until it became utterly fucking obvious that it made no difference, because as far as Dave was concerned, the contract always included a clause allowing some discreet playing away.

You might think most of that sounds as if it comes from a 50s guide to being a good wife, but unless you were brought up round here, you won't understand. Sure, we know about equality, but most of our mums worked not because they wanted careers, but because the cleaning and reception and waitressing jobs were the only way to pay the bills. Especially if, like Mum, that was the only income.

And that's another reason feminism never appealed. I'd seen Mum, coping without a bloke, and although we never talked about it, she made it clear that was second best. So I wanted a picture-perfect, squeaky-clean marriage, two point four children, cat, dog, goldfish, nice car, nice clothes, nice life – not just for me, but for her. And I suppose if you look at our family album, it looks exactly that. But it ain't nice, not with a philandering husband, a lonely child and a gaping hole in my life I'm filling with daft memories and an obsession for the Internet.

And I've been thinking, maybe it's time to start living.

And maybe that's where Gary comes in . . .

'I think Mo's boyfriend is going to propose to her,' Gabby said, shutting one of her glossy magazines and throwing it at the coffee table.

'Can't believe anyone would want to marry Mo.' Gary didn't take his eyes off the sports pages. He knew it'd wind her up, but he'd be out of her hair within the hour, and she was funny when she was riled.

'She's obviously got it more sussed than I have. Maybe I should pick up a few tips tonight.'

'Isn't that what you girls do on your nights out anyway? Plot on how to snare men before you head back to someone's house to cast spells in front of the video?'

'They're not very effective, are they?'

He looked up at her this time. She didn't seem to be joking; in fact, she looked seriously pissed off. He dragged himself out of the chair to sit opposite her on the arm of the sofa. 'Aw, Gabs, how can you say that when I have invited you to share not only my life, but also my lovely home?'

They both surveyed the living room, its windows steamy from the rain, mugs stacked in the usual gravity-defying installation on the floor, Saturday papers carpeting the floor, an ironing board so much a part of the furniture that it was piled with bills and pizza flyers, a cat litter tray with suspicious sandy mounds humming gently by the sink, and the 70s relic of a TV throwing out the fuzzy sound of football results.

'Yeah. Thanks. Just a shame I never realised that living in West London meant we had to pretend we were in an episode of *Steptoe and Son*.'

'Actually, Gabs, there is something I've been meaning to ask you. But . . . Oh, I dunno, maybe it's not the right time.'

'Well, you've started now.'

Gary took a showy deep breath. 'Gabs, will you . . . come to the pub quiz with me on Wednesday?'

'Oh, ha ha,' she said, throwing a cushion at him.

'Had you going, though, didn't I?'

'NO. And what makes you think I'd have you anyway?'

He stood up. 'Because I am irresistible.'

'I'd forgotten that. Saturday nights must be such a terrible ordeal for you . . . all those women desperate for a bit of uniform.'

'Well, I don't like to boast, but my rotas are published

on the Internet, just so my fans know when to hang around street corners and have road traffic accidents. . .'

'In that case, I don't think you should keep your public waiting,' Gabby said, reaching for the phone. 'Now piss off and leave me alone to swap spells with Mo.'

Boris has arrived, almost incontinent with excitement.

'Oooh, Trace, what do you think it could be? Maybe a big meal somewhere posh?'

I laugh. 'Isn't your belly big enough already?'

'Nah – now I've got an excuse.'

'Anyway, what's that got to do with the programme, unless it's one of those places they have in London where they sell spotted dick and custard served by women in suspender belts, who cane you if you don't clean your plate.' I look up at Jamie, who's already set up in the corner. 'It's not that, is it?'

'I'm saying nothing until Jenny gets here.'

'I don't care what it is,' Boris says, 'I haven't been out for weeks.'

'Your husband's almost as bad as mine for being away all the time.'

'The only difference is I miss mine,' she says, rubbing her bump, like it's a security blanket. 'But the more he works away now, the more time he can take off when the baby comes.'

'Men always say they'll be there. But they forget it all the minute you've given birth, the same way women forget how much it hurts until they get pregnant again.'

'Brian won't do that.' She gives me an odd look. 'And I don't care how much it hurts. It'll be worth it.'

I'm shocked at how serious she's become, and as I rack my brains for something to say to clear the air, the doorbell goes. I let Jenny in, and she rushes ahead of me with two carrier bags.

'This is so cool,' she tells us. 'Right, Jamie-boy, get that camera rolling so I can give them these.'

He obliges, then says 'Speed', which I've now learned means 'ACTION'. We take our cue, and start rummaging in our bags.

The first things to emerge are two white shirts – not classy, tailored, posh, evening out shirts, but cheap and nasty blouses with packaging creases still warping the cotton. Another rummage produces a pair of fishnet tights each, and as I pull out a tie in a depressingly familiar canary yellow, a terrible conclusion is forming in my mind.

'God. It's my worst nightmare. We are going to one of these school dinner places, aren't we? I thought they were for pervy businessmen who miss being at public school.'

'Hang on,' Boris says, back to her normal self, as she pulls an envelope from her carrier bag. 'This must be what we're doing. Oooh, it's just like *Blind Date*.' The way she says it, you'd have thought being like *Blind Date* was a good thing.

I reach in for my envelope, and tear it open. '"School Disco? A club night with all your favourite 80s tunes – only admitted if wearing school uniform?"' On the back, there's a Tube map.

We both look at Jenny, who grins back. 'Surprise!'

She's not joking. I haven't been to a London nightclub since I was twenty. And judging from the expression on Boris's face, that still makes me way more experienced than her.

I told you I hated surprises.

Roger watched the girls totter past them in their tiny skirts and ridiculous heels. He clicked his tongue sadly.

'If only I was ten ... no, twenty years younger. Like you, in fact, Gary.'

'I'm past it, too, mate.'

The two policemen walked past the alkies and the dope-heads by the park. They were always there, and Gary had even given directions based on them, 'turn left at the drunks, and the post office is up there on your right.'

'We're all in such a hurry to be adults, and once we get there, we spend the rest of our lives regretting it,' said Roger.

Gary thought he probably preferred it before when he and Roger spent their shifts in silence, before Roger got comfortable with him and confided pearls of worldly wisdom. Endlessly.

Five women – one sporting the full hen-night uniform of L plates, veil and last-chance sequinned boob tube – ran past them, turned back and wolf-whistled at Gary.

'What about that bird of yours? Has she stopped banging on about weddings yet?'

'She knows the score.'

'I bet she does. She knows she'll wear you down in the end. Oh, or get pregnant.'

Pregnant. Did women still do that, trick blokes into the full commitment thing with biological warfare? Maybe some did, but not Gabby. She was too ... equal. And, thank Christ, too young to be paranoid yet about running out of time.

'What about the other one? The one who got in touch from school?'

The M4's one of those roads that still seem romantic to me. Though it promises much more than it ever delivers.

If I ever go into London now, it's by train, I wouldn't dare drive in the city myself, but when I'd just started working at Gillard and Arburthnot, we used to go in a group in my friend's Renault 5. The bright lights. . .

It starts with the planes, you know, and the signs for

124

Heathrow. I fancied working at an airport, not as a stewardess or anything, that's no more than glorified waitressing, but on the ground, like in those TV programmes, escorting visiting celebrities, or rescuing lost kids.

It's getting dark outside, and the lights under the planes make them look even closer than they are. Then the neon signs in front of us become more distracting – office blocks and factories, ads for Lucozade and courier companies – and the road narrows towards the flyover. That always used to seem the gateway to the city, even though this bit of West London was universally accepted as a dive. Almost as bad as Notting Hill. My mum banned me from going to the Carnival, but I still went, and I never saw anyone who looked like Hugh Grant.

'We'll be there soon,' Jenny says. 'The club's in Hammersmith.'

I feel even more disappointed. At least if they're paying for us to go clubbing, it could be in the West End.

'Hammersmith?'

'It's pretty cool there, these days,' she says. 'Nigella Lawson lives there.'

'Who?' says Boris.

I'm surprised Boris doesn't know this one. 'You know – the Domestic Goddess? The posh woman whose dad was a fat Tory?' Hammersmith, eh? I can't see Nigella Lawson going to School Disco.

There are streetlamps over this bit of the motorway, and as the sodium flashes in and out of the car, I keep catching sight of our reflections; we look like a couple of specialist prostitutes.

Once, when I was at G&A, we found a stack of magazines left by this young bloke who'd been made redundant and had cleared his desk in front of everybody. Afterwards, we were raiding the drawers for all those useful bits and pieces people leave behind – the paperclips and the sewing kits and the pots of lip salve – and came across these magazines that looked as though they'd been run off on a photocopier, black and white with handwritten captions. All the pictures showed women of at least thirty in gymslips and straw hats submitting to various acts of corporal punishment. I'd seen more explicit things in my time (there was a weekly exploration of the more extreme products of the Scandinavian porn industry in the back of Mr Sutcliff's music class when I was in the 3rd year, thanks to Gary's older brother), but these were more shocking – for the tackiness of the whole thing, the outrageous cover price (about £3 and that was years ago) and most of all for the fact that Shaun, who I'd actually quite fancied, could possibly want to buy them.

And now that's what we'd been reduced to. If anything, Boris's bump makes her look more authentic than me – she could almost pass as a schoolgirl mum, that's one of the advantages of still having puppy fat into your thirties. But as for me – well, Shaun might have been tempted, but he'd have been in a minority of one.

I just look like mutton dressed as lamb.

The other one – the one that got away?

'What, Tracey, you mean?'

Gary kept wondering whether he shouldn't have followed his first instinct, and avoided e-mailing her back. He'd only done it to spite Gabby, but that was stupid, considering she'd never find out.

Then again, it was harmless. Tracey existed alongside the other cyber-women that he logged on to see every day. He knew they were real, but they were real somewhere else – in most cases, like Lolita ('legally yours – but only just') or Rosa ('bringing a taste of the Tropics to your laptop'), in another continent. Not that you could see the scenery from the cramped bedrooms where they flirted and posed, but he hoped they could hear the waves or smell the mountain air. Unless, of course, they were really in a call centre on an East End industrial estate.

But that would seem unfair, somehow.

OK, so with Tracey he knew exactly where she was, and it didn't exactly count as a faraway place. Not in geographical terms ... but even though she'd refused to go into any detail, the hints were there of a life – and a Tracey – so different from the one he'd fallen for, that she might as well have been on the moon.

Swapping e-mails was a bit like being in CID – without the paperwork – because she was playing her own game, holding back on the details that she obviously thought made her less appealing. The fact that nothing could make Tracey less appealing had escaped her. Now and again something would slip through between the lines – the fact she was married (well, of course she was, she was always bound to marry, and at an early age), the fact she had kids (ditto) and then this business about the reunion. Though she'd ended up being pretty forthcoming about that without him having to force it out of her.

He couldn't pretend it didn't intrigue him, the idea of going back, but this time with the car parked outside ready to speed you home to reality. He was pretty sure he'd have done well compared to the others, the well-paid job, the long-haul holidays, the flat that on paper was worth £120K (they didn't have to know it was next to a chippy, and backed on to the Tube line). And Gabby was a catch, a cut above the average, if only he could accept the fact she'd caught him good and proper too.

But it wouldn't be like that, if he went to the reunion, no form to fill in to calculate who'd scored top marks in the life exam. It was Tracey's show – hadn't it always been – and however superior he felt here, striding the streets like Blade Runner, he could imagine it melting away the instant he walked into the hall, and came face to face with the only bunch of people who knew the truth.

That he, Gary, the best-looking bloke in the whole year, had been dumped.

In favour of a teacher.

'So?' said Roger, and Gary realised he'd been waiting for more details.

'I've swapped the odd e-mail, but I've got Tracey exactly where I want her.'

In the past.

Chapter Fourteen

We push in past the long queue outside the club. I still feel like mutton but, looking at the queue, it seems I'm in good company.

The club PR people whisk us through a different way – apparently, when they've allowed filming before, crews have been swamped and followed like the Pied Piper.

'Weird,' Jenny says. 'That's exactly how kids behave in the playground.'

Boris looks nervous, and I wonder if they've thought through the possible consequences of plunging a pregnant woman into what Jamie says is well known as a snog and beer fest.

But the PR guy seems relaxed. 'It's a really different experience from other clubs. We hardly get any trouble. It's as though putting on a uniform makes everyone behave as if getting off their tits on snakebite – not that we sell it – is the most outrageous thing they can think of. So there's hardly any drugs.'

I guess he would say that, wouldn't he?

'You ready?' Jenny asks. We nod uncertainly, and, with the reassuring presence of Jamie and Cliff behind us, we take out first steps into the arena ...

The smells, sounds, thumping bass rhythms are standard

club fare – the only difference is the view. But what a difference . . .

Below us is a mass of white, more dazzling than a million sequinned and lycra outfits. It's like a giant vat of porridge which bubbles in time to the music, and there's steam rising off it, which reeks of sweat and lager.

I try to focus on the people who make up the human soup, and can see the occasional flash of a blue shirt among the white . . . though it's still before ten, odd pairs seem to be separating off, then returning to the mother ship.

Pippi Longstocking plaits bob up and down next to balding heads, jerking in time to the music.

And what music . . . it's naff and it's catchy, none of the dance music that finally forced me to accept the time had come to switch from One FM to Radio 2. New Romantics and one-hit wonders, it's wedding fare, without Barry Manilow.

'Here's your drinks, ladies.' Jenny's been to the bar and brought an orange juice for Boris, and a cloudy pint of beer for me. 'So what do you think?'

I'm about to come out with a snide remark about how dodgy the whole thing is, but when I open my mouth, all that comes out is 'Brilliant!' and Boris starts grinning as she drags me down towards the blob, to the opening chords of 'It's raining men'.

Gary saw them before Roger did, on the little marketplace just before the Broadway.

'Aye, aye,' he nudged Roger.

From a distance, the two figures fighting in slow motion seemed to be adult-sized, but as the two policemen approached them, it was clear they were children. But the ferocity was fully grown.

'Hey,' said Gary. 'Come on, lads, break it up.'

The presence of the two men stopped the boys, who looked twelve at most. But while the smaller one looked up hopefully – his cheek was already swelling, and sweat was making his face shine in the streetlamp – the other lad aimed another hard kick at his shin.

'Ow, fuck,' said the younger one, and went to wrestle his way back into the scrap he was already losing.

Gary looked round quickly to see Roger holding back, shaking his head in irritation, but with no obvious intention of intervening. Lazy old git.

'I said, BREAK IT UP,' Gary shouted, starting to move in between them. The older one had a livid scar across his chin that seemed completely out of place on his baby skin, like acne on a cherub. He locked defiant eyes with Gary, challenging him to go too far, but loosening his grip on the weedier kid, who seized the chance to dart behind Roger.

'What are you lads doing out at this time of night, anyway?' Roger managed to sound aggressive and pompous at the same time. He shuffled forward and bent down to pick up an empty bottle of vodka. 'Is this yours?'

'Not if it's fucking empty, wanker,' said the older one, who stuck two fingers up before striding off.

Gary shook his head. 'He hasn't even got the respect to run away.' He looked across at the other boy, whose breathing was slowing down. 'At least you've got a bit of a reprieve. Might be an idea for you to get off home, don't you think?'

The boy shrugged, and started to trudge back towards the Tube station.

'A thank-you would have been nice,' said Roger. As they walked away from the high street, a drinks can thrown from behind landed just short of Gary's ankles.

'Fuck off, pigs,' shouted a high-pitched voice, and they turned in time to catch the sight of the boy pulling faces and then running off.

Gary sighed. 'Another Saturday night. Welcome to the wonderful world of the Met.'

I don't usually drink beer because it makes me ill, but G and T feels all wrong for School Disco. I always thought it was a granny's drink at school, one step down the road to sweet sherry. Can't even remember when I changed my mind.

So now I feel gassy and I need a pee every ten minutes, but I also feel rejuvenated. The music's fantastic . . .

Boris can't help herself, she's screaming at the top of her voice 'La, la, la, la, la, la, la, modern girl . . .'

The men aren't bad, actually, even the older ones look cute in this get-up, which is slightly disturbing. But then all the girls look good too; there's something about the light in here, or the lack of it, I suppose, that makes everyone look, if not teenaged, then at least younger than I guess they really are.

Boris is banging her head up and down to the sound of Sheena Easton. And she's not even drinking. . .

Jenny and Jamie come back – they've been off filming some general crowd shots; I think they've been biding their time till I get pissed and stupid. They do some close-ups of Boris, then turn the camera on me.

'So what do you reckon, Tracey?'

'This is really getting me in the mood,' I say, it feels like the kind of thing they want to hear. 'You can't help yourself with this kind of music. And it's like being sixteen again . . . or maybe younger, because it's almost, I dunno, innocent here . . . apparently people hardly even do drugs. Not that I know much about drugs being a suburban housewife, obviously. But here, I don't feel like a housewife either . . . I suppose, it's just fun. And it's been a while since I've had some of that.'

Jenny nods the way she always does when she's happy

with the way an interview's gone, and I notice her reaching back to pinch Jamie gently on the arm to show she's finished this bit. I feel this irrational, slightly drunken jealousy.

The song switches to 'Girls just wanna have fun', and as I stand alongside a bopping Boris, a couple of girls come up to me and ask me what the filming's about.

'I'm doing a programme about school reunions,' I tell them

'Wow! Wicked,' says one, who has impossibly straight blonde hair. 'Is this your first time here?'

'Yep. What about you guys?'

'God, no, we come every week. It's great for pulling,' she shouts above the communal singing.

The other one points at Boris's bump. 'Though it looks like your mate's already scored.'

'I suppose that's true,' I shout back.

'We love the music. It's like, serious nostalgia, retro and everything. Takes us right back to when we were at school and everything.'

Boris seems to be slowing down a bit, but the girls are unstoppable.

'God, yeah. Though it's hard work remembering, isn't it?' says the blonde one.

I like the fact we're all owning up to that nostalgia, that desperation to be young again. 'You're dead right. It'll be seventeen years this summer since I left. What about you two?'

They look at me oddly.

'Um. Well, um, two.'

Two?

The other one looks uncomfortable, almost guilty. 'Well, four if you forget about the sixth form . . .'

Suddenly, I feel like mutton again. But I guess, that's kind of appropriate, in what I'm rapidly realising is a blatant meat market.

'Tracey?' I turn round to look at Boris, and she's slowed right down. In fact, she looks a bit sweaty. 'Tracey, I don't feel brilliant. Could we get a breath of fresh air?'

I look around for Jenny and Jamie, but they're miles away – well, only the other side of the room, towards the Tuck Shop, but by the time we'd got through the crowd, Boris's baby would probably be old enough for School Disco.

I grab her arm, which feels quite clammy, and clutching my beer in the other, we head for the exit. They'll find us.

It's still pretty warm outside, but at least we can kind of breathe out here.

'Is that any better?' I ask Boris, and I feel pretty stressed. Bloody stupid to take a pregnant woman to a nightclub anyway. I just hope it's all OK . . .

'Yeah, yes. Just a bit hot,' she says and she's looking less sick. 'But, what a laugh, eh? I'm coming back after the baby, with Brian.'

I think about putting her right, telling her that she probably won't go out for the first two years, but, hey, she'll find out soon enough. I notice that there's still a queue outside, though it's much smaller and these guys – it is mainly blokes – look more pissed and less well-dressed. They seem to have been hedging their bets with a half-uniform, instead of entering into the spirit of it. And by the sounds of things, they're now paying the price.

'Sold out, mate,' says a bouncer. 'It's just not going to happen tonight. You wanna get here a bit earlier next time. *And* you'll need a tie.'

There's half a dozen of them, and they look less friendly than the cutesy boys inside. Or maybe it's just that inside it's so unreal that no one looks threatening.

'Oh, go on,' says the bloke, but it's obvious from the

expression on the bouncer's broken-up face that cajoling, flattering and probably even bribery are not going to help.

'I told you, boys. Move along, you might still make the last Tube if you head off now.'

The leader, who's probably twenty-five or so, turns back to his mates, and there's this pause where it all seems calm, but I dunno, you can look back afterwards and think that you saw it coming, but do you? I think maybe I did, maybe I sniffed the testosterone before it ignited.

And then, like a dance troupe, off they go, legs, arms, feet, fists punching, and loud mouths screeching and swearing, the sounds carrying through the summer air.

I grab Boris by the arm, and pull her away past the guys, back up towards where I think Hammersmith is. I'm not scared, exactly, though they're not messing around, these guys, and the bouncer's response is to slam shut the doors, leaving the men jostling and itching to fight, but with no obvious target. I don't think we'd be in the firing line, they want enemies their own size, but the risk of being in the crossfire is enough for me to move away as fast as possible, and it's at this point that I realise that Boris pregnant is even more bovine than Boris as I remember her from school. She's dangerously slow.

'Fucking let us in,' one of them shouts, and the rest join in the cries, stamping and threatening some of the other no-hopers behind them in the queue, who're too drunk to have the sense to move away.

I'm looking round us, hoping we are going the right way, and wondering what the hell we do next, two grown women dressed as schoolgirls, in the middle of the night, a long way from home.

Then – who says they're never there where you need them – I see two coppers a way ahead of us, and they're coming this way, I'm sure they're speeding up but I can't tell for sure if that's because they've worked out what's going on, so I drag Boris along and start to shout.

'Police,' I cry in their direction, trying to make sure they hear us, but the guys outside the club don't. One of the policemen, a taller guy, breaks into a bit of a trot and behind him, one who looks older steps up his pace.

'Come here,' I shout, 'there's a punch-up at the club.'

The one lagging behind is pulling out his radio, and the running one catches up with us, looking quickly at Boris and taking in her bump, before anything else.

'Are you both all right?' he says and there's something about the voice, I dunno, there's something, a softer accent than pure Cockney, that makes me look upwards – and fuck me –

'Gary?'

He stiffens, but when he's once-overed Boris again for bleeding and obvious injuries, his eyes come back to me and his head twists in the weirdest double-take, and when he speaks, he really doesn't sound all that pleased.

'Tracey. Tracey Mortimer. What the hell ...?' But before we can even begin to go back down Memory Lane, there's the crash of breaking glass, and my first ever lover runs past me, into the firing line.

Chapter Fifteen

As reunions go it was pretty disappointing. Boris was so overwhelmed by the whole thing that she didn't realise it was Gary – but when the sounds of breaking glass (I wonder if they play Hazel O'Connor at School Disco) stopped, we headed back towards the club, where the older bloke's call for reinforcements had already paid off, because the guys who'd been fighting were now cuffed and outnumbered by men in uniform.

I identified Gary from his height and little curls of hair on the back of his neck, and then tried to catch his eye, while Boris shivered and looked progressively greener. She was desperate for Jenny and the others to emerge from the club, so we could all go back home, while I was determined to get some kind of acknowledgement – some kind of hope, maybe – from Gary before we left London.

But he was absorbed in his work, which, now the fuss had died down, seemed to consist of striding about and looking threatening. I'm ashamed to say this made me feel quite horny. I've never seen the appeal of fetish or S and M, but there was something about his macho air ... I guess it was a such different side to the Gary I knew, who was permanently nice at school. Well, until the day he wasn't ...

Just once I'm sure he looked at me. I've been trying to remember every fragment of that look – and to work out what it meant.

He'd gone by the time the crew came out. Boris went to rest in the car, while they made me do a last bit of filming inside, though Jenny looked really pissed off at the fact that it had all proved such an anticlimax ... Don't know what they were expecting. Maybe they hoped one of us would get off with some hooray Henry, or start smoking in the loos.

All the way home, I tried to freeze-frame Gary's expression.

He'd raised his eyebrows at me, I was pretty sure of that. An acknowledgement, a question, a shared joke, that after all those years we ended up meeting like that?

Then I think there was more of a stare, brief but hard and analytical, as though he was trying to look through me, to see ... what? It wasn't a nice feeling, and I tried not to look away, but I felt exposed and something else. Cheap?

And then just before he turned away, there was a softening – not a smile, I would certainly have remembered that, and kept it like a screensaver in my brain, returning to it over and over. But perhaps it was a second of recognition, a wrinkling of the eyes as he made a decision of some sort.

But what decision?

I'm surprised that it's not his looks I'm concentrating on – but they're the same, or at least, as instantly recognisable as the buildings at Crawley Park. Yes, changed a bit by time, but fundamentally the same layout and the same foundations.

It's Sunday afternoon, and I've lost count of the number of times I've logged in to my e-mail. Nothing. I know I could send one myself, but I have this feeling that I should wait for him to make the first move. Not a tactic I'm familiar with...

There's not much I'm sure of after last night, but I still think that somewhere in that short, sharp expression was the look of unfinished business. And I hope that means he will get in touch.

Jenny rolled away from Jamie's overheated body, trying not to wake him. He could fall asleep anywhere, but the slightest sound or movement would bring him hurtling grumpily back into consciousness.

Alec was bound to blame her for last night. The camera lens steaming up, Boris feeling faint, the punch-up outside, all were obviously going to be down to her, because she was ultimately responsible for everything on that shoot, and for the fact that it wasn't exactly going to provide as long a sequence as they'd planned. And, of course, she was still ultimately to blame for choosing Tracey at all.

'What?' whimpered Jamie, emerging suddenly from sleep.

'Sorry, honey. Just too stressed to drop off.'

She reached out to touch his forehead, burning as always. He emitted more heat than most radiators. Which might explain why he shared it around, like a one-man version of the National Grid.

He sat up in bed, and she saw his gaze drift to the alarm clock. Then he relaxed back on to the pillow. He could probably get away with staying till mid-afternoon. 'It wasn't that bad.'

'No, but it wasn't that good either.'

'Look, I've shot twenty rushes tapes already and we're still ages away from the reunion. And I know you don't like Tracey –'

'That's not fair.'

'But you don't really, do you? But I think she's OK, she'll come across fine.'

'Just 'cos you fancy her.'

'She's all right for her age, but a bit too needy for my liking.'

'So you don't deny fancying her, then?' Jenny was teasing, but only just.

'Hey, Jen, watch it, I don't do jealous women.'

She laughed. 'No, I guess there's not a lot of point me going down that road, is there?' It wasn't even that she wanted Jamie to herself, way too high maintenance. 'If only I'd waited till they got the commission for that history programme. I knew I shouldn't have stayed at Smart Alec Productions.'

'Nah, you'll be all right. And anyway, if you'd done that, you wouldn't have had the chance to work with me again, would you?' He smiled that smile of his that never failed.

'That would have been a blow,' she agreed.

'Anyway, if you're stressed, I've got the perfect solution,' he said, pulling the duvet over their heads.

Mum thinks I've got a hangover, so she's tutting around saying things to the kids like, 'Don't make any loud noises, your mummy's paying the price for her heavy night,' and then slamming the door behind me.

I won't deny that my head aches a bit, lager always does that, but it's annoying that I'm getting cast as irresponsible old soak when I behaved really well all night.

It's always been like that, though. At school, there were some girls who had amazing 'best mate' relationships with their mothers, and I'd love to have someone to talk to about the whole Gary business, but she knows so little about me that I know there's no point. I can't believe that we shared a house for two decades and all we've got to show for it is a common passion for Findus Crispy Pancakes.

You know the June Whitfield character in *Ab Fab*? I'd say that Mum knows even less about me than she did about Edina, or Edina did about Saffy.

Kelly's taking Mum really seriously, tiptoeing nervously about, carrying her notebook. She's getting obsessive about it, every time I look round she's huddled in a chair, writing.

And I realise with a horrible jolt that Kelly and I are just as far apart as Mum and me, and that she's probably going to grow up thinking all the same things, that I don't understand her and she can't talk to me.

But I don't think there's a thing I can do to change it.

The glare from the computer screen is really savage every time I log in, but I can't stop myself.

One new message.

I clench my fists in frustration as the computer refuses to download my inbox, and shut it all down and go back online. But who is going to e-mail me on a Sunday unless it's ...?

Boris.

'Bugger!' I swear out loud and when I turn round I notice Kelly's scribbling something else in that sodding book.

Gary staggered into the kitchen, rubbing his eyes.

'Any tea going?'

'Oh, the monster awakes. Kettle's just boiled, I'll make you one. So was it a hard night?'

He fell slowly backwards on to the sofa. 'Only the usual, being sworn at, spat at and generally abused. Plus a punch-up outside that School Disco place. Bunch of overgrown yobs dressed as schoolboys, getting sulky because they weren't letting them in.' Oh, and a momentary meeting with my first love on the Shepherds Bush Road. But something told Gary it was better to keep that part of the evening to himself.

Gabby handed the steaming mug over the top of the sofa. 'I fancy going there some time.'

'Really? You'd change your mind if you'd seen this bunch.'

'Yeah, but what about all those girls in uniform? Every bloke's fantasy, I would have thought.'

Gary shrugged. 'I don't have any desire to go back in time, thanks very much.' Not after last night.

'Oh, don't give me that. You'd love it. And don't forget this time round you've got the money to drink and smoke . . .'

'Yeah, I guess. Anyway, what about your night?'

'Just the usual spells. Couple of curses on Mo's supervisor in the adoption department. She's been getting a really hard time because of that court case, you know the one I told you about . . .'

She squeezed in next to him, and stroked his hand as she chatted on, her calm voice sing-songing with impersonations of her friends and their boyfriends and bosses, and the actors in the slushy video they'd watched. He loved the sound she made, but he wasn't taking in any of the words.

Tracey Mortimer was back like an old war wound, and just as hard to get rid of. On the Internet, she was harmless. In the flesh, it was something else.

She'd followed him back to the club. He felt her there before he saw her, and then he tried to sneak a glimpse without her noticing, but it was impossible, she was staring at him the whole time. He forgot how he normally walked, and felt instead that he was doing a bad impression of a policeman, striding around like he was in the drill yard at Hendon.

And when he did look, it was like racing into a tunnel

with no end, he couldn't tell how long it went on for, but he was paralysed. Maybe it was like this when you died, that 'seeing your whole life flash before you' people have described, when they've been brought back by doctors. Except he didn't see his whole life, just Tracey's eyes, and all the times he'd gazed into them, and all the things she'd been doing when they locked on his. Messing about, flirting, confiding, kissing, fucking, dumping him, taunting, teasing and, this time, asking for something, though he didn't know what.

He'd known all along it would be a mistake to see her, and now he knew his hunch was right. It was bloody awful the way those few minutes had churned everything up.

Did she look older? He thought maybe she had, tried to remember what impression he'd formed, in the second or so before he realised who she was. But that told him nothing, because he'd been assessing what she was telling him about the punch-up, and so she was no more or less than a witness. Who happened to be in school uniform. Which happened to show she had good legs. Which, a moment later, he realised were legs which had often been wrapped round his neck, once upon a time ...

So where the fuck did this leave him?

'You're not listening, are you?' Gabby said, but she didn't sound pissed off.

'Sorry, love, I kind of am, just knackered, really.'

'Well, you can go back to bed because – as I was just telling you when you'd gone into your spaced-out mode – I'm going shopping with Dee. OK?'

She kissed him on the cheek, and went into the hall. He heard her zipping up her boots and throwing her keys into her handbag. 'See you later, Gaz.'

'Bye, Gabs.'

As the door shut, the computer suddenly seemed to grow to dominate the living room.

He'd had the big question in his head, since he'd frog-marched the guys away from the club, to deliver them to the custody sergeant. But he was no closer to answering it.

There was no harm, he supposed, in logging on to see if she'd e-mailed *him*. Then he could take his decision based on that . . .

At least Boris is OK. I've mailed her back saying I think it's bloody outrageous that they dragged her to a club in her condition, but she's so laid back about it, that she says it doesn't matter, at least she's in one piece, and it's just a shame I couldn't stay longer because of her.

She's a sweetheart, Boris. She didn't even cross my mind for all those years, but now I realise what I've missed. I always thought she was a bit of a bleeding heart; she talked to everyone, even Suzanne, and that annoyed me. I'd have thought it would have been Melody whose friendship would pass the test of time, but once you took away the bitching and the fact we were both decent-looking, what did we have in common?

Boris is the first friend I've had in years . . . it's embarrassing to admit it, but it's true. I've always counted my mates as the girls at the office, then the ones at the shop, or the other mums from antenatal, but I hardly saw them, never rang them up for proper chats or anything like that. And with Boris, well, there's something there, a connection; maybe it's just shared history, and the fact that we're doing the programme, but I think there's more to it . . . I hope she feels the same way. Because it makes me feel nice.

I reply to Boris's latest message. She says the baby's having a manic afternoon, so I tell her maybe it's a boy, because Callum moved loads more than Kelly.

I send the message, and when the page reloads, there's the message.

From GARYANDGABBY, but there's no subject line. I click on it . . .

'ello, 'ello, 'ello . . . fancy bumping into you!

And that's it. One measly line. But it tells me all I need to know.

Chapter Sixteen

Where do you go to meet your first love after seventeen years?

I know I'm always disappearing into silly daydreams, but, for once, it's not just fantasy. It's actually going to happen.

I kind of knew it would as soon as he sent that e-mail. After bumping into him like that, what had we got to lose? But after the disaster of that first meeting, the stakes are so much higher to make the next time just right.

Only the next time is tomorrow.

I wanted to prove how sophisticated I am, to suggest the perfect venue, but all I could come up with is the Crown Hotel. The bloody Crown, where salesmen meet their bits on the side, and small-time manufacturing companies hold their annual dinner dances.

But Gary wanted to come to Bracewell – and it saves me having to get a babysitter, because Maureen next door will always take Callum for a couple of hours. I didn't even think about getting Mum involved ...

Once we'd worked out he'd come here, I had to think of a meeting place, somewhere no one would see us. All right, so we're just a couple of old, old friends meeting up, but I'm still married, and with Dave busy erecting things on the other side of the Irish sea, it wouldn't take much to get the gossip going if anyone saw me with Gary. The advantage of the Crown is that no one I know would be seen dead there, and there's a snug bar where even if someone did happen to have a brainstorm, and come for lunch, they still wouldn't see us unless they were looking. The disadvantage of the Crown is that it's tacky, it's old-fashioned and it smells.

I suppose if we enjoy tomorrow, then there's a chance that ... that what? This is what I keep coming back to. What am I hoping for? He's got a girlfriend, I'm a housewife and mother, it's not as though this can go anywhere, is it? I've been trying hard to work out what I want from it, and I don't *think* I'm living in cloud cuckoo land, hoping to be carried off on a white charger, but if this is just a get-together with an old school friend, why have I been unable to think about anything else since last week?

Whatever the reason, I know one thing. Having a TV crew there is NOT going to help.

Which is why I haven't told them.

Jamie walked in from the bar. 'OK, that lipstick camera's rigged up, and we've tested the mikes as well.'

Alec and Jenny faced each other in chilly silence, as though they'd been frozen mid-slanging match. Jamie stopped. 'Sorry, didn't realise I was interrupting something. I'll go, shall I?'

'No, don't mind us, Jamie. Jenny's just having another pop at me, aren't you, darling?'

'I can't actually believe you're going to go through with this, that's all!'

Alec shrugged. 'Yes, well, I've taken the decision, I'm the producer, and you're going to have to live with it.'

'I'm going to get a coffee,' she mumbled, leaving the

storeroom, which was crammed with monitors and tape machines.

'God, she's fucking hard work today,' said Alec.

'I kind of see her point, though, don't you? It could backfire really badly.'

'In which case, I'll take the rap, won't I, like I always do? Anyway that silly cow Tracey shouldn't have gone behind our backs, should she?'

'Maybe not . . . I'll just get off and see how the boys are doing with hiding the cables.'

In the bar, Jenny was sitting opposite the table where the crew was tidying up the cables. Jamie sat down next to her.

'There's nothing you can do when he's like that, Jen.'

'I can't fucking believe he's doing this. It's mad, the whole bloody programme could fall apart over it. Never mind the fact that it stinks. Morally.'

'Morally?'

'Well, I wouldn't expect *you* to understand that.' But she was smiling.

'It's a bit daft of Tracey, though. I mean, the company's spending a fortune on organising the reunion, it's not on to keep stuff from you.'

'Maybe not. But I'm sure she'd have told us in her own time.'

'She knows you can read her e-mails, though?'

'She must have forgotten. And, of course, it wasn't *me* reading them that was the problem, was it? I would have kept my gob shut.'

'Hmmm. Where is Annabel, anyway?'

'Still in London. She's only coming down for the fun and games tomorrow.'

The barman came over with her coffee. 'Going all right is it? I used to love that Jeremy Beadle, *Game for a Laugh*.'

When he'd gone, Jamie said 'Stroke of genius from Alec, though, this surveillance idea. Not to mention the cover story – the hotel have bought it totally. You've got to hand it to him.'

'Oh, yeah, he's brilliant at being a devious backstabbing cheat. But fooling the hotel's one thing. Dealing with Tracey when she finds out is going to be a totally different scenario.'

Suzanne watched as a man in a green sweatshirt worked his way through the jungle of plants in reception. He followed the same routine with each one, touching the leaves and the compost, stroking each one gently, then stepping back like an artist surveying the landscape. Every plant would be refreshed with water from a can, or a spray, or both. Discoloured leaves were removed, and tablet or two of food placed just under the soil by the rim of the container. With a final flourish, the man leaned in towards the plant and patted its bark or stem, as if to say goodbye, see you next week.

It was strangely relaxing to watch him tending his urban oasis, even though no one else had given the plants a second glance during the twenty minutes she'd now been waiting in the foyer. Suzanne pulled out her palmtop, selected her ideas file and scribbled in 'plant man – nurturing – dedication'. She'd always kept notes like these, either electronically, in notebooks or, back in the bad old Crawley Park days, in pink lockable diaries. In the last few years, it had started to pay off, as so many of the little homilies or observations could be used for speeches or in the articles she wrote for professional journals and, recently, the occasional Sunday supplement.

The woman behind the reception desk looked up. 'Are you *still* waiting?' she said, as if Suzanne was deliberately cluttering up her personal space.

'Suzanne?'

She turned. 'Mr Carmichael.'

He smiled. 'I think I'll be happy with Bob, now. Unless that makes you feel uncomfortable. Bit like calling your parents by their first names, I guess.'

'I'll try it. Bob.'

'Righto. I've had enough of the office, shall we go to a coffee shop round the corner?'

She nodded, and as they walked, Suzanne stole glances at him. Once her favourite teacher, then a terrible disappointment, then an object of snatched gossip in between revision periods and 'O' level exams – and now, more bizarre than all of those, a potential colleague.

He didn't look that different, the hair was lighter and the suit darker, and the cut of both was clearly more expensive. She knew most of his pubescent female pupils had thought he was tasty, but she'd been a late developer, and it was only now that she could see it – the strong jaw and the crinkly eyes which looked more inviting with age, in the annoying way that men's features often did. She'd never admired him for his looks, but for his intelligence. And his integrity. What a joke.

They arrived in the coffee bar, an Italian place with hissing espresso machines, steamy windows and a guy behind the bar who smiled at Bob and eyed Suzanne with unconcealed curiosity.

'Double espresso, and?'

'Cappuccino, please,' she said, taking a seat by the window.

'This is proving to be a year of reunions,' said Bob.

'So you already know? About Tracey?'

'Yes.' He smiled at her. 'I didn't think you'd got in touch after all this time to talk about education policy. Though we can, if you like.'

She felt herself blushing. 'Maybe another time.'

'I must say, though, I liked the sound of your speech. The one about Tracey. Something of an indictment of Crawley Park, and me, I suppose. Though you seem to have made the best of it.'

Suzanne gulped. 'I was very disappointed in you. For going off with Tracey. I mean, it never would have occurred to me to fancy a teacher, but when she ended up with you, it was like ... I thought you had more taste.' She stopped. She'd said too much.

Bob's eyes seemed to narrow in amusement. 'I think there was more to Tracey than maybe most people saw. Sure, she was a pain in the arse if she wasn't centre of attention, but all the stuff with you and with her ... I honestly don't think any of us realised it was as bad for you as you suggested in that speech.'

'Perhaps not. Anyway, Dick Phipps called me and said you didn't want to stop her doing it. Aren't you worried?'

'Suzanne, him calling you had nothing to do with me. He's scared of the scandal coming out, and making him look bad for letting me resign. I'm not that worried. She was over the age of consent, it was hardly the pinnacle of my career, but at least it wasn't illegal – and the rules were different in those days.'

'All the same, with your job and your profile ...'

'It's a long time ago. OK, ideally I wouldn't want it dragged out again, but if Tracey has a reason for doing this, then it's not up to me to get in her way. So what about you? Will you be going?'

'I don't know. I rang the TV company, and they're quite keen to interview me, as the programme's resident psychologist, which could raise the profile of Millennium Child. But then that speech could be a problem. If someone finds that, and puts two and two together, things could get messy.'

'And you don't want that?' He was still canny.

'No,' she lied. The truth was she didn't know what she wanted. She needed time to work it out. 'The charity's the biggest thing for me, now. Yes, I'd like to raise the profile of what we're doing, but not if it leaves behind a nasty taste in everyone's mouth.'

'Sometimes it is better to leave things as they are.' He sounded sad.

Suzanne studied his face. 'The thing Dick was most surprised about was that he thought you wanted to see her again.'

'Poor Dick. He never did understand deep feelings. That's why he taught Geography, I suppose.' He chuckled at his feeble joke. 'My subject was about learning from the past. Which is why I won't be going. I mean, I think I would like to see her again. I know it might seem a daft thing to want, but despite all the unpleasantness of what happened afterwards ... Tracey isn't someone you can forget.'

'No,' Suzanne agreed.

'But I'm not going to gatecrash her party. I'll find it hard to resist watching the programme, though.'

He looked at his watch. 'If you DO want to get involved in the citizenship group ... the one you arranged this meeting about –' Suzanne blushed slightly, '– then I'm sure you could make a contribution.'

'Thanks ... though it smacks a bit of the old school tie, doesn't it?'

'Well, if Eton and Harrow can abuse their positions, why shouldn't Crawley Park do the same?'

'Yes. You're right.' Suzanne stood up. 'I'd better head back to the office. Thanks for meeting me. And I'll think about the working party.'

'Thanks. You should be proud of yourself, you know. You're doing an important job ... ' He reached over to touch her hands, and then glanced at her wedding ring.

'And your husband's a lucky man, as well. See you again, perhaps, Suzanne ... '

The sun was warm when she left the café, so Suzanne decided to walk back to her office. She needed to think.

It was almost too easy. All she had to do was go through her contacts list, identify a likely journalist and tip them off. No one would find out it was her – after all, the whole school had known about the affair at the time, so there was no way of tracing it back. She didn't much like reporters, but they were scrupulous about protecting their sources.

She caught sight of herself in a shop window. Surely she was too grown-up now to want revenge. But then again, she'd fought for ten years to lose the persecution complex. The conviction that from the instant she stepped into a room, until the moment she left, she was a target; and the certainty that every giggle, nudge or whisper, was directed at her ...

The fear that everything she did – from the way she brushed her hair, to the way she held her pen – had the potential to increase the abuse, or to start a whole new campaign of mockery ...

The knowledge that the only way to avoid more hurt or humiliation, was to avoid human contact altogether, to avoid looking people in the eye in case they laughed back ... to avoid conversations with strangers in case she heard her words repeated and used against her ... and to avoid ever daring to believe that someone would want to be her friend, or could possibly fancy her ...

She'd spent five years in the shadow of Tracey Mortimer, and it had taken nearly twice as long to unlearn the lessons of Crawley Park. The only thing that had kept her going through those agonising classes and lonely breaktimes was fantasising about how she could get her own back. Mostly it involved a large pair of scissors (for cutting off all that wavy blonde hair) or a millionaire boyfriend (to take her to the school disco, and strike Tracey, Melody and the rest of their cronies, dumb with jealousy).

But she'd never imagined that the perfect opportunity would arise now, of all times, when she was happier than she'd ever been. What was it they said about revenge being better served cold?

Chapter Seventeen

I can tell it's going to be a big day when I wake up before Callum does.

As I come round in the mornings, before I even remember the basic stuff like who I am, where I live, or whether I can afford a lie-in, there's always this gut feeling that tells me what kind of a day it's going to be. Usually it's either vague contentment, or vague misery, and then as I wake up, my brain searches for clues to confirm my mood ... the thought process goes something like this: I'm sad ... I'm married ... to who ... to Dave ... oh yeah, that's right ... that's why I feel sad ...

Well, this morning, I wake up to a buzzy feeling, and the clue comes when I open my eyes to see the clothes I've decided to wear already hanging on one of the handles of the built-in wardrobe. You can say a lot against Dave, and I do all the time, but he's provided well for us. I have more cupboard space than a woman could wish for, with concealed lighting above the full-length mirrors that make me look quite glamorous on a good day.

I stretch my legs out to the very end of the bed – I love having the king-size to myself; it almost makes up for the lack of sex. I did enjoy sex when I was younger, but then I also enjoyed air hockey, and the opportunities for both are now fewer and further between.

When did it stop (the sex, not the air hockey)? Callum was a big baby, so that didn't help. And Dave seemed to go off the idea as well – eventually I think he found the Moben fitted furniture catalogue a more enticing prospect in the bedroom. Except when he's pissed, of course, but then for men like Dave, it's any port in a storm.

But in the last couple of months, I've noticed a gradual thawing in parts of my body I'd assumed were as chilly and out of reach as last summer's chicken wings at the bottom of the chest freezer. I suppose it's a reaction to being around decent-looking men for a change – Jamie, Alec and now Gary ...

And the thought of Gary and his handcuffs is definitely speeding up the defrosting process ...

I dress in my normal school clothes to deliver Kelly – we've got another psychology appointment due this week, which I'm not looking forward to, but she's drawn little stars around the family calendar in felt pen, so I guess she feels differently.

I bought an anti-wrinkle avocado face-pack in the supermarket yesterday, and I smooth it on before giving Callum a ridiculously early lunch. I don't go in for treatments as a whole, and he's so intrigued by my newly green face that I have to reel backwards like a boxer as he reaches out with his fists to try to touch my nose. Then I drop him off next door, and retreat to the bedroom to attempt a transformation.

Black linen trousers – it's sunny outside, but June's so unpredictable – and a slim-fitting camel-coloured shirt that flatters my skin and my hair, even if I do say so myself ... it can't look any worse than that stupid fake school uniform, after all.

And then the make-up that I rarely bother with these days. I'm going for the natural look, which takes about twice as many lotions and potions as the unnatural look, but for a lunch date, I can hardly wear full war-paint ... by the time I've finished, I've probably erased a couple of years, but I'm not sure whether it's taken away the pleasant easy-going years at the end of my teens, or the shittier ones at the start of my marriage, when I realised Dave was playing away.

I wouldn't exactly describe myself as rejuvenated, but the effect isn't bad.

'Right, guys. Operation Tracey begins in approximately –' Alec checked the clock on the wall '– three-quarters of an hour. Let's synchronise watches. 12.14, everybody.'

Jenny sighed deeply. He was loving every minute of this farce. But she was willing to bet he wouldn't be so keen on taking centre stage when it all went wrong.

'Now, we don't know exactly what Gary looks like now, but judging from Tracey's later photos he's tall and quite bulky, dark brown hair and decent-looking. If he – or anyone who fits that description – arrives before she does, stay at your tables until she gets here, that way there's no risk that the wrong person gets the seats.'

The stooges – three people drafted in from the Smart Alec Productions office for a day out – nodded.

'Now, Steve, you're all right with the briefcase camera?'

'Yep, Jamie tested it out earlier.'

Alec had called in the help of one of his old colleagues from news, Steve, to organise the undercover stuff. Jenny quite liked him; at least he'd used the cameras and the wires and all the other gadgets to trap villains. Typical Alec, to go well over the top with this – he didn't have the guts to do proper investigative stuff, but obviously liked the idea of messing about in the manly world of undercover journalism.

'And you're happy, Jamie?'

'Yep, the main mike and the back-up are fine, and the lipstick camera's giving pretty good pictures. All we need now are our victims ... '

I wanted to take a cab, but then Kelly will need picking up from school in a few hours, so it's not as though I can get pissed. Which is what I so desperately want to do. I was tempted to take a swig of gin before I left the house – wouldn't even have needed the tonic to go with it – but I suppose that the vague smell of alcohol on my breath wouldn't enhance the classy impression I'm trying to create.

I park the car near the town hall, and walk to the Crown. It's the only one of the pubs in town that we never went to when we were at school. Not that we were old enough to go to any of them, of course, but by the time we were fourteen, Melody and I never had a problem, and Gary and the other lads would sneak in behind us. But we didn't even think about trying it on in the Crown, because it was strictly for old farts.

Which, I guess, is exactly what we are now. Faintly embarrassing, trying to be cool, and probably failing in my case, and certainly way too old to be even thinking about sex. I catch sight of myself in a car window, and the shirt looks too tight, the trousers too dowdy, and the make-up not nearly thick enough.

I suddenly wonder what the fourteen-year-old Tracey Mortimer would make of Tracey Brown.

At first, she's horrified. Where's the house in *Homes and Gardens*, the Caribbean holidays, the designer clothes? Yes, the kids are there, she knew there'd be kids, but while Callum would have passed the test, Kelly would have been a serious disappointment. A cuckoo in the nest, not at all a natural successor as most popular girl in the school ... The teenaged Tracey was not, I must admit, particularly tolerant of anyone who didn't seize life by the bollocks ...

So I'm not sure she'd think much of me, either. Boring life, boring husband, boring children, boring job ...

But then again, you know, the boring Mrs Brown isn't sitting on her arse waiting for it to get fatter. Sure, she's had a quiet period, falling in love, giving birth, falling out of love, but now something of the old Tracey is returning. How many other suburban mummies would talk a TV company into making two programmes about her? Who else would have the nerve to get back in touch with the guy whose heart she broke seventeen years ago? Never mind invite him out on a date ...

I'm talking myself round. It's like I've turned a corner – actually, I have turned a corner, the one that leads from the town hall to the street where the Crown is, but that's not what I mean. No, it's more like the moment when Olivia Newton-John turns from feeble wally into leather-clad hussy, except in my case I've done it in reverse, spent the last few years in a daze of nappies and spinelessness. And now – about bloody time – I'm reverting to type.

Five to one. Gary had been determined to be late, but he couldn't skulk around outside much longer. It was strange enough being back in Bracewell, without hanging about like one of the more obvious boys from the Drugs Squad.

He'd never been in the Crown, but once inside it was exactly what he'd expected ... swirly maze of a carpet, ridiculously gilded reception desk with an over-decorated receptionist behind it, a vague institutional smell of cabbage and boiled beef wafting from what, judging from the sounds of clinking cutlery, was the dining room on the right.

So that meant the bar must be to the left. Gary lowered

his head to go through the doorway – built for a poorer nourished, shorter generation. The bar was dingy, and much busier than he'd expected, every table occupied. He couldn't see what attracted them. It couldn't be the atmosphere, because there wasn't one. He doubted it was the décor, with its horse-brasses and tobacco-stained paintwork. And, he thought, as he approached the bar, it wasn't the welcoming bar staff or the range of real ales.

'Half a lager, please.'

The barman looked at him strangely, confirming Gary's suspicion that he looked like a bad undercover detective. But that wasn't what was making him uneasy. He still wasn't sure what he was doing there. A gentle amble down Memory Lane? Not when the present was so much better. Or maybe a twisted little look at the way things could have turned out, if he hadn't made a run for it ...

But what if 'it' was still there, whatever it was that had driven him mad with hormones, and then nearly mad with grief?

What if after seventeen years, he still hadn't got Tracey Mortimer out of his system?

'Sorry, mate,' he called out to the barman, who was bending over to reach a glass. 'Can you make that a pint?'

I really wanted to do a last-minute check in the ladies before going in, but the Crown is so shit that I can't find them. I'm about to ask, when I spot Gary in the bar. Still good-looking, no doubt about it, though there's this sulky look on his face that, if you didn't know him, you'd think was bad temper. But it's just his way of covering up uncertainty. I recognise it from the days when I used to turn up at his house in a filthy mood, and he didn't know what the hell to do to placate me.

It's nice to know he's feeling nervous. Another sure sign: he's clutching his pint with both hands like he's afraid of dropping it, and casting these shifty little glances around the bar. It's surprisingly packed; maybe there's a convention of sprocket makers.

Right. Shoulders back, head up, lips forward. Advance.

'So, what's a nice guy like you doing in a shithole like this?' OK, cheap line, but kind of appropriate.

He turns, and I see it there, just before he pulls his face back together into a bland, Mr Plod expression, a flash of attraction that passes between us, and proves I've hung on to something special from the old days.

'Waiting for someone,' he says and I can't tell whether he's playing the game or not. He looks at me like he's trying to work out the same. Then he flashes those enormous teeth of his in this odd leering smile. 'So can I buy you a drink until she turns up?'

I nod, and just when I'm looking round to see if I can spot an empty table, a smartly dressed woman at the corner table stands up, sighing loudly. She continues sighing as she flounces past me and out of the bar, like an actor in a soap opera.

'Gin and tonic.' Well, one can't do me any harm. 'I'll just go and bag that table, shall I?'

I watch him as he orders. He doesn't seem to have put on any weight, maybe all that running after criminals keeps him fit. The thought of him chasing around London like Dennis Waterman in *The Sweeney* makes me laugh, but also makes me feel quite flushed. There's a reproduction Coca-Cola mirror on the wall opposite me, and I do look slightly pink and, I must admit, more alive than I remember seeing myself in a long while . . .

He sits down opposite me. 'So.'

'So.' I want him to take the lead.

'What shall we toast?'

'School discos?' We clink glasses. 'So did you bang them up? The guys from the punch-up?'

161

'Only the guy with the knife.'

'One of them had a knife? Bloody hell.' My big, brave, hunky hero.

'That's what it's like on the mean streets, Trace.'

Trace. He makes the 'a' really long, holding it in the back of his throat. It makes me tingle.

'So, do you like your job?' It's a lame question, but I can't ask the things I really want to know. Do you fancy me? Do I look the same? Does your girlfriend know you're here?

'The pay's good, and we have a laugh when we're not being gobbed at.'

Fucking hell, this is hard. What did we talk about when we were fifteen? Not school, not gossip, not music. I suppose mainly we snogged, and messed about, to postpone the moment when we were finally going to Do It.

'Poacher turned gamekeeper, eh?'

'They nearly didn't take me because of what happened. Even though I was seriously provoked – don't you think?' He stares at me, and I find it impossible to hold his gaze. He seems to enjoy it.

'I . . . it was a long time ago. And London? Do you like living there?'

'It's expensive and it's dirty. But when I come back here, I don't regret getting out.' He drinks some beer. 'You weren't going to stick around in Bracewell, either, were you?'

He's needling me, and I think he's doing it deliberately. 'Things change, don't they? I got out of Crawley Park, that was far enough for me.'

He snorts. 'Right. I suppose we all had to scale down our plans for world domination.'

'Well, I didn't get the grades to get on the world domination course.'

'Shame. You'd have thought old Carmichael could have

put a word in for you. Personal reference, if you like.'

This isn't going the way I'd hoped. I laugh, but it's not funny. 'So, are you still in touch with anyone else?'

'I exchange Christmas cards with Briggsy. And one of the lads invited me to his wedding a few years back – do you remember Darren Bostock? But I couldn't see the point. I've got different mates now, in the Met. People I've got something in common with.'

'Yeah. Yeah, I know what you mean.' Only I bloody don't know, do I, because if I had lots of those new mates, I'd hardly be organising a sodding reunion.

'What about you?'

'Well, Boris and I are pretty close.'

'I can't believe that was her, I didn't even notice, what with the punch-up to sort out. Say hi to her for me.'

'I will.'

What now? It's completely silent in the bar, and right now I'd even welcome some of that awful mood music to fill the gaps. Everyone else is on their own, the business-man opposite who's got his head buried in paperwork, and seems to be blocking the world out with his briefcase. The young girl reading an airport novel in the corner.

I try again. 'This place is like a morgue. I'm sure there are funkier places we could have met, but I'm not cool enough. They'd probably turn me away at the door as too old.'

He looks me up and down. 'You look good.' But he says it with a complete lack of interest, as if he's talking about gloss paint or motor oil.

'I was worried you wouldn't recognise me.'

'What, not recognise my first lurve?' He smiles into space. 'I'd recognise you anywhere, Trace. And do you know why?'

I don't think I want to, but I think he's going to tell me anyway, so I shake my head, with a smile as false and brittle as an air hostess's.

'Because it's very hard to wipe out the face of the person who humiliated me in front of all my friends.'

Shit.

'Who chased and pursued and flirted until she got what she wanted, and then dumped me two weeks before the exams.'

It's my imagination, but it feels like the whole bloody bar is listening to what he's saying. I even catch the barman looking over, but he darts back under the counter.

'I've tried hard, believe me, Trace. But then, I dunno, something will remind me. Maybe Gabby – that's my girlfriend by the way, gorgeous, she is – will switch on the radio and they're playing "True" by fucking Spandau Ballet, and I'll remember how it felt punching Bob sodding Carmichael in the face when what I really wanted to do was smash *your* face in.'

He's spitting the words at me now, though he hasn't raised his voice.

'Oh, don't worry, Trace. I'm not going to do it now. Because this meeting is exactly what I needed, to get you out of my system. You're just as small-town as I thought you'd be, and thank Christ you dumped me, because I can't think of anything much worse than being stuck here with you in Bracewell for the rest of my days.'

He stops and we both sit utterly still for I don't know how long. He looks even more surprised than I feel at what he's just said.

I gulp and I feel stupid, humiliated and, I hate to admit it, tearful. But I'm not going to let him know that.

I down the last of my drink. 'I guess you won't be wanting an invite to the reunion then, Gary.' I stand up. 'Thanks for coming. Have a nice life.'

The loos at the Crown definitely aren't off reception, I remember that at least, and try to head to the other end of the bar to find them before the bloody waterworks start.

So I stride briskly through the door marked toilets, as I battle against the unfamiliar vinegary sensation spreading from my throat to my nose, and then my eyes.

And walk straight into Jenny.

Chapter Eighteen

The shock of seeing Jenny stops the tears in their tracks. It's such a daft place for her to be, like seeing an elephant on the North Pole.

'What are you doing here?' She can't meet my eye.

'Oh. Um, working. What about you? You look very glamorous.'

'Thanks. What work?'

There's something wrong about this. I've had my ration of coincidence with bumping into Gary in London ...

'Yeah, um, we're ... sussing out where to stay for the reunion.'

We? Who else is here? I can't see them coming on a day trip from London just to look at hotels.

I'm suddenly sure that she's been following me. But then how did she know I was coming here? Unless ...

'Have you been reading my e-mails?' Shit, I'd forgotten that they could get into my account ... maybe they've seen the whole thing. How could I have been so stupid?

'No!' But Jenny's a terrible liar, considering she works in television. I've had years of practice with Dave, so I can spot someone this crap at it a mile off. And I think she realises it because she says, 'Let's get a drink, shall we?'

*

'I can't see us using any of that shite in the show,' said Alec, as the technician spot-checked the recordings from the secret camera. There was barely space for them and all the equipment in the storeroom.

Annabel looked upset. 'It might work,' but even she couldn't see how it would fit.

'Mind you, interesting about this other pupil he mentioned. Bob. Sounds like a teenage love triangle. Maybe we could work something up around that. What have you got on him?'

Annabel was flicking back through her notebook, shaking her head.

'Oh, for Christ's sake, Annabel, don't tell me she hasn't told you about him? Some researcher you are. And what's taking Jenny so long? You women spend half your lives in the toilets, don't you –'

'Now this is interesting . . .'

'That makes a change.'

Annabel ignored him. 'In my notes it says Bob Carmichael wasn't a pupil at all . . .' She paused for effect. 'He was her form tutor.'

Steve walked in from the bar, taking off his pin-striped jacket. 'Coast is clear now. How was it for you?'

'Dull as hell, mate. Except it seems our friend Tracey was a bit keener on teachers than she'd have had us believe. Bob Carmichael – I knew the name rang a bell.'

Steve said 'I tell you why that is. Bob Carmichael is one of the government's advisors. School standards and all that. We interviewed him for a documentary on Channel 4 last year.'

'No, this one is Tracey's old teacher . . . Unless of course it's one and the same . . . Now that would be a story!' The men chuckled to each other.

'Alec?' Annabel tugged on his arm and pointed at the monitor, where the secret camera showed Tracey sitting back down again. With Jenny.

'Oh, bugger,' Alec said. 'This does NOT bode well.'

'You *have* been reading my bloody e-mails, haven't you?'
How could I have forgotten that they had access to the
account? What a huge cock-up – I can't even organise a
secret tryst with an old lover without giving the game
away AND taking years of pent-up abuse . . .

At least Jenny has the decency to look a bit guilty.
'Yees. I'm sorry, Tracey. We weren't meaning to spy on
you, it's just to start with we didn't know if you'd got the
hang of the computer, so it was like a safety net. And then
the next thing, you're in touch with Gary, and then didn't
tell us, so we were worried you were keeping other things
from us and . . .' She tails off.

I suppose I can understand why she's been logging in
but I don't see why she had to follow me here. 'Well,
there won't be a happy bloody reunion between me and
Gary as it turns out so we've all been wasting our time.'

'Oh dear,' she says. 'Are you OK?' The way she's
looking at me makes me wonder if she heard the whole
saga. But then she can't have done, because she wasn't in
the bar. The place is deserted now, which is weird in
itself. I feel like I've gone into a topsy-turvy world where
I'm paranoid about everything . . .

'It wasn't quite the jolly chat I'd been hoping for, but
you win some, you lose some.' Actually, I feel like
screaming the place down but I'm not going to tell her
that.

'Maybe he'll come round,' she says 'I suppose it's not
always going to work as well as it has with you and Boris
– Helen, I mean. Anyway, we've got some good news . . .
Madness have agreed to play at the reunion! Isn't that brilliant?'

Yeah, brilliant . . . Even the fourteen-year-old Tracey

would have had her reservations – excitement at the fact a real life proper chart band was coming to Bracewell for *her* party, but irritation that it wasn't someone cool, like Joy Division or Morrissey ... though Madness are probably trendier now than they have been for twenty years, because the world seems obsessed with 80s nostalgia.

And I can't get excited about a band when my whole past has just been dragged out and hung out to dry. I want to take it out on someone – and, thinking about it, Jenny's the obvious person.

'I'm not even sure I want to go ahead with the bloody reunion if you're going to go behind my back.' She looks really nervous now, so I decide to rub it in. 'Anyway, what the hell did you turn up here for? If you wanted to eavesdrop, then you've missed the action, because he didn't hang around.'

'I'm sorry, Tracey.'

'Yeah, well. Whatever. I need to think about this whole bloody thing. I don't really know if I want to carry on with the programme. I'll be in touch, but don't hold your breath.'

I stand up, and there's that shifty barman again, watching but trying not to look nosy. He dips down below the counter as soon as he sees that I've clocked him ... so as I walk out, I lean right over.

'Sorry to interrupt your afternoon entertainment. Get a sodding video next time, instead!'

I storm out of the Crown, slamming the door behind me.

I know I've got to go home, but what I really want is to drive out of town to one of the old Roman Roads, put on a Black Sabbath tape, and put my foot down, until I'm as far away as I can get.

I'm breathing really heavily, and I can't work out what to do next, so I start walking back to the car. A hurricane of emotions is racing through my system, and it's so fast that I can't even identify what most of them are ... But the worst is this anger, and it's not even fair to say it's directed against Jenny or even Gary.

It's me I feel most angry with ... for not changing the password on my e-mails, for arranging this stupid meeting, for shitting all over Gary in 1984, and most of all, for having these unspecified, unacknowledged, unachievable hopes that one meeting with the man whose teenaged self I was once in love with could somehow change everything that's wrong with my life.

And then I see Alec's sports car.

'God, I really need a drink now,' said Jenny. 'Vodka and fresh orange, please.'

'I suppose they don't always go according to plan, do they?' said the barman. 'Does that mean I won't be on telly now?'

'Probably not.' Jenny turned round, as Alec and Jamie came into the bar. 'You owe me big time for getting us out of that.'

Jamie climbed under the table to start de-rigging, while Alec put his arm round Jenny. 'Yeah. Thanks – you did well there. I really thought she'd worked the whole thing out when we saw you on the monitor with her. But I reckon she'll come round ...'

'No, she fucking won't.'

They turned to see Tracey in the doorway. She walked across the bar to the table where Jamie was removing the microphone.

'You as well, Jamie. I thought we got on.'

Alec started blustering. 'It's not what it looks like ...'

'As the actress said to the bishop. I'm no TV expert, but I'd say this looks pretty much like you've been filming me without me knowing.'

Jenny looked away as Alec opened his mouth, but no sound came out.

'You can't even deny it. Bloody hell. What am I, to make you to go to all this trouble? Some kind of gangland hitman?'

'Blimey, that was close –' Annabel said as she walked through from the storeroom, then stopped in her tracks.

Tracey stared at her. 'No show without Punch. Well, actually there'll be no show at all now.' She headed towards the exit for the second time in ten minutes. 'Oh, Alec, just a little tip, from an amateur ... if you're going undercover ... don't leave a note for the traffic warden on your dashboard saying you're filming with a TV crew in the hotel.'

Chapter Nineteen

Poor Boris. She had to listen to me on the phone all last night and now here I am cluttering up her lovely living room with more of the same.

'You should sue them.' Her voice is as soothing as the decor, all plumped up cushions and cross-stitch wall hangings. Even Callum is sedated by it; he's sitting quietly on the floor stroking Pierrot, her Persian cat. 'It's invasion of privacy.'

'Yes, but I was the one who invited them to invade my privacy in the first place ...'

'It's not the same,' she says, but I wonder if she's only humouring me. 'As for Gary, well, he's obviously changed personality since he became a policeman. I always thought he was far too gentle – I mean ... '

'Far too gentle for me, do you mean?' I ask, and that chubby hand goes to her mouth as it always does, and she blushes gratifyingly.

'Well, yes ... but you're different now, too. You've mellowed.'

I wonder if she's right. I also wonder if it wasn't *me* that changed Gary for the worse. Or maybe I'm flattering myself to think losing me could be enough to change someone's personality. Once upon a time I would have been sure I could do that, but now. . .

'I don't feel very mellow at the moment. I just feel like I've cocked everything up.'

'It's the anti-climax. I'm sure there's a name for it and if there isn't, they'll probably invent one . . . Let's see . . . Post Reunion Aftermath Tension . . .'

'PRAT? You're not bloody joking. I must be so stupid to think that one little meeting will sort out all my problems.'

She pats my hand. 'I know, petal. But you don't have *that* many problems when you think about it. . . you still look great, you've got a nice house, two healthy, happy children-'

'That'll be why Kelly's seeing a shrink then, because she's so happy? And you've forgotten my lovely husband. Oooh, and my wonderful career in the stationery shop. I can't believe I'm born sometimes.'

'Oh, Tracey,' she says, softly, and with huge effort she pulls her front-loaded body forward, and puts her arms around me. 'Don't be sad.'

And it's been such a long time since anybody held me like that, expecting nothing back. I'm not even sure anyone ever has . . . Mum was too buttoned up for spontaneous affection, and with Dave, hugs were only ever a kind of foreplay.

I start crying and it feels as though I'll never stop . . .

'Justin, hi . . . this is Suzanne Marshall-Sharp from the Millennium Child Campaign. We met at that reception at Number 10 last December, yeah? That's right . . . So how's life treating you? I saw your pieces in the *Guardian* last week on homelessness. Cracking stuff . . . and I thought you might be just the person I'm looking for. I've got this story . . . well, it's not connected to the campaign as such, and it's very delicate, so I'm looking for a

173

journalist I can trust to tell it right ... I'd rather not go into the details over the phone, but it's about someone pretty high profile. And it's the kind of thing you'd be fighting the tabloids over ... hmmm, thought you might be interested ... shall we see if we can find a convenient time for a chat about it? Off the record, of course ... '

When I stop crying, I'm exhausted. I'd forgotten how knackering it is. Then we decide to change my life.

Boris says the way to change my life is to make a list, so that's what we're doing. It seems highly unlikely to me, but she swears by them, and now I'm looking, I see them everywhere in her house – by the phone, in the kitchen, next to the huge arrangement of flowers that she tells me Brian sends her every Wednesday, to make up for being away. She even shows me one she's got programmed into one of those little personal organiser things she carries in her handbag. Actually, she's got them sub-divided there into work, friends and family, and household.

'I don't know where I'd find the time,' I say, and then I get this pang because there's no longer any reason for me to spend hours on the Internet, composing pithy e-mails to Gary, so I will need something else to occupy me.

'Think of this as the A level of lists,' she says. 'We'll work our way up to it. Remember, I've been doing this more or less since I left school. It's sooo lovely when you can tick things off!' She goes rummaging in the drawers of this huge dresser she's got in the dining room, and pulls out a padded notebook featuring pictures of hedgehogs in bathing costumes at the seaside.

'Since when have you been a branch of WH Smith?'

'You can't make lists without paper!' she says, and it strikes me that this isn't just pregnancy-related hoarding. Boris has been nest-building all her life. 'Right then – what shall we call this list?'

'Crap things about Tracey?'

'No, let's call it "Wishlist". Things you'd like to change.'

'Being married – I wish I wasn't.'

'Well, we can always sort that out if you REALLY don't want to be ... but it's a big decision.'

Am I miserable enough to want a divorce? I suppose what I want is straight swap for the current husband. I'll trade you my good-looking, cocky middle-aged wideboy for a good Dad, someone sweet and funny and, above all, faithful ... dream on, Tracey, you've never gone for that type anyway. And if I divorced Dave, I'd probably just lose the house while he got away scot-free.

Oh, and I couldn't bear the knowing looks from Kelly's bloody psychologist.

'I'd like Kelly to be happier ...'

We both look at Callum, who is chattering happily into the pretend mobile phone he takes everywhere with him.

'Well, at least he's proof it's nothing *you*'ve done,' Boris says.

Maybe she's right, but it feels too easy to take responsibility only for the kid who's turned out right, and to let myself off the hook for the one with the problems.

'What else do you want to sort out? Work?'

'I don't really care about the job. It's only eight hours a week, anyway, and I was never going to be a career woman, was I?'

She smiles at me. 'It's not all it's cracked up to be, believe me.'

'So why did you and Brian wait this long for the baby?'

'Things don't always turn out as you expect them, Tracey,' she says, and I wait for her to explain. But she doesn't. 'OK, let's leave work for now, we can get you the chief exec's job at Boots once we've sorted the other stuff. What about the whole reunion thing?'

175

'Oh, don't. I had another message on the mobile this morning from Jenny, grovelling like mad. But they're wasting their time.'

She raises an eyebrow. 'I hope you don't mind me saying this, Tracey, but I think you've been looking for an excuse. Not that this isn't a bloody good one.'

That's another thing I suddenly remember about Boris. Behind that sugar-pink fairy godmother face, she lets nothing pass her by. It makes me feel uncomfortable. I know she could easily throw me off my high horse.

'I don't know why you say that.'

'Just a hunch. I suppose I think that you liked the idea in theory, but it's just not turned out to be what you had in mind. You can't recreate the past.'

'I wasn't really trying, I thought it would be fun –'

'Yes. I know. But it's not that easy to go back in time ... Anyway, if you're definitely not doing it, they're going to have a job on their hands letting everyone down. How many people are due to be coming?'

I can't bring myself to tell her that the last time Jenny talked about it, she had less than a dozen confirmed. So much for the Good Old Days. 'I don't think it'll be too much of a problem getting the word around ... '

'How many?' And the expression on her face shows she's going to keep going until she gets an answer.

'Erm. Ten.' I feel really stupid.

'Right.' She looks at me sympathetically. 'Is that another reason why you've been so down about the whole thing?'

I shrug. 'It doesn't really matter now, anyway.'

'OK, let's forget the programme. If you could have a reunion no one's filming, just for the sake of it, who would be there?'

'You, obviously.'

She grins. 'Goes without saying ... and? Melody?'

'No bloody way.'

She doesn't say anything, even though I can see she's dying to know why. 'Gary?'

I hesitate.

'I'll take that as a yes.'

'Bob?'

I laugh, despite myself. 'Gary AND Bob? We wouldn't need any fireworks, would we?' I congratulate myself for avoiding the question.

'Is there anyone else?'

There is, of course, but how can I say it without looking strange?

Boris waits. Then she says, 'Fantasy reunion. You know, whatever you want, never mind if it's possible or not. Dream a little.'

I feel the back of my throat go tight. 'OK, if you really want to know. Shrimp.'

She doesn't look surprised, just sad. 'Do you miss her?'

And I'm only in tears again, a one-woman bloody sprinkler system, but I can't seem to find the tap to switch it off. She holds me again.

'Yeah ... and I want to say sorry.'

'For what, honey?'

'For killing her.'

She pulls back to look at me. 'But she died in a crash. You didn't kill her.'

'I said the worst things. The worst things. And Ricky, you know, her brother, he blames me and he's right, because if I hadn't –'

'Tracey.' She sounds stern now. 'Stop it. You can't know what might have been. You can't. It gets you nowhere.' She's stroking my hair now, like Mum did when I was very small. 'Shrimp died because sometimes people die before they should. Not because of anything you or me or anyone did.'

She's got tears in her eyes now, and I know she's trying so hard, and I want to believe her, but I can't. So I pretend.

'I know,' I say.

'We need more tea,' she tells me, and she disappears into the kitchen, while I try to stop myself crying. When she comes back, she seems calmer too.

'The thing is, Tracey,' she says, 'I think that now the TV company have cocked up so badly, they owe you. But they still *need* you to do this programme, and I think they'll do pretty much anything to keep you on board. Which puts you in a very strong position.'

'I've got too much to think about at the moment.' It's a crap excuse.

'Maybe you have. But then again, maybe you could use them to get you through the problems. A holiday, say? I reckon they'd pay for that if it meant you'd stay with the programme; it's still cheaper than them starting over with someone else. And it stops you going to the papers.'

'That sounds like blackmail.'

She giggles, but behind the girly innocence, I catch a glimpse of the tough businesswoman I'd been struggling to believe she's turned into. 'That's not a very nice word. But I think we could make it work to your advantage ... and I was quite looking forward to the reunion, whether there's ten of us, or a hundred.'

'I'm just not sure I've got the energy.' And maybe it's all the crying, but I do feel completely worn down.

'You could let me ... negotiate on your behalf. I'm really bored at home waiting for junior to make an appearance.'

I'm torn between wanting to chuck the whole bloody thing in, and wondering whether she can really make it all right.

'Go on, Tracey ... give me, what, a few days? If I haven't sorted out something that makes you happy by, say, next Monday, then we can just forget the whole thing? You've got nothing to lose, have you, not really?'

She's smiling again, like it all makes perfect sense and I'd be a spoilsport to deprive her of her fun.

'Next Monday?' How can I refuse her?

She rubs her hands together, then reaches out to shake mine. 'Oh, brilliant! Tracey, you definitely won't regret it. I think we should toast it.'

I follow her through to her kitchen, where she starts the kind of proper tea-making ritual I thought you only found in Japan, but even watching her do it is soothing.

'Is that your phone?' she says, above the hiss of the water boiling in the kettle.

'Probably Jenny again – I'll put her straight on to my agent, shall I?' I shout through, as I retrieve the mobile from the depths of my handbag. 'Hello, Tracey speaking.'

'Mrs Brown? It's Mrs Fellowes from school, I've been trying to get you at home. It's Kelly. There's been an accident.'

Chapter Twenty

There's only one thing worse than finding out your six-year-old daughter's had an accident.

Finding out it wasn't an accident at all.

Boris drives me and Callum to the hospital, because I can barely speak, never mind steer. Mrs Fellowes told me on the phone not to worry, but that's like telling a baby not to cry, or an injured pet not to bite through its stitches. Boris lives half an hour away, but drives like a maniac through the country lanes.

And when I get to casualty, the nurse rushes me through, and I'm terrified that I won't be brave enough to cope with whatever it is I'm about to see, and then she moves back the cubicle partition and there's Kelly – sitting up on the bed, with a cut and emerging bruises to the side of her face, but otherwise apparently in one, rather pale and tearful, piece. In an instant, I run through the same checks I did when they gave her to me in the delivery room – two eyes and ears, one nose, ten fingers, ten toes (or at least, feet in undamaged patent leather shoes).

'Mummy, my head hurts,' she says, and for the second time in one day, I'm sobbing uncontrollably, while poor Callum looks on, completely unused to seeing me showing any emotion except irritation.

After a while, I hear a cough – one of those 'I'm making my presence felt' coughs rather than a 'I'm in hospital because I have a bad case of TB' coughs – and look round to see the school secretary, who I recognise from a fund-raising fête.

'Hello, Mrs Brown,' she says, and she sounds really nervous. 'Now, the doctor's checked Kiely over –'

'Kelly!' I shout back at her. 'Her name's Kelly.'

'So sorry, yes, but anyway, the doctor's checked Kelly, and they think they can discharge her, yes, she's had a bump on the head, but they think concussion's unlikely, but they want to have a word with you, and tell you what to watch out for, but they think it's best to take her home and keep an eye on her there.' Finally she stops talking long enough to breathe.

I'm relieved, but then most of that I could see for myself.

'What happened, Kelly, love?'

'Mrs Brown, shall we talk about that outside?'

'Kelly?' I reach out to hold her little hand, which is grubby with dirt and dried blood, and damp from tears. She grasps it back, then starts crying again.

I turn to the school secretary. 'What happened?'

'What did Mrs Fellowes say on the phone?'

'Just that there'd been an accident. Then I came straight here.'

She nods several times, as though she's thinking something over.

'Right. Right ... well, it's really quite early to say exactly what happened, obviously it was in the playground, and --'

'But, roughly?'

'OK. Well, roughly. Well, it looks as though what might have happened is that Kelly had her accident when, well, when two of the other little girls from her class got

181

behind her in the queue for the slide.'

It's not making any sense. 'Kelly?' But she just looks even more small and scared, like she does when she comes out of school alone, and can't see me or Callum waiting for her.

And then it dawns on me.

'These little girls ... This wasn't an accident at all, was it?' I can feel this anger like nothing I've ever felt before starting somewhere in my chest and spreading in waves like nausea through my body.

'As I say, Mrs Brown, I think it's a little early to say, but Mrs Fellowes has stayed behind at school to see if we can get to the bottom of this as quickly as we can.'

'Well, you might need a full-blown bloody inquiry but it's quite obvious to me what's going on. My daughter has been attacked and injured by *bullies*, because your precious school can't even keep a bunch of infants under control ... '

She won't look at me, and is shifting uncomfortably from side to side. The rational part of me – yes, there is one, though it's buried very deep – is pleading for her, saying it's not her fault, there are other people to blame. But the scary earth mother lioness part of me, that I didn't even realise existed until now, is having none of it.

'Get out. If you can't protect my child, then you've no place here with me and my daughter.' She opens her mouth to placate me, but I rush at her. I'm not going to thump her, but she's obviously not too confident, because she backs out of the cubicle without even looking behind her.

I'd forgotten about Boris, but even her tranquillising qualities aren't enough to stop these awful feelings of rage and ... something else ... guilt, yes, it's guilt.

'Boris ... we'll be fine now. We'll get a cab home. I think we need a bit of time ... ' and she understands, and leaves the cubicle without a word.

All I can do is turn towards Kelly and, tentatively, place my arms around her, and, like Boris did to me an hour ago, hold her until she stops crying.

Boris raced through the hospital corridors using her bump like a battering ram, sending patients and staff scattering in her wake. She was on a mission.

She broke the speed limit all the way home, but knew from experience that a whispered 'I'm in a terrible hurry,' and a coy glance down at her belly, would persuade most policemen not to give her a ticket.

Pierrot was waiting at the window when she pulled into the drive, and miaowed at her silently behind the double glazing. He wasn't going to like the new arrival any more than he liked the bell on his collar.

'Hello, baby,' she said, as he greeted her with a flourish of the tail and a rub around her waterlogged ankles. She smiled as she encountered the solid lump that stopped her taking off her boots. 'And hello, other baby ...'

Boris grabbed a packet of cookies from her biscuit stash, and took them upstairs to her office. Well, it was more of a cubby hole really, but painted a fresh yellow to stop it feeling cramped. Shelves ran from floor to ceiling, loaded with books on computer theory and business financing, with one solitary row of classic novels, and a small section on pregnancy and birth ... opposite her desk, there were carefully organised box files of paper and envelopes, plus two of the plywood boxes of mini-drawers IKEA sells by the pallet-load, which Boris had hand-painted to match the surroundings, and then filled with paper-clips, printer ribbons and sticky labels.

She switched on the computer, and picked up the phone. 'I'd like two numbers please. Yep, the first is for Gary Coombs, London – I think it's West London ... you don't? Oh, OK. Right, the second's for Crawley Park Comprehensive – sorry, College ... Thanks, that's brill –' Boris stopped, as she realised she was no longer talking to a human.

She hooked up her palmtop to the main computer, and transferred across the new file, headed Tracey's Wishlist.

'What do you think, Pierrot? I reckon we should rename this one, to reflect the urgency of the situation.'

She took a cookie from the packet, and crunched purposefully for a minute. Then she highlighted Wishlist on the screen, deleted it, and in its place, typed 'Reinventing Tracey'.

I'm glad Boris didn't insist on staying, because her sweetness would only make me feel even worse. All it does is show me how inadequate I am as a mother, to let this happen to my child.

Questions keep popping into my head – and I wish I could stop them but they come back again and again like those cockroaches that infest tower blocks and can't be eradicated even by an entire squad of pest-control officers.

Why Kelly? Why not someone else's daughter, the child of a junkie teenager, maybe, or the offspring of a shy weirdo, like Suzanne Sharp?

And it's worse than that. Because the question I keep asking myself and I want to ask her, except she's too young to understand, is: why the hell didn't she stand up for herself?

The white-haired nurse gives me a photocopied sheet about the symptoms of concussion. 'But we really don't think she'll have any after-effects. It really wasn't a very serious fall, so just keep an eye on her.' She smiles at Kelly, and strokes her hair. 'You'll soon be right as rain, won't you, my angel? Back to normal.'

Normal? I have to shut my mouth before a hollow laugh

escapes. I don't know what normal is anymore.

I take Kelly's hand, strap Callum into his pushchair, and head back through the chaos of the waiting room.

The cab driver grins at us, this blonde family straight out of a mail order catalogue. 'Been in the wars, then, love?'

Kelly darts out of sight into the back of the car. 'No need to be shy,' he says, looking more annoyed than amused, and I wonder if her whole life's going to be like this, avoiding attention.

He doesn't say anything else all the way home.

Tracey Mortimer, aged fourteen, would have hated the idea that she might end up 'normal'.

But right now, I'd do anything to achieve exactly that.

The mobile phone rang, and Boris checked who it was, then waited four rings before answering it.

'Hi,' she barked, as though she had far better things to do than eat the rest of the chocolate chip cookies.

'Helen, hello, it's Jenny.' Her tone was already apologetic. Boris sensed victory before she'd stated her demands.

'Jenny.' She left a long, painful gap in the conversation, as though she was not even convinced she should be talking to anyone from Smart Alec Productions. 'I've been talking to Tracey.'

'Yes. I feel terrible, Helen, I don't care what happens but I do want you to know that I argued against Alec, I think it was a terrible thing to do, and I really don't blame Tracey for being angry.'

'You're still working on the programme though?'

'Yes, touché. Not that we've got a programme anymore, not without Tracey. I know you're her friend, and I totally respect that. But do you think there's any way she'll come round?'

It really was going to be easy, thought Boris, feeling slightly disappointed. She'd geared herself up for a proper fight. Though there was still Tracey's marriage, job and children to sort out, not to mention the small matter of getting more than a dozen people to the reunion. 'I don't think she'll change her mind without a lot of ... input. It all depends on how far you're prepared to go to convince her you're not out to get her ... '

'But she might change her mind?' She sounded so desperate that Boris almost felt sympathetic. Then Jenny spoke again, this time much more quietly, so it was nearly a whisper. 'Between you and me, I don't think there's *anything* Alec wouldn't do to get Tracey back on board.'

There was only one cookie left now, and Boris sucked at it like it was a rusk, humming gently so Jenny would know she was still on the end of the line.

'Well, first of all, I think that the whole business has made Tracey very stressed. Her daughter's been taken to hospital today.'

'Shit. Is Kelly OK?'

'Yes, just a playground accident, cuts and bruises. But it's the last straw for Tracey, so even to get her into a position where she can make a decision about the programme, I think she needs a break ... ' Boris left it for Jenny to fill in the gap.

'I think I see what you're saying ... there's this health spa I know that might help restore her ... um ... equilibrium. And I'm sure it'd be much more fun if she didn't go on her own.'

'That could be just what we – she needs ... provided, of course, that a film crew don't come along for the ride.'

'There aren't many places to hide a secret camera in the sauna, Helen. Tell you what, I'll have a word with Alec, see how the budget's looking and then I'll come back to you. And, thanks ... '

Boris put the phone down and clicked on the file marked Reinventing Tracey. She typed in a summary of the phone call, and placed an electronic tick in the box alongside.

One down, four problems to go, she thought. Not bad for an afternoon's work.

Time for another packet of biscuits.

Chapter Twenty-One

I'd hoped for a Caribbean beach holiday, but Boris says long-haul is overrated, and a weekend at this health farm costs about the same, and there are no kids there, and no Rastas hanging round the beaches offering you the chance to 'ride the big bamboo'. I feel guilty about the no kids rule, and curious about the bamboo ... since Dave can in no sense be described as having a big bamboo (think twiglet at best). But Boris – who had her honeymoon in Barbados – says all the attention gets boring.

'You don't even have to say yes to going back to the programme,' she says. 'And if you do, then we can go back to the negotiating table and see what other bonuses we can arrange! It's a win-win situation.'

She makes me laugh when she uses daft phrases like that – it's probably the only sign that she's grown up since school, and done all that shoulder-pad, businesswoman stuff. It's hard to take her seriously, with her little-girl's voice, but judging from the way the TV company have been racing around trying to spoil me rotten, I'm the only one to feel like that.

I feel bad leaving Kelly, but Dave is coming back this weekend and Sandy the psychologist says one of the top items on Kelly's 'things that make me happy' list is 'playing with Daddy'. It's a kick in the teeth, but also, if I'm honest, not much of a surprise. It's the same with divorced couples, isn't it? Mum is Mrs Angry, who makes you tidy your bedroom while Dad's the fun one who takes you to the zoo or McDonalds.

Or in my case, Dad was the one who was never there, so my fantasies about how much more fun he'd be than my weary mother were unaffected by reality.

I was dreading the appointment with Sandy, because half of me wanted to shout and scream and threaten to sue her and the school for being unable to protect Kelly, and half of me thought I should be the one under attack for messing up her life. But it was Sandy who rang me the day after we came back from hospital.

'Mrs Brown, the school have told me what's happened, and I wanted to suggest coming round to your home before Kelly goes back, so we can try to come up with some strategies for her and for you ...'

How can you refuse? It sounded like a good enough idea, but when I put the phone down, I wondered if it would just give her more ammunition for labelling me a bad parent ... too much disinfectant, or too few room-fragrancing sprays? A garden too tidy for proper playing, or a hazard-filled bathroom without the right kind of children's toothbrushes?

But in the end, Kelly was too busy showing her the Barbie buggy my mum had bought her for being a brave girl at the hospital for Sandy to notice very much at all. Even the cup of tea I made went undrunk ... maybe she was so horrified by the unhygienic conditions in my kitchen to risk it.

'Mrs Brown, what I'd like to do if it's OK is maybe spend a little bit of time with Kelly, going through the work she's been doing, and then get back together so we can all chat about going back to school?'

So they trooped upstairs to Kelly's room, leaving me feeling a complete spare part. When they came back down again they seemed to be best mates, and it's daft but while Sandy was explaining how we all needed to work together, especially at playtimes, so Kelly could feel safe and make friends, all I could think about was what was so special about bloody Sandy, how come my daughter could giggle and play happily with her but not with me?

And then I realised I was jealous, and it seemed an even bigger sign of my inadequacy that I should be jealous of the woman who has come in to help Kelly overcome the problems I've probably caused in the first place.

'Kelly and I have been chatting about how she's going to work with me and Mrs Fellowes to see which children in her class might be nice new friends. And then we're going to try some drama so we can practise being less shy.'

'That sounds good,' was all I could muster.

'And I'm really impressed with the work Kelly's done in her book ... I think you're quite enjoying your home-work, aren't you?'

Kelly smiled shyly, and I reached out. 'Let's have a look then,' but she flinched and moved away.

'We've decided that Kelly's book should be private, Mrs Brown, so she can write down anything she likes. But if she wants to share parts of it with you, then she will.'

Private? She's six, what could she have she needs to keep private? It'll be different when she's fourteen, and full of sinful secrets. But now? When I looked at Kelly, she had this guilty expression, and I knew that there must be plenty in her notes that wasn't favourable to me. But I could tell by the conspiratorial glance she then shared with Sandy, that there would be no negotiation on this ...

I laughed, tried to make light of it. 'Oh, I wonder what kind of terrible secrets you've got in there. Go on, girls, tell me what you've been writing down.'

Sandy said, 'Well, I think we can tell Mummy that it makes you happy playing with the school guinea pigs.'

'Russell and Flo,' agreed Kelly, and I wondered if this was a sophisticated plot to make me procure some pets, and then loathed myself even more for being suspicious of the poor kid's motives.

'Yes, Russell and Flo. We often find, incidentally, Mrs Brown, that giving a child like Kelly direct caring responsibility for an animal like a guinea pig or a rabbit, can have a very positive effect on self-esteem. But obviously, that's something for you and your husband to discuss. What does he think about the situation at school?'

'He's obviously very concerned and we're going to talk about it when he's back from Ireland at the weekend.'

She nodded with intense sincerity. 'Yes, Kelly's explained that he's not around as much as you'd like.'

He's around quite often enough for my liking, but then Sandy continued, 'I think it can be difficult for children to understand why one parent might be absent some of the time, and it's very important to explain it in such a way that they realise it's not *their* fault ... especially when, like Kelly and your husband, there's such a strong bond.'

I raised my eyebrows – I couldn't help it. She nodded again. 'Yes, that's one of the really positive things to come out of our little chat upstairs. And, of course, I wouldn't want to suggest that your daughter's mental health should be weighed against the financial necessity of the arrangement, because obviously it's none of my business, but I do think it's something we could build on, the relationship between father and daughter.' Then, after a pause, she added. 'And of course, your own relationship with Kelly.'

Oh, of course. Mothers have the worst of both bloody worlds, don't they? All the responsibility, all the guilt, none of the credit.

191

'So the next stage will be for Kelly to return to school, and we're going to have a special class meeting about it. Mrs Fellowes and I will do some work on improving the supportive aspects of the pupils' behaviour. We're going to put in place some Circle Time exercises; I don't know if you've heard of the approach, but it can be incredibly effective in a situation like this –'

'Hang on a minute. That's all very nice, circles and whatever it is, but the most important thing for me is that the kids who did this, are taught a lesson. For all the problems that Kelly has, they must be pretty disturbed to be violent at this age ... you have to nip these things in the bud.'

She looked at me warily. 'I so agree that problems of this nature must absolutely not be allowed to drift. And I can assure you that the work we'll be doing has been proved through the research to be the most effective way forward. It's a holistic approach.'

'But the kids who pushed Kelly –'

'We don't know for sure they pushed her.'

'It's what she says, isn't it?'

'Ye-es, but there were no adult witnesses, and the rough and tumble of the playground does occasionally lead to the odd problem. I'm sure you remember from your own childhood –'

'So, are you saying the brats aren't going to be punished?'

She sighed. 'I understand your need for retribution, but we're trying to go on what is in Kelly's best interests, and, at this stage, if we can rebuild relationships in her class, then the prospects are much better. Wouldn't you agree?'

No, I wouldn't but it was obvious there wasn't any point in telling her that. Schools are dictatorships, and there's no point fighting the system.

So next Tuesday, Kelly goes back to school, and they're

going to sort her out by sitting in a big circle and telling each other how they feel. I try to think how that would have gone down at my school, and it doesn't look good. I reckon if I'd have heard some wimp of a kid saying how miserable they were at being teased, I'd have patted myself on the back and started looking forward to starting again at dinner time. Sure, we knew we'd be watched in the playground, but that just made it more of a challenge . . .

So now I'm abandoning my bullied daughter, the weekend before she goes back. But according to Sandy, she's better off with her dad anyway.

I wave goodbye to my little nuclear family, ignoring Dave's panicked, hard-done-by expression, and load my suitcase on to the back seat of Boris's car – there's no room in the boot because she's got this mammoth Samsonite thing. God knows what she's got in there. It makes no sense, as I thought health farms were places where you wandered round in a bathrobe and slippers, kind of like a cross between heaven and a maternity ward.

I haven't left the kids for a whole night since . . . well, it's been more than a year, and the last time was because the hen party I went to was in Slough, so there was no way of getting back. But the kids seem fine, excited by the novelty of undivided attention from their dad, though I suspect that'll change when they realise his idea of child-care is to put them to bed early and send them back there if they dare to creep downstairs and interrupt his beer-fuelled viewing of *Soccer Special* . . .

The journey takes about an hour, leaving behind the well-made roads and the rows of houses just like mine, for odd farms in the middle of fields where you have to drive slowly to give you room to escape, in case a wilful tractor is thundering towards you down the narrow lane.

And then there it is – a grey, Gothic building with

turrets and enormous wooden entrance doors, and an apparently endless supply of small men who race out as we arrive, to park the car and relieve us of our luggage – and, presumably, our emotional baggage too.

The reception area is wood-panelled and cosy, heated to sub-tropical levels, with a platter of pineapple, mango and other fruit I don't even recognise, next to the guest book.

'This is going to be good,' says Boris, as we check in. 'Last spa I went to was lovely on the outside, but inside the swimming pool area was all damp, and the walls were covered with yucky brown stains. And you had to PAY to rent a dressing gown. I mean, dressing gowns are as essential at health farms as sewing kits and shoeshine are in normal hotels. And they wanted to charge for them!'

The receptionist smiles soothingly, and reaches below the counter, emerging with bathrobes so fluffy that we can barely see over the top of them when we take them in our arms. 'Terry will show you to your room – and you'll find your treatment schedule laid out on your beds. I know you're going to enjoy your stay with us.' It's a cheesy thing to say, but I have a strong hunch she's going to be right.

Our room is larger than the whole ground floor of my house, and we have a double bed each, facing a widescreen telly, with a fridge instead of a bedside table either side. I can't resist looking inside.

'Bloody hell, Boris, I thought health farms were alcohol-free ...' There's a full-size bottle of champagne in mine, alongside some fresh juices and mini-bottles of spirits. I guess there must be the same in hers, and since she's pre-natally challenged, I can see myself having an interesting evening.

'Depends on the place. Wintersham House is more about pampering, though you can go for the diet detox option ... but we're getting the full Monty – unlimited food, booze, treatments. We must write a thank-you letter to Uncle Alec ... '

'Never mind him. It's you that deserves one ... well done for sorting it, Boris, this must be costing them a bomb.'

'Yep. And I reckon they'll have had to call in a load of favours to get this suite and these treatments at such short notice.' She picks up the timetable on her bed. 'There's a three-month waiting list for this two-person Thai massage.'

'Two person – what, we get done at once?'

She laughs. 'Er, no. It means you get two people giving you their undivided attention for two hours ... I challenge you to remember your name, never mind what you're stressed about, after that.'

I've been in a sauna before, down at the health centre when one of the girls from the shop talked us into going to a Step aerobics class, which I soon realised was the most pointless thing I have ever done. Afterwards, we sat there, our towels on top of the wooden slats, waiting for things to warm up, but there was so much through traffic that it never got properly hot. Then someone poured some water on the coals and the steam sizzled so much that it made my nose hurt. And this was meant to be relaxing?

But here there's a steam room as well, and it's wonderful. It feels like being a Roman or Greek goddess – which lot was it that went for mosaic tiles in a big way? Anyway, there are thousands of tiles covering these bed-like benches, circled around an ornate fountain, with steam rising from little pools of water collecting in ceramic bowls at the bottom. It's scented – at the moment the fragrance is rose, which the assistant says is fine for pregnant women. And in the ceiling there are twinkling fairy lights in different colours.

'Usually, steam rooms are like plastic pods,' Boris says, she knows about these things. 'A bit like being in the Tube with extremely sweaty people. So this is something else.'

I've had my head massage, followed by the two-person session, which made me feel very self-conscious at first, but pretty soon all my worries about it being a kind of posh-person's threesome disappeared with the rhythm of it. Dave, funnily enough, has never really seen the benefits of massage, unless it's me massaging his dick, of course.

Boris has gone for a manicure, which has transformed her chubby little fingers into Rouge Noir talons, and a pedicure – and the beauty therapist had to use a mirror to show her how it looks. But Boris is one of those women who really suits being pregnant – the bump doesn't look glued on, like it did with me, but a natural part of her that adds to the overall cuddly effect. She'd hate me for even thinking it, but in her yellow swimsuit, she's a dead ringer for La La from the Teletubbies.

'So is Brian excited about the baby?' I'm very curious about Brian, who I haven't met, and who doesn't seem to have made any sort of mark on their girly home.

'Hmmm,' she says. 'Yeah. It's what he's always wanted. A little boy ... or a girl, though I think he'd prefer a boy ... We don't like to talk about it too much, though. Superstitious, you know.'

'You're on the home strait now.'

'Maybe ... a lot can happen in six weeks, though, Tracey.' And she strokes the bump.

For the first time, I wonder about my two, and hope Dave is behaving himself. But then I know he'll call my mum the moment he runs into the slightest hitch. And she'll be round there like a shot, sympathising with him, because he's been abandoned; how can any woman be such an irresponsible hussy and just leave her children for a whole weekend? Never mind that one of the children wouldn't really care if she never saw me again ...

'Anyway, we've got something else to think about before my baby, haven't we?'

I know she means the reunion, and it's something I've been trying to avoid thinking about. 'Do you think I'm going to have to do it, now they've paid for this?'

She shakes her head. 'No way. You can kind of think of this as a bribe to stop you going to the papers and telling them all about their dirty tricks. But I do think it might be worth reconsidering ...'

'Really?' If I never see them again, it'd be too soon. Except Jamie, perhaps ... but then I really hate him for going along with the whole plot.

'If you think back to when we first got together, you were so excited about it, Trace. And I think that if *we* take over, make it how we want it to be, it could still be brilliant. I love parties.'

'I don't think I've got the energy. And you know that hardly anyone's said they're coming. I think I should be concentrating on Kelly.'

'Look, forget about the hassle of it for now. Just think about what you'd like it to be like – in your fantasies, imagine being there, the belle of the ball. I bet we can talk them into giving you a fantastic designer outfit – something *really* expensive ...'

I can't help myself thinking about what I'd wear if money was no object, and I was going to be centre stage ... something long, slinky and clingy, perhaps, with a split from ankle to thigh: my legs are still my best feature.

'And we quite liked School Disco, didn't we, apart from me having my funny turn? Well, it could be just like that ...'

'Except for the fact that there'll be nobody there except you and me dancing round our handbags ...' I suddenly come back down to earth with a hell of a thud.

'It's early days ... and if they'll pay me to organise it all, then I guarantee we'll get a full house. After all, who can turn me down?'

Through the steam, I see her determined expression, and I feel that resistance is futile ...

'I suppose there's no harm in trying. But if you haven't managed at least, I dunno, fifty people? Then I want a get-out clause.'

'Of course,' she says, and winks at me. But I realise that I've just proved her point about no one ever turning Boris down. And it makes me feel strangely reassured.

Chapter Twenty-Two

And so, Boris the fairy godmother waved her magic wand, and out of nowhere appeared 120 ex-Crawley Park pupils, who said they wouldn't miss the reunion for the world ... along with a designer promising to take the best of 80s style to create my dream outfit ... and a production team who can't do enough to keep me happy.

A month ago I wouldn't have thought any of it could really happen, and the fact that Boris has achieved any of it is amazing ... but it's still not enough.

Trouble is, I can't imagine what would be. Because if I could, I'm pretty sure Boris 'Jim'll fix it' Norris could sort it out for me. She seems to have this knack of working out what has to be done, then doing it, before anyone else has even noticed that anything's the matter. Though I can't help wondering if she should be working for something worthwhile, like the UN or a worldwide campaign to stop global warming, rather than ungrateful old Tracey.

Have you ever started something you can't stop? Who was the guy who invented the nuclear bomb? It's like him, he was messing about doing random bits of physics, thinking it was all pretty theoretical, and bang, he splits the atom, someone gets to hear about it, and before he can say

Enola Gay, they've blown up several million Japanese and triggered the arms race.

I don't want to sound melodramatic, but I keep wondering if the reunion's going to be my Hiroshima. I was wandering along, not happy exactly, but not too unhappy either, waiting for I don't know what. The kids to grow up a bit, and make me laugh by bringing home unsuitable blokes and slutty girls. The bills to get smaller so we can afford to go abroad, instead of to the West Country. Maybe I was even waiting for Dave to do what I've always known he was going to do, and decide that rather than bother with all the affairs, he might as well go the whole hog, and run off with a younger woman.

But the reunion's made me think, and once you start thinking, you can't stop. Pandora's box, that's what they call it, isn't it? Tracey's box is full of all these memories I thought were one thing – carefree, funny, joyful – but when I take them out and look at them properly, they're not what they seem.

It's like when people take their relics to the *Antiques Roadshow* thinking they'll be worth a mint. So they prepare those shocked expressions, 'Oh dear me, I should insure it for that much, goodness, I had no idea at all, but of course, I won't part with them.'

But then the expert gives them a strange look and says, 'Well, yes I know they *look* like van Goghs, but actually if you examine them under a magnifying glass, you'll see that the leaves on these sunflowers have in fact been ... airbrushed, and an airbrush is one of the tools that Vincent didn't have at his disposal.' And they try to control the grimace of acute disappointment before the cameras can zoom in, but it was there for long enough for everyone to see it, to mock and despise them for having ideas above their station, for daring to think they had something valuable, where any old idiot could see it was a fake.

And then the expert says, 'But I'm sure you wouldn't have wanted to sell it anyway,' and they feel obliged to respond, 'Oh, you're so right, how could we do without something that gives us so much pleasure.' The director shouts 'cut' and they have to watch from the sidelines, as someone else acts out the very scene they thought was theirs. 'My goodness, THAT much? It can't be true.'

And my memories don't stand up to any kind of proper examination, either. The bits I thought were funny seem to have warped over time, so when I think back to them, I can almost hear us cheering as someone else is crying ... taking the piss out of people like Suzanne Sharp no longer seems harmless and deserved. Maybe it's because of Kelly.

That seems to be the one thing Boris can't fix. And I can't get into her head ...

I have a terrible confession to make. I read her book.

I can't quite believe I did it, and I know it makes me just about the world's biggest scumbag. I could pretend that I was cleaning up and came across it open at a page, but it's not true. I waited until Callum was having his nap in the afternoon, and I went and searched for it. There's no way I would have stumbled on the book; it was hidden beneath her collection of Beanie babies.

Things that make me happy had been written in copper-plate by Sandy, and beneath it, in Kelly's own uneven writing, was a list ...

Playing with daddy
Jolene
Barbie buggy
Russel and Flo (ginny pigs)
Choklut rice crispie cakes we made at nanas
Wekends

I turned the page, and there, below Sandy's second heading, were **Things that make me unhappy.**

Dinner time at shcool

Felling lonely
Carrotts
Callum wen he is crying two mutch
Wassps
Zoey and Cahtherine and Emmily espeshully at dinner time
Peeple hoo are horrible too animuls

I can't decide what would be worse – to be under the things she doesn't like or not to feature at all. I don't seem to count enough to be on either list.

I turn the page and find a kind of diary. It's obviously something Sandy has suggested after the playground incident, and she's begun by writing another one of those neat headings.

Going to Hospital
I went to hopsital becos Emmily tripped me up in the playgrownd and I hit my head and it hurt and then the sekreterry took me to the hopsital and mummy was there and she lookd upset and Callum and my face went a funny colur all blue and swelld up and then I had days of school.

Underneath, she's drawn a little picture of her face, adding a black eye with felt tip pen. On the opposite page, there's another heading: **Going back to school**.

I donnt wont to go back too school but Mummy and Daddy and Sandy and evrywun says I haff to and I think its unfair becos they donnt go and they donnt haff Emmily and Cahtherine and Zoey beeing horrible
Today I went too school and everwun was nise but then Cahtherine sed I hadunt orta tell tales any morr and it skaired me but I think I will tell sandy becos she will be nise and help me get morr freinds.

I turn over and there's only one more heading. **Making new friends.**

I haff been making new freinds at school theres Sasha

202

who is nise but her freinnd Rosie is not as nise to me and
I think she is jellus and today I saw her torking too Zoey
and it skaired me agen becos what if they gang up on me
and then we had sercle time we sit in a big sercle and we
all haff to say wot we are feelling and I sed I like having
Sasha and Rosie as my new freinnds and Mrs Felloos
smiled a lot and sed that's nise evrywun we are all frein-
nds in our class but its not true reely but evrywun sed oh
yes we are all very happy and I think I am kind of happy
now but also wot if Rosie is horrible it will be the same as
it wos beforr and then I donnt wont to go ever ever agen

And underneath that, of course there's no way of telling
when she wrote it, the shortest sentence yet.

I hate Rosie and I donnt never wont to go back

I was prepared for the shit-shovelling, and for the vomit,
and the sleepless nights. But what nobody could ever have
prepared me for was this powerlessness ... I sit on her
bed with the notebook in my hands, and I can't decide
whether to cry or to go down to that bloody school, find
Rosie (or Zoë, or Catherine, or Emily) and give them a
taste of their own medicine.

Boris limbo-ed her way from under the steering wheel,
and out of the car door. She was terrified that one day the
baby would grow just one extra millimetre while she was
driving, and trap her there so the only way she could get
out would be by calling in the fire brigade to cut the roof
off. It was almost as scary as those ridiculously tiny
ladies' loos, which she'd found stressful enough before
she was pregnant, and now made her feel like an elephant
in a phone box.

Hammersmith looked different by day. She'd driven
round the roundabout where the Apollo was, past the club
where they'd gone to School Disco, and, as Gary had
suggested, she was planning to park in Tescos. Maybe she

could do her shopping on the way back ... though she was getting very tired these days, so after a hefty lunch, she'd probably be fit for nothing except a nap in the car before heading home again.

An elderly man smiled benevolently at Boris and her bump, as she ignored the signs saying the car park was only for customers, and turned down the alleyway that would take her to the restaurant. Turn left at the end, and it's the second building, ten yards along. Typical policeman, she was surprised his directions didn't tell her the exact number of paces, or the OS grid reference.

The maître d' opened the door for her as she approached. Lovely! The restaurant was all blond wood, and chrome buckets of fresh gerbera flowers, with purple-painted screens surrounding each pair of leather banquettes. Soft classical music played in the background, and there was a strong smell of garlic and baking bread. It was exactly her kind of place, but she was surprised that it was Gary's sort of place, too. Still, people changed.

'The reservation's in the name of Coombs,' she said as the maître d' took her coat.

'Excellent, your husband's already here. Can't keep you waiting in your condition, after all.'

He showed her to their table, and Gary stood up, a filled-out version of the fifth-year lad she remembered, with better manners. Police training obviously had its advantages. He stepped out from the table and kissed her on both cheeks. Very London.

'My, Boris, haven't you grown!' he said, smirking. The maître d' gave them an odd look, and handed them the menus before retreating.

'He thinks we're married,' Boris explained.

'Well, YOU are.'

'And what about you, Mr Coombs, are you a confirmed bachelor gay?'

'I don't think Gabby would call me that.'

Boris grinned. 'And how long have you and ... Gabby been an item?'

'Eighteen months or so. We met when we went on a raid to snatch some kid – she's a social worker, you see.'

'Very right on. And is she the one?'

Gary shrugged. 'No such thing. Not as far as I'm concerned. But she's all right. Decent company. Sharp.'

'And does she feel as ... non-committal?'

'Nah ... no offence, Boris, but she's a woman. And I haven't met one that thinks like blokes do, that can take it or leave it, not since ...' And he stopped mid-sentence.

'Since Tracey? That was what you were going to say, wasn't it?'

He shrugged again. That was one thing that city-living and the Met hadn't got rid of, Boris thought, the nonchalant gesture that professed he didn't care, but made it obvious that really he did.

'Yeah. That's what you're here to talk about, isn't it? I mean, it's great to see you after all these years, but you didn't ask to meet me just to go over old times?'

Boris giggled. 'You're right, of course, Gary. But slow down. We haven't even ordered our lunch yet.'

Andrew Grey was not the most patient of men.

'Can't you give me a bit more of a clue?' he pleaded with Suzanne.

'No, I'm sorry. But I promise July the twenty-first will be worth waiting for.' It was their third meeting and she still didn't feel she could trust him. Maybe the surroundings didn't help – talking in a proper greasy spoon added to the seedy atmosphere of their chats, but didn't exactly enhance the feeling of mutual respect. He'd dressed down so he wouldn't stand out, a flasher's mac shielding the designer suit, and the matching designer aftershave rendered inert by the stench of cooking oil and tea. She felt trapped between *Brief Encounter* and *Lock, Stock and Two Smoking Barrels*.

'I still don't see why you want me to give up a whole Saturday for it ...'

'Well, if you're not sure you can spare the time, there are a couple of other journalists I could talk to. No hard feelings ....'

'No, no, I'm not saying that. But it'll be someone big enough to make the splash?'

'Andrew, I wouldn't lead you up the garden path. I've got my reputation to think of.'

'Except you want to stay anonymous.'

'But *you'd* know, I'm sure you'd find a way of getting word round that I wasn't to be trusted, even if you didn't say why. I'm not that naive.'

'I'm not sure the interest hasn't gone out of education stories, anyway,' he said, stubbing out his cigarette with an affected flourish. He really was not an attractive man, for all the labels and the pricey men's grooming products he clearly used.

'This is NOT an education story. This is a scandal,' said Suzanne. 'Sex, politics and past history people have tried to keep hidden. Blockbusters have been made around less than this.'

'Sex, eh?'

'Yes, sex. But you've already pushed me too far, Andrew. Just wait your turn – in two weeks' time you'll have the exclusive and you'll wonder why you ever doubted me.'

'And what about you, Suzanne?' His eyes narrowed, closing off the only mildly attractive part of an otherwise featureless face. 'What are you getting out of giving me this great scoop?'

'I don't think it's any of your business,' she snapped back.

It was quite simple, she thought, as she left the café. One word covered it.

Revenge.

They both ordered mushroom and marsala soup as a starter, followed by the duck for him and the salmon for her. Boris chose a poppy-seed roll, Gary one flavoured with Mediterranean herbs.

'It beats chips and gravy,' Boris said, dipping her bread in the little dish of oil on the beech table.

'Don't know if it does, you know. Just more expensive.'

Boris gave him a sly smile. 'If you're so keen on the good old days, you ought to come to the reunion ...'

Shrug. 'Can't see Tracey wanting me there. Not after the row at the Crown.'

Boris looked at him carefully. 'I wasn't there.'

'I bet she told you, though.'

'I'd like to hear your version.'

'Are you sure you're not really a head teacher, Boris?'

A waitress appeared, carrying two wide white bowls of steaming chestnut-brown soup. In the centre of each, a carefully placed dollop of thick cream, and a single, perfect wild mushroom.

'I'm completely sure. Are *you* sure you haven't picked up tips on avoiding questions from your criminal clients, Gary?'

'Fair point.' He took a spoonful of soup and moaned gently with pleasure.

'You're still saying that's no better than the school canteen?'

He studied the dish. 'I don't know what happened, Boris, I really don't. I suppose I'd thought I might tick her off a bit ... it was pretty humiliating the way she did it. You've got to admit it.'

'Hmmm. But it was also seventeen years ago.'

'I know, I know. I never thought about her, you know.'

Boris looked at him. 'Are you sure about that?'

'Well, hardly ever ... OK. Now and then. But only, I dunno, if I was having a row with Gabby or something, getting angry, and then, I'd think back to the angriest I've been, and, well, you know when that would have been.'

Boris nodded. She knew.

'But you know, I've moved on. It's good, my life. And when I got that e-mail, I was intrigued, but nothing else.'

'Why did you e-mail her back, then?'

He laughed. 'Stupid, stupid thing to do. It was after I fell out with Gabby over the washing-up. I suppose ... I just wanted to prove I wasn't ... ' He waved his spoon around, struggling for the right word.

'Hen-pecked?'

Another shrug. 'I never expected to see her. But when I did, it seemed like ... fate? I dunno. I hate all that horoscope bollocks, so does Gabby, I mean, that's one of the things I lo ... I like about her. She's sensible, you know, more like a bloke than some daft girl. No offence.'

'None taken. But you're a true Scorpio, Gary, with a temper like yours.'

'Yeah, yeah ... so, like I say, I really don't believe in any of that shit, but to see her there, there had to be a reason for it, didn't there?'

'Go on.'

'I didn't plan it. To have a go at her. But seeing her like that – she didn't look any different. None of us do, do we, not to each other? You don't, except for the obvious ... '

Boris nodded. 'Do you think we'll feel the same when we're sixty – that we all still look sixteen?'

'I dunno. Probably. But she really does look the same, and we were sitting there and ... ' Shrug. 'Something just snapped. And all the stuff I wanted to say back when it happened, but didn't have the guts to, it all came out, and she just sat there, and I felt so much better to get it out of my system, I caught the train back and this huge weight had been lifted.'

'She didn't feel the same, funnily enough.'

'No. No, I don't suppose she did. If it's any consolation, that feeling didn't last. When I thought about it, it seemed like a pretty shit thing to do. But I couldn't help myself.'

They sat in silence, until the waitress took away their empty bowls.

'Do you want to know what I think, Gary?'

Shrug, but with a smile this time. 'Not necessarily, but I'm sure you're going to tell me anyway . . .'

The waitress returned with their main courses, plates piled high with fish and fowl, plus side plates of potato dauphinoise, green beans and honeyed carrots.

Boris loaded her fork with crumbly salmon and fresh salsa. She took a bite. 'Yummm . . . I think the reason you had such a go at Tracey is that you haven't got over her yet . . . oh, do stop shrugging, Gary, it's driving me mad, how does your girlfriend put up with it?'

He went to shrug and stopped midway.

'And I think you're going to find it almost impossible to move on until you and Tracey have made your peace.'

'I don't think –'

'Well, I do. And between you and me, things aren't going too well for Tracey at the moment. You know she's got a little girl, Kelly?'

'She didn't mention her kids,' said Gary, and they both considered the implications of this. 'I kind of guessed.'

'Well, she's got a daughter, and a baby boy. But Kelly's nothing like Tracey – dear little thing but so shy.'

'Tracey's daughter, shy?'

'I know. But it's worse than that. I was with her when she got a call to the hospital – some bullies had pushed the poor kid over, and she'd hit her head.'

'Shit.'

'She's OK. But she's six years old.'

'Bloody hell.' He shook his head. 'Bloody hell, we weren't like that, were we, Boris?'

'I hope not. She's having a tough time, though, Tracey is. I worry about her – I know she always seemed hard, but I think it's just a defence mechanism. And the reunion ... she's worried about that too, what it'll say about her if no one comes ...'

'I don't know ...'

'I have got a lot of people on the list now. But they're not the people that were important to her.' Boris paused for a second. He didn't interrupt, which had to be a good sign. 'At least think about it.'

'You don't give up, do you, Boris?'

'No,' she said, not looking even slightly guilty.

'I've only got one question ...' said Gary. 'If you want the people there that were important to Tracey ... shouldn't you be inviting Carmichael?'

Chapter Twenty-Three

It's reaching the point of no return. Well, OK, if I'm honest, that probably happened a month ago, when Smart Alec Productions paid for the health farm, but I've tried to hang on to the illusion of freedom, like a tiger at Whipsnade. After today, though, there's definitely no way I can back out of the programme.

It's the last bit of filming before the twenty-first, this afternoon there's the fitting for this mad 80s fashion creation that Boris talked me into, and before that, there's some psychology interview about why people organise reunions. I'm buggered if I know.

I've managed to avoid seeing Annabel and Alec and Jamie in person since the whole secret filming business, and though I know I'm the one in the right, I am still feeling nervous about meeting them again. Annabel because she's irritating and now that I know it's too late for them to throw me off the programme, I'll be permanently tempted to tell her to shut up. It's the same but worse with Alec – he's an odious tosser and I'm dying to tell him. But he's got the power to make me look a complete hag AND a nasty bitch in the finished programme, if I get on the wrong side of him. I know, I've seen *Big Brother*. So I have to bite my tongue until the programme's gone out. Then he's getting both barrels.

But it's different with Jamie. I feel so disappointed. I thought he and Jenny were above all that. I wasn't exactly great mates with Jenny, but she seemed a decent human being, and I felt the same about Jamie.

Sorry, that's not strictly true. The difference with Jamie was that I thought he seemed a decent human being. *And* I wanted to rip his clothes off. And knowing the warped way my mind works, now I know he's a scumbag, I'll have an even harder job keeping my hands to myself.

Bob Carmichael turned the invitation over in his hands. His hands had aged pretty well, he thought, none of the dried-out-leaf wrinkles he saw on other men's hands when they shook his. His nails had always been strong, like his teeth and the bones that refused to break, even when he was going through that phase of doing dangerous things, jumping out of planes and hang-gliding and water-skiing . . .

His Post Tracey Phase . . . otherwise known as a death wish. Strange how she hit him harder than anyone since. Not that there'd been very many.

He was still attractive. He saw it in women's faces, a momentary contraction of the muscles around the eyes as they clocked him and decided that he wasn't bad at all, considering his age. He'd even overheard his research assistant, Heather, choose him over three younger men in the team, when they were playing 'Fantasy Fucks', a strange game invented by the girls in the Joined-Up Thinking Unit. They spent their fag breaks deciding who was untouchable, and who was fanciable. He'd been quite chuffed to be near the top of their wishlist.

He couldn't go to the reunion, of course. He'd thought it through quite carefully, trying to work out whether to ring up for an invitation, and decided it was way too dangerous.

Sure, if it came out, it came out and just as he'd told Phipps, he'd been ready for it for seventeen years. But there was no sense actively encouraging the premature end to his career. And ultimately when the programme came out, he'd get the chance to see what Tracey was like now. Which is the only reason he'd have wanted to go.

Dirty sad old git that he was.

But then an invitation arrived anyway. He had no idea who'd sent it. The envelope had been handwritten, and was marked personal, so for once his nosy PA hadn't opened it first.

And all there was inside was the ticket. No note, no letter of explanation, just this small piece of card, embossed like a wedding invite, with the date, time and address of the Crawley Park Comp Reunion, 'sponsored by Channel 5'.

The TV company? Dick Phipps's idea of a joke?

Or Tracey? He liked this idea the best, of Tracey somehow coming across his picture in the paper and cutting it out and agonising over whether to invite him. Though he had to admit he couldn't imagine Tracey buying the kind of newspaper that printed his photograph. He'd never made it into the *News of the World*, though maybe she'd seen him in the line-up next to Cherie that they printed in the *Daily Express* ...

Anyhow, it hardly mattered who sent it. Because he couldn't go.

His hand hovered above the bin. But instead of throwing the invitation away, Bob opened his top drawer, and tucked it under the £20 he kept for the odd random taxi home.

No harm keeping it as a souvenir.

Jenny picks me up to take me to the interview. She says they've found somewhere 'perfect' to do it, and I don't try

213

all that hard to suppress a sneer that creeps on to my face.

I have a near-permanent sneer on my face these days; when I get up it's there, and when I go to bed I feel as though I have to wipe it off with my bumper pot of Nivea. My mum used to threaten me with the wind changing, and that seems to have actually happened.

We don't talk much on the way. The pretence that we're girly friends and *isn't this filming the best fun ever*, has been dropped since what Boris now calls the Crown Affair. So she has the businesslike manner of someone doing her job, and I feel not unlike a child being ferried to the dentist or the piano teacher. I know there's no way round it, and it probably won't be that bad, but that doesn't mean I'm going to enjoy it.

'You've read the briefing notes?'

Jenny sent me this mammoth e-mail full of ideas about what I should ask the psychologist. 'I waded through them, yes, but I don't know if I'll remember it all.'

'I'm sure Alec'll prompt you if you don't,' she says. We've turned off the motorway, and into the outskirts of some nondescript town.

'Is he being a pain in the arse as usual?'

'He's my boss, you can't expect me to comment ....' But then Jenny gives me a sideways look. 'Yes. It's funny, but early on, me and Annabel were convinced you'd fancy him. He can be a bit of a smooth talker.'

Was that only three months ago? 'Yes, but he can also be a bit of a wanker.'

She grins at me then opens her mouth as if she's going to say something, but seems to change her mind.

'What were you going to say?'

She shakes her head. 'It's nothing ...'

'Go on.'

'I don't suppose I should tell you this, really, because it makes me look like I'm dobbing everyone else in it. But it's

214

important to me that you know I really didn't want to do what we did at the pub. I argued with Alec for days, I thought it was a shit thing to do. But, he's my boss, you know; at the end of the day what he says goes ... I am really sorry we did it.'

I do believe her, but it doesn't make much difference now. 'Yeah, well. I suppose it's not your fault.'

'I think Alec learned his lesson, though. The thought of the whole programme being off, with all that filming down the pan, was pretty effective in teaching him a few ethics.'

So I've been a positive influence on that ratbag's moral development. What an achievement.

'And Boris is coming along later?' Jenny says, after a while.

'Yeah, another antenatal this morning. But she's coming to the fitting.'

'You two seem thick as thieves these days ... must be nice to get back in touch with someone after all those years and find you still have so much in common.'

Except we seem to have more in common now than we ever did then ...

Jenny steers into an industrial estate, which is not what I'm expecting at all. It doesn't look as if it's a short cut to anywhere but more warehouses. I'd been thinking more of an empty classroom, or a Victorian schoolhouse or something. But we pull up alongside Alec's bloody car next to a low-rise pre-fab.

'Exciting location ...' I say and Jenny just grins at me.

We walk in through a side door, and as my eyes adjust to the light, I feel as though I've drunk an Alice in Wonderland potion, and shrunk to about two-thirds my normal size. I'm surrounded by enormous gun-metal grey lockers and PE benches and doors where the handles are level with my chest. It's like being eleven again.

'Isn't it brilliant?' Jenny says. 'It's all the leftovers from the Millennium Dome, they had one display all about schools, so they built everything big so adults would feel child-sized – even the school bell.'

She points and I look up and see it, one of those bright red metal bells that splits your ears when it goes off. And as my head drops to ground level, I see something which is even more effective in taking me back. A distant figure, with long red hair, talking to Alec, gesticulating wildly.

'Bit of a surprise for you, Tracey,' Jenny says, touching me on the elbow to propel me forward. 'The psychologist we've told you so much about, also happens to be your old classmate, Suzanne.'

And the red-haired figure steps from the shadow and holds out her hand to shake mine.

'Tracey ... I can't believe how long it's been,' she smiles. But it's not a real smile, and I can see she's clocking me as much as I'm clocking her. It makes me feel very uncomfortable.

While they're setting up the lights for the interview, Suzanne – who now has a double-barrelled name because she found someone desperate enough to marry her – offers titbits about her life, and I do the same. We're unnaturally polite to each other.

'You look great,' I say, and she does, actually. Slim where we used to tease her for being skinny, and the hair looks more of a statement now, instead of an affliction, though Christ knows how much mousse she must use to control her curls. But the compliment seems to make her even more suspicious, as if I'm about to follow it up with a killer insult.

'Thank you. You haven't changed a bit,' she says, and I'm sure that's not a good thing as far as she's concerned.

'And you're a psychologist, now?' I feel like the Queen, asking questions to pass the time, without caring about the answer.

'Yes. I've done direct work with children, and now I run a charity.' Again she refuses to look at me, except through hooded eyes. It's years since I've seen the silly cow but that hangdog face is so familiar.

'Really?'

'Yes. I help children who have been bullied,' she says, and gives me a significant look. And then I realise why her defensive expression rings so many bells.

It's exactly the same one I see on Kelly's face every time I wave her off in the playground.

'We're ready for you both now.' Alec is grinning enthusiastically but there's tension in his smile. He looks worried that I might flip any minute. Serves him right.

Jenny sits us down in orange plastic chairs modelled on ones from primary school, but large enough to accommodate adult bums. 'So, you'll start with some general stuff about memories and how those are important to people's own idea about themselves, and then move on to some of the stuff about what changes when people actually have a reunion.'

I can't see the point of any of this myself, but Jenny told me that since all the reality TV shows, they're trying to make it feel that there's more to the programme than entertainment. I don't even think it's going to be that entertaining anyway.

'Speed,' says Jamie, and his voice still sends little electric pulses through my body. Damn.

'Um. Right. Are people's memories of school usually good?'

Suzanne looks pretty startled at the question, which is odd, because I get the impression she's much more experienced with the media than I am.

She shakes her head slightly. 'I think the idea that school days are the happiest of your life is responsible for a great deal of *unhappiness*. The trouble is that as soon as we walk out of the school gates, and we literally put those days behind us, we put on the rose-tinted specs and forget all the petty rules and restrictions, the lack of power, the terrible pressure to conform. And instead, we invent for ourselves this strange mixture of memories that are more about children's books and magazine articles than our own experiences. And yet again we conform by agreeing about what fun it all was. A lot of us are in denial about our pasts.'

Rightio. It wasn't exactly what I was expecting, and judging from the silence that follows, it wasn't what anyone else was expecting either. I'm trying to find a way of following that, when Alec says 'Suzanne, um, that's great and everything, very interesting indeed ... but I wonder if we could be a little bit more ... upbeat?'

She stares at him. 'You'd like me to dumb down, would you?'

He flinches, but then smiles. 'If that's how you see it, then, yes. We can get the message across about things not always being sweetness and light, but I happen to think we can do it more subtly ... ' He turns to me. 'Tracey, why don't you start with why grown adults might want to dress as schoolgirls, like at School Disco?'

Or maybe why middle-aged men like ogling grown women dressed as schoolgirls ... But I'm bored already, so the sooner me and Suzanne provide the desired combination of silly questions and 'upbeat' answers, the sooner we'll be able to leave Alec to his sexual fantasies ...

It takes about twenty minutes before he shouts 'cut', and Suzanne's done a much jollier interview, all about reclaiming lost youth and comparing your wrinkles.

'So are you coming to the reunion?' I ask her.

'I think so, yes. If I can bring my husband.' She sounds incredibly smug when she says the word 'husband'.

'Mine's coming,' I say, keeping up. 'And my kids, for the early part at least.'

That's trumped her, as she obviously hasn't got any.

'Lovely,' she says and for the first time, there's a real interest there. 'How old are they?'

'Kelly's six coming up to seven, and Callum's nearly twenty months.'

'Oh, so you're nearly finished with the really messy bit, then? I love them when they start talking to you properly. And the kids we work with, they tend to be pretty bright, and you can make such a massive difference in such a short time ... it's great, seeing them blossom.'

'Really?' Her enthusiasm surprises me. 'But surely there's not much you can do with these kids, is there? I mean, if they're shy, then they're shy, if they're not popular, that's the end of it.'

Her face hardens again. 'It's not that simple, Tracey, though I'd have expected you to think like that, I suppose. Change is always possible. I've found that out myself. Fortunately, now, there's much more effort going into trying to intervene earlier, so children don't have to endure what I went through.'

'I didn't mean ...'

'I think I know what you meant, Tracey.' She starts walking away. 'I'll see you next week.' She doesn't sound as though it's something she's looking forward to.

I suppose she's right. She certainly seems changed from school, though sadly she hasn't lost the priggish, superior tone. But if she has worked with kids like Kelly, maybe I ought to ask for advice.

The thought does make me feel queasy, and I'm not sure I could bear the smugness that would probably unleash ...

'That went well,' says Jenny, bouncing over. 'Alec's very pleased. Now, if you're ready, I'm at your service to take you to the dress fitting.'

Chapter Twenty-Four

It's not very promising. I was expecting a flash boutique in Bond Street, like the ones I read about in the magazines on the rare occasions I go to get my hair cut.

Instead, the 'designer' they've commissioned to make my reunion outfit, is based a few miles from the warehouse, in a suburban wedding shop. When they told me to send in my measurements because she was too busy to meet me, I'd imagined she was making couture numbers for 'It' girls. Instead, it seems she probably had a few too many frou-frou numbers to make for the Berkshire equivalents of Essex girls.

'Bella' is the last shop on a run-down terrace, past an old-fashioned ironmongers, and one of those café-bakeries where the most advanced thing they do is pump air-filled cream into ready-made doughnuts.

Boris is already in the café.

'How did you get on?' we both shriek, simultaneously, as I rush up to the plastic table where she's nursing a cup of tea and a sandwich with orange cheese.

'You first,' she says, and I notice she looks pretty worn out. Not surprising, at her stage, though. Jenny disappears to get a couple of coffees.

'It was *Suzanne Sharp*,' I say, then realise from the

looks on the old biddies around us that I'm talking too loud. 'She's only a psychologist now. Bizarre. She was really odd with me, too.'

'In what way? And what was she like?'

'She looked OK, actually. The same but smarter. Expensive clothes, and she'd had something done to de-fuzz her hair. And she was narky, you know the way she always was. Superior. Anyway, you can see her yourself at the reunion. What about you? How was the hospital?'

'Oh, you know. Boring. They want to keep an eye on my blood pressure, I'm probably just a bit too porky.'

She grins at me, but high blood pressure's not great, is it? Even I remember that from the baby manuals. 'When are they seeing you again?'

'They just want me to go to the nurse every day or so.'

'Every day? Boris, that sounds bad.'

'No . . . it's just something they want to monitor.'

'But that –'

'It's not going to help to talk about it,' she snaps. 'Sorry. I'm stressed enough without discussing it, that's all.'

Jenny comes back with the drinks in two chipped mugs. 'I've spoken to the lads, they reckon their ETA is about ten minutes, and they'll set up in her workshop before we go up . . . so, you looking forward to seeing your outfit?'

I look over at Boris, but her face is calm again, the tension's passed. 'I don't have a clue what to expect . . . but judging from the window display, it's going to be fluffy. And I don't really do fluffy.'

'Bella comes highly recommended,' Jenny says. 'You can't always judge a book by its cover, you know.'

'And you haven't set me up with something awful? Because if I don't like it, I'm not wearing it!'

'Stone-washed denim,' Boris says, suddenly. 'I always wanted a stone-washed denim jacket. Maybe that'll be what she's made.'

'Er, I hope not. I don't want to look like Bananarama.'

'White was very popular, wasn't it?' Jenny says. 'And no, that's not a hint. It's not what we've told her to do. All we've done is give her your vital statistics and a picture of you, and let her loose ...'

'But you did tell her I wanted to look "sexy", didn't you?'

Boris is in a world of her own. 'Maybe there'll be a ra-ra skirt. I did have one of those, it was pink. With polka dots ...'

'What were we like? I had pink pedal-pushers.'

'The 80s look is the big thing this summer, apparently,' says Jenny. 'So whatever Bella's done, you'll be the height of fashion.'

'How's the rest of it going?' Boris asks her. She's finally handed over the last preparations to the company, and, judging from the dark patches under her eyes, it's a good job she has.

'Bit like organising a wedding – not that I ever have, of course, but it's just as worrying. And you've done a fantastic job on the guest list.'

'Nothing to it.'

I feel a bit left out. 'Just hope I recognise some of the people at *my* reunion ...'

'Don't worry,' says Boris, with a wink that makes me sure she's got something else up her sleeve. 'You will.'

The electronic door chime plays 'Here comes the bride' and through the window, I can see a small woman rushing through from the back. She's got Goth-black cropped hair, and she's wearing a tight cerise satin bodice with a pair of black jeans. Not at all what I was expecting.

'Hi, Tracey,' she says to me. 'I recognise you from your picture. Come up.'

We walk through the showroom, which is painted sugar-pink and has a chaise-longue by one wall. A little girl's dream ... but Bella looks like the wicked witch.

The door at the end leads up narrow stairs. This seems more like it. The walls are painted crimson, and framed prints of designs from *My Fair Lady* hang all the way up.

'It's been brilliant to let my imagination run riot,' she says, 'Much more fun than all those blancmange frocks.'

I follow her into the room on the left of the staircase, and shut my eyes until they're accustomed to the bright lights the crews have already set up. 'I hope you haven't gone overboard ...'

'Oh, don't worry. I think you'll like it.'

Behind me, Boris is breathing heavily. She just squeezes into the room, leaving Jenny hovering on the landing.

I peer around the room for clues. It's cluttered and chaotic, with fabric and shoes strewn all over the floor. It's also a bit of a fire hazard, with huge pillar candles balancing on magazines and pattern books, and a couple of those headless tailor's dummies, both covered with sheets. I guess this must be my outfit, but the cotton shrouds aren't giving anything away. On one of the walls, there's a noticeboard crammed with photos and newspaper cuttings and even an album cover ... Kim Wilde's back-combed halo dominates the image ...

'Is that a clue?' I say, wracking my brains for memories of what she used to wear. There's a glimpse of a striped T-shirt at the bottom of the cover, and it rings a few bells. And wasn't there some jacket with enormous lapels?

'ARE YOU RUNNING?' Jenny shouts from the hall. 'Just pick up actuality, Jamie.'

I catch Jamie's eye and before I remember I'm annoyed with him, we share a look of irritation. 'Yeah, I'm running,' he says.

223

Bella smiles at me. In this light, I can see her face is heavily lined, and she must be at least fifty. I hope I can get away with those clothes when I'm fifty ...

'I must admit that Kim Wilde wasn't my immediate thought when it came to designing for you ... but I started to warm to the idea when I noticed that the two of you do actually have very similar bone structure ...'

And as she's talking I remember, that Gary once told me I reminded him of her.

Boris says 'She presents gardening programmes now, you know, I saw her on one of those daytime shows the other day. Very nice. Down to earth.'

Bella nods. 'Yes, well, the inspiration for your design, Tracey, came from the way she looked fifteen years ago ... it's a bit of a cheat, really.'

She tiptoes over the debris to the covered dummies. 'I actually copied a dress from one of her album covers ... naughty, I know, but it was so perfect. And then, to jazz it up a bit, I took a bit of inspiration from that Adam Ant chap. I think he was a fashion student, wasn't he? Anyway, my dear, I do hope you like them ... would you like to do the honours?'

She places the corner of the sheet from the first dummy in my hand and pats me on the shoulder. 'Go on.'

I pull, and the sheet drops to the floor, revealing an ornate 'dandy highwayman's' jacket, with epaulettes and gold buttons. It's over the top, dressing-up box stuff, but also gorgeous. 'Do I have to wear the stripe across me nose as well?'

'Do you like it?'

'Definitely ... can I try it on?' She lifts the jacket off, and when I put my arms into it and shake my way into it, Boris laughs. 'I love it, Tracey, you look so funky.' And when I look at myself in the cheval mirror, I have to admit it fits well and looks good even over my T-shirt and jeans.

Bella fusses around me. 'I might take quarter of an inch off the arms ...' Then she stands behind the other dummy. 'But if you want to be the centre of attention, I think it's this that's going to achieve it ...' She pulls off the second sheet.

'Wow,' says Boris.

It's a knee-length sleeveless black leather dress, close-fitting, cut off at sharp angles by the arms to make a feature of my shoulders ... it's certainly sexy, and I have a vague memory of Kim Wilde wearing the same thing, standing on a rubbish-strewn building site. I reach forward to touch the leather, which is baby's bottom soft.

And then she turns the mannequin round, and I remember what was really show-stopping about that dress ... apart from three shoestring leather straps holding it together, the whole back from neck to lower waist is exposed. It's stunning.

'Better book myself a few sunbeds before next week, if I'm going to carry this one off,' I say to Boris.

And my inner Tracey Mortimer is smiling a wicked smile.

Chapter Twenty-Five

It's The Day Before. I'm sitting at the kitchen table smoking a cigarette. Another thing I haven't done since the day of my wedding.

You know what I said about how my biggest worry then was what if Dave didn't turn up?

Well, imagine that feeling, multiplied by, oh 125. Along with the knowledge that the last time I was worried about the VIP turning up, he did, and set the tone for the next miserable nine years. That might give you an idea of how I feel.

The dress looked great, by the way. I'm lucky because I lose weight when I'm stressed, and I think Bella poured all her frustrations at creating chiffon fantasies into my outfit. By the time she'd fiddled about, pulling the seams even tighter, I was worried all that stretched leather would make me look too much like a baby seal. Instead, I was visual Viagra. Even Jamie looked impressed.

And since then I've been almost too nervous to speak – that really doesn't suit me. Dave arrived home last night; he was irritated at having to come back when the rest of the lads had a big pissed-up weekend planned, but then he saw the dress, and keeps stroking it and trying to get me to try it on. Men are so bloody predictable.

I tried stockings and suspenders once, when I was sixteen. I went to Marks and Spencer's, and bought black stockings patterned with little dots that made me look like I was suffering from a skin disease, and a white lacy suspender belt. I felt uncomfortable and ridiculous, but Gary could hardly contain himself. And he was my age . . . I can understand it with the dirty older man (and yes, it wasn't long before I tried the same trick on Bob, to the same effect) but they've been reared on black and white pin-ups of 40s starlets. Why would my age group, used to full frontals and money shots, react the same way? Is it something instinctive? Could you parade up and down in a suspender belt in front of an Amazonian hill tribe, and get the same response?

I used to think about things like this all the time, trying to understand men. The last time I wore stockings was my wedding day, and that's also just about the last time I bothered to try to understand the male psyche. Maybe Callum will give me a clue when he grows up, but I suppose by then it'll be too late for me.

I've tried to work out who I'd really want to see after all these years and the list is very short. Gary's off the list, been there, done that, and it was hardly a roaring success. Briggsy, maybe, but what would be the point without Gary? Suzanne I didn't want to see in the first place. I have a horrible feeling that Melody will be on the guest list, though hopefully all that sunbathing will have taken its toll and she'll look much older. And she's so bony, maybe she'll look like a whippet. Bone structure's a mixed blessing.

And what about Bob? Where is he now? I suppose he's probably aged less than me and Boris. After all, Dick Phipps looked exactly the same when I saw him again. I'd kind of like to see Bob . . . he was always a gentleman to me, whatever people said. The first guy to make me feel like a woman instead of a girl ...

The only person left that I would really like to see is poor Shrimp. And she's dead.

I can hear Kelly upstairs, running up and down the landing. She's brightened up so much since school broke up on Wednesday – a different child, almost. I just wish I could stop worrying about her being lonely ... she seems happy enough in her own little world. But it can't be much fun, really. And all you need is *one* good friend ...

Which is exactly what I've been looking for ever since Shrimp, I suppose. Only this time, I won't let anyone down. Whatever happens tomorrow, the most important person there will be Boris.

My old, new friend.

'What about you, Bob?'

'Eh?' Bob Carmichael peered up from the report he was proof-reading. *Building Bridges, a school-based approach to community relations.* Yet another government publication that would use up a few hundred trees, and sit unread in a few thousand staff pigeon holes. At least it was another entry on his bibliography.

'What are you doing to celebrate finishing the sodding report?' Heather, his research assistant, had already had a few at lunchtime, while he'd been checking the final draft. 'You should come out with us later on, we're going to a party in Fulham – probably going on into Saturday night, too.'

She was only half-joking; after all, he knew she'd chosen him as one of her 'Fantasy Fucks'. But he didn't think the rest of her twentysomething friends would appreciate his presence. 'I think I'll go home and open a nice bottle of red I've had waiting for exactly this kind of occasion.'

'Boring or what? Don't you ever let your hair down?'

But Heather didn't wait for an answer, and moved into the next office to round up more party animals.

Bob grinned to himself. If only you knew. He read on ... 'the importance of the partnership approach have been accepted by all parties in the multi-agency pilot study'. How had they missed that? He crossed out 'have' with the pencil, which snapped under the pressure, so he reached into his drawer for another one. And spotted the invitation.

He hadn't forgotten it, exactly. Ruled it out, obviously, but not forgotten it. Bob imagined Tracey was already making preparations, with her girlfriends gathered around, starting a marathon of buffing and shaving and painting and conditioning.

They'd never got it, Dick and the rest, never seen past the cloud of 'Impulse' and the stream of smart-arse abuse she gave every teacher ... but Tracey was brighter than a class full of insufferable Suzanne Sharps. She had this natural spark – much more appealing than intellectual prowess – that he'd never seen in anyone else. Not to mention the sweetest grin.

But Tracey Mortimer was never right as a romantic heroine. Not passive enough. And the name hardly trips off the tongue like Lo-li-ta. And she came from the wrong part of town.

Fucking hell, Bob thought, he'd been thirty, it wasn't *West Side Story*, star-crossed lovers at the mercy of society's disapproval. He was old enough to know better before it even started, or, given that it had, old enough to take control, and take the punishment if this really mattered more than anything, more than his career and his reputation. Surely he'd owed her that.

OK, so she dumped him before he had the chance to whisk her away to a better life, but he might still have been able to pull it off.

He pulled out another pencil, and slammed the drawer shut. But even as he scribbled 'has' in the margin instead of 'have', he knew the carefully chosen bottles of wine in his cellar wouldn't be able to compete with the invitation burning a hole in his desk.

'Has Christian even visited a state school before?' Charlotte asked.

Suzanne tried to gauge from the look on her secretary's face if she was being sarcastic, but the sun was reflecting off the silver café table, and so she could barely look in Charlotte's direction. 'I don't think so.'

'So he'll be seeing your humble origins!' Now she definitely sounded as though she was taking the piss.

'It's not where you start, it's where you finish, Charlotte. Corny, but true. If anything, it'll just prove to him that I was made of better stuff than all the other hopeless cases I was there with.'

'And what about the bitch you did your speech about? Is she going to be there?'

Suzanne sipped her prosecco, which had gone unpleasantly warm and flat at the bottom of the glass. Only Christian knew who 'Stacey' really was, thank God.

'I'm not quite sure, but that's all water under the bridge. You can't let your past rule your present.' Suzanne hoped she sounded convincing. Because she hadn't yet convinced herself.

'I've told you, Gary, I'm not coming. I get enough dysfunctional families during the week, without spending time with your dysfunctional friends from school. No way.'

They were sitting on what the estate agents lovingly called 'outside space', but was actually a tiny area of flat roof overlooking a traffic-clogged main road. The potted herbs had withered in the heat and pollution, but Gary and Gabby still insisted on having their Friday night Budweisers al fresco.

'I don't even want to go any more, but I told Boris I would.'

'Can't believe any grown woman would still let people call her Boris.'

'You'll love Boris.'

'No, I won't, because I won't be meeting her.'

Gary stared at the bus spewing blue smoke from its exhaust. *Convenient for public transport.* He decided to try a change of tack. 'You know my first love is going to be there.'

She stopped picking the dead bits out of the mint plant. 'What, the legendary Tracey? You saying I should be worried?'

'Well, I'm happy enough as I am, but she can be seriously determined when she puts her mind to it.'

'If she's a threat after all these years, then you're not really a great loss, are you, petal?'

'It's not really about that. It's more that ... well, I want to show you off, don't I? Show the rejects of Crawley Park that one of us at least had it in us to get the girl and get the hell out of there ...'

She was trying not to smile at the compliment. 'School reunions, eh? It's got nothing to do with reliving old memories ... it's all about settling old scores.'

'So will you help me settle this one?'

'I'll think about it ... in the morning. If you get the drinks in tonight!'

I'm helping Kelly choose her outfit, when Dave bellows up the stairs, 'Boris is on the phone.'

I wasn't expecting to hear from her till later, because I know she's been busy with her check-up at the surgery, this time with the legendary Brian, who arrived back last night, and is going to stay close to home while they wait for the Big Day. I'm looking forward to meeting this paragon of manhood.

'Hi, Boris, how ya doing?'

'Not good, Trace,' she says and in those three words I pick up so many things. The hiss of a mobile and the labouring of a car engine and the grind of hot rush hour traffic. But most of all the tininess of her voice. She sounds more like a little girl than she ever did when she was a little girl.

'What?'

The wait for the answer is the longest I can remember. 'Brian's driving me into the hospital now. My blood pressure's off the scale. I don't know ...'

And then she starts to cry, single sobs at first and then big growling sentences of crying that I can't make sense of. In the background, Brian is telling her to try to calm down, it can't help her blood pressure any to get all upset.

'Boris, listen. I'll come down to the hospital, Dave'll just have to babysit. You're going to be in the right place, they can monitor you and the little one and the rest of the pregnancy's gone fine, so there's no reason at all that once they've got you in there, everything shouldn't go according to plan.' I gulp as I realise that there's no way she's going to be at the reunion with me.

I know it's selfish, but all I can think about is that I am going to be totally, completely, utterly alone for a party that I no longer even want.

My reassurances don't seem to have helped either. Boris sounds like a wounded seal, and I only catch the odd word. 'But ... baby ... before ... can't come ... want you there ... no good ..'

'Boris, breathe deeply for a minute then you can tell me what you're worried about.' But the tears are still coming, and I wonder if the phone will stop working under the deluge.

There's a rustling and then a male voice. 'Tracey, it's Brian. Sorry we haven't met yet. You can't come to the hospital, I'm afraid. That's what Helen's trying to say. They're probably going to induce the baby.'

'Induce it? But ... can't they wait?'

There's silence and it sounds like the phone's gone dead until I hear a horn blaring and Brian shouts, 'Fucking wanker. Not you, Tracey. The thing is ... Helen hasn't told you, has she, but you see, it's happened before. And last time ... well, the thing is, last time, our son ... our son, he was called Harry, and he didn't make it.'

This is still sinking in as there's a pause, and then Brian seems to catch his breath, and says, 'I can't drive and talk, sorry, Tracey. We don't need a road accident on top of everything else. I'll call you as soon as there's any news.'

And I just catch another heartbreaking sob from Boris before the line really does go dead.

Chapter Twenty-Six

I haven't slept much, and it shows. There's gob all over my pillow from the few minutes of kip I did manage, and on my cheek you can see the creases in the fabric where I was lying on my face. I'm sure this never happened when I was younger.

Poor Boris. I've tried ringing the hospital, but they're not giving anything away, and her mobile's switched off. I don't know what I'd say if I did get through. I thought we were close friends, and yet she couldn't even tell me she'd lost a baby. I just assumed the reason she'd left it later to have kids was because she'd been too busy living it up. But I never bothered to ask, did I? Some friend. I've learned nothing from what happened with Shrimp. Nothing at all.

'Mummy?' Kelly's hovering at the door. 'You excited?'

I summon a smile from somewhere, and she comes and joins me on the bed, giving me a kiss. 'Ugh, Mummy, you smell funny.'

I lick my hand and sniff it; I read in a magazine that it's the best way to test your own breath, and sure enough, it smells as sour as a cat's bottom. I suppose I always thought that motherhood would make me too wise to want to drink myself into a stupor before going to bed without brushing my teeth. Silly Mummy.

'So do you, Kelly!' I tell her, but she knows I'm messing, and starts giggling. Not going to school has turned her back into a child I still don't understand, but can recognise as my own.

I let her pull me out of bed, and then follow her slowly down the stairs. The hangover's not as bad as I'd feared, but I still don't have a clue how I'm going to make it through breakfast, never mind the whole reunion.

Downstairs, Dave is doing his best husband and father act, feeding Callum cereal using the aeroplane trick 'coming into land, open wide . . .' which never works for me, but right now seems to be achieving remarkable results on the plate-clearing front.

'You decided to get into the reliving your youth stuff a bit early last night. Paying for it now, though?' Amazing how quickly he can extract himself from my good books.

'Just make me a coffee.'

'What did your last servant –'

'I've asked you for a coffee once – *once* – in nine bloody years of marriage. Is it too much to ask?'

Kelly covers her ears and Dave sighs, pulling her to him. 'What's got into Mummy?' he says, brightly, then murmurs, 'Too many bloody gin and tonics.'

I get my coffee, after much more clattering of crockery and cutlery, but it's thin and rancid-smelling, with most of the granules stuck to the side of the mug, spreading in the steam like bacteria under a microscope. Other men would have satisfied my craving by doing sexy things with cafetières or even espresso machines. I bet Jamie's got one.

I look at the clock. I'm running out of time to get ready, before the cab comes to take me to Crawley Park for a photo call.

I hold my nose and drink the coffee, trying to suck out the caffeine.

It's going to be a long day.

Fortunately for the taxi driver, I'm getting changed at school, so he's spared the sight of too much of my flesh in daylight. In three-quarters of an hour, I've managed to shower, shave my legs and underarms, put on some body lotion, drag my jeans over the slimy residue, and then throw all the gels and serums and sprays I can find into a Tesco carrier bag.

'What are you doing going into school on a Saturday?' he asks me, catching my eye in his mirror as I rummage around in the bag of tricks, pulling out concealer and some French stuff with egg white that tightens your skin. It's got its work cut out with me.

'It's a reunion.'

'Oh, I thought maybe you was a teacher. So – how long's it been?'

I think about asking him to guess, but when I see myself in the mirror, I decide that the way I look this morning, I won't like the answer. 'Seventeen years.' I slather on a generous coating of the patent rejuvenating egg white stuff. No wonder I look so old.

'Bet it'll feel like yesterday when you're there, though.'

Will it? Maybe when the others are there, it'll take me back. Because right now it feels a lot longer than seventeen years.

I use the chrome back of my hairbrush as a mirror to work out which bits of my face are crying out for concealer, though it occurs to me that it might be quicker to apply it all over.

The roads are pretty quiet this morning, less traffic than I'd expected, and I think of Boris and Brian going through the jams to get to the hospital last night.

'Could we do a bit of a diversion before we go to school?'

He looks a bit doubtful. 'It's on account.'

'Yeah, they'll never notice. But I'll make up the difference if it takes too long to get back.'

They've done a *Changing Rooms* on the hospital reception since I had Callum, all glass bricks and soothing water colours. But once I've followed my nose back to Rosebud ward, it's just as horrible as ever, stinking of disinfectant, with the radiators on full blast, even though it's a hot July day. A zombied pregnant woman nearly walks into me, pulling her drip along behind her like a wilful Great Dane.

I stick my head round the bay where they used to put the women who were confined to bed for the duration. But there's no one there.

I walk towards the reception desk, where a tired-looking midwife is hitching up her trousers to scratch her ankle.

'I'm looking for my frien – ... sister.' If she's that ill, there's no way I'll be allowed anywhere near her unless I'm a blood relative. 'Boris ... Helen Morris. Um. Norris.'

She gives me a funny look, the same one she probably gives to women who come in and can't decide if they're having contractions or not. 'And you're sure she's your sister?'

I nod, and I guess I look the part – frazzled and surviving on no sleep, exactly the right attitude for a dutiful sister in the midst of a crisis.

'She's in Lily room,' she says, pointing down the corridor.

Of course ... a private room. Had to be really, Brian's never there, but at least he's earning enough to keep their grief ring-fenced from the common herd.

'Don't stay too long,' she shouts after me.

The door's not really closed, just pushed to, and I can't hear any wailing or arguing through the crack. I knock gently but don't wait.

Boris is on some kind of monitor, and when I walk in she moves her head extremely slowly, as though she's scared of breaking something if she reacts too fast.

'Tracey,' she says, quietly, and I flatter myself that she sounds pleased.

At the window, there's a tall man, silhouetted against the sunlight. He turns round. Brian. Nice-looking, bit bashed about – I'd guess he was a rugby player who stopped before he got a cauliflower ear. Bit too 'casual sportswear' for my liking, but he's not looking very crisp now. I guess he's been at the hospital all night.

I lean over to kiss Boris's cheek, and squeeze her shoulder through the cotton nightie. Then I reach across her bump to shake Brian's hand.

'I wish we weren't meeting here,' I say, and he looks through me. 'What's the latest?'

Boris nods at Brian to explain. She looks as though even talking is a dangerous waste of what little energy she's got left.

He sits down and stares sadly at Boris's belly. 'We're expecting the consultant any moment. And he's got to decide whether to induce or do a caesarean.'

'So the baby's definitely got to come out now? At least it won't be very premature.' Last night I dragged out one of my old pregnancy books, and looked up high blood pressure. The index referred me to dire warnings about pre-eclampsia, which was one of those words they mouthed grimly at antenatal classes, the way actors do with *Macbeth*. As if even to say it could bring disaster.

'I wanted to do it properly,' Boris whispers.

'I just want the baby to be born alive,' Brian says, and then bites his tongue at how harsh it sounds, reaching across to kiss her cheek, muttering 'Sorry.' Looks like foot-in-mouth disease is one thing Boris has in common with her husband.

'You're in the right place,' I say, resorting to cliché.

'We were last time, too.'

None of us can think of anything more to say. I wish I hadn't come – Lily room already feels like a funeral parlour.

I wave vaguely at the window. 'My taxi ...'

They both nod at me, and Boris smiles. 'I wish I was coming with you, Tracey. I can't believe I'm not going to be there.'

'Nor can I.' I feel the sudden pressure of tears behind my eyes, but I won't let myself cry. 'At least you'll be able to watch the video!' It's a very feeble attempt to be cheerful. But Boris tries to smile, to make *me* feel better, which makes me feel even worse.

'I'll be thinking about you.' I place my hand on her belly as gently as I can, and I'm surprised at how hot it feels. 'And about you, baby ... I look forward to meeting you.'

I don't think Brian even notices I'm leaving the room.

The taxi driver is happily watching the total on his meter mount up when I get back to the car.

I clamber in, and jam myself into the corner as far as I can so it's hard for him to see me in the mirror. A few tears have defied my grim attempts to stay unemotional, and my nose has gone red with the effort of holding the other tears in. I smear on even more concealer. I've used most of a stick on my face, and the rest seems to have collected under my nails.

'Any more unscheduled stops?' he asks, hopefully.

'No, thanks.' I sniff, staring at cars, road signs, anything I can see out of the window that has no emotional significance whatsoever. But the signs point to the maternity unit, and the car in front has a 'baby on board' sticker in its window. So I fix my eyes on the back of the passenger seat, with its torn leatherette upholstery and fabric head rest.

I concentrate on individual threads of cotton until they all swim in and out of focus, and I feel slightly sick and maybe I even fall into some kind of trance, because it's only when the driver pulls on the handbrake that I realise we're there.

He pulls up just inside the school gates, and gets me to sign the account. When I get out, the car park's busier than it usually is on a school day – but instead of Minis and Clios and Fiestas, the space is taken up by Volvos and Saabs, a couple of big lorries and a generator. There's even a catering van.

The only person I can see is a teenager wearing a fluorescent bib marked 'Marshal'. He's hovering at the end of the car park, smoking inexpertly.

He sees me, and tries to hide the cigarette behind his back. It's depressing to think he sees me as an authority figure.

'Don't worry, I don't want to interrupt your fag break,' I say, and wink at him.

His face relaxes and he takes a long drag, which makes his face colour up. I'm much happier now I realise he's trying to impress me.

'I'm here for the reunion.'

'You press? You're a bit early.'

'Er, no. It's actually MY reunion. I'm Tracey – I was a pupil here, oooh, seventeen years ago – except we used to smoke by the bins at the back of the canteen.'

He frowns at me, and I think he's struggling with the concept of anyone being daring enough to smoke seventeen years ago, i.e. before he was even born.

I give up on conversation – this is less rewarding than talking to Callum. 'I'll go and see how they're getting on with setting things up.'

I walk round the other side of the hall, where the windows are, and it's as if I've stepped on to a Hollywood film set. People striding around with supreme self-importance, carrying the tools of the trade – clipboards, cables, clipboards, lights, clipboards, loudspeakers. Oh, and did I mention the clipboards?

It's at this point that my stomach starts to feel like a washing machine on spin cycle. All this here because of little me. Well, little me, and the need for Alec's grubby production company to squeeze money out of Channel 5.

I want to run away but my legs are refusing to co-operate. So I stand like a statue at the edge of the action, and everything seems to slow down, the rushing figures I don't recognise are going blurry and an echoing voice seems to be calling out from somewhere else ... 'Tracey ... Tracey ...'

I think I'm going to be sick.

'Feeling any better?' Jenny asks me. We're sitting in the staff room, which has been relabelled the Green Room, and has a new keypad lock on the door to make sure no pupils, press or even guests get to raid the secret supplies of booze ... I've been told the code, which proves they see me as part of the production team now. Though I bet I'm the only one not getting paid a penny.

'Yeah. I had a really bad night because of Boris –'

'What about her?'

Oh shit. 'You hadn't heard? She's been admitted to the general and they think they're going to induce her, because of her high blood pressure.'

'God. How awful. I'd better tell Alec.'

'I'm sure he'll be very concerned ... about how it affects his precious programme.'

She looks as though she's going to argue back, but then she just shrugs. 'Anyway, we need to get you back to

241

looking human, and the good news is our floor manager is also a dab hand with a make-up sponge. So she's the next step in your preparations for ordeal by journalists . . .'

Chapter Twenty-Seven

I don't think I'm up to a press conference. It sounds like the worst job interview in the world, combined with meeting the parents of a new boyfriend, who has just revealed that they're highly religious and still wish he was marrying the vicar's daughter.

Brenda the floor manager, whose abilities with a make-up brush have not been exaggerated, used to go out with a journalist.

'They're bastards. Think Alec times ten,' she says, as she blends foundation around my albino-rabbit eyes. She's had to remove all the stuff I'd smeared on in the taxi. Her own make-up is so perfect that I have no idea how old she is.

Up till now I haven't had chance to worry about it, which is a good thing, but then again I haven't had time to prepare for it, which is a bad thing.

'The men are bad, but the women are definitely the worst ones – they suck up to you and pretend to be your friend, and then stab you in the back.'

'I guess things didn't work out with the boyfriend, then?'

She snorts at me. 'I learned the hard way.'

By the time she's finished my face, I look as though I've

been on a long relaxing holiday, but my insides are churning even more violently than before. Brenda takes me to the classroom where we're doing the press conference. Annabel is waiting for me, with ten noisy children.

'Surprise,' she says. It's that all right. They're about twelve, and dressed in school uniform even though it's Saturday AND the holidays ... 'Meet the kids from the current class 1G. We thought it'd be fun to get some of them in for the photographs.'

Fun for who? The children and I eye each other suspiciously. They're much better-looking than we were, less smudged and warped. The girls are well-groomed; I'm sure a couple of them are wearing lipstick, and even the boys look clean. They're already flirting, and sending each other signals as blatant as any you'd see in any nightclub. It makes me want to run home and wrap Kelly up to stop her growing. Like Chinese foot-binding.

'So who is your form tutor then?' I ask them, not knowing what else to talk about.

'Miss Nicholls,' says one of the girls with lipstick. 'She's a frigid bitch.' Everyone laughs at this.

'Oh. Well, that's teachers for you. At least if they don't have sex, they won't breed more teachers.'

I think I've gone too far, and the kids look from me to the cocky girl, waiting for a response.

She's weighing it up and after a bloody long wait, she finally grants me a sly smirk. 'Yeah, right,' she says, and I know I'm in the gang.

Annabel walks towards the door. 'I'll leave you *children* to get on with it then,' she says, making it clear she's including me in that. 'We're expecting the journalists in about ten minutes, so I'll bring them up in one big group.'

Now that I'm officially cool, the kids all talk at once, telling me about their friends and their pets and their siblings and their favourite bands, and they're not nearly as grown-up as they're trying to be. Bless 'em. It's nice to let it wash over me, the trivia of these lives about to be hit by the juggernaut of puberty, while I try to second-guess what these reporters will ask me.

What would I ask myself? With my insider knowledge of what makes me tick, what would be the worst questions they could come up with to throw me off course?

When was the last time you had sex?

Not really an obvious question at a school reunion, but it would certainly throw me. Though maybe it's not really that embarrassing that me and Dave no longer bother to do it after nine years ... it's probably worse that I haven't found anyone else to shag.

Whatever happened to your first love?

Actually, even that's not a real toughie, is it? He's a policeman living with his girlfriend in London. 'And is he coming tonight?' 'No, I think he's working a night shift ... yes, it is a shame, but then again, I don't think we'd have much in common any more. People change, don't they? What if he had a horrible beer gut now?' I almost convince myself.

What's the secret of a lasting friendship?

I keep thinking about Shrimp, and about Boris, and it makes me feel sick. What's the right answer to a question like that? Something that makes me sound wise and balanced and mature, instead of the way I feel, which is shallow and clueless and lonely.

'The secret of lasting friendship is to know that people change, but to hang on to the things that made you friends in the first place.'

I like how that sounds ... I almost come across like someone you'd want as your friend.

'I'd better get off before anyone clocks my car. Guests aren't meant to come here till seven o'clock. Ring me when the press conference is over, and I'll give you your next clue!' Suzanne still felt unsettled by her thirst for revenge. But it was also exciting.

Andrew pouted. 'You really are making a meal out of this. Why can't you just tell me now what the bloody story is?'

'Because it's more fun this way.'

'For you. Not for me. This isn't the way I work, being led on a wild goose chase. I should be at a wedding this afternoon.'

He was very tiresome, and Suzanne wished she'd chosen someone else for the story, but within twelve hours, Andrew would have served his purpose, and she would never have to have anything more to do with him. Best that way, so that no one could ever make the connection with her.

'Ring me,' she said, and opened the passenger door to let him out. 'I'll meet you at my Mum's later on . . .'

The cloak and dagger stuff was a good distraction from the reality of what she was doing. She'd even kept it from Christian, who never disapproved of anything she did. She was thirty-three, with years of professional compassion behind her. Wasn't it time to bury the hatchet?

But one image in her head was stopping her. It had haunted her for nearly two decades, and for Suzanne, if plotting and stitching Tracey up could eliminate it from her memory, then the end would definitely justify the means.

She watched Andrew trudge over to his own car, get in and then drive through the school gates.

Somewhere inside, Tracey Mortimer was about to meet Andrew. And with it, her nemesis.

It had been a long time coming.

It had taken Suzanne ten days to believe Gary Coombs

could fancy her. And ten years to get over the fact he didn't.

The note had looked genuine enough.

Will you come to the Easter Disco with me?
Gary

He'd slipped it into her Maths exercise book before it was handed back. She hadn't actually seen him do it, but when she went to check the mark she'd been given for her algebra homework, the note fluttered to the floor like a feather. She read it while she was leaning down beside her desk, and by the time she surfaced again, her face was as red as her hair.

Suzanne had never dared to fancy any boy, because she was sure no boy could fancy her back. And even if they did, they'd never admit it. It would be utterly uncool to want to go out with the class swot. But as she absorbed the content of the note, repeating each word to herself, she wondered ... if there was *anyone* with enough credibility to get away with dating her, it was Gary. So handsome and so smooth that he could do as he pleased ... and, in the process, he might just remove her from the bullies' firing line ...

She dared to catch his eye once during the lesson, and he blushed. It made sense. Maths was the best time to send the note. It was her weakest subject, and his strongest, and the only one where Tracey and her cronies didn't rule the roost, because they were in the bottom set. Suzanne knew Tracey had her eye on Gary, and she'd assumed he felt the same way ... but what if he really did want someone more ... intelligent?

The hardest thing about school was having no one to talk to, and the note reinforced her isolation. So she tried to interrogate it, to read between the lines (there were only two, after all) to see if it was truth or dare.

Her first step was to check the handwriting to see if the

note had actually been written by Gary. At least that was easy. Mr Phipps always kept his pile of marking stacked in alphabetical order, so she brushed against his desk to knock them over. Gary's book was near the top when she gathered them up again.

Yep, it was definitely his writing – angular, heavy-handed.

Back home, she couldn't concentrate on her homework. Not even English, her favourite subject. The possibility of going to the disco with Gary kept distracting her. To start with, it was unreal, like the idea of going to the disco with Sting or Martin Kemp. But, as she worked out the details – what she would wear, what he would wear, how they would get to the disco, and, most exciting, the reactions when they finally arrived – the picture forming in her mind became clearer. And sharper. And suddenly, terrifyingly attainable.

Three days later, Suzanne did something she hadn't done since primary school. Initiated a conversation with someone in her class. OK, so it was only Boris, but it was still a breakthrough.

She cornered her at break time. 'Helen. . .?' she said, and Boris didn't turn round, because no one ever called her Helen any more. Suzanne tried again. 'Boris?'

'Hmmm?' Boris looked startled that Suzanne had spoken, but not hostile.

'Just wondering if you wanted to share some cake with me? It was Mum's birthday yesterday, so she's put chocolate cake in with my packed lunch, but I'll never manage it on my own.' It wasn't true, of course, but Suzanne had guessed that it was the best way to attract the attention of the fattest – and least vindictive – girl in 3G.

Boris thought it over. 'Has it got buttercream?'

'Yes. And icing.'

'OK, then.'

At lunchtime, they headed to the back of the field. They hadn't discussed it, but Suzanne knew Boris would appreciate being as far away as possible, in case anyone saw them together. Maybe all that would change when she was going out with Gary. It would be nice to have friends.

Suzanne had cut the cake into several odd-shaped pieces, to disguise the fact that it was shop-bought. But she realised immediately that it didn't matter to Boris, who was wide-eyed at the sheer quantity.

'Tuck in – I don't even like chocolate,' Suzanne lied. Then she watched in awe as Boris polished off half the cake without speaking, licking the sugary filling off her fingers as purposefully as a kitten. She looked up and grinned.

'Boris ...? What would you do ...? I mean, if you thought that maybe ...?' It was an awful struggle to know where to start, so finally Suzanne rummaged around in her bag, pulled out the note, and handed it over.

Boris unravelled it and looked even more impressed than she had at the cake. 'Have you stolen this?'

It wasn't what Suzanne had hoped to hear. 'No ... no, he slipped into my exercise book in Maths.'

'Wow!'

'You don't think it could be a practical joke, do you?'

Boris thought about it for a second, then reached over to pick up another piece of cake. She finished it before she spoke again. 'Prob'bly not, but there's only one way to find out. Write one back.'

It took Suzanne all weekend to write it. She bought a couple of teenage magazines with what was left of her pocket money after paying for the cake. They suggested playing it cool.

On Monday, she tried to catch his eye in Maths, but he ignored her. Embarrassed? Annoyed because she hadn't even replied. On Tuesday, she did the same, and this time he blushed, as he had the week before. It gave her courage.

On Wednesday, she offered to hand out the exercise books, and slipped her own note into Gary's book. It was written on a piece of pink paper, folded in half so no one else would see it poking out of the cardboard cover. She'd practised her writing, tearing the mistakes into confetti-sized pieces so her Mum wouldn't be able to decipher the message. In any case, all it said was, *'Yes, I'll come, from Suzie'* In a daring moment, she added *'xx'* after her name.

She liked the idea of being Suzie, it sounded better alongside Gary's name, and it also sounded like someone else, the person she wanted to be. Suzie wouldn't get top marks, in fact, Suzie might sometimes be so busy going out and having fun that her homework would be late. But Suzie wouldn't care.

She had to lean back in her seat to see his reaction. He opened the book, saw the pink paper, then shut the book immediately, checking that no one else was watching. Suzanne looked away, and when she felt brave enough to turn round again, she knew she'd made a mistake. He was frowning, and when he realised she was facing him, he shrugged, asking silently what she meant. And she knew all she could do was wait.

It didn't take long. On Thursday, when Suzanne walked into Mr Carmichael's room for registration, everyone was waiting for her. Boris looked nervous, Gary looked embarrassed. And Tracey looked triumphant. In her hand was a piece of pink paper.

'Well, well, well, Suzanne ... I think we need a little chat about *my* boyfriend ...'

Annabel returns eventually with five blokes and a girl. One of the guys I recognise, it's Tone, the local radio reporter from last time I was here. None of them look nearly as threatening as I'd been expecting.

'Hello, Tracey,' Tone says. He seems pleased that he's got one over the other hacks by knowing me already. 'The big day, eh?'

What an idiot. I smile sweetly.

Annabel introduces me to the journalists – the girl is from the local rag, there's a young-ish man from the evening paper in Reading, two photographers dragging huge canvas bags behind them, trying to outdo each other with the lengths of their lenses. And then there's this shifty guy, much better dressed than the rest. Andrew is a freelance 'all the way from London,' Annabel says, and it's clear she's only interested in what he thinks. I get the impression she's disappointed at the turnout.

'Let's do the Q and A first, and then the snappers can do their stuff? If that's OK with you all?' Annabel says, but she's only looking at Andrew.

He goes up to one of the photographers – obviously the one he's decided has the biggest equipment – and says, 'Dunno who I'm going to flog this too, yet, but would you shoot a roll for me too? Can't guarantee nothing, but it could bring in a bob or two.'

The guy shrugs, but takes Andrew's card. 'All right then.'

Tone sets up his tape recorder, and the kids have gone silent and surly again.

'So who's firing the first question, then?' asks Annabel.

'Tracey, what's been the biggest surprise of the preparation for your reunion so far?' Tone puts on this kind of transatlantic DJ voice, but it's so different from the way he looks – like a train-spotter – that I have to work hard not to laugh.

Where would I start, if I was going to answer truthfully? The fact that I seem to be the only person who enjoyed school? The fact that my first boyfriend still hates me with a vengeance after seventeen years? Or maybe the fact that I've forgotten what it's like to have a friend?

'It's probably not what you'd think, but the biggest surprise has been how much hard work it is making a television programme. You wouldn't believe it. Endless filming appointments, a compulsory trip to a health farm to make me look more glamorous, my own designer-made dress for tonight ... it's been exhausting. So if anyone's thinking of signing up for something similar – in the words of the *Grange Hill* anti-drugs campaigns – JUST SAY NO!'

They all grin. I know I'm going to be what Annabel calls 'good copy'.

The questions don't get any tougher. The girl from the weekly waffles on about the improvements to the school, and whether I'm surprised about Crawley Park now being a media college. The bloke from the evening paper is talking about old friends and what's happened to them – are any of them famous? Am I surprised by how successful some former pupils are? I talk a bit about Boris running her own company, and try hard to concentrate on not thinking about what is happening to her right now ...

Andrew's been the least talkative, which seems odd as he works for the nationals. I do a quick one-to-one radio interview, then when we do the photographs – which involve me posing with today's class 1G – he hangs around.

Annabel looks concerned. 'Have you got what you wanted, Andrew?'

'Not yet ...' he says, but flashes her a smile. 'I thought I'd come back later on – soak up the atmosphere. I think this will make more of a long feature than a shorter news piece.'

'Well, strictly speaking, we're not letting any journalists come back for the reunion itself – we don't want to do ourselves out of publicity when the programme itself goes out.'

Andrew shakes his head. 'Oh, don't worry. I'm not talking about gossiping about who gets off with who ... my main outlet is the *Guardian* features pages, you know. And I promise there won't be anything there that isn't ... original journalism!'

'Let me have a word with Alec about it,' she says, but I can see slimy Andrew getting his way. There's something about him that doesn't ring true, but then I remember what Brenda said, and I guess looking shifty is an occupational hazard for journalists.

'Delighted to meet you, Tracey,' he says, kissing my cheek. 'Maybe we can catch up again later on.'

Hope not. 'Yes, that'll be great.'

I'm getting good at saying the opposite of what I really mean.

I ring the hospital.

'Hello, I'm Helen Norris's sister – I was in earlier?'

It's a different nurse, but she seems to accept this.

'I wondered if there was any news about whether she's being induced or whatever?

'Hang on a tick ...' The phone clunks as she puts it down. After a couple of minutes she comes back. 'Mrs Norris has gone to theatre. The doctor thought that would be better than her having to go through labour like the last time ...'

'What, do you mean the baby's ...?' I can't say it.

'Look, I'm afraid I can't tell you any more at the moment. I'm sure her husband will call you when there's any news.'

'But, can't you tell me –'

'I'm sorry,' she says, firmly. 'You're going to have to wait. There's really nothing you can do.'

Chapter Twenty-Eight

I'm queuing at the location catering van, for food I don't really want. But it's like the medicine I force down everyone else's necks in winter – Kelly's, Callum's, Dave's – unappealing, but an insurance policy against feeling even worse.

I suppose I'd hoped for something more Hollywood than the veggie burger they give me when I reach the counter, but then this is Channel 5, and I'm hardly Gwyneth Paltrow. And I don't think I'd feel any more tempted by sushi prepared on the bellies of virgins, or whatever it is they'd serve up to celebs. The burger tastes as though it's already been reduced to the food groups we studied in Home Economics, so all that's on my tongue is protein, fat, carbohydrate. But after a while, my stomach feels less empty, so I have to conclude that it wasn't raw emotion making me feel quite so grim. It was hunger. I am that shallow.

Annabel has left me alone, and I've barely seen Alec. It's a stunning day, temperatures as high as I remember in the summer of '76, when the tar melted and we had stand-pipes because there wasn't enough water. My jeans are sticking to my legs, and despite the sun, the layer of sweat on my thighs makes me shiver. I'm in a bad way.

I look for somewhere quiet, and find one of the benches facing the back of the playing field, where we used to sit and watch the lads playing football. We'd cram on as many people as we could, which was fine for me because I was always in the middle, but the girls at the end would be perched on one buttock each, trying to keep their balance. And when one of the boys scored between the goalposts marked by two green jumpers, we'd all leap up, and they'd be toppled off like the losers in a game of musical chairs ...

It feels decadent to have the whole bench to myself, and eventually I can't resist lying along it full-length, like a tramp. I close my eyes and imagine I'm not on my own. Boris should be next to me, of course, and Shrimp and Melody and Gary ...

But why would he be here instead of on the pitch? I invent a convenient twisted ankle. Or maybe a groin strain. By the fifth year we were certainly busy enough below the waist for him to suffer one of those.

He's got his arm around me, and is playing with my hair, twisting it round, and watching it spring back. On my other side is Shrimp, taller and less skeletal than the last time I saw her. Not to mention 100 per cent more alive. She's stretching out her ankle-socked legs to try to catch the sun, but it's like trying to brown a jacket potato in a microwave.

Boris is next, her exact opposite in the Crawley Park hall of mirrors, pink to Shrimp's yellow, fat to her thin. But they're both grinning. And on the other side of Gary, is Melody. No surprises there, that girl always gravitates to the men, never mind that they're going out with her best mate. Though with Shrimp and Boris here, is she really my best mate? It always was a 'marriage' of convenience.

'It's been too long,' Shrimp says, and it makes me jump.

'Bloody right,' says Melody. She's the only one who looks her age, a fan of crows' feet around her eyes, and the puckered proof of twenty years' chain-smoking around her mouth. The rosebud lips are starved of colour, and the rest of her skin is grey on the cheeks, and mottled with pink thread veins around the chin and nose.

She budges herself a bit closer to Gary, even though there's room for another Boris at her end of the bench. But he's still transfixed by my hair, and doesn't even seem to notice she's there.

Boris isn't pregnant any more. 'So what are you up to these days, Melody?'

Melody curls her lip. 'Shelf-stacking.' She sounds defensive and defiant.

Ye-es!!!!

'It's not easy affording three kids on my own, and the child support don't seem to get very far with chasing their dads ...' She has this sour look about her that I don't remember from the old days.

Boris leans across to pat her on the hand. 'Still, they must bring you so much pleasure ... what about you. Shrimp? Any kids yet?'

Shrimp shakes her head. 'No ... don't forget we always had a houseful at home. I'm a traveller, really. Bit of this, bit of that. I don't get back very often. You're lucky to get me here .... Bet you never thought I'd end up a free spirit!'

'It's exactly what I hoped you'd end up being,' I tell her, putting my arm around her skinny shoulders.

I suppose my kids will do the same, backpack their way into adulthood before avoiding it again for three years at university. Following the same well-worn path to the same places, propped up by the money Dave and I should have used to enjoy the life we've been cheated out of by early parenthood.

But good on Shrimp for escaping the family rat-race.

'And Gary's a copper in London,' Boris tells the others, who start laughing.

'I know,' he says, joining in. 'I suppose I've got Trace to thank – or to blame, really. I could have ended up patrolling this estate for the rest of my life, if it hadn't been for what happened . . .'

He tails off, but he's still smiling at me.

'It's funny how things turn out,' he says, and kisses me on the cheek. I want to turn my head enough for our lips to meet, but it seems wrong to force things.

'Feels odd being back,' Boris says. 'On our own, I mean. It's too quiet.'

Melody says, 'I see hundreds of the brats every day. I only live over there –' and she points to the other side of the field, where the old estate houses are packed together, like beach huts. 'I remember what it's like to be fifteen, which none of you seem to . . . It wasn't that great. What's happened to you, Gary? Don't you remember what she did?'

Gary looks at me, and I known damn well he remembers, but he's been trying really hard to keep things light-hearted. She's a stirring bitch. 'Fuck off, Melody. You're in no position to slag me off anyway. Who was it I caught trying to grope my husband on my wedding day? And you were my fucking bridesmaid!'

Boris turns on her. 'Melody, is that right?'

'Takes two to tango. Dave didn't seem to object . . .'

'You didn't really give him much option, from what I remember . . .'

Shrimp holds up her tiny hands. 'This isn't really what we're here for, is it, girls? It's water under the bridge.'

She's right, and I'm surprised at how easy it is to let the resentment flow away, especially when Melody's life is obviously so much grimmer than mine. I brush it aside with a flick of my hair.

We sit in silence, peering out at the estate that we've all escaped, except Melody. Along from the older houses is a cluster of better homes, more *Brookside* than pre-fab, and you can even see proper cars parked in driveways, not the old wrecks our families were so proud of, the ones made mainly of fibreglass filler. Maybe even Crawley Park is pulling itself out of the gutter.

I catch sight of another figure out of the corner of my eye, and turn my head slowly. I already know who it is from the height, and the way he's stooping to try to conceal his size.

He's aged, too, but less than Melody. Seventeen years is less cruel when you're going from thirty to forty-seven, than from sixteen to thirty-three . . .

'Tracey . . .' he says. And when I look back to the bench, I realise that the others have gone. And I'm on my own with Mr Carmichael. Not, of course, for the first time.

Afterwards, people who didn't know me thought it must have been Bob who'd done all the running. The sophisti-cated teacher seducing the vulnerable schoolgirl. But that's so far from the truth. I'd defy most blokes to resist the campaign I mounted for Mr Carmichael. Not because I'm gorgeous – sure, I was pretty but aren't teachers trained to resist the attractions of pretty sixteen-year-olds? – but because I was determined.

It had started as a joke – a competition between Melody and me to see which of us could make a teacher blush. We each chose our prey, and set about being as provocative and flirty as we could. Melody chose Bob (mine was one of the PE teachers), and he held up really well, however much she tossed her hair and thrust forward her chest and crossed her legs. But by Day 2, I found myself feeling jealous. It was completely out of the blue. First of all I was angry I hadn't chosen him, and then I started to feel protective towards him; I wanted to tell him that Melody was only playing with him, would chew him and then spit him out . . .

But he resisted all her ploys, and that tipped the balance for me. I had to have him. And there are plenty of good excuses to spend time alone with your teacher when you're in your final year – especially if you've never been academic, but seem to experience an apparent change of heart about learning. Teachers love that – the idea that they are inspiring you, making a difference.

But it wasn't really as cynical as that sounds. Because I think I'd always seen something in Bob that was missing from my life. He was popular, anyway, despite his sarcasm and the insistence on homework coming in on time. Kids respected him. And while I'd always fancied Gary in a straightforward physical way, with Bob it was the first time I'd found a man's mind as attractive as his body. Probably the last time, too, thinking about it.

I set the pace. I hung around after school to talk about how unhappy I was at home, how I felt I'd wasted my education, how I felt frustrated by my friends and their lack of aspiration. And if in the beginning some of it was exaggerated or even made up to appeal to him, the basic emotions were genuine enough. I did feel lost; I did hate living with my mother; I did find spending my time with Melody was a frightening premonition of where my life was headed; and I did worry what would happen once I was out there in The Real World where, even then, I sensed my pole position in the Crawley Park circuit would count for nothing.

I kissed him on the Monday, the night after my mum had threatened to throw me out because she found the Pill in my bedside drawer.

It was after school, we were sitting close together,

going through my options – would the social help me get somewhere of my own? Could I sign on the dole before I left school? I knew it was just another one of Mum's threats, it would blow over once I'd been humble enough, but Bob didn't, and he was so kind and concerned that I did what I'd wanted to do all along. He started to respond, and then pulled away. He actually looked quite hurt. Until then, perhaps he hadn't realised that I wanted more than advice.

He tried to ignore me, and I let it happen. After about a week, I hovered around at the end of class.

'Can I talk to you?'

'Not here,' he said. 'Daisy's, at five?'

We met at Daisy's Café for four nights, one after the other, right at the back where no one could see us, but with my history exercise book open on the table, just in case. He drank black coffee, and I had a Coke float. I know he struggled with his conscience ... but I was sixteen, it was immoral rather than illegal.

He never really stood a chance ...

Chapter Twenty-Nine

'I didn't invite you.'

He doesn't look surprised. 'No? That's a little dis-appointing. May I join you?' he says, pointing at the bench. I don't reply, and he sits down where Melody was, a Gary-sized gap between us.

'I wonder who did invite me. Dick Phipps has been in touch about it, he wanted me to talk you out of it. And then I had a visit from Suzanne Sharp –'

'God, really? I saw her too, last week. The TV company made me go and interview her about the psych-ology of school reunions. It must be her. What is she up to?'

'I would say perhaps it's an attempt to cause trouble . . . which is partly why I've come now instead of later. Though I can't really say why I've come at all.'

I hear some of the words he's choosing, as he always does, with precision. But I'm mainly listening to the sounds he's making, the voice that was always like crème brûlée in a world of Angel Delight. Dense and creamy compared to the thin, sickly way everyone else spoke, including me.

'To see me?' It sounds vain, but what else could it be?

He raises his eyebrows. 'Yes. But why now? It wouldn't have been that difficult to find you, Tracey. So why did I wait until it was on a plate, so to speak?'

Did I mention that nothing was ever straightforward for Bob? That no emotion or reaction or even a sneeze or a cough, and certainly no orgasm, could escape his analysis. I'm surprised he hasn't got tired of it over the years, outgrown it like kids who finally learn to stop asking 'why' because more often than not, there's no answer.

He looks me up and down, slowly and carefully, as though he's taking in a painting. He never hurried anything – including making love. Of course, that couldn't have been more of a contrast to Gary and my mates; we tore around as though we were trying to beat some kind of life deadline.

'I'm glad I've come, though. It's wonderful to see you.' He doesn't try to touch me, it's as though just seeing me is enough. Maybe he's impotent by now, it happens when men hit middle age, doesn't it? But something about him, his confidence, his bearing, makes me pretty sure he can still get it up.

'It's a shock . . .' I start, feeling the need to say something, but with no real idea of what's appropriate. What's the etiquette for conversation with a man who lost his job because of your relationship? And who you rejected as soon as that happened?

He puts his finger to his lips. 'Don't say anything, Tracey. I didn't want to upset you by coming. I suppose it was fairly selfish, really, to turn up and expect a warm welcome.'

'I'd have thought I'd have been the last person you'd want to see again.'

'What happened was my fault, Tracey. There's no question about it. You were my pupil, it's against the rules and it's morally wrong.' He speaks evenly, no hint of anger. Given the amount of consideration he gives to selecting which daily paper to buy each morning, I can't begin to imagine how many hours he must have devoted to thinking about our affair. 'Though I don't regret it. Do you?'

His eyes are a surprisingly bright blue, like Paul Newman's, and when I look into them, I remember the moment I stopped seeing him as a teacher, and started weighing him up as a potential lover. Back when I had some power over men.

'No, Bob. And I think it's a bit insulting to take all the blame. I had a part in where we ended up, didn't I?'

I realise I want to kiss him. It's a shock, and what's worse is that I am convinced he knows it. He always could see through me. While poor Gary fumbled about, wondering what I was plotting, Bob could scan me like an X-ray machine, not just my body but my soul, and I felt naked. And I loved it.

Back then I thought it was about his age, and I assumed that all men would be able to do it, when they'd been around the block a few times. But it's not like that. It's more supernatural, a gift, like water-divining or clairvoyance.

'I don't want to insult you, Tracey.'

There were six other Traceys in my year; it was a common name, in both senses of the word. It's always placed me – and a million other girls – as being born somewhere between the moon landings and Donny Osmond's first album. But he spoke it as though it could easily have inspired Shakespeare to write one of his finer sonnets, or would have been a fit name for a princess in one of his History lessons. And he's doing it now, hypnotising me. I try to shake myself out of it. I'm over-tired; just a minute ago I was daydreaming about dead schoolgirls coming back to life. I have to pull myself back to reality.

'So, are you married now?'

He shakes his head, neither sad nor happy. 'No. I was

263

with someone until last year, but she wanted children. You can imagine, no doubt, how long it would take me to decide positively I wanted to bring a new life into the world. And you, Tracey?' He nods at the wedding ring. 'How long have you been married?'

'Nine years.' I try to say this as neutrally as possible, but I hear a sourness creeping into my voice. 'I didn't think so hard about kids. I've got a daughter who will be seven in August. And a son who'll be two in September.'

'Perfect. One of each. I can imagine you with a son. And your husband?'

What about him? Is he worthy? Definitely not. Is he what you wanted? Ditto. Would you rather it was someone else? Like the person sitting next to you?

'Dave. He's a builder. Works away a lot.'

There are conversations going on between us that can't be heard, like those dog whistles which are beyond the range of human ears.

'And do you work?'

'Part-time, two half days, in a stationery suppliers' shop. Gets me out of the house, but it's not a career. Then again, I was never really cut out for one of those, was I?'

'I never understood how someone so attractive and confident could have such low expectations, Tracey. If I could have given you anything in return for our relationship, it would have been broader horizons.' Now he does look sad.

'If it's any consolation, I think I might finally be growing up. Though it's taken me seventeen years ...'

'I think the benefits of growing up have been exaggerated over the years. And by having children, you've gone a lot further along those lines than I have, after all.'

'Yup, I am now the original boring conventional Stepford wife. Bet you're glad we never stayed the course ...'

For the first time, he reaches across to me, and touches

me gently on the cheek. When he takes his fingers away, my face feels hot. 'You're none of those things, Tracey. Except original.'

But he hasn't denied feeling relieved that we never ended up together. Then again he said he didn't regret the relationship. But maybe he's being kind.

I have to stop this stupid agonising. 'So, what do you do, Bob? I always worried about how what we did would affect your career.'

He looks at me suspiciously, but then starts to chuckle. And before long, the chuckle transforms itself into a low laugh, and then into full-blown hysteria.

And I find myself joining in. I don't have the faintest idea what it is we're both laughing about, but it's unstoppable, and my stomach aches with the force of it, and I try to get my breath back, but every time I look at his face, it's as red as mine feels from the exertion, and I start again . . .

When we finally get our breath back, we sit in silence for a while, and no matter how hard I try to banish the image from my mind, the flushed camaraderie reminds me overwhelmingly of the moment immediately after we first had sex. And when I finally trust myself to look him in the eye again, I have this strong feeling that he is thinking the same thing.

'So what's the joke?' I ask him, eventually.

'Oh, God, Tracey. It's going to sound so feeble now. The joke is that if it wasn't for you, I'd probably still be here, waiting for Dick Phipps to retire and give me the chance to apply for head of Humanities. But I'm actually better off than I could ever have imagined: I work shorter hours, and I don't have to go anywhere near a classroom.'

Another person whose life I've changed. How weird is this? Suzanne, Gary and now Bob. I seem to have done for people's careers what Carole Smillie's done for their bathrooms. While mine remains resolutely avocado.

'So what is it you do?'

'I work for the government. You couldn't make it up, could you? I have an office near Westminster, and I advise them on how to get people talking to each other, how to get schools working the way they want them to. It's stating the obvious, but for a fat salary.'

This is not making me feel too good. How come everyone else has made it, and I'm sitting here with a grotty husband, two un-designer children, and a life that struggles even to reach the pinnacles of being mundane?

'Good for you.' I say. I don't really mean it.

'None of it's really that satisfying. And I hate the publicity – I used to worry about them finding out. About us, you know ... but it wears off, after a while.'

'I'm surprised you risked coming.'

'Tracey,' he says, staring very deliberately into my eyes. 'I've wanted to come and find you since I left. I really have. And if they find out now, then I wouldn't be ashamed. I think it would almost enhance my reputation. But I don't want you dragged through the mud, which is why I'm going now, before anyone makes the connection.'

Do I believe him? I suppose the fact he came at all is a sign that I meant something to him ... or maybe just the desire of a middle-aged man to revisit the ultimate conquest?

'Yes, probably best for you to get back to the metropolis. Before the tedium starts rubbing off on you.' When he looks hurt, I add, 'Joke!' Even though it's not.

He gets up from the bench, and I want to pull him back, stop him going. For good. 'Tracey, it's not too late. I was only a bit younger than you when I got out of all this. I mean, I didn't want to, but in the end, I could never have been happy here, unless it was with you.' He stops, seems embarrassed. 'Anyway, that's the past. But you can do whatever you like. You always had more balls than me, didn't you?' He punches me on the arm, trying to be light-hearted.

'Yeah, I guess. See you around,' I say, knowing I won't.

He hesitates, then pulls out his wallet. 'This seems very formal, but if you want to get in touch, if I can give you any help, whatever, anything, here's my card.' It's classy parchment paper, embossed with 'Robert Carmichael, Senior Consultant.' He scribbles a mobile number on the back.

'I mean it,' he says and leans across to kiss me on the cheek, and I wonder if this is any more real than when Gary did this in my imagination a few minutes ago ... but this time I do what I wanted to do then, and turn my head slightly so his lips brush against mine. It's as awkward and as thrilling as it was in 1984, and it's over as quickly.

'Whoops,' I say, as if was an accident.

He looks at me, then leans forward again, planting a tiny kiss on my nose, as an indulgent grandfather might to his first granddaughter.

'You've got my number,' Bob says, then turns and walks steadily back towards the school.

I follow him, at a distance of a few paces. We cross the playground, where people are still striding purposefully along with bits of paper and equipment. Alec is shouting at someone who is holding a pile of T-shirts. As we head towards the car park, I spot Andrew the reporter standing next to a BMW, talking into a mobile. Next to it, is an old MG, and I know instantly it must belong to Bob – he was always one for classic cars.

I watch Bob head towards it. He has to squeeze right past Andrew to open the door, interrupting the reporter's phone call. But instead of moving out of the way, Andrew stares at him, then rings off abruptly.

He keeps watching as Bob reverses out of the parking space and drives through the school gates. And the look on Andrew's face – as if he's just worked out something that's been puzzling him for a while – makes me wonder if he's *really* only here to write a feature about nostalgia.

Chapter Thirty

Alec is having a temper tantrum because they've cocked up with the T-shirts he'd ordered.

He'd wanted a hundred with 'TRACEY SAYS REUNITE' across the front and back, Katherine Hamnett-style. Instead, they read 'TRACEY SAYS RELAX', which seems fine to me, better even, but he's a seriously stressed impresario today, so nearly right is not good enough.

'Someone ought to take his Diet Coke away,' I tell Jenny. She reckons we should ignore him. There's plenty around to distract us. The crew for Madness has turned up, and they're running sound checks, doing all kinds of technical things I don't understand, but it looks impressive, and there's a nice rhythm in the way they work that's soothing to watch. They seem to get things done without talking to each other.

Andrew drove off soon after Bob, and I can't get either of them out of my head. What's a London hotshot doing here in the sticks, months before the programme goes out? I mentioned it to Jenny, and she said it was kind of unusual, but maybe he wanted the exclusive, and now I'm thinking, that's exactly what I'm worried about.

It's time to get changed into my dress, and when I take

my jeans off, Bob's card is in the pocket. I stare at it, put it into my handbag, for safe keeping. I can't believe how it's making me feel. What did he say to me? 'It's not too late.'

It's rubbish, really. I mean, it is too late, for me. What am I going to do, leave the kids in Dave's incapable hands, ably unsupported by my mother, while I follow Dick Whittington's path to London? Live in a penthouse apartment with Bob, go to restaurants which cost more for lunch than I spend over a month at the supermarket, and discuss the single currency and illegal immigration with Cherie Blair?

But the Mortimer streak keeps returning, the part of me that loved Bob asking *why* all the time, because it was what I wanted to do, but didn't dare, because that would have been admitting I didn't understand anything much. And the old Tracey wants to know why? Why I can't be living a better life? Why the girls' magazines promising fun and glamour didn't live up to their word, and why they've been replaced by the women's glossies promising success at wiping out germs? Why Suzanne, why Gary, why Bob and why NOT me?

But then there's Boris. And if I'm fighting for life to be fair for everyone who went to Crawley Park, then she's got to be higher on the list of deserving causes than me. Because right now, a surgeon's probably cutting her open to remove another dead baby. And I know a baby's all she really wants. Sure, she's got the money and the house and she's got the husband, who I'm pretty sure from one meeting is too dull to go off shagging the way Dave does. But it's nothing for her, without a little Boris or Brian, someone with another chance to live all the dreams she's been happy to give up on.

And while I think of it, there's Shrimp.

So instead of envying Gary and Suzanne, not to mention

Cherie and Tony, maybe the question I should be asking is why Shrimp, why Boris, why NOT me?

'Bet you were a right goody-two shoes at school,' said Gabby.

'Just shows how little you know me,' Gary said, hitting his indicator and moving into the fast lane.

'Don't tell me, you were actually a rebel without a cause, were you, terrifying the poor residents of Bracewell with your gangland threats? Somehow I can't see it, Gary.'

'Let's just say I haven't always been on the right side of the law.'

'You're not saying you once stole a pencil sharpener from the newsagent, are you? Or – hang on – maybe you wrote rude remarks about one of the teachers in the boys' toilets.'

'You're just so funny, aren't you?'

'Go on, Gary, tell me. I like the idea of you being a wild child,' she said, moving her hand across to his knee, and then up towards his groin. 'It's so sexy ...'

'You keep your hands to yourself, madam. There's nothing sexy about a conviction for dangerous driving.'

'You see, you're too bloody sensible. I can't believe you've ever done anything illegal.'

'Not even twocking then?'

'Nicking a car? I don't think so,' she laughed, but Gary didn't. He kept his eyes straight ahead at the road. 'Gary? You are joking, right?'

'And what if I'm not? Does that make me so much cooler all of a sudden?'

'Well ... if you want an honest answer, then ... yes. It makes you more ... rounded, as a person.'

'So by that logic, if I'd been done for GBH I would have been chat show material? Grow up, Gabby.'

'Ooh, sense of humour failure or what? It's just really interesting, with you being in the Met, I assumed you'd been part of the establishment all your life.'

Gary groaned.

'Come on, Gary. I'm not taking the piss or anything. Plus there's more street cred for me as a social worker to have an ex-con as a boyfriend than a copper, you've got to admit it.'

He steered the car carefully back into the middle lane. 'I wasn't convicted, actually. Sorry if that disappoints you.'

'You're going to have to tell me the details, now, mate.'

'What's it worth?'

Gabby moved her hand back towards his groin. 'Are we talking sexual favours?'

'Might be . . .'

'I'll give you a blow job at the hotel . . .'

Gary sighed. 'OK . . . you win.'

'You drive such a hard bargain, Gary. Go on, then, spill . . .'

'Right. Well, I took a car, I drove it around the estate, not all that quickly, got caught, got taken in for questioning, got a few thumps from my dad, disappointed looks from my mum, and then a few days worrying about what was going to happen. And then, I got cautioned.'

'Is that it?'

'Sorry I didn't end up in Strangeways, but, yeah. That's it. And don't think you can get away with backing out of the blow job.'

'How old were you?'

'Sixteen. Which was also handy, because the Met were willing to overlook a little . . . youthful misbehaviour.'

'I bet the owner didn't see it like that.'

'No, well, actually he was pretty determined that the police shouldn't press charges.'

272

'You knew him, then?'

For the first time, Gary looked embarrassed. 'Yeah, as it happens. The car was my form teacher's.'

Melody never could keep a secret, and when Tracey refused to give her the lowdown on the night of passion at Mr Carmichael's house, it was only a matter of time.

But how? If there was one thing Melody liked more than sex, it was attention, and the best place to get maximum attention was surely morning assembly. So she waited until Bob, as head of year, was explaining the arrangements for the 'O' level revision sessions, before whispering in Gary's ear, 'You wanna know why Tracey doesn't fancy you no more?'

Gary's answer – 'Eh?' – wasn't exactly what she'd been expecting, so she assumed he hadn't heard her properly.

'I said ... don't you wanna know why Tracey's gone off you?'

Gary hadn't even realised she had. 'What?'

Melody was losing patience. 'It's because ...' she started, and this time it was loud enough for everyone in the front two rows to hear, 'she's fucking HIM.' She was pointing towards the stage.

In the few seconds that followed, big things changed. Tracey realised her best friend was definitely not to be trusted. Bob realised his teaching career was over. And Gary realised that nice guys came last.

No more Mr Nice Guy.

He leaped up on to the stage, and the apologetic expression on his teacher's face told him all he needed to know. Gary broke his nose with a single punch. As the noise in the hall rose to such a pitch that even the head teacher came out to find out what was happening, Gary ran from the school hall, found the red Triumph Herald in the car park, and finally put into practice the hot-wiring skills his older brother had been trying to pass down for the last three years.

He did three circuits of the estate, and then, in front of most of the fifth year, he drove Mr Carmichael's Triumph slowly, but surely, into the school gates.

Andrew walked up the path to Suzanne's mother's house. Bees buzzed around the geraniums which filled half a dozen hanging baskets. When he rang the doorbell, it played 'Home, sweet home'.

Suzanne answered the door, and showed him into the front room, which was obviously only ever used for visitors. It was as quiet as a library.

'It's Bob Carmichael, isn't it? Your classmate was shagging him?'

It was almost a relief that he'd guessed, rather than Suzanne having to spell it out. It made her feel less responsible. She nodded. 'You're not as stupid as you look, Andrew.'

'He was there, you know.'

She looked surprised. 'What, this afternoon?'

'Why, had you planned for him to turn up later and be on camera, too? You're a bit of a snide bitch on the side, aren't you?'

'No, I didn't –'

'Oh, don't worry, I mean it as a term of endearment. It's good stuff, just like you promised. And I'll deliver, too. No name, no pack drill.' He sat down in the carvery chair at the head of the table. 'And you're sure no one else is on to this?'

Suzanne sat down next to him, her chair creaking. 'How could they know? It was all hushed up at school, lots of rumours but nothing concrete. Only a few of us knew, for sure, because we talked to the police.'

'It gets better.'

She glared at him. 'Don't get too excited. There was nothing against him, she wasn't underage when it started, or if she was, they couldn't prove it. And she was hardly a virgin by the time he got in there.'

'Bob Carmichael, though, eh? The rumour was that he was gay, not a child molester.'

'Yes, well. Congratulations on being so quick on the uptake. You won't be wanting tea, will you, you'd better get back to London so you can write your piece?'

'Anyone would think you're trying to get rid of me.'

'We had our deal, and I don't really want you here, Andrew.'

He grasped the chair arms with his neatly manicured hands, and relaxed back into the seat. 'My, my, we're not feeling very friendly now, are we? What did she do to you, eh, Suzanne? Or was it him? What did they do that made you want revenge so badly? Because you're so right-on, aren't you? You've staked out the moral high ground, with your charity, but this isn't exactly whiter than white.'

'I'm not interested in your clever-dick analysis, Andrew. You've got your story, and now I'd like you to leave.'

He raised his arms behind his back, yawned, then stretched out like a cat. 'Yeah, sure, OK. You've got your reasons. People always do, or I wouldn't be in business, would I?'

Suzanne stood up, folding her arms in front of her chest, then immediately unfolding them when she caught a glimpse of herself in the mantel mirror, and realised how much she looked like her mother. Andrew walked ahead of her, back towards the front door, and then on to the gravel pathway.

'See you later,' he said, grinning.

'What do you mean?'

'Well, I wouldn't tell you how to do your job, so I'm sure you won't tell me how to do mine. But it's important when you're looking into a story to make sure you get both sides. One of the first things they taught me in journalism training. And, as I know exactly where Tracey is going to be later on, it would be silly to waste the opportunity to strike while the iron's hot.'

'But you don't have to do it tonight ... I mean, you promised –'

'To keep you out of it? Yes, of course. I will. But I've got to check it all out, and you shouldn't exactly be surprised if it gets messy. I mean, that must be what you wanted all along?'

He waved at her, then headed back to his BMW, leaving Suzanne standing in the doorway, wondering what she'd started.

Chapter Thirty-One

'You know the routine, Trace,' says Cliff, sticking his hand down my bra without ceremony. 'Hey, this might be the last time we're ever this close.'

'Oh, shame,' I say. Cliff is so staggeringly unsexy that having him groping around in my cleavage doesn't bother me at all.

'This radio mike's smarter, because it's got a switch,' he says, clipping the microphone just under the neck of my leather dress. 'If you remember to flick it off, we won't have to listen to you going for a pee.'

Attaching the radio transmitter thing to my expensive designer outfit is more difficult, until Cliff sticks it to the small of my back using that extra thick black masking tape they carry round for these occasions. And, presumably, for impromptu bondage sessions. Cliff looks like the type. Though Jamie wouldn't need to tie me up.

Bob appearing like that has clearly unleashed even more hormones.

Alec comes into the dressing room. The same dressing room where I fought thirty other girls for space by the mirror to apply my Egyptian kohl when I played Joseph's wife.

'Can't you do better than that?' he says, pointing at the

microphone box. It doesn't look brilliant, I must admit, makes my back look slightly deformed, but I can't see an alternative.

'Where else are we meant to put it?' Jamie says. 'No, seriously, Alec, I bow to your superior brain and salary. Tell me where to stick it, and I will.'

Jenny and I wait for Alec to reply. He opens and shuts his mouth like a fish, but nothing comes out. It reminds me of when I confronted them all at the Crown. There is nowhere else to put the box, and for once, he's been shown up for what he is. Someone who likes dishing it out, but can't take it himself.

Eventually, Alec points at the Adam Ant jacket hanging on a chair. 'Just make sure she wears that most of the time,' he says to Jenny before he struts out of the room. He doesn't even bother to talk to me anymore.

'Who's she, the cat's mother?' I say, even though it would be much more dignified to ignore him.

The worst bit, when you're throwing a party, is the time before everyone arrives. And this time of course, it's even more of a nightmare, because I've had no control of the guest list or the music or the venue. And yet I'm supposed to be entertaining. That's the contract, that's why they chose me to do the bloody thing, and that's why Jamie and the boys are going to be following me round like ducklings who're convinced I'm their mother.

'I bet you're nervous,' Jenny says. I feel sorry for her. It can't be easy being piggy in the middle between me, and Annabel and Alec. The gruesome twosome. They deserve each other, but you can tell that they'll be so much more successful than poor Jen, who's burdened with far too many scruples.

'Yeah . . . I suppose I am.'

'Mummy!' I turn round and there's my family, followed

by Annabel. Kelly runs up to me, she's wearing one of the 'Tracey says Relax' T-shirts, even though it's so big that it trails round her ankles. 'You look lovely, Mummy.'

Brenda's given me another going over with the foundation, so thick this time that it wouldn't have disgraced Barbara Cartland, and I do look nice, in an actressy way. And I think that's the way I have to look at it tonight: I'm going on stage, playing a part, in return for the dress and the party and all the other things I don't really want.

Dave's wearing a Mod-style suit with a skinny tie, and he's eyeing me up like I'm one of the Dublin girls he's hoping to shag after a night on the beer. And I suppose I look the type, except I'm wearing real leather, not the cheap plastic stuff that makes you sweat really badly. I'm not slagging them off, it's only what I used to do every Saturday night, and Dave's still a prize. Rich enough to buy all the drinks, good-looking enough to maintain a girl's status in the pulling pecking order, and confident enough to suggest that sex would be better than the average fumble. His technique wouldn't disappoint them, either, I'll grant him that.

'Scrub up well, you do, Tracey,' he says, as though this is a compliment.

Only Callum is holding back. 'Come here, Cal,' I say, and he recoils as though I've hit him. 'It's Mummy, come on, love, nothing to be scared of,' and I crouch down, reaching out my hand. He turns his face away, but recognises my leg and races forward to grab it. I hope he's not going to turn into a shy kid. Don't think I could cope with two like Kelly.

'It's looking amazing out there,' Dave says. 'Like a proper gig. Racks of big lights and everything.' He's as much of a kid as Callum, but right now that doesn't make him any more appealing.

'Yeah. I'm sure they'll let you bang on the drums, too,

279

if you ask them nicely.' I smile at him, and he really can't tell if I'm being sweet or sarcastic.

'People should start arriving soon,' Annabel says.

In under half an hour, in fact. It's 6.34. Who are the people she's talking about? I've got no idea who's coming, except the devious Andrew, and probably Melody and Dick Phipps. If only Boris was here, I could ask her for some clues.

If only Boris was here.

'Time to get out there,' Jenny says. 'The longer you sit worrying, the worse it's going to get. The only way to deal with nerves is to face them head on.'

She's probably right. So, with Jamie behind us, I lead the brood out into the arena, like a scaled-down version of the Von Trapp Family Singers ... I've been in the dressing room for a good hour, and even in that time, the transformation in the hall is enough to make me blink.

They've turned the space into a real disco. Dave was right about the lights – they've taken the lamps that were already there, and added dozens more, mounted on tall scaffolding towers. There are pools of coloured light falling on the stage, on shifting areas of the floor, and then a whole set of screens at the opposite end of the hall which seem to be lit from within.

As we step in the centre of the empty parquet dance floor, the speakers start to buzz, as though we've triggered some kind of invisible switch, and I recognise the first notes of the first song ... I look at Dave and realise he does, too.

Kelly clamps her hands to her ears. 'Ugh, Mummy, it's too loud, it's too loud.'

'Don't be daft, Kelly,' Dave shouts over the top of the opening rhythms, and she looks at him, shocked at the uncharacteristic knock-back. 'So, Tracey, d'ya wanna dance?'

And to the astonishment of our children, who I hate to admit have probably never seen us embrace, we start circling round each other to the sound of Cyndi Lauper.

Girls just wanna have fun . . .

Dave grabs me by the waist and we dance and something about the way the music is pounding from the speakers, gets into my head and my body and I can't help myself . . .

Just wanna . . .

I'm heading back towards the old days and the old feelings. The sensations from the beat and the light and even, I'm surprised to notice, from my husband's fingers pressing against my flesh through the leather, are making it real . . .

The DJ mixes from Cyndi into 'Feels like Heaven'. Dave and I pull apart and we're both flushed and embarrassed. We've created the two kids who're watching us suspiciously from the edge of the hall, and yet a couple of minutes of teenage fondling has deprived us of the power of speech.

'Look, Mummy,' Kelly calls above the music, pointing towards the screens at the end of the hall.

The blank white spaces have been replaced by projected images, which keep changing, and it takes me a moment to realise that it's pictures of us . . . of me, and Gary, and Boris, and all the others . . . they've blown them up so when I go and stand next to them, they're bigger than life-size, and slightly fuzzy, but then so are the memories . . .

'That's your mummy,' Dave says, lifting Callum up so he can touch my foot-long nose. 'Isn't she pretty?'

I'm drawn into the pictures, looking for something I can't place in my teenage face . . . what was it that made me so certain that life was mine for the taking? It wasn't innocence, I'd sussed out how the world worked well before I arrived at Crawley Park. And it wasn't confidence, because I've still got plenty of that . . . Maybe I just felt safe in the knowledge that whatever happened, I could take control, exactly as I had taken control of Class 1G.

There are pictures there I don't recognise – Boris must have organised a trawl around everyone who's coming. Shrimp and I on the ferry to Calais, flaunting our daring 'flick combs' that we were convinced were as cool as banned flick knives – until you pressed the switch, and revealed you were in possession of an illegal styling device. Half a dozen girls, me and Melody at the centre, doing the can-can – we must be in the third year then, judging from the haircuts. And one of me and Gary on the bench at the back – the same bench I imagined us all on a few hours ago – seconds away from a snog . . .

'I hope he's not coming, whoever he is,' Dave says. 'Might have to deck him for getting there first.'

He really is a dickhead, but he means well. All this Memory Lane stuff is obviously turning me into a big softy, because I don't feel angry with him. I feel sorry for him.

'I don't think there's any danger of him coming, Dave. So you'll have no reason to defend my honour!'

Jenny appears from the car park. 'You like the display, then? We thought you would! The one of you and Gary is priceless.'

'I wasn't bad, was I?'

She shakes her head. 'Don't go all maudlin on us already . . . you're not bad now, either. Have you seen the way the sound guys are ogling you in that dress? It's nothing to do with age, Tracey, you've either got it or you ain't – and you definitely have.'

Did I say before that I'm starting to like Jenny?

'Anyway, I didn't come in here to boost your ego. Your first guests are arriving, so you ought to come and meet them.'

It's real, now, no more kidding myself that this is just a family party on a slightly bigger scale. I follow her out into the car park, and I'm aware of Jamie and Cliff right behind me. The sunlight is a shock, and it takes my eyes a while to adjust to the row of people – five, no, four, standing just outside the doors.

Jenny sees this, and buys me some time. 'Now then, not all of this lot were actually in your year, so you are excused if you don't remember all of them.'

The man furthest away from me immediately makes me uneasy. He's more familiar than the others, but I can't work out why. Just occasionally, you see someone you recognise, and even though you can't remember who they are, you feel an overwhelming emotion associated with them – whether it's laughter or misery or humiliation.

With him, I feel guilt.

'OK, you guys, looks like you're going to have to give Tracey a clue.'

The first one steps forward. A plump guy, dressed for the occasion in a frilly New Romantic shirt (at least I hope that's why he's wearing it), with the first hints of a receding hairline. 'Tracey – it's Bodger – from your Maths set? Remember?'

Oh yes, Bodger Lewis, the guy who never got anything right. He hasn't changed that much, looking at him. Maths was my worst subject, and so it was only in that set that I ever came into contact with the real low-life of Crawley Park. The people destined for the custard cream factory.

'And this is my missus, Angela,' he says, proudly dragging forward a girl with long mousy hair. 'You wouldn't have known her, she was still at primary when we left. Bit of a looker, eh?'

'Hi,' I say, dredging up some enthusiasm. They look well-suited, anyway; neither has any obvious signs of a personality.

283

The next girl in line doesn't look familiar, either. 'Tracey, well done for getting this going – it's brilliant. Maybe we should do a quick chorus of "Joseph" while we're at it, do you think?' She seems slightly irritated that I don't rush forward to hug her, but I've just realised who the last guy is, and the blood is rushing to my head. 'I'm Kathy, I was a sheaf of corn, along with Melody. Great laugh, eh? I gave them some photos to use as well, of the performance.'

'Lovely,' I say. The last bloke is waiting his turn, and I'm taking in his height and his thin legs in the drainpipe trousers and the cliff edges that form his cheekbones.

'And I'm –'

'I know who you are,' I say, quietly. 'You're Ricky. You're Shrimp's brother.'

Chapter Thirty-Two

I hate Shrimp. I hate her bike. I hate the way she reckons she's better than me now she's got it, when everyone knows she's poor and she lives in a smelly house and she needs me to make anyone even want to talk to her or be her friend. But she's acting like I'm the sad one.

It's only because she's got all those brothers and sisters; my mum says her mum and dad breed like rabbits, and someone should cut his bits off to stop them having any more. Mum never wanted any more after me, she says. Sometimes I think that's a good thing, perhaps it's because she thinks I'm the best, how could she get a nicer daughter than me? And sometimes I wonder if I'm so awful that that's why she didn't want any more. Actually, she says that herself sometimes when she gets angry.

Not that she could have any more anyway, because Dad left her when I was a baby. She says sometimes that that's my fault, too.

'Tracey Mortimer, are you with us, or are you with the Woolwich?' That wanker Phipps thinks he's so funny, but he doesn't know that we all call him Fister because he lives at home with his mother, so we all know he's queer, and in one of Gary's brother's magazines that he found in the shed on the allotments during the holidays, there was a picture of men fisting, and it was so disgusting that we thought only horrible people would do it, and then someone said Phipps sounded a bit like Fist and it was better than the old nickname we had for him, which was Pipsqueak.

'Yes, sir.'

'Well, that's excellent, Miss Mortimer. So perhaps you'd like to take us through the differences between sedimentary and igneous rock?'

I can't see the point of Geography, apart from maps and capital cities. That's kind of useful, but the rest is just invented by people like Fister to justify us having to have two lessons a week of it. Most of school is pointless, except Home Ec. is nice; last week we made a mixed grill, and some of the boys didn't even know how to use it, and their sausages were so burned that they looked like turds and would have tasted like them too, except then I nicked some from Suzanne Sharp, for Gary and Briggsy, and she knew what happened but she didn't dare tell.

'Not sure, sir.'

'Would anyone like to enlighten Miss Mortimer?'

Oh, and there she goes, Suzanne Sharp shoving her hand in the air. Hee hee, I wonder if she'd fist Fister, in return for extra lessons. She's even more annoying this year because she's got a bra, nothing to put in it, hardly, it's a double A, we hid it in the changing rooms, under the showers, and she had to go without all day because it was too wet to wear.

But my mum won't get me a bra. Cow. And I'll need one soon.

Don't suppose Shrimp will, ever. Her mum's got no tits, and neither has her sister Debbie, who's fourteen.

She's next to me and it's really hard not to give her the look we always give each other when Suzanne is spouting in lessons . . . we developed it in the first week of the first year, and it involves raising your eyebrows, crossing your eyes in a mad squint, flaring your nostrils and curling up your lips. It's harder than it looks.

But we're not speaking, and that even rules out taking the piss out of Spazzy Suzanne.

It'll blow over, but she's being really stubborn this time. It started at morning break because I wanted to sit round the back where Gary was, but she said it was boring and I said she was boring and she said I was obsessed with lads and didn't care what she wanted and if I was that bothered, then maybe Gary should be my best mate, not her.

Or something like that.

And I said – I didn't really mean it – that he'd be a better best mate, because at least he's not a skinny minny, or too broke to be any fun.

I said it because I knew it would hurt her feelings. I get that sometimes; I know exactly what's going to upset people the most, and I just say it, and I quite like it when they react . . . But then after that I feel really, really bad. Not about Suzanne or the teachers, they know they're winding me up, and they could stop if they really wanted, but with my friends and my mum, I feel mean.

It's said now, anyway, and she's obviously in a right mood because she lasted not even looking at me all through French; and then, dinner time, I had to go and hang about with Melody and the others, and she just sat there very quietly eating her chips and gravy (she always eats that, it must get so boring) and then she went to the *library* till the bell rang.

And then there was registration and Maths, and now it's double Geography, and then hometime. Usually we walk out together to where the road splits, but I'm pretty sure she's going to keep up the bad mood until tomorrow, try to make me feel guilty.

Well, she can suit herself. She'll come running back tomorrow. We're best mates. She's just not going to find anyone else who knows her like I do.

'Hello, Tracey,' Ricky says. He always looked more like Shrimp than her other brothers and sister, so seeing him gives me the creeps. It's like coming face to face with what she might have been if she'd had the chance to grow up. And it's nearly twenty years since I've seen him.

'Um, Bodger, Kathy? Shall I show you where the cloakroom is?' Jenny comes to my rescue, yet again, and I wonder how much she knows. They follow her into the building, and Ricky and I face each other, awkward.

'Why have you come?' I ask, eventually.

I know what I think he's come for. He's come to go over it again, to watch me squirm as he repeats all the reasons why it's my fault. But he doesn't know that there's no need – that I remember every word he said the last time. At Shrimp's funeral.

He starts walking, and so do I, and then I remember the crew behind me. I turn to Jamie, look straight at him. 'Give me a bit of space, guys ... please?'

To my surprise, Jamie nods, and then stops walking. Maybe he still feels bad about Gary and the Crown Affair.

Ricky and I walk until we reach the start of the playground. I wonder if Shrimp would have been quite this tall? He's well over six foot, and if anyone ever deserved the label, 'lanky streak of piss', it's him. He's got a wedding ring on one spaghetti finger. We all succumb in the end.

'Boris invited me.'

Boris. The images of surgeons and knives and blood and blue babies drift back into my head and I shake it, as though that'll send them away, like it does water from your ears when you've been swimming. All it does is

288

remind me that last night's hangover still hasn't gone.

'She invited lots of people,' I say and nod back towards the car park, which is starting to fill up. 'It still doesn't explain why you've come.'

'Because Boris thought I oughta ... that there are things that oughta be said.'

'I doubt that.' It had all been fine, Shrimp's funeral. Well, as fine as it can be when it's the funeral of an eleven-year-old girl knocked off her bike as she cycled home from school. When that girl was your best friend, who you thought would live for ever, just like you, and when you know that the last words you spoke to her were 'I don't want you as my best mate, anyway, you're ugly, skinny, and you've never got any money, anyway. So we can't have any fun because you're TOO POOR!'

It's bad enough carrying that around with you while you wait for the news, and hope that there's something the hospital can do, and then it sinks in that there's going to be no miracle recovery, no medical history made, just another statistic ...

But then you go to her house before the funeral, and you see her, or rather, her body in the coffin, and despite your fears, she looks more peaceful than she ever did when she was alive, because she was always fidgeting, Shrimp was, as if she knew she had only a limited amount of time and a lot of activity to get through.

And the funeral's grim, and there's loads of tears, but it's comforting somehow, all that ritual. Incense, altar boys, and more crying. And then when they take you back to their house for the wake, and it's wrong to be there without Shrimp, and the aunts and the cousins are talking to me about how lovely it is to have a best friend, and how brave of me to come, but time will heal, there'll be other best friends, though you'll never forget Louise ...

And then Ricky appears and starts pointing. 'What are

you doing here? It's YOUR bloody fault, they said at school that you and her had a row that day, and she was always careful on her bike, so it must have been YOUR bloody fault and you should have seen her with her head caved in, she wasn't Lou any more, even before they switched her machine off and it's YOUR bloody fault and you should know that and bloody live with it for the whole of the rest of your life and even then it won't be long enough because it's YOUR bloody fault she's dead.'

So I can't see what there could have been left unsaid.

Ricky raises one eyebrow, the way Shrimp used to, when she was trying to work out something really tricky. 'No, no, I think you need to listen to me, Tracey.'

'I know what I did, Ricky. You can't make me feel any worse than I did then, and I still feel the same – like, there are photos of me and Shrimp ... Louise as part of the display they've set up, and when I saw it, yeah, I felt it bad over again. And I'm sorry. So if that's all you wanted-'

He puts his hands up to stop me. 'You're wrong, Tracey. I wanted to say sorry to you.'

'What?'

'It was nobody's bloody fault, Tracey.'

'You don't mean that. We both know that if I hadn't –'

'She always used to go on about how no one could get a bloody word in edgeways with you, Tracey Mortimer.'

I look at him, trying to work out why he's smiling. It doesn't make sense. 'OK.'

'Tracey, we were kids. Kids say stuff they don't mean.'

I nod. That's what got poor Shrimp killed – me saying things I didn't mean. What did they say in the war? *Careless talk costs lives.*

He smiles again. 'It's easier to blame someone. Especially when you're young. You know.' Ricky seems to be struggling, but I bite my lip to stop myself butting in. 'I did think it was your fault, for … I don't know, maybe a couple of months. But Dad kept telling me, over and over, it was a bloody accident.'

I stare at his lips, watching them form the words I suppose I've always wanted to hear, but unable to believe it's Ricky Shrimpton saying them.

'And he was right, Tracey. Lou died in an accident. Maybe she was in a mood because you'd had a row. But then again, she might have been wondering what she was having for tea, or what bloody single to buy.'

'Don't Stand So Close To Me'. That's what single she was going to buy, with her birthday money from her grandparents. We'd been talking about it all week.

'You move on, Tracey. We all did. I feel crap every time I remember I haven't thought about her for a few days. Don't bring her back, though.'

'No,' is all I can say.

'When Boris came to see me, I was gobsmacked. I was, that you were still thinking it was your bloody fault. It's been twenty bloody years. But then I had a think about how I feel crap when *I* forget her – and, well, it don't seem so daft.'

And despite the make-up I can feel weighing down my skin, I start to cry, and Ricky walks right up to me, and hugs me so tight I can feel his ribs through his shirt.

'I came for Lou, Tracey, I came to tell you that it wasn't your bloody fault. And that she'd be well pissed off that you was still thinking it was.'

This crying business is starting to become a habit, but for the first time, it makes me feel better.

Chapter Thirty-Three

I try to convince him, but Ricky doesn't want to stick around. He's got to meet his partner down the pub, and he says she went to Bracewell High School, our deadly rival, so she wouldn't be seen dead here, even now. But I think it's because staying here is too much of a reminder of what Shrimp should have been.

I won't have any guests, the rate I keep sending them away.

As I head back towards the hall, I'm surprised that Jamie and Cliff are still there, facing me, but after what happened at the Crown, surely they wouldn't have been filming me. Would they?

I walk right into Briggsy.

'Tracey Mortimer!' he says, as though he's surprised. Dopey bastard, it is my reunion, after all.

'Gavin Briggs!' We perform a stage hug. 'I could say you haven't changed a bit, but you're fatter and uglier.'

'Yeah, and you're still an old dog.'

We've always talked to each other like this. It's a sign of affection.

I lead him through to the bar area they've set up behind the water feature in the school reception – a distinct improvement over the usual displays of dodgy pottery by fourteen-year-olds.

'The booze is on me . . . the bar's free till nine o'clock!' It's the first time I've had a drink since last night, and I feel slightly sick at the thought, but then I think it might be the best thing to calm my nerves. So I order a double G and T and get a bottle of Bud for Briggsy.

'So,' I say, as we walk back into the hall, which now has about a dozen people in there, a few of whom I vaguely recognise. They're playing 'Oh what a night', which is hardly an 80s track, but I think they played it at School Disco, too. In keeping with tradition, all the guests are clinging to the wall like houseflies. The free bar should fix that before long . . .

'So,' he says. I was lying before about him looking different. Actually, he looks pretty much the same as he always did, though the stubble on his face suggests he finally does have a real need to shave every day. Even in the fifth year, his chin had only the slightest hint of fluff, however hard he tried to coax the bristles with razors he nicked from Superdrug.

He was a slow developer, bless him, Robin to Gary's Batman. It works that way, doesn't it? A good-looking one to pull in the opposite sex, and then a nice or clever or funny one to keep them there. When I first met Dave, he had a sidekick called Trev, and, I guess I already knew, aged eleven, that Shrimp would be perfect as mine. Perhaps that's why Melody and me were never going to work. We were always competing, and maybe the friendship thing only works if you know instinctively who's top dog . . .

'It's been a darned long time, Briggsy . . . but it's good to have you back. What are you up to these days?'

'Engineering foreman.' He looks proud, and I guess he should be.

'Foreman, eh? I thought you'd never work again once

the YTS stopped paying your wages.'

'Yeah, well. I heard that the only reason you kept your job was cos you nobbed the boss every payday ...'

'Found anyone desperate enough to nob YOU, yet?'

He holds up his ring finger. 'Yeah, and she married me too.'

'I'm really surprised they let you go dating at the school for the blind, mate.'

'And which guy did you snare?'

'He's ...' I look around but I can't see him anywhere. Which is annoying, because from a distance, with the light behind him, and if you don't actually have the misfortune to have a conversation with him, he looks like a good choice of husband ' ...here, but he must have taken the kids to the loo, or something.'

'Kids, too? You don't scrub up too bad, considering ...'

It's the nearest to a compliment he's ever given me, and makes me feel all warm inside, and a bit embarrassed. 'Awwww ... you don't mean it?'

'Yeah, I do. Though I always preferred the younger model myself ...' And then he tails off ...

'What?'

'Um ... well, looks like Gary does, too ...'

And I turn round, and there's Gary and this stunning woman. Five ten tall, easy, and she's not even wearing heels. This must be Gabby.

Gary sees me too, and shuffles forward, with Gabby trailing behind. Finally, when he's close enough to me to talk, but still out of punching range, he says, 'Hi. Hope you don't mind me coming. But Boris said it wouldn't be the same without all the old gang ...'

Annabel cornered Dave and the kids on the grassy bank near the cricket nets. The light was fading, so it was only

Kelly's T-shirt that made them visible.

'Hello, you three, wondered where you'd got to ... I was looking for Tracey actually.'

'Haven't seen her,' said Dave, without looking round. He was smoking a cigarette and holding a pint in the other hand. 'If you find her, tell her it must be her turn to watch the kids for a bit.'

'OK,' Annabel said, vowing yet again never to have children. Men were so lazy. 'By the way, have you ever met Suzanne, she was in Tracey's class? And this is her husband, Christian.'

Dave finally turned to see a stylish couple hovering behind Annabel. 'Nice to meet you,' he mumbled unconvincingly. 'I'm Dave, Tracey's house husband.'

Christian laughed too loudly, like a privately educated donkey. 'Excellent. I'm Suzanne's toyboy, but one day, I might get promotion to be her house husband too!'

'I don't think Dave's serious, darling,' said Suzanne, walking over to where the children were playing with grass. 'Are you Kelly? I used to know your mummy when she was a little girl ... I'm Suzanne.'

Kelly gave her a suspicious look. 'Don't bother with her, she's very awkward with strangers,' Dave said. 'You'll get more out of Callum and he can't even talk properly yet.'

Suzanne ignored them. 'That's a pretty daisy chain, Kelly. Would you show me how to make one?'

'Ah, well, if Suzanne can't get anything out of her, no one can,' said Christian. 'Bit of a speciality of hers. She runs a whole charity for children with problems, bullying and what not. Though when we get round to it, ours will be supremely well adjusted, won't they, darling?'

Dave shrugged. 'Well, me and Tracey aren't exactly backward at coming forward, but it hasn't stopped Kelly being a nervous wreck. We've even had a shrink in to talk to her, but she still won't say boo to a goose.'

'Oh, for God's sake!' Suzanne turned on him. 'It's hardly surprising she's like that if you talk about her as though she isn't here. Hasn't it occurred to you that some children are just quieter than others? It's not a crime.'

'Temper, temper,' Dave said. 'Not setting a very good example yourself, are you?'

Suzanne tossed her hair in irritation. 'I know it's not easy being a parent, but Kelly needs your support.'

'She needs to toughen up a bit. Or she'll always be miserable.'

'Maybe I could talk to her . . .'

Christian leaned across to touch her arm. 'Always on duty, eh, darling? We're at a party, let's just leave it for now.'

'No, fine,' Dave said. 'I'd love to see what you can do in ten minutes when we've been bringing her up for nearly seven years . . . and while you're at it, why don't you take Callum too? Then I can go and get pissed. When you've finished, you'll probably find me propping up the bar. Which is all you think the likes of us are fit for, isn't it?'

And before they could answer, he started walking back towards the school building.

I don't know where to look. Gabby's entered into the spirit of the reunion with a tiny pleated skirt, which skims the very top of her cellulite-free thighs, and a tight white shirt tied Britney-style at her waist, revealing a belly-button ring, which is the only bulge on her otherwise flat stomach. Her blouse also shows off her cleavage – her breasts are smaller than mine, but she hasn't got a bra on and they still bob happily along without any help. Mine rest on the bottom of my ribcage, unless I enlist the help of underwires . . .

'So what do you do, Gabby?' I ask her on our way back

from the bar. She's drinking fizzy water because she's driving.

'I'm a social worker – child protection.'

Bloody hell, a do-gooder as well as a supermodel look-alike. Haven't you done well, Gary?

'That must be stressful.' I can see why he wasn't too impressed at meeting me now, and it makes me feel better and worse at the same time. Better because there wouldn't have been much I could have done to tempt him away from this goddess. Worse because ... well, I used to be the one who could get any man she chose. And I chose Dave.

'Well, yeah, but I'm an adrenalin junkie, and it has its fringe benefits.' She looks over her shoulder at Gary. 'Like the hunky policemen we get to meet ...'

'Right ...' Gary and Briggsy catch us up as we enter the school hall. Now they're playing 'Venus' which every 80s schoolgirl knows actually has to be sung as follows:

I'm your penis, I'm your bra-a, your desire!

I'm about to sing it to Gabby, but then I do a quick sum in my mind, work out she was barely walking when the song came out, and decide not to bother.

'Shit, is that Nigel?' Briggsy says, pointing to a bulky guy strutting his stuff in one of the spotlights. 'NIGEL!' He shouts across the dance floor, and goes running over there, joining in. They're worse than a couple of embarrassing middle-aged dads trying to look cool at the PTA disco. Not that I know, of course, as I never saw my dad dance. I bet he would have been good, though. I must have got it from somewhere.

Gabby runs after him, and I'm relieved to see that she dances almost as badly as Nigel and Briggsy. The goddess has a flaw. But she's also sensitive – I realise that she's probably left Gary and me alone deliberately. Say what you like about do-gooders, but they've got hearts of gold.

'Thanks for coming.'

'No, well, no . . . thank Boris. She talked me into it. I –'

Boris to the rescue again.

'Gary, I know it's a bit late . . .' I cringe as I say it, but I also know it has to be said. ' . . . but I owe you an apology. For what happened. For dumping you for Bob . . .'

He looks down at me, and shrugs. I can't believe he's a bloody policeman, to me he's no different from the wet-behind-the-ears sixteen-year-old who was genuinely shocked the first time I suggested giving him a blow job. Not for long, mind you. They learn fast not to look a gift horse in the mouth.

He watches the lads on the dance floor, then looks back at me and shrugs again. 'It's OK, you know . . . I was upset, yeah, course I was. And . . . what I said and every-thing, in the pub. It wasn't on, to come out with all that. Should have said it there and then, when we were sixteen, not bottle it up. My mum always said bottling it up is stupid. Sorry.'

He leans over and kisses me on the cheek. And it's weird, but I know that, as far as Gary's concerned, that is that. Seventeen years of heartache and agonising and envy and bitterness, not to mention a touch of joy-riding. All finito.

The song finishes, and the others come back, casting slightly nervous glances at us, then relaxing when they see us grinning.

'Things are really hotting up here at the great Crawley Park reunion,' says the DJ. 'And it's not long to wait now till the highlight of the night – hang on to your baggy trousers because in less than half an hour, I'll be making way for absolute . . . MADNESS!'

There's a loud cheer, and I realise how many guests are actually here – I count seventy or eighty altogether . . .

Now the group around me keeps growing, people are coming up and chatting ... Steve the plumber, Shazza the midwife, Colin the security guard, Rachel the aerobics instructor, Darren the postman ...

It's kind of fun, all these faces from the past popping up and repeating the same false compliments – you haven't changed a bit, it's brilliant what you've done to get this sorted, you can't have had two kids and still look that good – so that by the end you're almost believing it.

And then someone appears to shatter the whole bloody thing.

Dave the builder.

But where are the kids?

Chapter Thirty-Four

'Where the fuck are the kids?' I scream at Dave.

'Oh you're all right, Trace,' he slurs, and I want to hit him. 'They're in good hands. Better hands than ours, according to your mate. I've left them with the perfect parents – Christian and Suzanne ...'

'Suzanne?'

He takes a swig of lager. 'You were at school with her. Stuck-up bitch with ginger hair. Reckons we've messed up with Kelly, so I thought I'd let her have a go at it ...'

Suzanne Sharp.

Sod bloody Madness. I've got a score to settle.

'There,' Suzanne said, winding the daisy chain three times around Kelly's neck. 'That looks really pretty.' She rummaged around in her Anya Hindmarch flowerpot handbag for a mirror. 'Look ...'

The sun was nearly gone, and it had left a pink mid-summer haze, turning everything mellow. Suzanne could see Christian tickling Callum's feet with a blade of grass, and could hear them laughing. She was sitting with her legs stretched out on the earth, which was radiating heat like an oven with an open door. But she knew the whole thing was unreal.

Christian didn't know any better. He thought that this tickling and giggling and messing around was what parenthood was about. But he worked in banking – admittedly with a bunch of grown-up children – where everyone acted as though Thatcher was still in Number 10.

'It's nice,' said Kelly.

This was the reality. Or, at least, it could be. A kid who was a bag of nerves, and who knew already what a disappointment she was to her parents, and yet had no way of knowing how to change.

Suzanne had worked with enough of them to know that look. At Kelly's age you could still reach them, there'd be occasional signs of hope and expectation. Once they hit their teens, the dead eyes gave it away. She'd seen the same flat expression on the faces of prisoners of war – or, at its most extreme, on the newsreel footage from the liberation of the concentration camps.

Tracey's kids were like two sides of the coin – with one they got lucky, the other they lost. Usually it was the boys who failed the social skills test, using tantrums and train-spotting to connect with the world. People found it harder to accept with girls. They were going against all the unwritten rules – women are the communicators who oil the wheels, and when girls failed at the very things they should have excelled at, adults closed in on them, like high court judges on female bank robbers or serial killers. You have broken the rules, you deserve to be punished.

'So apart from making daisy chains, what do you like doing, Kelly?'

Kelly rolled her eyes. 'Trying to remember . . . I wrote it all down, for Sandy. She's my cyker . . . cykergist. At school. You know.'

'Psychologist?'

'Yes, Sandy made me write it all down. If I had it here I'd show you.' She looked disappointed.

'It doesn't really matter, Kelly. Let me see, when I was the same age as you, I used to like ... reading. Do you like reading?'

'Yes. A bit. Mummy doesn't like me reading all the time, though.'

Suzanne sniffed. 'No, I can imagine that. And I always loved animals. Ponies and rabbits, especially.'

Kelly smiled as if she'd discovered a kindred spirit. 'Guinea pigs. I love them. They're all ... roly poly. More gentler than rabbits. The rabbits at school growl sometimes.'

'And what about dancing? Do you like dancing, Kelly?'

'On my own, in my room. Not where people can see, though. Makes me feel silly.'

'No one can see here, though. We could have a dance here.'

Kelly looked doubtful. 'There's no music.'

'We could sing some, make our own. It'd be fun.'

'Fun.' There wasn't even in a question in Kelly's voice, but it was clearly an alien word. In some ways, the kids who threw dolls or wooden bricks or even plastic chairs at you were easier to deal with than the ones who quietly accepted their friendless fate.

Suzanne stood up, shook the grass from her skirt, and held out a hand to Kelly. No six-year-old child was a lost cause.

Even when her mother was Tracey Mortimer.

I don't know what I'm going to say to bloody Suzanne when I find her. I've left Dave chatting with his new best mates. After a couple of jokes and a couple of burps, I could just see Briggsy and Gary thinking what a good bloke he was. Just wait till he tries to pull Gabby. Then they'll realise what he's really like.

I'm prowling the school site when I run into Jenny and

the crew – they've been keeping their distance, which impresses me.

'How's it going?' I ask Jenny.

'Yeah, fine,' she says. 'You all seem to be getting on better.'

'Suppose so. There's a lot of water under the bridge.'

'And nice of Gary to apologise like that ...' she says, and when I turn to stare at her, she adds 'Oh, don't worry, we won't be using it.'

But I've just remembered the fucking radio mike. No wonder they haven't been stalking my every move – it's just as good for them to stand back and film from a distance as I bare my soul and settle old scores, because perfect sound is being transmitted back to their camera. I can't even slag them off this time – it's not as if they sneaked it on to me when I wasn't looking.

'Right,' I say.

'Actually, can we do a little catch-up now?' Jenny says, and Jamie turns the camera on me. 'So is it turning out the way you expected?'

I know what to say by now, and from somewhere I dredge up a 'ring of confidence' smile. 'Yeah, it's amazing ... I was worried that maybe I wouldn't recognise people, or that I wouldn't have anything to say to them. But it must be that shared experience that means we all still have so much in common. And it's gonna get better later because of course this is the first time I've seen most of us legally drunk!'

'And I believe it's also the first time you've seen your first boyfriend since you left school,' she says, winking at me.

'It's sooo weird,' I say, remembering not to answer yes or no. 'Gary was my heart-throb all the way through school, and he hasn't changed at all. Still drop dead gorgeous, I could definitely still fall for him. But he's got a girlfriend, and I'm married, of course, so there's no danger of history repeating himself. It's great to see him, though. And I might see if I can grab him for a slow dance later on ...'

Jenny nods. 'Thanks, Tracey.'

'Would you do me a favour for a few minutes? I'm going to nip off to find the kids, and it'd be nice to be properly on my own just for a bit ... without the camera. Is that OK?'

'Sure,' she says. 'Must get a bit tedious, and we could do with a break ... just give me a shout when you're back. And make sure you don't stay too long; Madness are on soon.'

They head for the bar, and I switch the mike off, then I walk towards the playing fields. I can hear Callum laughing hysterically and when I look over, he's chasing a lanky guy around. That must be Christian. Nicer-looking than Suzanne deserves, and young too. As I watch them, he pretends to trip over and Callum leaps on him, pummelling little fists on the guy's chest.

A little further away, I suddenly see Kelly's profile skipping along the horizon, followed by Suzanne. They're moving quite fast, and as I approach them, I realise they're singing ...

'What's new, pussycat?'

'Who-oh oh a ...'

It's one of Kelly's favourite songs; my mum loves Tom Jones, and every time we go round there, Kelly demands she puts it on. But it's unusual to see her bopping, that oversize T-shirt she's got on is flying up and down. She's jumping about like Tigger.

Suzanne sees me first, she must have sensed I was there, and she stops moving. But Kelly carries on leaping about and singing – the same chorus over and over because she can't remember the verse – until I'm really close and call out her name.

'Kelly.'

She looks up and stops dead. Her shoulders slump and she blushes, as though she's really embarrassed that I've caught her doing something she shouldn't.

'Hello, Tracey,' Suzanne says, and the way she's standing I can't see the expression on her face. She reaches out to hold my daughter's hand. 'Kelly and I have been having our own disco.' Kelly grins at her.

I don't know why, but this makes me feel even angrier. Who the hell does she think she is, playing with my daughter? Maybe she thinks she needs to tell me how it's done, how to be a mother ...

'Kelly, go and play with Callum,' I say, pointing back to where her brother is. She squints at me, then lets go of Suzanne's hand, and trudges off.

'Your husband didn't seem to mind, Tracey.'

He wouldn't, would he? 'I mind. I don't want to leave my child with just anybody.'

'I am trained in working with ...' she starts, but I'm frowning so hard that she trails off. 'No harm done, anyway.'

She begins to walk off in the same direction. 'Hang on,' I shout. 'I want to know what the hell you think you were playing at, inviting Bob Carmichael.'

She stops. 'I ... I don't know what you mean,' she says, without turning round to face me.

'Yeah, right, really you don't. He turned up, and I certainly didn't invite him.'

I walk around so I can see her. She's got that irritating look that always used to make me mad at school – martyred and superior at the same time.

'Tracey, I can't think where you got the idea that I would invite anyone to YOUR reunion. What's it got to do with me?'

'Good question. I've been wondering about that ever since he said you'd been to see him.'

'Oh. Well, I wanted to talk to him about this working party he's involved in. It's an area I'm very interested in developing.' But even she doesn't look as though she believes what she's saying.

'Don't talk shit, Suzanne. I know we didn't see eye to eye at school, but I can't see what you're trying to achieve by messing about with my life. And you fucked up anyway – if you wanted to embarrass me, or make things awkward, well, it hasn't worked, because Bob's been and gone. I think you should do the same, don't you? I've never wanted you around before, and I don't now.'

She stares back at me. 'You really don't scare me any more, Tracey, however much you shout. I didn't ask Bob Carmichael, but I don't actually care whether you believe me or not.' Then she starts walking towards me. 'You're right, I did go to meet him, I can't explain why, but when I heard about the reunion, it brought a lot of stuff back that I'd tried to forget. You made more or less every day here a bloody misery –'

'Don't talk shit, Suzanne, you –'

'No, you listen to me for once,' she says. She's not even shouting. The only sign that she's losing it, is that her accent's slipping back into how it sounded when we were all at school, rather than the artificial 'posh' tone she used when we were filming the interview for the programme. 'I used to feel sick before I came into school and it was because of you. Because you're an ignorant, callous bitch. I dare say you haven't even thought about any of that since we left, but it's stayed with me, all right. I've talked to lots of bullies over the last few years, and most of them are the same – stupid people with no understanding of anybody else, except if there's something in it for them. All the shit you put me through, it was just a power game for you, wasn't it? A way of proving you were in charge, and sod what effect it had on me, or anyone else.'

She pauses for breath, and I wonder if I should say something. But what? She's exaggerating. Bloody drama queen. Sure, there were moments when I couldn't resist showing her up, but she deserved it, everyone agreed with me. She was such an easy target, but that was her choice. I can't believe she's been agonising about it for seventeen years. It's bloody tragic, but it's not down to me. She's the weirdo.

'Well, Suzanne, this is all very interesting, but I'd better get back to my party.'

'Oh no, you don't ...' she says, and she runs in front of me, trying to block my path ' ... I haven't finished.' She's close enough now to lower her voice to a whisper. 'So I fought to get over it, to get back some of the self-respect you systematically took away from me for FIVE years. And then when I heard about the reunion, I couldn't work out what to do. It brought it all back to the surface, and I was scared that it might just make me feel like shit all over again.

'But now I've got Christian,' she nods over to where Kelly and Callum and her husband are messing about. 'And friends, and a good job, and a life ... and I thought I'd risk it. And do you know, it's been the best thing I could have done. Do you want to know why?'

I open my mouth to tell her I don't, thanks all the same, but she keeps going.

'Because I look at you now, and I realise you're nothing. Sure, you were queen bee for a few years ruling a bunch of kids who knew no better. But the minute we walked through those gates for the last time, you lost your crown, and while the rest of us got on with our lives, you were stuck here, weren't you, in your head? Stuck in the

307

days when Tracey ruled the world.

'Well, guess what? She doesn't any more, and if you thought this whole reunion thing was going to give you another crack at things, you're so wrong. Because we've all come to look at how badly you fucked up. And didn't you do us proud? A no-hoper husband who couldn't get shot of your kids soon enough so he could get pissed. No friends that I can see. And a daughter who looks as terrified of you as I was. And why's that? Because she's got a bit of sensitivity, some intelligence, a bit of imagination? Oh well, I'm sure you'll manage to bully it out of her before too much longer, Tracey. Then one day, she might be just like you. There's something to look forward to.'

This time she pauses to let me respond, but I don't know what to say. Of course, she's wrong. Really, badly wrong. About me, about the reunion, about Kelly. But I don't know where to start, and what I really want to do – to slap her and pinch her and pull her hair – is not going to win me this argument.

'Speechless, eh?' And she grins. 'That really is a first.'

I wonder if I should remind her of my stage fright in *Joseph*, but I don't get chance.

'You know, I hoped that at the end of this, I'd be able to feel sorry for you, because pity is a wonderful revenge. But I don't. For all the pleasure of seeing you for what you really are, I also feel very sad. Because I'm about to walk away.

'But you can't. And neither can your children.'

Chapter Thirty-Five

I watch her walk back to her perfect husband and my imperfect kids. She lifts Kelly up, and says something that makes her laugh, then leans over to kiss Christian.

Maybe they'll decide I'm such a bad parent that they'll wander off into the sunset with my two, and give them a posh upbringing. Take Kelly to junior yoga, and Callum to toddler pottery, feed them polenta and sun-dried tomatoes, send them to private school.

And then what do I do?

Leave Dave, for a start. He's an average dad, but an utterly useless husband, and if I wasn't tied to him by their genes, I'd be off. Where, that's the harder question? Would I have the guts to go and join Bob in London? To start over with a man just old enough to be my father, and probably repeat the whole kids thing, but this time have a Chloe and a Sam, as well as the money to give them the benefits of a proper middle-class childhood? It's all cloud cuckoo land.

I can hear Kelly laughing, and it hurts. I wonder if Suzanne sees every giggle as proof that she's right after all, that my daughter prefers a woman she's never met before to me. That I am the terrible mother she thinks I am.

Part of me wants to go and seize Kelly and Callum back, drag them off to the green room, and force them to play nicely with Annabel's sister, who's been drafted in as babysitter for the night. But I can't bring myself to spoil one of Kelly's rare moments of fun. For all of Suzanne's insufferable smugness, she seems to have a way with my daughter ...

And anyway, the words I intend to use to explain my state of mind to darling Dave are not suitable for the ears of young children.

I start to head back, keeping my distance, and pulling my Ant-jacket back around me. Now the sun's gone, it feels quite cold. Or maybe I'm shivering because I can see my future.

I've lost sight of the Perfect Family by now; there's hardly anyone milling about outside, and I can hear someone speaking rather than music on the loudspeakers. I speed up a bit.

'...it's typical Tracey that she's never around when you want her. But it's also typical Tracey that she can gather together such an amazing bunch of people for a reunion.'

I peer in through the doors, and realise it's Briggsy on stage, loving the attention. I want to jump up beside him, tell them it's not me who sorted this out, it's Boris, and we should all go to the hospital now and stand outside, chanting slogans of support to show how much she's loved. Because that's what she needs right now.

'And it doesn't stop with the memories ... because now, to take us all back to the time when we were pulling hair and eating dirt, we're going one step beyond – with MADNESS!'

There's a split-second pause when nothing happens ... and then everything goes mental. Lights, drums and the cheering of a free booze-fuelled crowd who're determined to make as much racket as a Wembley-stadium full of

310

fans. I feel a rush of excitement pass through my body, as they play the opening notes to 'Baggy trousers'. Then I think of the kids, and start panicking – where has Suzanne taken them? All this noise must be terrifying, especially for Callum.

As well as the lights on stage, there are spotlights streaking their way across the people in the hall, and I scan the room for them and Suzanne and Christian. And for Dave. But I can't see any of them . . . part of me wants to rush to the front of the stage, to relish the moment, to reach out to Suggs and the nutty boys who are here – in front of us, in our old school – because of me. Maybe I could climb up with them, and take Gary with me, and pretend, just for a minute, that we're still teenagers and there's everything to play for.

But we're not, and my head is starting to fill with horror stories . . . Callum running away from the music straight into the path of a car . . . Kelly too scared to stay around the masses of people, and walking out of the school gates into the clutches of a passing paedophile . . .

Where the bloody hell is Dave?

'It's a bit loud for you two in there,' said Suzanne. 'Christian, are you sure you can't see him – he's not in the bar, is he?'

'No. And I've been back to look for Tracey but she's not on the playing field any more.'

Callum had run out of steam, and decided to lie down on the concrete.

'Oh, God, I'd better put them in the car.' Suzanne found the keys in her bag and clicked the alarm. 'Let's go and give your brother somewhere to have a nap, and then we'll find Mummy, OK, Kelly?'

'OK.' Kelly clambered into the back seat, and stuck her thumb in her mouth. Suzanne and Christian took one end each of Callum, and hauled him into the front, without him waking up. Once they'd covered him with the dog blanket, a seatbelt fastened loosely over the top, they closed the door and sat on the bonnet, exhausted.

'So why did you send Kelly back to me?' Christian asked. 'Girls' talk?'

'Hardly. No, I had things I'd wanted to say to Tracey for seventeen years, and it seemed like a good opportunity.'

'And do you feel any better for getting it off your chest?'

Suzanne sighed. 'Not as good as I'd hoped. I mean, yeah, it was nice to do the talking for a change – she didn't get a word in edgeways. But it was a bit like kicking someone when they're already down. If you look at the two of us, who's come out of it better?'

'But you've put some ghosts to rest?'

'I suppose so ... feel more sorry for these two than anything,' she said, tapping gently on the car window.

'You can't help everyone, Suz. Sometimes you've got to walk away. And once we've found their dad – God help them – I think we should leave, go back to London and you can put Crawley Park and Tracey Mortimer and the whole inferiority complex thing behind you.'

'I don't know that it's going to be that easy.'

Christian leaned across and planted a kiss on her lips. 'I can think of one way to make a new start. To have our own.'

'Ye-es ...' Suzanne said, meaning 'no'. 'Let's talk about it when we get home.'

I feel slightly unsteady on my feet – a combination of the heels and the gin. But I can't go slowly, when there's so much at stake. I've managed to calm myself down a little bit about the kids – Suzanne might be an appalling stuck-up bitch, but she obviously knows about children, so I guess it's the best place for them while I sort out my husband. I just hope Kelly doesn't start talking about anger management, or Callum doesn't end up wanting to watch Channel 4.

And I can't pretend I'm worried about Dave. I'm angry with him, and I want to have a go at him for abandoning the kids. And ask him what the hell he's doing abandoning them when I'm not going to be allowed to leave my own party before the end, and he's probably already too pissed to be in charge of a packet of fags, never mind two children.

All right, *I* know we've got Annabel's sister ready to look after them, and Mum due to pick them up at nine-thirty, but I deliberately didn't tell him. Thought it was about time he took some responsibility. Huh.

He's not in the bar, which was the most likely location. So I head out the other side of the school, towards the terrapins, which were decrepit enough in my day, but now look as though they're held together by chewing gum. The least fashionable subjects were always shunted off into the mobile classrooms, like incontinent relatives hidden in a granny flat. In our day it was Maths and German. I jump up to look through the grimy windows, and see scruffy posters blu-tacked to the walls. 'Grape varieties of the Rhineland,' says one. 'German composers through history,' reads another. I'm sure that one was up there back when *we* were struggling with our verb endings.

Beyond the terrapins is the science block, with the dining room, gym and changing rooms in the basement. I'm sure there should be some kind of health and safety regulation forbidding food, chemicals and sweaty socks in the same building.

It's really the last area where there's anywhere to skulk, though I don't know how he'd know to go there. Devious instinct, perhaps? By the bins was our equivalent of the bike sheds – they moved the bike sheds halfway through my time here, once they cottoned on to the smoking and snogging going on. It was a bit smelly by the bins, but when the men came to empty them, we could nip round to hide in the little porch where the PE teachers used to store metal cages of outdoor sports kit, to protect them from the rain. But that was pretty cramped, so it was first-come-first-served. Until we were in the fifth year; then we could pull rank.

I had my first kiss there, the Old Spice aerosol-induced one with Briggsy. Actually, it was Melody's idea. Not the deodorant, but the snogging. And before any of us knew what was going on, she was diving on top of Gary, making strange humming noises. Not to be outdone, Briggsy pressed his face hard on to mine, as though I was a pane of glass, and he was trying to terrify someone on the other side of it by squishing it into a hideous expression. His teeth ground into my jaw, and then a hard tongue tried to force itself between my lips, and I was so shocked, that I let it. Once inside, it circled inside my mouth like a washing-up brush trying to reach every corner of a saucepan covered in sticky scrambled egg.

We were twelve. I didn't ever think I'd forgive Melody for that. It should have been me and Gary sharing our first kiss – and although it was some consolation when we finally lost our virginity together a few years later, it set a precedent. Shrimp would never have done that.

I can still hear pounding from the hall; it's hard to identify the song, but from the whooping that's accompanying it, a good time is being had by all. I walk past the bin store. Nothing.

Maybe the bastard's gone home. Conveniently forgotten about being a dad, got the hump and caught a taxi. But then I look at my watch, and it's not nine o'clock yet ... I can't see him leaving before the free drinks run out. My feet are killing me now, so I sit on the steps upwind of the last bin, and massage them. Through a process of elimination, I realise the band's playing 'House of Fun'. How appropriate. Everything – sex, smoking, all the grown-up things – were much more fun when we were too young to do them. Before it all became a chore.

'Shhhhh . . .'

It's a woman's voice, followed by giggling. Coming from the porch area. There's something about it that's familiar but . . . I drag myself to my feet, and I hear my knees cracking so loudly I'm convinced whoever's hiding must hear it too. I tiptoe along the path that's been worn away by generations of kids doing the same hop-skip-jump from the bins to the safe haven of the PE porch.

It's a couple. Obviously deciding to go for the full reunion experience, complete with groping and the risk of discovery. I never remember being terribly excited about the idea of being discovered during sex when I was a teenager, but I suppose it was such a constant risk that there was no novelty value attached. It's only when we get middle-aged that we have to find new ways to summon up a bit of adrenalin.

They've got their backs to me, and what I see immediately is dark hair, white shirts, pale skin, pieces of a kaleidoscope that suddenly click together to form an image so vivid, so painful and so unmistakable that I want to vomit.

Dave.

And Melody.

Chapter Thirty-Six

On my wedding day, I didn't ever want to stop running, but it was hard work in a long dress. So I decided it was all Melody's fault.

If you are in love with someone – which I suppose I must have been then, though I can't remember what it felt like – and if you've only been married for three hours and twenty-five minutes, then it's the obvious thing to do.

My mum told Melody to clear off, and she did, and we invented a migraine for her to explain her absence, and that was that. One less bridesmaid. I wonder why Mum did it, but then I think after the shock of me and Bob, she never thought I'd get married, so she wasn't going to let it all go wrong for the sake of some random grope.

A couple of years ago, I found out that they can use computers to remove unwanted relatives or friends from your favourite photographs, basically rewrite history, and I considered having it done, because some of my nicest pictures have got *her* on them. Kelly loves taking out the album to swoon over the images of my day as a fairy-tale princess. And seeing Melody there riles me.

But in the end I decided it was a waste of money. I'd already done it, mentally. So when I looked at the photos, she was still there, of course, but only in the way a head-stone is there, in the background of the churchyard. She became an object, quite a decorative one I'll admit, but less significant than my bouquet of flowers. Kelly picked up on it too, bless her, only asked me about the lady in the sky-blue dress twice before she started to concentrate all her questions on the child bridesmaid standing next to her.

The trouble is, I'd applied my mental airbrush to far more than the wedding pictures. I'd removed all trace from my brain – or so I thought until a few moments ago – of Dave's hand disappearing up her bunched satin skirt. And of his rubbery lips planting kisses on the cleavage I'd been kind enough to allow her bridesmaid's dress to reveal.

I'd also removed what had drawn me towards the fire escape in the first place. The sound of Dave whispering, 'Mel, I want you so much.' He would have been on pretty safe ground in assuming no one would hear him above the disco, if Groovy Graham hadn't just put on my favourite slow dance record, sending me outside to find my new husband.

'I know this much is true . . .'

I saw something on the news once about pornographers using the Internet, and how even if they think they've been really clever and wiped all trace of what they've been up to, there'll always be something in the computer's brain that an expert can dredge up, to prove their guilt. I think it's the same with me – except it was my poor, deluded brain that decided to erase Dave's guilt, to go along with the farce that our marriage has been from Day One.

As I run back to the hall, I look down and realise my feet are bare, and one of them is bleeding. I'm still holding on to my strappy shoes. Madness are playing 'My girl's mad at me'.

*

Andrew stood at the back of the hall, trying to spot Tracey. He'd had a hectic afternoon checking things out, and he still didn't have all the information he wanted, but he was pretty sure it wouldn't take much to make her confirm the story ... he'd deliberately left it a while before coming to the party, because there was a fair chance she'd be pissed by now.

But she was proving irritatingly elusive. One person he'd asked had assured him you wouldn't be able to miss her – she was wearing a leather dress, apparently – which made Andrew curse because he hadn't brought his digital camera.

Still, if he played it right, he might be able to get pictures from the TV company anyway. He had to judge it carefully, but he was pretty certain they'd run with the idea that all publicity was good publicity, and so the kind of publicity he was about to guarantee for Tracey and her reunion could only be a gift.

It wasn't his kind of story, really, he'd left the grimy door-stepping behind him when he left the provinces for London to pursue serious journalism, but this was a scoop that had everything – sex, politics, power – and it was bound to bring him big bucks. Which was a good job because the exhaust on the car was about to fall off, and the parts for BMWs didn't come cheap.

No, she definitely wasn't there. He walked back through the bar, which was almost empty. A handwritten sign pinned to the front of the beer pumps explained why – 'sorry, all drinks after 9pm to be paid for'. Lots of people in pretend school uniform, but no tarty blonde in a leather number. Married, two kids, part-time job in an office supplies shop – she really was so average it was untrue. Except for shagging the teacher. Maybe even that passed for normal at Crawley Park.

Through the doors from reception, Andrew could see

Suzanne standing by her car, talking to a guy who must be her husband. That was the story that *really* interested him – what had she got against Tracey that would make her be willing to stitch her classmate up so badly? He'd never push it, of course, when it came to protecting his sources, he'd be as good as his word. It was every journalist's heroic daydream, to be pulled up before a judge demanding to know where a story came from. In Andrew's version, he would refuse to divulge their name in a speech so moving, so honourable, that the court would break into spontaneous applause before he was sent down for ... what, a couple of days, maximum. And while the old lags offered him the pick of the prison food, out of respect for his dignified stand, there'd be questions in the House, and he'd become a cause célèbre of press freedom, before being released in a blaze of glory.

But maybe it wouldn't happen with this one. And he was getting bored.

He bought himself a mineral water, and stood in the doorway. Perhaps Suzanne would know where she was.

Andrew walked towards their car. 'Hello,' he said, and Suzanne turned and when she realised why she recognised the voice, gave him a venomous stare.

'Sorry to bother you both, but I'm looking for Mrs Brown. For Tracey? And I can't seem to find her. I wonder if you've seen her.'

The blond man smiled politely. 'Snap! We're trying to find her too, but she seems to have disappeared off the planet. We've got two sleepy kids in here who want their mummy,' he said, pointing into the car. Suzanne pursed her lips.

'Oh, right ...' Andrew said, peering through the window. A chunky toddler was out cold in the front, a trail of dribble snaking down his chin. In the back, a girl looked back at him through saucer eyes. 'Bless 'em.

What's she like, abandoning her babies? We'll have to do something about that ...'

My foot has started to hurt now, I've picked out a fragment of glass that I must have trodden in as I made a run for it. But I can feel my heel slipping about in the blood that's collected in the sole, and it'll probably soak through and be ruined. I'll have to keep it as a souvenir of the night my marriage died. Very fitting.

I thought they might at least try to come after me, but there are no cries of my name, no footsteps behind me, no demand to 'wait, I can explain', just the creak of my heels as I trudge back. My head's clearer now, my sore foot has sobered me up, and I've called Mum to ask if she can come straight away to pick the kids up. All I've got to do is find Suzanne.

I've got to time it carefully now. Mum says she'll be fifteen minutes, but I don't want to get involved in a debate about what's wrong, or why I don't want a lift back with her.

Because I'm getting out. Fuck the reunion, fuck the TV programme, especially fuck Dave. I'm walking out of those bloody gates again but this time I'm not looking back.

Which is all very well, except I don't have a clue where I'm going.

'Is that her?' Christian said. 'She seems to be limping.'

Suzanne looked up. 'Thank God for that. I was starting to think we'd have to call social services.' She turned to Andrew. 'Do you mind leaving us alone to sort this out please?' she snarled.

'Darling ...' Christian frowned. 'Sorry, she's not normally this rude. It's been a long day, you know, and I think –'

'Shut up,' Suzanne said. 'We don't owe him an

apology.'

'What, you know him?' He glanced from his wife to the stranger, and back again. Neither said anything. 'Oh hell's bells, what is going on?' The only thing he could be sure of was that the faltering figure drifting towards them was definitely Tracey. 'Yoo-hoo .... Over here,' he shouted, desperate for certainty.

Who's that? It looks like Suzanne's dopey husband, and actually, that looks like Suzanne next to him, so it makes sense. Where are the kids? They don't seem to be panicking about anything, maybe they're in the car. Or maybe Mum's already here.

There's a third guy, and as I approach I realise it's that scummy reporter. How bloody cosy. Suzanne's got the most unbelievable nerve – first, she tries to set me up, then she gives me a going-over at my party and now she's chatting away to some bloke who is probably even now plotting to put me on the front pages.

Unless ... it was her who tipped him off in the first place ...

'Tracey,' says her husband. He has the most annoying posh voice. 'We haven't met properly, I'm Christian. Are you all right? You seem to have hurt your foot.'

'It's fine,' I say, and I look into the car. Kelly and Callum are asleep.

'The kids are a bit tired, but we couldn't find Dave, so we thought they might be happier away from the noise. Are you *sure* you're OK? It looks as though you're bleeding.' He turns to Suzanne, who is much quieter than she was on the playing field. 'Because Suzanne's a first-aider, aren't you, darling?'

'I've had enough help from your wife for one day.'

'Really?' he says, and the sarcasm's escaped him completely. 'That's my Suz. She was telling me about

Kelly's problems, but I'm sure it'll –'

'That's not what I mean. I'm talking about the help with publicity.'

Andrew glances at her for just long enough to tell me it's true. But Christian blunders on. 'Darling?'

'Oh, hasn't she introduced you to her partner in crime?'

'Tracey, I don't know what you're talking about,' she says, in such a patronising voice I want to slap her. But now is not the time.

'Yeah, right.'

Andrew steps forward. 'Mrs Brown, I was just asking your guests here if they knew where you were, because I was keen to catch you for a private word . . .'

'You had your chance at the press conference.'

'This is rather more personal . . .'

'Well, I'm sure it's not so personal you can't talk to me here . . . in front of one of my oldest friends.' Poor Christian has the same expression as Stan Laurel, and I half expect him to scratch his chin.

'Mrs Brown, I really think . . .'

'I'm afraid I'm in the most terrible rush, I can't neglect my guests, so this is your one chance.'

Andrew sighs, takes a deep breath and says, 'OK. I'm following up a story about you and Bob Carmichael, the government adviser. I understand he used to be a teacher here, and that you had a relationship, and I wanted to give you the chance to put your side of things . . .'

Now Christian's mouth is hanging open, and Suzanne tries to look surprised.

'I think you're barking up the wrong tree,' I say, and turn to go.

'I've got evidence, Mrs Brown. So whatever you say, I'm afraid the story is likely to be published. But you were very young, and I don't think it'll reflect badly on you, especially if you're willing to talk to me.'

I suppose I knew this, really. The penny's dropping with Christian, too. 'Suz?' he says, 'Darling, did you know about this?' He nods towards Andrew. 'And did you know about him?'

'Don't be ridiculous,' she snaps.

I turn on her. 'What, so are you denying that you met Bob and talked about the reunion last month?'

'No, I – '

'Suzanne?' Christian says, using her full name like a parent telling off a naughty child.

'And I suppose you'd say it's a coincidence that you're chatting to this scumbag journalist?'

She stares at me. 'It doesn't matter,' I say. 'You can stuff your stupid story, print it, what do I care? I know who my friends are, and who they aren't –' I pause for a meaningful look at Suzanne, 'and nothing else much matters. Especially something that happened seventeen years ago.'

Andrew waits for a second, then reaches in his pocket, and pulls out a business card. 'I'd advise you to think about this more carefully ... when you're a bit calmer. All my numbers are on here. But don't leave it too long.' And he walks off, leaving the three of us in silence.

I suddenly feel overwhelmingly tired.

'Tracey,' Christian says my name, and despite the annoying accent, he sounds worried. 'What an awful thing to happen ... I'm sure Suzanne's got nothing to do with this, but, honestly, if there's anything we can do ...'

'Actually, there is ... I need some space ... to think, but my mum's coming to pick up the kids. To save waking them up twice, would you mind waiting for her and telling her I'm fine, but I had something to do? She's due any minute, in a beige Metro?'

Suzanne leaps in. 'Oh, yes, of course ... no problem. We'll make sure they're fine ...' If I needed more proof

323

she's guilty, this is it. But it doesn't seem to matter any more.

I blow kisses at my sleeping children, and hobble slowly out into the night.

Chapter Thirty-Seven

Once I've made my grand gesture, I don't have a clue what to do next, so I hide in the bushes to make sure everything's all right when Mum arrives. Even at this distance, I can see that she's angry, she's all smiles with Suzanne, but her body language is screaming 'how could she be so irresponsible?' It doesn't help that she's right.

When she drives off, sending aggressive puffs of smoke from the car exhaust as she accelerates away, I crawl out of the undergrowth. Dave still hasn't appeared; the kids could have been on their way to join the white-slave trade for all he cares. What now? I limp to the late-night shop round the corner, and buy tissues for my foot and a packet of fags.

'You been at this reunion?' asks the guy behind the counter, pointing at my Adam Ant jacket. 'We had a bloke in here earlier, journalist he was, nosing around about some girl who used to go to Crawley Park, shagging her teacher he reckoned.'

'Really?' He's been bloody everywhere.

'Yeah. Couldn't tell him anything. Only been here three months. Four-sixty, love, please.'

The fag is disgusting, but it buys me thinking time. You see, when I say I don't have a clue what to do next, that's not strictly true. I know exactly what I *want* to do, and I'm trying to work out some convincing reasons why I shouldn't.

What I want to do is call Bob. Apart from anything else, he does need to know that this bastard Andrew is on to him. But it's not really that at all . . .

I also want to call him, just because I want to call him. Because through all the grimness of today, the Gary–Shrimp–Suzanne–Dave–Melody moments, it's been the only thing I've hung on to, the certainty that what we had, even if it took less than a term to go from flirtation (mine) to resignation (his), was real. And more than any of the other reunion stuff – with the exception of Boris – it still means something to me today.

Boris. That's the other thing. I feel terrible because there've been whole stretches of this evening when I haven't specifically thought about her, even though I've had this constant sense that something is missing. But what am I meant to do? I'd be as out of place at the hospital as I was here, at my own party, attended by my own kids and my own husband.

I pull out Bob's card, and examine it under the street-lamp. It's the loops that do it . . . on the back, he's written 'mobile' followed by the number, and the 'b' and the 'l' are both topped by curly loops, and it reminds me of the only love letters I've ever had, each one on the thickest paper, crammed into parchment envelopes, addressed to Tracey with a final flourish on the 'y'.

I key the number into my phone, but have to smoke another fag before I finally press send.

It rings four times, enough to make me think again, but as I'm about to cut it off, he answers. 'Hello.' His voice sounds flat, and I can hear traffic in the background.

'Bob.' I say. And then I'm tongue-tied.

'Tracey?' He says my name as though he can't quite

believe it. 'What – where are you? What's happened?'

'Nothing ... everything. I don't know.' Pull yourself together, Tracey, for Christ's sake. 'They know. A reporter, he turned up at the reunion, and he knows about us. And he wanted me to talk about it, but I didn't, but he says he's going to publish anyway, and it's going to ruin your life, and –'

'Tracey, shhh ... listen, where are you?'

'Outside school, I had to make a run for it. And I'm leaving Dave, I found him with Melody, I think it's been going on all the time we've been married. And I need to know what's happened to Boris; I've been so selfish, and she's lost her baby and I've been too busy obsessing about myself to even make sure or go to the hospital in case she needs me. Oh, Bob, I'm such a bitch. They all think so, even bloody Suzanne, and they all blame me for messing up my kids, and they're right, you know.' I feel like I'm about to cry, and I look down at the pavement, and see the blood crusted along the side of my shoes, and that does it. 'And I've cut my foot open.'

There's a pause, and then he says. 'Have you got any money?'

'Yes,' I whimper, hating myself for being pathetic.

'Take a cab to the hospital. Is Boris at the general?'

'Yes.'

'Right, get yourself to casualty, and I'll meet you there. We can get you patched up and then we'll see if we can find out what's happened to her.'

'But I can't ... what about the TV crew?'

'Sod the TV crew. This is your life we're talking about, not someone else's light entertainment. You've had a shock. They'll understand.'

I can't see Alec understanding. But somehow that doesn't make me any keener to go back to the party. It still seems wrong. 'But you're in London ...' I bite my lip in the pause that follows. Please argue back. Please look after me. Please take control.

'No ... no, I'm not, not tonight ... I decided to book myself into a hotel, Marshall House? I can be at the hospital in twenty minutes.' It's his turn to sound lost, as the implications of the hotel booking hang in the digital signal passing between our phones. 'A treat to myself, really, it's not like I was expecting that anything would happen, you know, with you and ... anyway, ring a cab and I'll see you in A and E. OK?'

'OK,' I say, relieved to be told what to do. Maybe that's where I went wrong after Crawley Park – playing the field, trying to make my own decisions – when all I really wanted was a replacement for Mr Carmichael. Or maybe even a replacement for my dad.

In the cab I started worrying that my stupid outfit would be horribly embarrassing once I got to casualty, but it's such bedlam, the girl on reception doesn't even seem to notice.

'Description of injuries?'

'I've cut my foot on some glass.'

She raises her eyebrows. 'How badly?'

'Well, it keeps starting to bleed again. I think it might need stitches.'

'It's your decision, of course,' she says, as though she wouldn't trust me to decide on a lipstick colour, never mind anything relating to health, 'but you couldn't have chosen a worse time to come into casualty with a minor injury. It's likely to be a long wait.' She nods in the direction of the waiting room behind me, where the patients are considerably less photogenic than the average extras for a medical drama.

'I'll try my luck.'

I find the ladies' toilets, which are only averagely dirty,

and try to lift my foot into the basin to clean it up a bit. But the leather dress isn't exactly designed for high kicks, so I have to hitch up the skirt part around my waist. I wash away the worst of the dried blood, and I'm surprised at how deep the cut actually looks – before long it fills up again, and I wedge a pile of green paper towels into the front of my shoe and limp back out.

I don't have any change for the vending machine, so coffee or vegetable soup isn't an option, though I realise how hungry I am. Life-changing trauma can make you peckish. I pick up a pile of magazines, and flip through them, without reading any more than the ridiculous head-lines. My aunt is my gay lover. DIY plastic surgery: I gave myself a facelift. And even – this one made me laugh out loud, but no one in the waiting room seemed to notice – my husband's other woman is a Dalek. There's a picture of a middle-aged couple, sitting down to breakfast, along-side a life-size model of a robot.

I could fill an entire magazine on my own. Page 2, my infant daughter's bullying hell. Page 3, my husband has been shagging my bridesmaid. Pages 4–5, lessons in love from my form teacher. And on the back page, the problem page letter: how I failed my friend in her hour of need.

'Tracey.'

He looks dishevelled, and older than he did six hours earlier. And worried about me. I realise that second that he won't be going back to his hotel room alone. I feel better when I know this – my foot still hurts, so do all the things that make me such a brilliant subject for a whole host of 'true confession' articles – but at least I know I don't have to go home tonight . . .

But then I come over all shy, worried he can read my mind. 'Hi.'

He sits down on the plastic chair next to me, and the whole row shakes slightly. 'How's the foot?'

'It's sore, but I don't think it's going to fall off. It's just everything else happening that's made me overreact.'

He puts his hand over mine, and I'm relieved that they're young man's hands, warm and firm, and free of liver spots. 'I don't think any of it's an overreaction. But we can sort most of it out, even the newspapers. We're all grown-ups now.' He taps my knee. 'Let's have a look, then.'

I take off my shoe and hold my foot up. The bleeding's stopped again.

'Ugh. Not very nice, but I think you could die of a hospital super-bug if we stay here. How about we go and see what we can find out about Helen?'

Without me having to ask, he stands on the side of my bad foot, and supports me. We tell the receptionist to take my name off the list, then head for the lifts.

'I've never been to a maternity ward before,' he says, and I wonder what he's done with the last seventeen years. Sure, he's got the flash job and the flash lifestyle, but is that all there is? Nice hotels are all very well, but what's the point if you're on your own?

'Don't worry, they keep the muff shots out of view,' I tell him, and I feel the spark returning, momentarily. But as we step out of the lift, it disappears again. I nudge him towards the desk. 'Will you ask? I can't bear it ...'

I can't even bear to stand near enough to hear the midwife say the words. Through the window, I try to locate Crawley Park in the distance, but there are too many different orange lights out there, too many people getting on with their Saturday nights, trying to forget the life and death stuff that's staring us in the face on Rosebud ward ...

'Tracey ...' I turn around slowly, but when I finally face him, he's smiling. Insensitive bastard. I know he's trying to help, but –

'Tracey, Boris is asleep. But if they can find Brian, we might be able to take a peep at the baby.'

Baby?

'Tracey? If that's what you want?'

I walk up to the desk, to ask the midwife, in case Bob's misunderstood.

'Could you tell me what's happened with Mrs Norris?'

She lets out a low moan. 'I've told your husband already. She's tired after the caesarean but we're monitoring her, and everything seems fine. And the baby's small, but she's fine, too.'

Another nurse comes back and says Brian's asleep as well. But we should ring in the morning and see about popping in then.

Back in the lift, Bob and I don't know what to say to each other. It groans and clunks its way back to reception, and then he leads the way out to where he's parked. When we reach the car, I stand on one leg like a stork, folding my injured foot up behind me, embarrassed.

'So ... can I offer you a lift?'

I smile. 'I hear there are some nice hotels around here?'

Chapter Thirty-Eight

From a distance, the hotel looks like a wedding cake. But inside, Marshall House is very masculine, all mahogany and chrome, with a strong smell of furniture polish.

The night porter lets us in. He takes in my jacket and my lack of luggage, and gives Bob a man-to-man glance, avoiding my eye entirely.

'Sleep well,' he tells us, handing over a key mounted on a Bible-sized wedge of wood.

The journey from the hospital has been short on conversation, and Bob even switched on the CD player to fill the gap that threatened to last for twenty minutes. But it's Bob Dylan, and as he wails about rolling stones, it makes me wonder what I'm doing here, with a man old enough to be my father.

We take the lift to the second floor, even though my foot hardly hurts now any more. He opens the door, switches on the lights, then gestures for me to go in ahead of him. Always the gentleman.

It's not just a room, it's a suite. I step into the hallway, which widens out to become a lounge. The room is lit by a mad modern chandelier, with tiny ultra-bright bulbs on the end of a dozen tangled wires. Underneath, there's a huge leather sofa, a big TV and a thick creamy sheepskin rug on the wooden floor. To the right, there's an archway, and I peep through to see an enormous bed, one of the French ones shaped like a boat, and it looks like it's been carved from a single chunk of oak. On top, there are half a dozen pillows and a huge duvet, all covered in crisp white cotton, plumped up with fresh air and feathers.

I turn away. There's just something about it that's too scary... too horizontal ... too bed-like, for me to feel comfortable with it. So much for big, brave, Tracey Mortimer, who'd always fantasised about fucking in a posh hotel.

Bob puts his hand on my arm. 'I am more than happy to sleep on the sofa.'

I shake my head. 'No ... no. If anyone's going to do that, it'll be me. You must have paid a fortune for this suite. I'm not tired, anyway. Though I am hungry.'

'Well, that's something I think I can help with.' He walks across to where the TV is, and just behind it, there's an icebox, a miniature version of those trendy American retro fridges. He opens it, and empties slabs of chocolate and fruit on to the floor. 'Can I get you a drink?'

'God, yes.' I grab one of the bars, perch myself on the arm of the sofa, and break off pieces of dark chocolate, though what I really want to do is cram it all into my mouth at once. I take off my shoes, and when I let them rest on the floor, it's warm underfoot. It makes me smile, and he notices as he comes over with a gin and tonic. He didn't even have to ask.

'They've installed some kind of Swedish heating in all the floors – the attention to detail is amazing.' Then he grins, looks embarrassed. 'How middle-aged am I, Tracey? Mind you, the power shower IS incredible ... I promise this isn't part of a seduction routine, but if you do want to change out of that ... outfit, and have a bath or whatever, there's a spare one of those huge bathrobes I'm told women love.'

'You saying I smell?'

'No, I –' and he stops when he realises I'm winding him up.

A bath would send me to sleep, and that's not what I want to do until I've worked out exactly *where* – but a shower sounds a good idea.

The bathroom is as uncompromising as the rest of the suite, and the lack of a shower curtain throws me. There is a bath, but it's tucked behind the door, and is clearly not the main event. In the world of designer hotels, baths are obviously for wimps. The room itself is the size of my lounge, and is coated floor to ceiling with mosaic tiles in different shades of blue ... the floor slopes away to a drainage hole, and along the walls are a variety of nozzles which I suspect will spurt hot water at me if I can work out how to switch them on.

Apparently I'm not the first guest to be confused, because just by the door, there's a chrome plate engraved with the words 'guidance on using the wet room is available from reception'. Which makes me laugh for two reasons – why build a bathroom that people need instructions to use, and has anyone ever had the guts to ring through to admit they don't know how to work the shower?

I strip off, laying my dress and underwear to the side of the marble basin, and it's impossible to avoid seeing myself in the mirrors running alongside it. Actually, it's not as bad as it could be. Or maybe the lights and the mirror are designed to give that impression, to make you feel as glossy and beautifully finished as the room itself.

What do I look like to him? The last time he saw my body I was sixteen – tits pointing to heaven, cellulite-free skin, and a heartbreakingly flat stomach. And now? It could be worse. I turn slowly in front of the mirror, and my skin still looks soft, only the very top of my thighs resemble orange peel, and my stomach's rounder, but not fat.

It's the bits you can't see in the mirror that have probably changed the most – and no one but Dave has seen them since they were stretched and torn by childbirth. I wonder sometimes whether men talk about down there, compare notes on size and shape, as women do obsessively about dicks. The thought makes me shudder – we have no way of knowing how we measure up, but that particular part of me definitely belongs to Tracey Brown, rather than Tracey Mortimer.

My breasts are bigger than the last time he saw me, but they've not yet travelled as far as my waist. And I like my back, and the way my hair skims my shoulders and sways with me as I move. I suppose it all depends on whether Bob fancied me for myself, or fancied me because I was sixteen. And if I believe it's the latter, then what am I doing in a hotel room with him?

I step into the shower area, and tucked inside are a series of buttons – this really is a boys' toys bathroom. I press the largest one ... there's a low roar and then this torrent of warm water jets out of the nozzles in the ceiling and the walls. I hadn't realised there were that many holes, but it doesn't take long for pleasure to overcome surprise. I turn the big central dial towards the red indicator, and the water heats up, but without the spray becoming less intense, like it always does in the shower at home. I cover my body with designer soap from the built in shelf, and play around with the different buttons – one increases the pressure so it's like standing under a waterfall, and another one makes jets burst out of different nozzles in orgasmic spurts ... steam is filling the bathroom, and I don't ever want to come out.

335

I don't know how long I stay in there, but by the time I force myself to switch the shower off, I feel as if I've just swum in a lake, or run through a forest – alive, invigorated, cleaner than I've ever been. And in the mirror, my face is flushed and my hair hangs together in a horsetail, darkened by the water. I unhook the huge bathrobe, which has been warmed on the towel rail, and when I lose myself in the thick white towelling, I feel as innocent as a newborn.

'Better?' Bob asks as I walk back into the suite. He is sitting on the sofa, reading a magazine. Or pretending to – I get the impression he's as nervous as I am. There's jazz coming from the CD player.

'Much.' I sit beside him, and it feels strange being naked under the robe. I drain the glass, and the kick of the gin and tonic warms hits my near-empty stomach. 'Shall we go to bed?'

'Are you sure?'

'No ...' I say, and his face falls. 'But I feel like taking a risk.' I take his hand and we walk through to the gigantic bed.

I'd never fucked in a bed before. When you grow up, you forget how teenaged sex is all snatched knee-tremblers in the back of friends' cars – if you're lucky enough to have friends old and rich enough – or sessions on the sofa when you're babysitting for well-meaning neighbours. Mum would never let Gary in my bedroom, and he had to share his with his brother. It's a wonder I ever lost my virginity.

But a bed was different. Grown-up. Scary. That was more frightening than the idea of sleeping with my teacher. Melody covered for me, which was a calculated risk. Once I'd told her, I knew she'd do anything to keep the gory details coming, and she loved the fact she had to herself the juiciest piece of gossip in the history of Crawley Park. But there was always a danger that the temptation to share it would become too much ... that night, though, she kept it to herself, and Mum thought I was round at hers playing records.

I hadn't had long to prepare. He finally gave in at teatime on Friday. At seven o'clock on Saturday night, I went to the bus stop to wait for him to pick me up. I don't think he wanted to give himself time to change his mind.

Bob lived in the old part of town, in a small terraced house – they're pricey now, but no one wanted to live in them then; they wanted draught-free homes with upstairs bathrooms.

He bought a Chinese takeaway on the journey to his place, and I wanted to eat it from the cartons on our laps, but he insisted on serving it properly, on plates. He'd lit a candle in the middle of the old dining table, and put jazz on his record player. I still don't actually like jazz, but it always makes me feel grown-up.

I don't know who was more nervous – I suspect it was him. He treated me like a 'real' date, complimenting me on my hair and my clothes (a new top from Chelsea Girl, designed to show my cleavage), topping up my glass with white wine, but insisting I drink exactly twice as much water, to stop me feeling drunk then or hungover the next day.

The next day. There was only one thing between me and the next day. The night. And that was what was scaring me the most.

At least he didn't bore me with moral dilemmas – four nights of agonising at Daisy's café had convinced him I knew what I was doing, and that we were destined to be together.

This time, it was him that took the lead. He kissed me, and I could see the clock on the mantelpiece, 8.35pm, which felt terribly early to be going to bed, but then again, why would you wait if you had a house to yourself?

He led me upstairs and into his bedroom, which was painted white, with a big wooden bedstead by the window. He switched off the lights, and sat with me on the bed, kissing me and stroking my hair, and murmuring my name. Then he started to undress me, carefully, down to my bra and knickers. He pulled the duvet down on to me, as he undressed to his underpants, and then we moved together, skin to skin . . .

The feeling of a man's body against mine, against the cotton sheets, in this silent, private room, is something I'll never forget. He smelled of a woody aftershave, and as I explored his upper body with my hands, I was surprised at how hairy he was – Gary was very different. Bob's skin was rougher, but in the dark it didn't feel like he was my teacher any more.

He was slow and methodical, working his way around every inch of skin with his fingers, but with no sense of urgency. I felt excited but frustrated – sex was about lust, wasn't it, about explosions of need and passion? So I reached down to his pants, and touched his cock, and he whimpered.

He unhooked my bra, while I removed my knickers, and when he was quite naked too, we rubbed up against each other again . . . it was so different from the snatched moments of sex in impossible positions that Gary and I had been grabbing.

'Are you sure?' he asked me. I kissed him back.

When he entered me, it was familiar and yet different – better, more 'right', somehow. He was smaller down there than Gary, but I don't buy into the whole size-matters thing, anyway. Especially when Gary, like most sixteen-year-olds, had less self-control than a compulsive gambler or drug addict.

It wasn't rushed, though to start with I felt I should thrash around and make the noises you see in the films . . . but he slowed me down by saying my name over and over again. And when I came, I opened my eyes and the light from the streetlamp lit up his, boring into me, a look of satisfaction at what he'd done.

Afterwards he kept saying my name, and we did it again and again till we fell asleep.

When I woke up, I felt different. For the first time I had actually 'slept' with a man, and I put my head on the pillow as close to him as possible, so I could take in the warm, bitter-almond scent of his breath. He woke up almost instantly, and when he saw my face, he started, then smiled.

In the morning, when we did it again, we could see each other in the daylight.

Bob fiddles with the control panel so there are two pools of light on the duvet, spotlights for the main attraction. I sit on the bed, and he moves around to my side, and kisses me. My body remembers and when he pulls the dressing gown open, my nipples are gratifyingly erect.

'Oh, Tracey,' he says. 'It's been too long.'

Chapter Thirty-Nine

I wake up to sunshine pouring on to the duvet. It's the perfect day for ending a marriage.

Bob is still asleep. I think about leaving a note, but it seems underhand. It's just that now I know what I have to do, I don't want to waste any time.

I tiptoe into the bathroom. My foot is throbbing, but the cut seems to have started to heal. I look exactly as you'd expect someone to look who's spent the night with a former lover. My hair is all over the place, there are signs of stubble burn on my chin and around my lips, and my face is flushed and tired at the same time. I try to restore some order with Bob's comb, and I thank God for hotel freebies, because moisturiser and cologne help to tip the balance from dirty slut to plain old dirty stop-out.

I'm feeling quite pleased with the minor transformation, when I think about getting dressed. Shit. All I have is a pair of stupid pointy shoes, a leather dress and a ridiculous jacket. It is not an ideal outfit for a Sunday morning.

I carry the clothes back into the bedroom, and Bob stirs.

'Hello,' I say, as he opens his eyes.

'Hello.' He reaches out his hand to touch mine, but he looks sad. Or perhaps it's a relief. He knows as well as I do that last night was a one-off. There will be no fairy-tale happy ever after.

'I ought to get home. Stuff to sort out, you know.'

'I know,' he agrees. 'Can't I at least tempt you to breakfast in bed?' But he knows the answer. 'Then you must let me give you a lift back,' he says, and pushes back the bedclothes.

'No, honestly. I've got the money for a cab. I don't want to drag you out of bed, especially when you've paid for this suite – don't leave until they throw you out!'

But I wish I hadn't said it, because when I think about it, what can be more miserable than having breakfast on your own in the most perfect bed, when the person you've spent the night with, is no more than a dent in the pillow.

'Well, I'm not letting you leave like that.' He swings his body out of bed, and I look away. He doesn't belong to me; it seems wrong to see him naked now. He bends down to pick up his underpants and puts them on, before grabbing a holdall off the floor, and rummaging around inside. He pulls out a grey fleece, and a carrier bag. 'Here, wear this . . . and then put the jacket in here. I'm sure you want to keep it as a souvenir – unless the TV company are going to want it back!'

Shit. I've hardly thought about the programme since I walked out of the school gates, but what the hell did they do when I left? I take my mobile out of my handbag, and remember that I switched it off when we got to the hospital. How many messages are there on it from Jenny and Alec? I drop it as though it's a grenade.

'Do you think they could sue me for walking out like that?'

He looks up from buttoning his shirt. 'I don't know. I doubt it. Did you sign a contract?'

'Only something giving them permission to film me and the kids.'

'You'll probably be OK. I can't see them suing you,

anyway, not exactly good publicity, is it?'

I pull the fleece over my head – it swamps me, which is a good thing. Only a short piece of the leather skirt is still visible. 'And what about you? The reporter and everything?'

Bob sighs. 'Can't stop them, if they really want to publish it. It's true, after all. I had a quick word with our press officer on my way over to the hospital last night, so he's briefed.' He walks across the room to me, and reaches for my hand again. 'I'm sorry, Tracey. It might get a bit messy. But I'll help out, you know. If the papers arrive, you ring me, and I'll arrange for you and the kids to go away for a while.'

'Don't apologise. It's my fault. Anyway, a bunch of journalists don't scare me.'

'Atta girl,' he says, and rumples my hair. 'Are you sure about the lift?'

'Yeah ... I mean, there could be reporters there or anything. And if Dave's come home, it could make things messier than they need to be.'

He smiles at me. 'I meant what I said about not settling for what you've got, Tracey. The prospect of life with a raddled ex-teacher is no more tempting, I understand that, but you've got so much time left. Do me a favour, and don't waste it on that wanker.'

'OK,' I say, and I kiss him on the forehead. He winces slightly, and when I leave the room to call a taxi in reception, I think there are tears in his eyes. They make them look bluer than ever.

It's still only eight o'clock, but Mum is looking out for me when the taxi pulls up. She's shaking her head as I walk up the drive.

'What the hell do you think you're –'

'Mum, I'm not listening,' I say, as I barge past her into the lounge. When she continues to rant, I hum loudly, and stick my fingers in my ears, until her mouth stops moving.

'Put the kettle on,' I tell her. She looks shocked at being ordered about, but then meekly does as she's told. I wonder why I've never tried this before.

I look around the room, and it tires me out. It feels like a compromise, with its washed-out colours and seen-better-days furniture. Now that Callum's growing up, maybe it's time to redecorate – white walls, beech tables ... this time, I'll do it how I want it.

She comes back with two cups. The tea is very sweet, and makes me realise I'm hungry again.

'I'm not telling you where I went, Mum, so don't ask.'

'But -'

'It doesn't matter. It's irrelevant.'

She sighs, but gives a half nod at the same time.

'Is Dave here?'

'No. I don't know where he is. I can't believe that you both abandoned your children like that, you're not kids any more, you have responsibilities.'

'I don't care what you think.'

'Now, there's no need -'

'Mum, I've decided to throw Dave out. He's unfaithful and he doesn't love me. And I don't love him. There's no point.'

She shakes her head. 'I don't think you realise how hard it is bringing children up on your own. You should -'

'I do know. I've been doing it for the best part of a year. If anything, it'll be easier when I don't have to change my routines every time he heads back from Dublin on a whim.'

She tuts.

'Mum, I want you on my side with this. I will need you. But I can't carry on with the marriage.' I pause until she looks up at me. 'Last night, I found him with Melody.'

'Oh.'

'I don't know if it's been going on since the wedding, or if they were just meeting up for old times' sake. I don't care, actually. If it isn't her, it's been someone else. Or lots of someone elses.'

'If people split up every time the husband had an affair, there'd be no marriages left,' she sniffs. Poor Mum. She never had the option of standing by her man; she didn't see him for dust.

'Maybe. But I don't want to live like this any more. And I don't want the kids to grow up thinking it's normal for their parents to have nothing to say to each other.'

'I had to fight to bring you up,' she starts, and then stops. I realise she's trying not to cry. 'I didn't think the same would happen to you.'

'I know, Mum. But if it's a choice between having a miserable mum and a crap dad under the same roof, or a single mother who's committed to you, I'd go for the second.'

She frowns. 'If I didn't know you better, Tracey, I'd say that was almost a compliment.'

I grin at her. 'I must be going soft in my old age.'

If this was a movie, we'd probably fall into each other's arms, but instead we sit there feeling awkward.

'Oh, I forgot,' she says. 'That girl from the TV company came round last night, told me to get you to ring her as soon as you got in.'

I have a shower before I dare make the phone call. Compared to the jet-extravaganza at the hotel, it's a feeble dribble, but I still feel better afterwards. I put on a pair of cutesy brushed cotton pyjamas from my underwear drawer, which makes me feel less like a harlot, then I sit with my brush, trying to tidy up my barbed-wire hair.

By 8.45, I've run out of excuses. I take the phone into the kitchen, and then I remember the packet of cigarettes I bought last night. I retrieve them from my handbag, along with the discarded radio mike, and dial Jenny's number.

She answers immediately. 'Fucking hell, Tracey. It'd better be good.'

'I'm sorry.'

'That's a start, I suppose.'

I know I've messed them about, but her attitude is already rubbing me up the wrong way. 'Look, I'm sorry I left, but there's no need to be so rude. It hasn't been an easy couple of days.'

There's a pause. 'OK. So what happened?'

'I found Dave with Melody.'

'With? As in . . .?'

'Use your imagination. And then . . . well, then . . . I suppose you'll find out soon enough. One of the journalists at the press conference had found out something about the past. Something that's no one's business, but anyway, there it is, it's out now.'

'Is it about Robert Carmichael?'

I nearly drop the phone. 'How do you know?'

'Something Gary said to you the day you met him at the pub. I did a bit of research, and it didn't take much imagination to work out what he was on about. It's OK, I didn't tell the others.'

'They'll know soon enough.' Last night feels like a long time ago. 'How's Alec?'

'Oh, God, he was beside himself.' Jenny sounded amused. 'But seriously, Tracey, we're all in the shit over this. I don't know what we're going to do. We carried on filming, did loads of interviews with people. But without you there, it's going to look really rubbish.'

'I know. I do feel bad. I'll do anything I can now,

though. Maybe I should dress up again and do the interview as if I'm still there?'

I hear her laugh. 'You're a bloody fast learner, Tracey, I'll say that for you. And I suppose if this story about you and the teacher's going to come out, we might well end up with better ratings than we ever thought we'd get. By the way, any news on Boris?'

Boris. The one light at the end of the grimy tunnel of my life. 'Yeah. It's all fine. She's got a baby girl . . .'

'That's brilliant.' I'm sure I can hear someone else in the background.

'Are you all right, Jenny?'

'Yes. . .' more giggling. 'Yes, I'm fine. Look, I'd better go. I'll talk to Alec and we'll be in touch. Oh, and Jamie says he wants his radio mike back . . .'

I ring Boris's mobile, and eventually Brian answers.

'Tracey,' he says, and passes the phone over to Boris. She sounds knackered but elated.

'She's perfect,' she sighs, and I hope she is. If anyone deserves something beautiful, it's Boris.

'And what about you? Are you OK?'

'Hmm . . . the drugs are wonderful. I can't feel a thing.'

'And have you thought of a name?'

'Yes . . . we thought we'd call her . . . Louise. The whole reunion thing got me thinking, and I always loved Shrimp. It's another chance.'

She's such a bleeding heart, but I feel a lump in my throat. 'Lovely.'

'Anyway, what did I miss?'

Ten minutes later, I'm still talking, and when I get to the bit accusing Suzanne of being a scheming, manipulative bitch for inviting Bob, the line goes quiet, and I think she's fallen asleep.

'Boris?'

'Oh, Tracey . . .' she moans, and I worry that I'm tiring her out.

'What? Look, I'll leave you to rest.'

'No . . . no, the thing is. You see, it wasn't Suzanne that invited Bob. It was me.'

'You? But, why?'

'I don't know . . . I suppose, I had a hunch that meeting Bob again might just trigger something, I dunno, make you realise how awful Dave really was.'

I'm thinking about it as she's talking. 'I'm so sorry, Tracey. I had no idea what was going to happen. Typical me, meddling where I'm not wanted.'

'No . . . no, don't apologise, Boris . . .' It's probably the biggest favour she could have done me.

When the kids get up, they head straight for the garden, and I drag out the paddling pool Mum kept from thirty years ago. This must be the first summer since Kelly was born that there hasn't been a hosepipe ban, so we fill the pool, and Mum and I take turns to watch them.

Dave finally turns up at two o'clock. I don't even realise he's let himself in, until I see him through the kitchen window, taking a can of lager out of the fridge.

'What the fuck are you doing here?' I walk through the back door towards him. His face is unshaven, and there are dark circles under his eyes. I try not to think about how – or where – he spent the night. Though it's not as if I have any right to claim the moral high ground.

'Chill out, Trace,' he says. He's laughing at me.

'You're unbelievable. How dare you come back here after what happened last night?' I'm trying to keep my voice down, but the kids are watching from the garden, even though Mum's trying to distract them by splashing about.

'Erm . . . because I live here? It's no big deal, Melody

and me hadn't seen each other for years. It was meant to be a reunion, so that's what we were doing. Reuniting. Like you and your mate Suzanne! There was nothing to it. Don't tell me you haven't kissed anyone else in nine years . . .'

'Our marriage is over, Dave. I want you to leave.'

He doesn't even have the grace to react to this, but turns round to go outside.

'Did you hear me?' I shout. 'Are you fucking deaf as well as stupid?'

He turns back, and there's something about the long-suffering expression on his face that tips me over the edge. On the breakfast bar, Kelly's craft scissors are lying abandoned on top of a scrapbook. I grab them, and leap forward towards him.

'Trace?' he says, quietly.

'I am not messing around. You leave NOW or I won't be responsible.'

He's shaking his head at me, but he doesn't know whether to take me seriously or not. 'I can't go now. I haven't got any clothes or anything. Don't be hysterical.'

This time I jump even closer. 'I am not hysterical, I am fucking serious. GET OUT.'

He shrugs, and brushes past me on his way into the garden. Maybe it's my hangover but when I walk outside, everything is brighter, hotter, louder. The orange ducks floating on the magnified plastic-blue water in the paddling pool; the sunlight on my skin making me sweat and shiver at the same time. And, as Dave turns to sneer, the click of the ring pull on his can of lager, and the hissy release of gas as the beer bubbles to the surface. And the anger inside me spills over.

Before I really know what I'm doing, I rush towards him, I don't have a plan except to wipe that grin from his face, and it's only after I see this unfamiliar look pass

348

across his eyes – the ones I once stared into for hours, believing they held all the answers – that I remember I still have those craft scissors in my hand, and realise the look was fear.

I move backwards, shocked at myself, but it's too late for Dave to recover. He tries hard, but he's toppling backwards, fear replaced by confusion and then by an expectant wince, as he tumbles into the paddling pool. There's a satisfying splash of water followed by an 'oof' as the cushion of air breaks his fall. It's like a clip from *You've Been Framed*.

For a second or two, we're all paralysed, and I notice that Kelly, Callum and Dave's mouths are all pursed in the same 'O' shape. It's like a game of grandmother's footsteps, and I'm just wondering what the hell to do next, how to stop this causing the kids some awful trauma that the bloody educational psychologist will blame for everything they do wrong over the next twenty years, when Grandmother comes to the rescue.

'Silly Daddy,' she says, and then starts to giggle. It sounds forced at first, but then Kelly and Callum look down at their father, and the sight of him wet through, his legs waving in the air like a beetle's as he tries to right himself, suddenly seems funny rather than shocking.

'Silly Daddy,' Kelly agrees, between giggles, and Callum points his fingers at the pool, as Dave finally manages to heave himself out. He forces his mouth from the 'O' to a kind of crooked smile, but his eyes are cold.

I look down at the scissors in my hand, and when I unfurl my fingers, I see that the metal has left indentations in my palm. As I let it drop on to the grass, I feel a kind of release.

'I think you should go,' I say, under my breath, though the kids are now past hearing, as they keep trying to stop laughing, clutching at their sides, but then starting off again when they look at each other.

He opens his mouth as if he's about to say something, but then looks down at his dripping clothes, thinks better of it, and starts trudging towards the back door. I spot Callum's Winnie the Pooh bath towel neatly folded on the plastic garden chair – Mum must have brought it out with her – and pick it up.

'Dave,' I say, and he turns. I think he's expecting me to beg, to have a change of heart, to apologise, something. But all I do is throw over the towel, and, instinctively, he reaches out his hands to catch it. 'You'll be needing this to dry yourself off.'

'Fuck you,' he mouths. But he knows he's beaten, and I wait until I hear the front door slam. I bend down to pick up his can, still trickling frothy beer on to the grass. I walk into the kitchen to throw it away. Then I go to the fridge, take the other half-dozen tins of his favourite lager, and throw them in the bin, too.

Chapter Forty

'It's rude to stare,' my mum says, barely under her breath, as we walk down the detergent aisle.

'Leave it.' I'm getting used to the attention. Four days after they showed *The Trouble with Tracey*, and the public attention I always craved is mine – in my home town, at least.

The reaction's been mixed. It certainly wasn't the programme Smart Alec said they were going to make, but some of the critics (the ones who weren't too snobby to review a show on Channel 5) reckoned it was better for that. They changed the name from *Reunited!* to *The Trouble with Tracey* pretty much straight after the disasters of July 21st ... I wasn't all that comfortable with it to begin with – I was worried they'd stitch me up, make me look terrible, but then Boris pointed out that I couldn't look any worse I did in the newspapers.

August's the silly season, you see, and so a story that at any other time might have been confined to the inside pages of one tabloid hit the headlines in almost all of them. The odious Andrew made sure of that. He waited a while, and I wondered if someone had put pressure on him – I've watched enough thrillers to know that governments can cover up pretty much anything. But it seems Bob's reputation wasn't worth going to any trouble over, and as for mine ... I guess no one was ever going to lose any sleep over that.

Bob's still there, though. I'd even hazard a guess that the whole thing won't do him any harm in the long run. Sure, shagging your pupils isn't recommended by the Department for Education, but things were different in the 80s, weren't they? Everyone was out for what they could get, and you grabbed what was offered. We both survived the first wave of articles, and I was amazed that no one came out of the woodwork to put the knife in. Suzanne kept her mouth shut, and so did Dick Phipps.

It did mean that the last few weeks leading up to the programme have been mad. The press officer helped me choose the right interviews – I've done *Richard and Judy*, *Woman's Hour* and a couple of news programmes, plus a really fun make-over for a glossy magazine. I stopped short at Adam Ant jackets this time round. Oh, and the locals – telly, radio and papers. They've proved the most enthusiastic of all ...

All the publicity meant they got a huge audience for the programme – in Bracewell, there was a story going round that the electrical shops were getting loads of phone calls from people who still hadn't got round to tuning Channel 5, fourteen years after it went on air, just for TTWT. Or Twit, as we took to calling it.

I quite enjoyed the editing, too, I had a few trips up to London with the kids, all paid for. Mum would take them to the Tower of London or the Zoo, and I got to sit in a darkened room in Soho, eating free Danish pastries, and helping them write the script. They even took me to 'The Ivy', which is this restaurant where all the actors go. Nicole Kidman was there, but I didn't even consider racing over to her table to ask for her autograph. That's how sophisticated I am now.

Instead of two shows, they made a single programme, a whole hour long. I don't know if it's an accurate picture of me – how can you ever tell? The guy from the *Sunday Telegraph* said I made Maureen from the Driving School programme look self-aware, but then the *Sun* said every bloke in the land would understand why 'Bonking Bob' (as he is now known, bless him) couldn't keep it in his trousers. Which is a compliment, kind of. And I've memorised what the nice woman from the *Daily Telegraph* said about me, after we met for lunch. 'Tracey's taken the knocks – from a marriage break-up to a summer of press persecution – but she's still the kind of woman you'd always invite on a girls' night out. Streetwise, witty, a true child of Thatcher's generation – and anyone who judges her as lacking in any way is simply a snob.' She confided during our interview that the critic for the *Sunday Telegraph* is her ex-husband, so I had a feeling her verdict might be more sympathetic than his . . .

She's right, though, it's been a hell of a summer. The divorce is coming along nicely, and Dave agreed to a very attractive maintenance deal on condition I didn't drag him through the mud on the programme. I was true to my word – there's not a snide script line about him in the whole thing – but he's done a great job on his own of looking like a scumbag. And the beauty of it is, he doesn't even realise it. He rang me the other day and told me he's taking a copy over to Ireland with him to show the lads. He is a very stupid man.

The kids are doing better than I'd feared. They see about as much of him now as they used to, except now he has to make an effort to find things to do – the whole Sunday afternoon circuit of McDonald's, cinema, safari park, Wacky Warehouse. Towards the end of August, Suzanne got in touch to offer Kelly a place on some special week-long holiday for kids who've had problems, and she said she wanted to go. It hasn't turned her into a rampant extrovert, but she's made friends of another little girl who lives a few miles away, and she even had her round here for a birthday tea. She hardly ever talks to Jolene any more.

Suzanne was obviously feeling seriously guilty about the whole set-up with Andrew, because she also went into Kelly's school to do a talk before the programme went out, and it went pretty well – she managed to convince the kids that Kelly's appearance in Twit made her more of an object of admiration rather than one of ridicule ... so far, so good.

I heard from Gary the other day. Well, from him and Gabby, actually. It was an invitation to their engagement party. The silly bugger finally decided to take the plunge. I don't think I'll go – I'm probably not the best person to celebrate the joys of marriage at the moment – but I can't help wondering whether the reunion might have helped him make up his mind. Even if it was just the shock of seeing me, and realising what a close shave he'd had ...

'No, you can't have those, Kelly.' She's trying to sneak a Barbie princess outfit on to the conveyor belt. I hate the way supermarkets sell things like that. It's emotional blackmail. But for all my irritation, I like the fact that she'll misbehave now. Who knows, maybe one day she might even get in trouble at school.

We load the stuff into the car, and I drop Mum and the kids back. I've got a busy afternoon – including my first job interview in six years.

It's the strangest thing. On Tuesday, the day after the programme went out, I had a call from Berkshire FM, one of the local radio stations I've done interviews with. They'd had this idea for a new show, *Old School Ties*, which will reunite listeners, mainly former classmates, but also people who used to work together, or old neighbours or whatever. And they'd been so impressed with my interviews, and my performance on the TV show, that they'd like to audition me to be a possible presenter. If I was interested . . .

Well, what do you think? Was I interested in swapping my thrilling part-time job in the stationery shop for a job involving gossiping for an hour a day to a captive audience, on five times the money? I really had to think about it . . .

It's not certain, but I rang Jenny and she said she thinks it sounds as though they've built the whole show around me, so my chances must be good.

'Don't undersell yourself,' she told me. 'The Tracey Mortimer name is worth a lot now, you know. You're a valuable commodity.'

How strange is that? I won't believe it until they give me a contract to sign. Or until I'm sitting in front of the microphone . . .

But then part of me also wonders if I wasn't always destined for more than life as plain old Tracey Brown. If maybe I took a few wrong turnings, but my route out of tedium was always there for the taking.

And no matter how horrible it's been at times over the last five months, I don't regret a second of it – not because of the job, or the designer outfits or the health farm, but because without the reunion, I'd never have found Boris. It's taken her a while to get fit again, but Louise is amazing, a really happy baby, and so charming that she's even managed to lure Brian away from spending so many nights on the road selling software.

Smart Alec invited me to a launch party on the night the programme went out, but I decided I really wanted to watch the programme at home, with the kids, Mum and Boris. When Mum had taken Kelly and Callum to bed, we sat up drinking fizzy wine, and going over the stories that weren't in the programme. Shrimp. Melody. And Boris's favourite, the banishment of Dave ...

'And I threw the towel at him, and I said ...'

Boris picked up my cue, 'You'll be needing this to dry yourself off!' And we both collapsed in hysterics, until I started worrying that her caesarean scar wouldn't take the strain.

I had another swig of wine, and Boris grinned at me. It was the first time she'd been drunk since the baby was born.

She reached out to me, and kissed me on the cheek. 'Welcome back, Tracey Mortimer. I've missed you.'

And I realised I'd missed me too.